"Reisman writes beautifully, a prose of restraint and grace. The achievement of this novel is that you are completely inside it from the moment you begin. . . . This is a story that has the shape of life as it is truly lived." —Anna Quindlen, *Book-of-the-Month Club News*

"This is a stealth novel. The characters creep up on you, and before you know it you are inhabiting their world, attuned to intimate details, desires and desperate measures invisible to outside eyes. A lovely read." —Ann-Marie MacDonald, author of *Fall on Your Knees* and *The Way the Crow Flies*

"A superb new writer. . . . Reisman, whose sensually charged, often outright stunning style strongly evokes Virginia Woolf . . . proves herself a rare master of internal drama, able to isolate the moment that effects a sea of change within a lifetime of compromise." —*Vogue*

"Reisman's hypnotic prose makes her . . . characters live. And her sympathy and wealth of detail make the Cohens' world our own: specific, inescapably flawed, unpredictably meaningful and very, very real." —*People*

"There is not a false move in Nancy Reisman's *The First Desire*, one of the best tales I have ever read both about belonging to a family and about what the book calls 'the second desire,' the wish to be invisible, to disappear from that family, and to vanish into the American landscape." —Charles Baxter, author of *The Feast of Love*

NANCY REISMAN

The First Desire

Nancy Reisman is the author of *House Fires*, a short story
collection that won the 1999 Iowa Short Fiction Award.
Her work has appeared in, among other anthologies
and journals, *Best American Short Stories 2001*, *Tin House*, and
The Kenyon Review. She has received fellowships from the
National Endowment for the Arts and the Fine Arts
Work Center in Provincetown. She teaches creative
writing at Vanderbilt University in Nashville.

The First Desire

A Novel

NANCY REISMAN

ANCHOR BOOKS
A Division of Random House, Inc.
New York

FIRST ANCHOR BOOKS EDITION, SEPTEMBER 2005

Portions of this work have previously appeared in *Five Points*, *Michigan Quarterly Review*,
Tin House, *Best American Short Stories 2001* (New York: Mariner Books, 2001) and *Bestial Noise:
The Tin House Reader* (New York: Bloomsbury, 2003).

Grateful acknowledgment is made to Farrar, Straus and Giroux, LLC. for permission to
reprint an excerpt from the poem "Crusoe in England" from *The Complete Poems: 1927–1979* by
Elizabeth Bishop. Copyright © 1979, 1983 by Alice Helen Methfessel. Reprinted by
permission of Farrar, Straus and Giroux, LLC.

The Library of Congress has cataloged the Pantheon edition as follows:
Reisman, Nancy, 1961–
The first desire / Nancy Reisman.
p. cm.
1. Jews—New York (State)—Fiction. 2. Jewish families—Fiction.
3. Missing persons—Fiction. 4. Buffalo (N.Y.)—Fiction. I. Title.
PS3568.E5135F57 2004
813'.54—dc22
2004044665

ISBN-13: 978-1-400-07799-1

Book design by Iris Weinstein

www.anchorbooks.com

for Rena and Robert,
for Janet and Lo,
and for all of our loved ones

My island seemed to be
a sort of cloud-dump. All the hemisphere's
left-over clouds arrived and hung
above . . .

—ELIZABETH BISHOP,
"Crusoe in England"

The First Desire

PART ONE

Niagara

Late 1920s

CHAPTER 1

Sadie

1929

July, the air grassy and mild, the sort of morning Sadie waits for through the deep of Buffalo winters—mornings when it seems the city has surrendered to pleasure, to color and light. The harsh seasons are unimaginable. It's as if *this* is how all of life is meant to be; as if drinking coffee and reading, gardening and casual piano playing, are her true occupations; as if cardinals flashing through the yards and the lush green of lawns and the maple's fat leaves signal a permanent arrival. There are dahlias on the dining table, yellow and red, late strawberries. It's still early, and Sadie has an hour, maybe two, before the day's obligations intrude. The easy time, she thinks, the garden time. It's something she associates with marriage—not the image of a couple in the garden, but the luxury of time alone at her own house. A luxury apparent only after her mother's death, for which of course there is no compensation; but here is the second summer of such mornings, a time not yet occluded by children. She is twenty-four years old. Here is her coffee, the morning paper; in the back hall there are red geraniums to plant in a window box. The day is already bright, and she opens the living room drapes to the grass and pansies and oaks, and stops. There's a man on her lawn: light brown suit, cigar in hand, facing away from her. Slim and coltish, an impatience in his stance, a lack of definition she usually associates with faces but here sees even in the posture, the lines of his shoulders. It's Irving, her baby brother.

She glances at the new aqua-colored divan. The smallest of diversions, the look away. *Close the curtains,* she thinks, *try again later.* As if he will vanish. As if in ten minutes or an hour she'll open the curtains onto a lawn empty of everything but border pansies and white petunias. Pretend the man on the lawn is instead a strolling neighbor pausing to relight his cigar. Because the cigar is out. But Irving makes no gesture to relight it, and he is in fact Irving: Sadie has only one brother and there is no mistaking him. Irving, whom she did not expect to see at all today, let alone at this hour, miles from the family house, dampening his shoes in the grass.

She wishes it were noon. She wishes he were standing in a coffee shop: she is often happy to see him in coffee shops, in the company of pastry. They could eat Danish and argue about new pictures, and Irving could imitate Chaplin, walking with fast small steps and tipping his hat to make her laugh. Irving on the lawn cannot be a good thing.

In her nightgown and robe she opens the front door. A spread of bright petunias hems the grass. "Irving?"

He turns, ashes the burnt-out cigar, checks the bottom of his shoes, as if he has stepped in something unpleasant. For an instant he's a puzzled tan flamingo. And then he is Irving again, but he doesn't look her in the eye. What? A death? He'd have spoken by now if it were, and no one's been ill; there's evasion in his manner, but not the air of drowning. That half-embarrassed staring at his shoe—it's more than a small gambling debt. A girl in trouble? Which would be dreadful, of course, more than a little shocking, but not out of character.

"Have some coffee," Sadie says. And now he glances at her—still the puzzled look—crosses the thick grass, wipes his shoes on the front mat, and follows her voice through the hall to the dining room. She seats him at the head of the table, makes a ritual of pouring the coffee, stirring in the sugar and cream. He could be like this when he was a boy, couldn't he? Quiet, half-elsewhere until he'd had his breakfast, though at her table he fidgets, toying with his spoon until she sits down next to him.

"Haven't seen Goldie, have you?" he says.

Goldie, their oldest sister. Goldie, who lives with him, with their father and the others. "Goldie?"

"Hasn't been home for a while. Three days, actually."

"What do you mean?"

"She went out—to shop, I think, or Celia thinks. She had a shopping bag with her, Celia said."

"But Celia doesn't know."

"No. Celia doesn't."

"But she thinks Goldie went shopping."

"Went shopping and didn't come back."

"Three days ago."

"Well, two or three days."

"Three days ago was Sunday. Where does she shop on Sunday? She's never shopped on Sunday."

"She went somewhere then. Maybe"—and here Irving hesitates—"maybe to the Falls."

"And didn't come back," Sadie says.

"No."

"She often does go to the Falls," Sadie says. "Often has."

She pours more coffee, and focuses on the burgundy rings edging the saucers, the lips of the cups. One teaspoon of sugar for Irving. "Did she go to the Falls alone, or go shopping alone, whatever it is she did?"

He shrugs.

"No one called? No one came by for her?"

He fiddles with the unlit cigar. "I was out. I wasn't there."

"For three days you were out."

"More or less," he says. "Asleep when I was there."

"But you must have noticed."

"Goldie harps," he says. "I avoid her."

OTHER MEMBERS of the family are prone to disappearing, usually in absurd ways. Celia's age means nothing—she's twenty-seven but impulsive—and she turns up on docked streetcars and in speakeasies and sometimes at barbershops after following men. When Irving disappears, he returns whiskey-soaked. But Goldie's smart, the oldest, the responsible one, thank God uncrazy: she does not disappear. Maybe she told Celia she'd visit a friend and Celia forgot. Or Celia changed the story, blending it with other stories, as is her habit. And anyway what does *shopping* mean? On a Sunday in a city bursting with Catholics, Lutherans, Episcopalians, a city bound to Sunday as the Lord's day. True, Goldie might have gone to a Jewish shop, or to the bakery: Celia could mean *bakery* by *shopping*. Sometimes you have to unravel Celia's code. Last year she called Goldie's piano lessons *harbor walks*.

Sadie hesitates. The crisis has begun and will be with them now. But she can stir the sugar in slowly, she can wait and drink coffee and slowly dress and then the control of speed will end, all control will end. She'll have to give over to this thing, this disappearance and its ripple effects, to the strangeness of her other sisters, to her father's strong will or denial—you never know which it will be—to Irving wandering and returning, with rumor and inebriation. Give over and do what must be done. Do not speculate.

So she delays. The two of them, Sadie and Irving, sit leisurely over coffee, suspend the moment, as if nothing is happening and someone else is actually in charge. July. There's a brief ease that feels lifted from childhood, when she and Irving seemed a family within the family—a relaxed, affectionate little clan apart from their older sisters. Yet even as Sadie recognizes the sensation it fades, and she offers him jam and toast, the newspaper to read while she dresses for the day.

Alone in her bedroom, she senses that the morning has already become brittle and opaque, as if coated with burned milk. There's a bright fast ribbon of glee at the thought of canceling dinner with her mother-in-law, then the brittleness again.

IT'S A COUPLE of miles to the family house on Lancaster, far enough to be another neighborhood, another set of shops and

parks and schools if not a distinctly separate life. But often returning to Lancaster causes time to slip, and she needs to be mindful:
she needs the linen dress and gold clip earrings, the lipstick and
heels and whatever else she can summon. From the outside, the
Lancaster house is disarming, a solid, well-kept wood-frame, off-
white, surrounded by clipped green lawn and old elms, the shade
of maples and oaks and the clean-swept front porch suggesting
restful lives. Today the house is quiet, the foyer, the hallway and
front parlor slightly disordered, but only that. The smell of burnt
coffee wafts in from the kitchen; the house is alive with the smell.
Her sisters always seem to drink coffee burnt, as if there is no other
way. As Sadie passes the shaded dining room, the dark woodwork
and table and cabinets hushing the place into a season other than
summer, Irving hangs behind her and it seems—is she imagining
this?—that she might turn and find herself alone.

"Where are they?" she says.

Irving's examining his wing tips again. "The store. Papa's at the
store."

She pictures her father—impeccable in a wheat brown suit, his
dark shoes and spectacles and pale forehead shining in the heat,
salt-and-pepper mustache exactingly trimmed—checking velvet-
lined jewelry cases for dust, squinting at smudges on the glass. "For
how long?"

"He expects me there later."

"He opened for the day?" But her father has done as much at
other times, worse times, leaving a pale gray blur in his place.
From the parlor there's a glint of orange, which travels in Sadie's
direction: Celia's cat, slinking through the hall, now sniffing at
Sadie's pumps. "And Jo? What happened to Jo?"

Irving doesn't answer. The orange cat presses against Sadie,
rubbing itself across her shin, turning, rubbing itself the other
way. This is distracting: a tingling runs up Sadie's leg to the rest of
her, pleasant and more pleasant and then unnerving, that strong
tingling and the cat rubbing itself and loudly purring.

From the kitchen there's a clinking sound and the plash of
water pouring into water. "Celia?" Sadie calls. She makes her way
past the closets to the back stairwell and the kitchen, the cat

closely escorting her. There are white daisies in a water glass on the enamel tabletop, squares of light through thick-paned windows, a trail of garden soil along the floor to the back entry and the porch. Celia's at the sink, scrubbing a saucepan, flecks of oatmeal sticking to her wrists. Her face is a clear white oval, eyes hazel and unrevealing, her dress pink cotton, unfamiliar, oddly girlish. Today she's combed her hair.

"Jo's at work," Celia says.

"When did she leave?" Sadie says.

"The usual time."

Both of them, then, Jo off to her secretarial job, their father to the jewelry store, as if nothing is wrong, and Goldie will reappear any moment, ready to look after the house and check in with Celia. It's tempting, she admits, to take their behavior as reassurance and assume that Irving has misread the signs, but she knows better: this is not the sort of thing Irving misreads.

"Let's sort this out," Sadie says. "Let's sit down and sort this out."

Celia dries her hands, picks up the orange cat. Vera, she calls it. She is unnerved, you can see by the way she clings to the cat, the way she sidles up to Sadie and eyes the kitchen door.

"What's this about Goldie shopping?" Sadie says.

Celia talks at the windows and the door—or maybe it's to the yard beyond, the garden where she spends her summer. "She went shopping."

"On Sunday?"

Yes. Probably. Or Monday. No, Celia can't pinpoint the day for sure, it's possible that she saw Goldie again after the shopping, but that's not what she remembers. She does not know what Goldie shopped for. And she does not know where else Goldie might go— but here Celia refocuses on the floor.

And Sadie knows better than to expect answers from Celia now, with that look and the cat purring against her chest. She's too distracted, and even when she isn't she's still ruled by impulse, a tendency to lie. But you have to make the effort.

"What was she wearing?" Sadie says.

"Brown skirt, white blouse."

"She was wearing a brown skirt and a white blouse?"

"When she went shopping."

And now Sadie is imagining a cigarette, the moment of inhaling and the way everything in a room eases back a step; and the instant you exhale, with the smoke, the harsh pressure that's accumulated in your temples. "And Sunday? Celia, what was she wearing Sunday?"

"What?"

"What was she wearing?"

"She forgot her hat. I know she forgot her hat."

"Goldie hates wearing hats," Sadie says. "Almost never wears hats."

"That's how I know."

SADIE STARTS with Goldie's room—which is neatly made up and at a glance unrevealing—and riffles through the plain dresses in the closet, most of them blue or brown or white. The dun-brown skirt and white blouse hang on the back of the door. In the wide oak bureau there's costume jewelry—blue glass beads and paste pearls— an old cosmetics puff, an empty compact, a used red lipstick, darned stockings. The blouses are mostly mended, overwashed, none of them new. Beige and white and beige, despite the bright beads. Sadie can't tell if there's anything missing. Goldie's underclothes are ragged at the hems, graying and stained—embarrassing, she'll have to talk to Goldie about this, really Goldie must buy new—but the drawer is full. The dust motes seem thicker than usual—or is she imagining this also? As if it's been longer than two days since Goldie stayed here, certainly since she cleaned the room. Sadie pulls back the bedspread, fingers the linens, which have been slept in. It occurs to her she can't name what she's checking for. Blood? Stains from a man? There is the light, talc-speckled musk of Goldie herself, faint wrinkles in the sheets.

She is here but not here, which means what? Best if it means nothing, if you can stay suspended in the blankness of not answering. Yet there is somewhere an answer, disagreeable if not disastrous. Maybe she did stay at a friend's. But if not? Illness? A hospital? There's a history of hospital visits, their mother's, no one likes hospitals, but a hospital would call to let them know. The pillowcase tells her nothing: one long brown hair curves across a seam. Sadie does not want to consider the worst scenarios—one mustn't dwell—but the worst is always possible; there's a low beating fear, isn't there, just below the surface when you simply cross the street, or your husband crosses the street, that threat of slipping away altogether? And what of visits to Niagara Falls alone, after months of moodiness and low-grade secrecy, after mourning your mother, and not marrying, and joining reading groups with women who are most likely Socialists? "Missing" and "Niagara Falls" ought never to appear in the same sentence, though here, now, they have, and Sadie can't dodge the image of the rapids off Goat Island, the Niagara River wild; or the image of Goldie in her plain blue dress, dropping into the great stream, bobbing through the white water and careening over the Falls, smashing up at the bottom, frayed underwear surfacing downstream.

White sheets. Orderly corners. Clean quilt. No books, though Goldie reads voraciously and leaves books everywhere. No handwriting anywhere, no note of course, nothing hidden in with the shoes. It's the shoes that seem strangest to Sadie. She picks one up, slides her foot out of her own shoe and into Goldie's, which is slightly wider and longer, thicker-soled, hardly dainty. There is no feeling of Goldie in it, Sadie thinks. There ought to be.

Celia is upstairs now, pacing, her steps clunky and distinct, and beyond Goldie's bedroom door there's a series of meows, at first clearly the cat's and then what must be Celia mewing back. Sadie slips her own shoe on and pulls the door open to the hall, where Irving is leaning against the door frame, rolling a small glass marble back and forth over his palm.

"Is there anything else you can think of?" Sadie says.

"I don't know," Celia says. "No. I don't think so. No."

Irving shrugs.

"You've talked to police?" Sadie says. But of course they have not.

FINE, THEN, a cigarette. Sadie would like one and will have one, and her husband when he smells it on her clothes will simply have to keep mum. She sits in the front parlor and lights a cigarette and

Celia has one too, identical lipstick marks on white paper—when did Celia manage to get Sadie's lipstick out of her handbag? Irving sinks into the sofa, toying with a pipe. They smoke and gaze at the piano, which is mahogany and silent and in need of dusting. She does not think of Niagara Falls. She makes a list: Jo, Papa, library, hospitals, police, newspapers. Irving says their father knows nothing and though Irving is often unreliable, in this instance he is probably right. Sadie herself is more likely to know Goldie's secrets, if in fact Goldie has secrets, or *had* secrets—given the possibility that she's dead, which is jumping to conclusions, which Sadie mustn't do. Someone has misplaced the ashtray, and she needs to ash her cigarette. It seems that if Goldie were in the house, the ashtray would be apparent, the piano keys dusted and covered, or, better, played. Celia would not smoke: she doesn't when Goldie is around, and it's probably better that way, given Celia's vast ability to forget.

BY THE TIME Sadie leaves the house, the air outside has warmed and thickened, the breeze has dropped, and the sun is too hot, glinting off the Ford and forcing her to squint. Sadie drives south and east, downtown to the offices of Schumacher, Stein & Dobkin. On the second floor, beyond the gold-stenciled glass door and the small, formal reception area, her sister Jo hunches over her typewriter in the posture of a crabbed old woman. Jo is not an old woman, she's in her mid-twenties and she'd be attractive if she cared—gold-flecked hazel eyes, a delicate face. Her loveliness surfaces when it seems she doesn't know you're there. The moment the receptionist greets Sadie—an overly solicitous "How are you today?"—Jo glances up from the secretarial pool, and her face closes.

"What do you know," Jo says.

Sadie calls past the receptionist, "Can you take a break?"

Jo waves her back to the secretarial pool—now abandoned for lunch—and seats Sadie at an empty desk. "I don't have much to tell you," Jo says, as if Sadie has posed the real question. "She just stopped coming home. I thought she was scratching an itch."

Sadie imagines Celia's cat then—all that leg rubbing and mewing. Pictures dogs in the park. Jo's conversation always seems so unsavory. "What itch?"

"How would I know?" Jo looks as if she's sucking a lemon, and there's something stunned about her, something Sadie didn't notice at first, a slight tremor in her hands, which Jo attempts to hide, holding one hand over the other, rubbing her fingers as if to make them stop.

"I'm not saying you would," Sadie says, but this seems a portal to their regular squabbling, she doesn't want to go this way: they can accuse each other of nothing for hours. "What do you think we should do?"

At this Jo eases back. She doesn't know, though it's clear their father will not act; he hasn't even called Moshe Schumacher, her boss, and—like it or not—his closest friend. At the moment Moshe Schumacher is in court, but when he gets back, Jo will talk to him. He knows a lot of people, Jo says, police captains and such.

"Good. Thank you," Sadie says. This seems to have no softening effect. "What about last week?"

Jo shakes her head, and the sour look appears and recedes. If she knows more about Goldie's disappearance, she's convincing in her lies.

"How about last Monday?" Sadie asks. "Tuesday?"

There's a tiny twitch below Jo's left eye when Sadie gets to Wednesday, but Jo says, "Nothing special," and presses her lips together.

IT'S NO BETTER with their father. Sadie's sweating below the jewelry store's ceiling fan, while at the main display case he shows engagement rings to a plump businessman. This is not the sort of conversation one interrupts, although in truth her father has no conversations one should interrupt. She idles at a smaller display case—lockets and bracelets—and watches him behave as he always does with customers, solicitous and patient (more serious with men, more charming with women). He seems no different than he did two weeks ago: it's as if Goldie has merely stormed off to the neighbor's, as she did once when she was fifteen. And for a moment this vision seems plausible. But her father behaved the same way through their mother's last months and barely averted collapse.

She waits until he's made the sale. Kisses him on the cheek, and he blinks, as if he's suddenly remembered his life, the strangeness and shock of being a man with a family.

"Papa, what happened with Goldie?" she says.

"We did not have words."

"But what happened?"

"This is not like her." And then he's tight-jawed and silent and it's clear that he's taken Goldie's absence as an affront. On the far counter, black-and-white lists—inventory sheets—fan out, dropping angled shadows over the pearls. He's checking, then, to see if Goldie's taken anything; or is it to tally up how much, without her, he's got left?

From the jewelry store Sadie telephones her husband's office, but Bill is with a patient and he's booked all afternoon. She leaves a message with his secretary: a family matter has come up, today's plans have changed. The store's back office seems cooler than the front, but the air is still close, and while her father and Irving call out inventory numbers, Sadie swallows a quietly rising hysteria. Here is her compact. Here is her lipstick.

She drives over to the central police precinct, the day still hot, though high clouds have moved in from the lake, and with them a light breeze: the city is oblivious to anything but summer. She makes the report to the police alone, all the while thinking *Wait*, as if waiting means Goldie will reappear in another day, or two days. The look the officer gives her says the same thing: wait.

He's in his early twenties, no older than she is: young to be so matter-of-fact. "Women do all sorts of things," he says.

"What do you mean?" Sadie says, but he shrugs, as if he's already forgotten what he's suggesting.

"She's old-fashioned," Sadie says. "Old country." Which is both true and untrue: born in Russia, sure, and unstylish in her dress, but there's that whiff of socialism.

Sadie offers up a photograph, attempts charm. It's Goldie posed straight-backed on a garden bench, gaze direct and luminous. "She liked to visit the Falls. She might have. My brother says she'd have taken a trolley, she'd do that sometimes."

The officer nods and promises to check with Niagara Falls police—he is not unkind—but by any chance could Mrs. Feldstein's sister have gone to Canada?

To get a better look at the Falls? Not likely, Sadie thinks, not impossible, but that isn't what he means, is it? There's a blank second—she's at a loss, though she knows the question is hiding something—and then the words tilt and she can see behind them the suggestion of rum-running. "I can't imagine why," Sadie says.

"No? Well, river agents haven't mentioned a woman."

"Of course not." *She's a badly dressed librarian. Isn't she?*

Sadie leaves the precinct angry enough to be calm, and stops at the downtown hospitals, shows one nurse after another the photo of Goldie on the garden bench. In the late afternoon she places newspaper classifieds in the *Courier* and the *Buffalo Evening News* and the *Jewish Review.*

> *Missing: woman, 33 years old, of Jewish descent,*
> *5'2", dark hair and eyes, slim, last seen Sunday or*
> *Monday, possibly wearing a blue shirtwaist. May*
> *have visited Niagara Falls.*

It is almost five o'clock and she has not eaten today. She returns to her own house, where the lawn, the maples and petunias uphold July and the geraniums wait for their window box. She tries Bill's office again, then takes off her shoes and lies down on the aqua sofa in her clothes. Tomorrow, or maybe sooner, she'll have to go back to Lancaster, but the new sofa is soft, the fabric slightly cool, the desire to sleep irresistible. It occurs to Sadie that if Goldie *is* in Canada, she could be in a hotel room—maybe in a bed as lovely as this sofa—sleeping off the family. It also occurs to Sadie, this time without glee, that she must cancel dinner, that her mother-in-law will be unhappy and will not disguise her displeasure.

When Sadie's husband, Bill, wakes her, in that first moment it's just the end of a nap—she's forgotten everything but the drifting—there's simply Bill waking her: light reflecting off his glasses, a scent of soap and musk, his palm on her arm, his palm on her cheek. There are his lips, a darkened pink, and she kisses him, there's a sweet warmth to kissing him: she would like him to lie beside her now, she would like to lean her head against his chest and listen to his heartbeat and doze for a while and kiss him again. And then she remembers. It's six o'clock, early for him. In the next instant she anticipates an answer—he must have news—but he does not, only that he'll talk to the police himself, only that there's no word from the hospitals. He's home and *Let's not worry about dinner,* or his mother. He spoke with Jo. Celia is fine. They will be fine, he says, and with such authority that Sadie nods in agreement. But as she sits up, she notices her conversation with Irving still hangs over the dining table, anything but fine. And she wonders how the day would have unfolded had she not opened the curtains or let him in. Would this house, at least, be untainted? She blinks, and there is within her a welling desire to erase the day, or at least to air the rooms of the conversation with Irving, and clean them, and launder the clothes she's worn since morning. To bathe and begin again with an unsullied dress.

CHAPTER 2

Jo

JULY 1929

The newspapers love girl bandits, and so does Jo: she tries to get to the dailies before her father, who will take too much time and then toss them out. It's better if she can escape to her room with the *Evening News* or the *Courier*—or if she's lucky a paper from New York—and read the latest story: a bobbed redhead in New York, only seventeen, breaking in on a poker game; a young brunette holding up a jeweler in the Bronx; a college coed robbing a bank in Buda, Texas. They seem brazen, undaunted, these girls. Over days Jo follows their unraveling fates: they sometimes find leniency and sometimes are stuck, sentenced as harshly as men, and then disappear from the papers altogether. Other news bores her, and when girl bandits are absent from the paper, she drifts off instead, continuing in her mind old stories of women and guns and of other places she might live: her own flat, maybe near the Hippodrome— or better, a Hippodrome in another city—so she might go to the pictures whenever she likes. She imagines a pearl-handled revolver, smooth and cool to the touch, imagines herself downtown, disguised as a cabbie, talking only to shopgirls and the vendor in the theater ticket booth, planning the daring rescue of a gun girl in need, maybe even the Bobbed Bandit (still wearing her trial dress and bright orange stockings, a hat woven through with roses). It starts at the eleventh hour: the sentencing has not yet occurred, and the Bobbed Bandit is quick and feline and scared. Here is Jo, whisking her upstate and west, offering her protection and disguise—blue stockings, gardenias. Or for a less elaborate scheme, there's the story of the girl once arrested in Buffalo who called herself Vera La Mont. Here's Vera in the blue stockings, a white gardenia tucked into her hair, lounging in a darkened corner of the theater, Jo as the usher, the theater manager, the favorite companion.

These are stories in which she might truly belong, unlike the daily life she occupies. But there's no clear path between the stories and the business of waking and eating breakfast and working at the law firm; Lancaster; the women she actually knows. The only person she has whisked anywhere is Celia (away from a bank, yes, but only from the front entrance and a man Celia followed). And the only girl bandit she's met is a client of Moshe Schumacher's, a sniveling upper-crust girl who shoplifted a party dress. Jo's life is small, she knows this, but can't small things change? She's secretly saving for her own apartment: she doesn't run the house, she won't inherit the store—she's a spare daughter. Why shouldn't she go? Her father will object, of course. Marriage, he'll tell her, she must wait until marriage. Which Sadie can apparently stomach—life with a Bill, who pulls teeth for a living—but Jo can't fathom it, and she's already twenty-six. So her savings slowly accumulate. Her plan is to stay mum until she has enough money and a good lead on an apartment. When her father objects, she will throw a fit. If necessary, she will include in her fit the fact that Lillian Schumacher, his tartish girlfriend, lives alone.

But Goldie is gone, and this Jo did not foresee; she wouldn't have predicted such a thing or the resulting cold fear. Though Jo *had* seen changes; shouldn't she have been prepared? Last winter, wandering seized Goldie, a wandering not unlike Celia's: distraction, day-long absences, returns with freezing hands and muddy shoes and raw sorrow in her face. There had been wandering and sorrow woven into Celia from childhood, but never Goldie, the oldest, the reliable one. In January, Jo had noticed Goldie disappearing on Sundays, and then found evidence of weekday absences—dishes unwashed, groceries sparse, a glimpse of Goldie downtown boarding an unfamiliar streetcar. Separately Goldie and Celia left the house and separately they returned, both windblown, red-cheeked, their attentions fixed on invisible remote points. Often they seemed peaceful but agitated easily, as if sheltered by a kind of dream bubble; if you placed an index finger lightly on the surface, it would burst and they would give you scathing looks. If they came home distraught, you did not know why and might never learn. Later, if you talked to Goldie, she seemed calm and reasonable. Purposeful on workdays, dressed for the library in pressed skirts and blouses, neatly pinning her hair, never missing her streetcar. Only after work did the day loosen. Goldie remained capable: she laundered clothes, marketed, fed the cat and rescued it from trees. She cooked the family meals, but no longer rushed to ensure supper was ready by the time their father returned home. And their father waited, saying nothing, busying himself with his papers and clearing his throat.

A few times Jo followed Goldie, only to find her strolling quietly along the river or the harbor, despite the ice and grit of the waterfront, the rough winds off the lake. In early spring, Goldie chose the mud browns and old snow of Delaware Park, sat on benches with books. It was that mundane, and perhaps that easily understood—a half-deserted park, a certain aloneness—but here too the air was damp and chilly, and Goldie seemed impervious.

You couldn't exactly say Goldie was *going off*. Instead she seemed relentlessly herself: more bookish, more sealed in her opinions, more lost in her music. She took to playing the piano daily, with an intense and dreamy concentration, breaking a silence that had descended after their mother's death. Playing Mozart instead of tending to the housecleaning or to their father's tea (which Jo—and, in truth, their father—could brew perfectly well but generally refused to). Celia lay on the sofa, listening. And sometimes Jo too would watch Goldie play, Goldie's chapped hands oddly beautiful, and Goldie seemed entirely elsewhere, ignoring all of them.

THERE WAS a man, there had to be, probably the piano teacher. Jo had seen them together once, at the Regent Theatre, where he played. He and Goldie had merely exchanged hellos, but hellos that held no room for anyone else but the two of them, hellos that left Jo and Celia behind in the theater aisle. So maybe Goldie has gone to him, maybe it's that simple (if stupid). Maybe Jo should have told Sadie. Or not. Even this morning, Celia insisted Goldie was fine, and Celia—at least an unmuddled Celia—might really know. But Celia's been upset, and upset confuses her thinking: you have to catch her in a moment of clarity, before the facts mire and disintegrate. You have to catch her when she doesn't need rescue.

If Goldie is dead it was not a simple death. She isn't the weepy, frail sort, or the brazen, gun-blazing sort. She wouldn't take her own life, not Goldie—she's too practical for that, too canny. But something might have happened. This is what frightens Jo most: there are always violent strangers.

Her mother would have known in a minute whether to be frightened or not; would have wiped her hands on her apron and walked to the front door and gazed out, listening—to the trees, or to Goldie herself, somewhere in the distance (they always seemed of one mind)—then either nodded and returned to her tasks or tossed down the apron and hurried off, leaving Jo to keep an eye on Celia. In that doorway, Jo listens and waits, but the leaves sound like small waves and carry no other meaning.

THE LAWYERS' OFFICE can be deadening, but this week it seems better than the house, where her jitteriness expands to fill each room and interrupts even the stories she tells herself. At the office, typing and filing anesthetize her, and while she cannot dream up girl bandit rescues, she can conjure the interiors of different theaters—the Regent, the Great Lakes, the Hippodrome—the plush seats and unspooling movie light, the thick peripheral dark, piano music rising. In the months after their mother died, she and Celia and Goldie—sometimes even Sadie—spent free afternoons together at the pictures, and it was easy for them together: sitting with her sisters in the theater Jo felt less lonely, and less in need of being alone. Those days had the quality of shared sleep. And if, at her desk, she keeps her mind fixed on those matinees, she will make it through her morning, her afternoon, her typing and filing and dictation from Attorney Schumacher.

Still, her lunch break comes as a shock. When she stops typing, she finds herself blinking at the stark light of Goldie's absence, and her hands are trembling again. What caused the wandering? It appeared as winter stars appear, suddenly visible, and then began to take the place of Goldie herself, until only odd bits of Goldie remained in the house on Lancaster. Not unlike her mother, who seems now to reside only in the wallpaper and the samovar and lace tablecloths. At the office, the air is heavy and unmoving, too hot, and for a moment the relationships of floor to desk, desk to chair, wall to window seem jumbled. What presses in on her is at once heavy and perilously empty, and nameless: she feels it as a near cracking of her ribs and a hard suck of air, imagines tumbling down the basement stairs at Lancaster. Where she will be stranded if Goldie doesn't return.

What about last Wednesday? Yesterday, when Sadie asked, Jo couldn't say, except that on Wednesdays Goldie seemed especially distant. What detail of last Wednesday had she missed? It was an ordinary day. A nothing day. Last week a nothing week. Yet if someone other than Sadie asked, if Vera La Mont were to ask, Jo would say *something* had changed. If her own mother asked, she'd say here are the pieces: distraction, wandering, piano, argument. But if her mother could ask, there would be no change. Goldie would be her same irritating self.

Jo leaves the office for a bench on the square, her lunch in a paper sack, but she does not want lunch. There's a patch of green lawn and the shade of an oak into which, on a simpler day, one might disappear.

.   .   .

MOST PEOPLE, Jo suspects, are untrustworthy, and she prefers them silent, prefers silence to speech, but often her own words emerge snappishly—or, when she is upset, strangled—with a sharpness and pitch she regrets. After lunch, after Moshe Schumacher has spoken to the precinct lieutenant about Goldie and called his streetwise clients, Jo's thank-you is a small pinched burp. She gazes at his oversized suit, notes a tea stain on his necktie in the shape of a bug. The stain begins to blur: she is staring, her eyes seem filmy and strange, and he waits for her to say more. He stubs out his cigar, asks her if she'd like to sit down.

"She's not dead," Jo says.

"No," Moshe Schumacher says. "This would be a hasty conclusion."

"She's too stubborn to be dead."

"I see."

The plush chairs in his office seem out of a hotel lobby, and not of this place, not at all of this life, the overstuffed room itself momentarily strange to her. In her hands there is a small tremor, but her hands seem separate from her arms and certainly from her voice. She knots her fingers behind her back, tries to still them, and her fingers flutter, tap her knuckles. In her mind she hears the tapping as a marching band's tinny drumroll. Fourth of July, the sky overcast, a city parade—what is the point of parades?—and Goldie on the front porch reading another fat book by a Russian.

"Do you want to go home?" Moshe Schumacher says. The words come to her but the breeze through the back windows is lifting the drapes, making pattering sounds like slow flapping wings over the drumroll. Jo shakes her head and burps out another "thank you" and returns to the plain front office and her typing desk, where her hands will occasionally cooperate.

At the end of the day, she does not go directly home, but instead to a sweetshop three blocks from the office, and buys a small bag of chocolates. There is in the first taste, finally, an easing of fear: the dense, melting sweetness a kind of knowledge, a fat drop of her secret life.

. . .

SHE KNOWS exactly where the piano teacher lives and she ought
to go there immediately, but it's as if she is underwater, and the
small blue house the pianist shares with his father hovers far above
the surface, untouchable. Even telephoning seems impossible,
though what if Goldie is there? In love and probably moronic but
there nonetheless, a streetcar away. She must be told to come
home, where she belongs and Jo does not. But if Goldie is not
there, where would she be? Nowhere Jo can imagine, nowhere,
and now the trembling starts again, and she calms herself with the
thought of Goldie in the blue house. Like a lucky stone you carry
in your pocket and occasionally touch: for this moment, hoping is
better than knowing.

Jo waits until Saturday evening and finds the piano teacher at
the Regent Theatre, where he still plays in the evenings. When
he's finished for the night, he collects his music and closes the
piano, and she follows him into the red-carpeted lobby. Dark-
haired, thirty maybe, his face sculpted enough for the pictures—
though altogether too melancholy.

"Goldie's my sister," she tells him, though this isn't the first
time they've met.

He nods, lowers his eyes. "How is Goldie?"

"You tell me," Jo says. She doesn't mean to be sharp, but there
it is, the edgy, threatening undertone.

"Tell you? Tell you what?" Furrowed brows, a slight catching of
his breath, nothing false in his puzzlement. At the end of the
lobby a clerk wipes down the concession stand, while the last of
the audience leaks into the street.

"What happened?" she says.

"She missed her piano lesson. I don't know why."

From her pocketbook Jo pulls a sheet of newspaper with
Sadie's classified ad. "We haven't seen her since last weekend." He
covers his mouth with his hand and then his eyes fill. She can't
look at him; really, he ought to be more poised. He's bewildered,
and she does not want bewilderment: it makes her brutish. She
would like to kick him.

"Doesn't your father like her?" Jo says.

He looks at her curiously, those big eyes staring. "You're not much like your sister, are you?"

Her fingers begin to flutter. "Lookit," she says. "I didn't say anything to my father. About you. My sister Celia didn't either."

But there's no change in his expression, he's pale and shocked looking and she feels like she's swallowed bad milk. His shoes are scuffed brown leather, ordinary and strangely sad.

"She was wandering around town more, you know? More than usual. Near the water."

He shakes his head. "I haven't heard from her."

"No quarrel?"

"No."

When she steps onto the damp street, Jo's throat closes.

SHE HAS NEVER actually touched a gun: she doesn't know anything about relative weights and calibers, about bullets or the steadiness and strength required to pull a trigger. The guns she imagines have the heft of a bread knife, slim and light and easy to wield. That's not the part of the fantasy she cares about anyway: usually, the gun she imagines carrying is more like a pearl-handled wand. At times she's imagined the lobby of Buffalo Savings Bank, herself disguised with a mask and a man's suit, holding out her bread knife–gun; imagined the moment when the customers and tellers freeze and beg for mercy and hand over precious things, the moment when she dashes out to the waiting DeSoto and disappears into another city, a flurry of lights, a restaurant with a private table. The mask melts away. There is the question of what to order. Roast duck. Roast lamb. Baked salmon. What sort of breads the waiters should bring, what sorts of desserts. And for a companion a loyal brown-eyed girl appears, a girl strikingly like the ticket vendor at the Hippodrome. She offers Jo a rose, the kind the Bobbed Bandit wove into her hat.

Only on the days when the next-door neighbor's dog falls into spasms of barking does Jo imagine herself pulling a trigger, as a sharpshooter taking aim from an attic window with an Annie Oakley rifle. She would catch the dog on the first shot, silencing him.

His bark is harsh, piercing, and though his owners know better, he still gets loose, still torments Celia's cat. How many times has he chased the cat up a tree? Four? Five? And each time Goldie's negotiated with Ruby Berman to tie up the dog, then pulled the heavy ladder to the maple or the elm and climbed. Using bits of fish, she's coaxed the cat down to a reachable branch. All the while Celia's paced the yard and glared at the Bermans' house, calling in a squeaky voice *Kitty kitty kitty* and smoking Jo's cigarettes. Eventually Goldie would lift the distraught cat down from the tree, the fat orange thing racing into the house and hiding. In the upstairs hall, Celia's *Kitty kitty kitty* became a halting lullaby.

But now Goldie is gone, it's Sunday and the cat's in the maple again, the dog scrabbling at the trunk and Celia yelling to no avail. Jo shouts and throws stones at his feet until he backs away. She leaves Celia with a handful of stones to throw and raps on the Bermans' door.

Ruby Berman emerges, a round woman in her thirties with a mop of walnut hair and an always-red face, and today a stained cooking apron.

"Your dog got loose again," Jo says.

"Baby!" Ruby yells, and the dog barks from the edge of the lawn. "The boys must have let him out. They forget."

"Cat's in the tree again."

"Baby! Jo, I'm sorry."

"I'm not like Goldie," Jo says. "I'll call the pound."

Ruby smoothes her hair, gazes past Jo toward the beige pavement and the arching elms. "Sadie came by. Talked to me about Goldie."

"Did she?"

"I hope Goldie's all right," Ruby says.

"*Kitty kitty kitty,*" Celia calls.

Jo knots her fingers together. "You going to tie up your dog?"

"*Kitty kitty kitty. Jo?*"

Ruby sighs, wipes her hands on her apron, and starts after the dog, who dashes away behind the shrubs. From the toolshed, Jo drags out the heavy ladder.

.　.　.

VERA LA MONT was born Estelle Mackosky. She was young, and perhaps stupid—or perhaps in love with a stupid man—holding up Hoyler's Jewelers and remaining in Buffalo. She should have fled. Chicago, or Philadelphia, or Miami. Still, there must have been more to her, to use a stage name in her hometown. It's been years now since Vera's arrest and trial. Years since the papers reported anything about her.

CHAPTER 3

Irving

JULY 1929

Two pairs will not beat a full house, but the hand seems good enough to bet on, to meet Leo's three raises. Irving knows that unless he's sure, Leo doesn't raise more than twice, but the pair of sevens, the pair of tens fan out as shining promises. And it's Irving's turn for promises realized, for more than distraction and Artie Mankowitz's bootleg gin. He's betting petty cash, five dollars from his father's store, five dollars he'll replace in the morning, before his father makes the daily count. The cards feel slick in his hand, beautiful. The other players—Marty and Lenny and Eli—have the flat bored look of men waiting to pay rent, having all dropped their bluffs. Leo you cannot read, and he could reverse himself, defy his own habits. Once in the game Leo plays without pity, which is why before dealing he offered to lower the stakes for the night, why on the sideboard he set out lemonade as well as gin, why he directly told Irving to sit out any hand he wanted. This is Leo's nod to Goldie's disappearance. He is, after all, Irving's best friend. But Irving wants a night without her absence pressing in, it's *his turn;* he's mixed his lemonade with gin and played house stakes for every hand. He is trying to listen to the cards, as Leo says, though mostly he studies the precise patterning on the tens, the vertical rows of diamonds and clubs, the two-figure inset, rubs their glossy backs, and finds all signs inscrutable. Two solid pairs. He bets and loses the rest of the cash. "Good pairs—breaks your heart," Eli says, and Leo pours more gin and lemonade. "Just watch out next week," Irving says, and Leo says, "I will."

If Irving's father paid him well enough, he wouldn't dip into petty cash. If his father paid him well enough, all sorts of problems would vanish: the salary is just enough to keep him in good shoes, not enough for his own flat, or for a real city life. But his father is waiting for something more, for proof of Irving's worthiness, probably in the form of marriage. "You like that Rachel Brownstein?" his father says, and in fact Irving does, she's brown-eyed and sweet-faced and curvy, but you know at a glance she's too good for nightclubs, too earnest in her prayers. She's the kind who swoons over babies and goes to temple by choice. True, Rachel has his mother's quiet steadiness, but his mother's dead: now even his father seems to want a good time (why else would he take up with Lillian Schumacher?).

"Rachel's a nice girl," Irving says.

"Good. You should take her out."

Only if it comes to that. He's worked four years in the store and will someday inherit it, but someday is unimaginable. And if he dates Rachel Brownstein, how much of a raise can he expect? His father will still treat him as a boy. No, he deserves the petty cash.

Beyond Leo's flat the night stretches, a wide swath of dark broken by yellow dots and squares, and empty of money. Irving finishes his lemonade and collects his jacket, but in Leo's tiny foyer he hesitates, considers asking Leo for a loan, that five dollars just for a few days. Yet if he borrows, Leo won't let him play again, not until he's paid it back and then some. Marty and Eli and Lenny are broke, and anyway would call him a mooch, the excuse of Goldie notwithstanding.

"Next week," he tells Leo, accepts the pat on the back and Leo's "See you at Minnie's?"—the speakeasy where Leo always pays.

Irving takes a streetcar down Elmwood to Lancaster, the night air mild, lake water and grass mixed with trash and motor oil, passing whiffs of stale coffee. It's two a.m. and the gin is curdling into a nasty headache, and if he does not clean the store at seven his father will ask why. What makes his father think he belongs there anyway? True, Irving likes persuading customers to buy, he's got a way with the women, he's inherited his father's good looks; true, he loves the opals, the sapphires, the gold cuff links; but most of the time the store bores him. Mundane cleaning and paperwork, mail to be sorted, bank deposits readied, the slips dutifully returned to his father. The long wait for customers. The simplest work at the bench makes him impatient, all those tedious fine movements while you hold the rest of your body still. As if you are half-dead. He would rather own a nightclub: *that* would be something.

In the dark house, he checks the extra tea tin for grocery change (fifteen cents), the table and chairs for his sisters' pocketbooks, then the dining room, the parlor, the coatrack. Tiptoes into Goldie's deserted room and tries the top dresser drawer, her closet: in a skirt pocket he finds a quarter. Jo and Celia are light sleepers, their rooms impossible, which is too bad. Once in his own bedroom he checks his suit jackets and trousers, tries former hiding places for cash—the night-table drawer, the small bookshelf, the bowl of marbles—all of which he's scoured before. At the bottom of the marble bowl he finds another dime, though this requires emptying the bowl, sprawling on the carpet, and grabbing at runaway marbles to keep them from rolling onto the wood floor. They shoot off in opposite directions, as if conspiring. He is twenty years old. His hands are damp, the marbles slippery.

He undresses and lies in bed near the open window, not sleeping, watching the silhouettes of leaves and the occasional flicker of streetlamps. He does not feel like Irving: the name seems to loosen from his body in the dark. Torso, face, legs, arms, his skin sensitive to the warm air, his muscles tense; and the plain bed, which could be in any room on any summer night, his body any man's. Why then this particular house, this particular Irving life? Why not be called Leo, or anything else. *Irving* is simply a cloak to wear in the world of his father, though the name is less alien when Sadie says it, or, before, his mother, or at times Goldie, the ones with a soft spot for him, who might give him things on the sly. Even then he is part Irving, part opaque unknowing.

Sadie will have five dollars but whether she'll help him is uncertain: she is still in a state. They've all been in a state about Goldie—Irving himself is clumsier, more easily spooked—and it has become tiresome. This week, Sadie's more tightly wound—a pogo stick mood—which will make her either generous or deaf to him. It is not a good time to ask, but asking is the least desperate choice.

For a few hours he skates at the edge of sleep, close enough to feel the pieces of his life begin to move and recombine—marbles rolling toward Goldie, toward Leo, Lillian Schumacher's red mouth, the watchful faces of kings—but then he veers back into wakefulness. At five-thirty he shaves and bathes, dresses and descends to the kitchen, where Jo is eating toast and poring over a Sears catalogue. She studies him warily, eases back in her chair and closes the catalogue without marking her place. "You're early," she says.

"Cleaning this morning," he says.

"You might try the house." She's reverted to her natural rudeness, a perversely reassuring state. This cheers him. She bites into her toast and ignores him, idly flipping through the catalogue again. Irving packs bread and cheese, stops to pet the cat, and leaves through the kitchen door, feeling oddly hopeful.

The streetcar is empty, the city still quiet, though in minutes it will crowd up and erase this version of itself. These are moments he loves, though with money in his pocket he would love them more. At the store he sweeps the carpet and polishes the cases, sweeps the front sidewalk, wipes smudges from the windows. He can't call Sadie until Bill's left their house: Bill is unyielding, a killjoy. Irving waits. Eats a slice of bread—that's all he can stomach—and straightens the office and arranges his father's tools. Finally it is eight o'clock; Bill ought to be at work. Irving picks up the store telephone and the operator connects him to Sadie.

He feigns a measured calm. "Sadie, there's a problem."

"Goldie?"

"No, no, not so serious, but I don't want Papa upset. I made a mistake."

"Oh?"

"Don't think I'm a dope. I misplaced some petty cash."

She sighs. "Irving, how did you manage that?"

"I don't exactly know. I lost it."

"How much?"

"Five dollars."

"Papa gave you five dollars out of petty cash?"

"No. It didn't work that way."

"God, Irving. He'll be livid."

"That's the problem."

He can cover the money from the drawer until the daily cash-out, unless there's a big sale and Papa makes an early deposit. Replacing the five dollars "as soon as possible would be good," he says. "You wouldn't have five dollars, would you?"

"Promise me you won't lose a cent."

"I swear," Irving says. "I promise."

She tells him she'll be there. By noon, she says, and for the moment he is safe.

After he opens, morning at the store is slow drudgery, a few earring sales, his father hunched over the jeweler's bench, setting stones in engagement rings, a faint breeze through the front screen door and outside high sun, dollops of cloud. A far better day for Crystal Beach: no suit-wearing, hardly any clothes at all, cool water, the sun warming your skin, plenty of girls. *That's* how you clear a hangover, how you turn your luck around.

And maybe Crystal Beach is where Goldie's taken herself: it would be a fine choice. He never figured her to be the one to go, not like this—eloping with her piano player maybe, and why not? Irving's been half-ready for Celia to lose herself in trouble, of course: ignoring train crossings, walking on river ice, trusting a thug. But Celia is fine—maybe her oddness protects her. And Goldie? Goldie, whose bossiness can kill you—if she knew about the petty cash she'd make him earn it back—but she is sweet when she relents. Goldie, who in his schoolboy days would kiss him on the forehead. For a while, he hasn't paid attention to her, and now he wants to pay *less* attention: the way she surfaces can be alarming. Last weekend at the burlesque he was watching a woman's legs and wondering how close they came to the shape of Goldie's. He doesn't know the shape of Goldie's thighs and it occurs to him that he wants to, and also that this is not brotherly. Another man would be ashamed of the thought, and he is not, just troubled by the uncertainty of form, the inability to imagine her. Perhaps he should try to have more shame. He isn't a bad man. It's true he drinks, but so does the whole city; it's true he's drawn to looser women than Rachel Brownstein, but so is his father; it's true he does not love his sisters enough, but what is enough? There seems not to *be* enough, it's infinite what they'll take if you let them. He shuts and bolts a door and still his sisters appear, squeezing through the door frame like mice. Mice on pogo sticks. Mice skating through marbles.

At eleven o'clock Lillian Schumacher walks in, today wearing beige linen, and garnets his father bought last winter in New York. She's more subdued than usual, no hint of flirtation, no winsome glances or outright winks, no throaty laugh, but she's still Lillian, you can always see the spark: even when she's serious you know she likes pleasure. This time she asks to see gold earrings.

"We have some beauties," Irving says, and pulls out the tray. She holds one and then another pair up against the garnets.

"How is your father?" she says.

"He's in back," Irving says. "It's a strange time, Miss Schumacher."

"I'm sorry," she says. Her voice is, it seems, a summons to his father, which is too bad.

From the back hall his father says, "I'll help Miss Schumacher now, Irving. Thank you."

Irving crosses behind the counter to the far corner and the tabletop file and sorts June receipts. The timing is not ideal. Sadie is due in soon, and Sadie does not have a full appreciation of Lillian Schumacher. You can't really blame her: their father has taken up with Lillian too soon, you might say, and Lillian's reputation does not help. Irving himself has a great appreciation, though it's unpleasant to see his sisters anywhere near Lillian: they seem to contort. He tries to avoid such convergences, though now he must stay and wait for Sadie. Perhaps his father will take Lillian to an early lunch, missing Sadie, leaving plenty of time to replace the five dollars (provided he doesn't take lunch money from petty cash, in which case Irving will be forced to lie). Over the receipts Irving can see his father's stance relax, his father murmuring to Lillian. It's the point at which either they leave for the workroom or Irving does. Irving hesitates and his father glares over Lillian's shoulder at him. "Call me if you need me," Irving says and carries the file box into the back room.

None of the space here is his, really; the back room is split into an enclosed office and a workroom, both fully his father's, sparer than the plush front room. There's a wooden table and a samovar in the office, and a high glass window spilling checked light onto the floor. This is where Irving prefers to sit, where he sweats on the June receipts as he orders them by week, day, and letter, where he hears Sadie's "Hello, Papa" and a clipped "Hello, Miss Schumacher." Sadie inquires too sweetly about Irving—she's staving off a fit, no doubt—and then the soft footsteps over carpet shift to a hard click on the office's wood floor.

Sadie's in a pale pink summer suit, cream heels, and a small cream hat, in defiance of her state, but her face seems pinched, eyelids puffy. "Company today?" She glances toward the front room.

Irving rises from the table and kisses her on the cheek. "You're gorgeous," he says. "Do you have time to sit?"

"Just a minute."

He slides the desk chair to the table and opens a tin of sugar cookies.

"How often is she here?" Sadie says.

"Not so much." His tone is conspiratorial. "Once in a while."

She shakes her head, takes a sugar cookie from the tin, and draws her wallet out of her pocketbook, and in those gestures dismisses Lillian Schumacher. Fit averted. She counts out five one-dollar bills and pushes them toward Irving and tucks her wallet back into her pocketbook. He immediately slides the dollars out of view.

"I'm meeting a few of the girls," she says. Her mah-jongg friends, doctors' wives. "Bill thinks it's a good idea."

"It's a fine idea," Irving says and squeezes her arm. "Wish I could go with you."

"We'll try lunch next week," she says. "Depending." And then she's on her feet again. She waves toward the empty space where she'd left the money. "That's done with?"

"Thank you." He kisses her again, her scent faintly lilac.

And then she's gone, reduced to a voice trailing back from the front room. "I've just seen Celia, she's fine." There's a low murmur from his father and nothing from Lillian Schumacher, then Sadie's clear "Papa, I'll talk to you later," the door opening, the door closed.

His father appears in the office an instant too soon, after Irving's put the cash in the box, while he's placing the box back in the desk drawer.

"Today I'll go to lunch," his father says. His eyes are slightly bloodshot—could he, too, be hung over? Unlikely. "An hour. And you are doing what?"

"Putting the cash box in the drawer," Irving says. Innocent, even virtuous: as if he has just washed the windows.

"Why is that?"

"Oh, Sadie," Irving says. "She wanted to return a dollar, the one she took for her newspaper ad, the Missing Persons. She didn't want to trouble you."

His father sighs, ushers him aside, counts the money in the box. "You know better," he says. "Next time you come to me."

"Papa, of course."

His father's eyebrows are raised, lips pursed: there's no mistaking the skepticism. "Irvy," he says, "just watch the front. Miss Schumacher is waiting."

CHAPTER 4

Sadie

1929 (LATER SUMMER)

Sadie thinks of her body as a willful, erratic lap-dog, which sometimes cooperates and some-times does not. She's never sure what will happen when Bill climbs into bed with her. The first time, her wedding night, when Bill touched her breasts she was seized with a ticklishness so profound she had to dash to the bathroom to avoid wetting the bed. Sometimes she wakes, her skin sensitive, the texture of the sheets suddenly extravagant, a bodily dreaminess overtaking her. In that state she imagines kissing, a melting, a soft-focus drifting as in Impressionist paintings. This is how she used to imagine marital relations: a light, sugary closeness with the smooth movements of a waltz. Instead there's a saltiness to Bill's skin, and his eyes move from intensity to intensity, as if he is listening to a booming, dramatic inner music—hardly a waltz—and often when he touches her the melting sensation becomes a kind of fever, a possession not unlike wild sleeping, frightening, pleasurable, especially in release from the fever. She isn't always sure if the pleasure is worth the fright, though: the moments of lostness make her wary, distrustful of the whole business. When her body refuses to be lost, she watches the fever overtake her husband, allows the pleasure of his touch, his skin against her skin, but remains detached, as if the true Sadie is perched on the windowsill.

There are bedroom sounds, Bill's moaning and occasional bellows, at first alarming though now familiar, her own murmuring and sounds beyond a murmur, which she would not call bleating but would certainly rather not make: these are part of the lostness. She and Bill do not talk about what happens between them, but seem to have a code of hand holding, glasses of water, reading or not reading in bed, proximity or distance in sleep. Tonight, if they did speak, if Sadie could name what there is to name, she might say there's already too much lostness, even a sister is lost, she can't bear such immersion. But she doesn't say this and Bill's kisses are melting kisses; he touches her, there's the rising fever, a kind of racing heat, and he enters her. His solidity and the tang of his skin are a familiar return, both exciting and comforting, but as he's moving inside her the fever turns to panic, as if she is falling into canyons of space and can't stop falling. And now she is crying instead of murmuring, and Bill has stopped moving, he's hushing and rocking her, and the panic becomes a night desert stretching infinitely. Behind it Bill's voice says, "Darling, what is it?"

A choking. Her throat seems paralyzed and she shakes her head. "I don't know," she says, and then, absurdly, "a desert."

"What?" Bill offers her a glass of water.

And then the fever is gone. She kisses him, apologizes, rubs circles on his back, touches him lightly *down there*, the way she does when she's ready to start. Then it's as if she's perched on the windowsill again, observing the ceiling shadows and the alterations in Bill's face. After quiet feverless lovemaking, when Bill has fallen asleep, she runs a bath.

In the tub her legs float. She will not envision a death. There are already enough dead. A dead mother is plenty. Isn't it better to conjure the image of Goldie returning, walking into the Lancaster house with a shopping bag, bread from the bakery (a vision that exonerates Celia too)? Goldie cooks dinner—in truth, a mixed blessing, she never did get the knack—quietly reads in the kitchen while the kettle begins to boil. In her presence there's the shock of the ordinary—*she's here, she's back*—you're too stunned to say anything. Look, there she is, hair pinned up, thick brown waves dislodging the clips. Ten minutes later: there she is, still, her slim muscular arms, narrow hands, the chipped tooth, the plump lower lip. Goldie. Wouldn't you at first accept her back, with gratitude? *Thank God, we were worried.* Only later, when it's clear she's not an apparition and will stay at least the night, after she's cooked that first mediocre supper, the doubts creep in: will she leave again? And with doubts, the rage that she disappeared in the first place, your blank ignorance as to why. Is there nothing you can do to make her stay? And if not, if it's that random, what are you doing accepting her back so easily? How little she must value you to do something like this. How dare she.

Sadie finds herself soaped up and jammed between *how dare she* and *dead*, the white bath bubbles making tiny popping sounds. And here she pulls up short: this will not do. She has a husband and a house, and a garden in which crabgrass has begun to encroach on the petunias. She must stay in possession of herself.

AT 6 A.M. the telephone rings, a jarring trill in the living room. She swivels to the side of the bed, a swish of pale blue nightgown— the blue surprises her, she'd forgotten she'd put that on after the bath. Bill's already out of bed and she hears the rush of water from the bathroom faucet and the squeak of the turning tap, the stopped rush, footsteps down the hall and stairs to the ringing telephone. As she rounds the stairs, he's half-turned in the dim room, glow of white undershirt, thin belly and muscled arms, cheek curve, rim of wire glasses. Bill says, "Yes," and "What have you heard?" and "Papa Abe, what have you heard?" He turns in Sadie's direction: there's a wide smear of shaving foam on his chin and right cheek, as if he's dipped his face in meringue. When he shakes his head, a small dollop flies onto the carpet. "It's a little early, Papa," he says. "She's here." He gives Sadie the telephone, slippery from his wet hands.

"There is no tea." Her father's voice is a low blast through the receiver: it seems he is shouting. "A little coffee only." Apparently no one at the Lancaster house has marketed, something Goldie does twice a week.

"Good morning, Papa," Sadie says. "Why don't you have your tea downtown? I'll see what I can do."

"We always have tea," her father says.

"I know." She lowers her voice, in the unlikely chance that her father will follow her example. "What else do you need?"

Bill sighs from the staircase and in the sigh she hears mild outrage, which surfaces whenever her family makes odd requests—but it's outrage undercut by shaving foam.

"You come see," her father shouts. And then, mystified, "Did no one teach Celia to cook?"

SHE DEVOTES the afternoon to the Lancaster house: inventories the pantry, plans for the week. Celia follows. "Papa says you're out of tea," Sadie says.

"Um hmm," Celia says.

"You knew that?"

"It's been a couple of days."

"You should buy some, then."

And Celia's face opens in surprise, as if Sadie's suggested raising sheep. She wrinkles her nose and retreats upstairs when Sadie offers to market with her, though the grocer on Elmwood isn't far or strange—the family has shopped there for years. It's historical fact: Celia has marketed. And Celia has cooked, though admittedly her concentration's spotty. But maybe it's Sadie's mood Celia is responding to, the undeniable impatience: even the cat seems wary.

There is something satisfying in shopping alone, isn't there? No one slowing her pace or complicating simple tasks. Though as a girl she'd look forward to marketing with her mother, who'd joke with the store owners and chat with her friends, all of whom shopped at the same time every week. The best days coincided with Sadie's father's trips to New York: then her mother always seemed lighter, their routine chores oddly festive. While marketing, her mother would laugh easily and give her lemon drops, and the grocery became a kind of party, apples and beets passing for decoration.

Today the grocery is altogether ordinary, the narrow aisles

crowded, the owners preoccupied. Sadie hurries through, then to the closest bakery, stopping short of going to the butcher. And when she returns to the house, there is at first a silence, though it's already dinnertime. Her father's not even home. She brews tea, puts eggs and potatoes on to boil, and it occurs to her that these are Goldie's tasks and gestures. She watches her own hands as she sorts lettuce, separating the tender leaves from the bitter ones. Here she is in Goldie's place, doing Goldie's work in Goldie's manner: she concentrates, pours water on the lettuce, and the periphery of the kitchen begins to fall away as she repeats Goldie's name to herself. There is the sound-thought, the leaves, the water, and for a moment nothing else but the fervent will to make Goldie appear; it's the kind of consuming wish she felt as a child. But while she's drying the lettuce leaves, she notices a faint smell of tobacco smoke: Jo's in her usual spot on the back porch, with a cigarette, watching through the window. And then Jo's leaning in the kitchen door, blowing smoke into the house. She doesn't say hello, or offer help, just leans into the doorjamb and observes. The set of her shoulders makes you want to smack her. *No wonder Goldie's gone—* but there's the trap, speculating again.

"Papa's late today?" Sadie says.

"You could say that," Jo says.

"I have to get home."

"You know where he is, don't you? With her." The cigarette hangs from Jo's lips. She forms a circle with her left index finger and thumb, and pushes her right index finger in and out of the circle, and a thin line of smoke curves above her head. "You know who I'm talking about, don't you?"

"I don't want to discuss this."

"No, you wouldn't."

"And please stop doing that. It's disgusting," Sadie says. "I've left you food for this week. Market before you run out."

"Me? I got work to do. I work."

"Celia's not going to do it."

Celia is in the back garden, the light now a thickening yellow: from the kitchen window she appears slightly gilded, weeding the snapdragon bed.

"No," Jo says.

"Who's going to do it?"

Jo stubs out her cigarette in the sink.

"Goldie's gone," Sadie says.

But Jo stands at the sink watching Celia through the window, absently fingering the wet tobacco, and it seems she has left the room.

SADIE VISITS and revisits the stark police precinct, sometimes bringing bakery sweets, which have the effect of increased friendliness but no Goldie. She places classified ads in Rochester and Cleveland, New York and Chicago. There is nothing, though by late July the telephone's become tyrannical: inane calls from Lancaster, two or three times a day (Irving's drinking, Jo's annoyed, no one made Shabbos dinner); and nagging calls from her mother-in-law, whose sufferings calcified long ago. Once Sadie's called to retrieve Celia from a barbershop, where Celia has followed a stranger—a handsome one—and stationed herself. No word from Goldie, or anyone who knows Goldie. Once a day, Sadie lets herself fall on the sofa and wills the world to stop. The world does not respond. After ten minutes she's up again, in search of the armoring lipstick and her shoes, and maybe one of those bakery treats.

At least she has the separation of neighborhoods, of her house itself, some measure of privacy—yet even that is subject to interruption. In early August, weeks after Goldie's disappearance, Bill announces, "We'll be having dinner with my mother and Mrs. Teitelbaum on Thursday, Sadie. You know the sort of things she likes."

Sadie's at her writing desk, addressing letters to police departments in Syracuse and Albany and Toronto. Why should she entertain anyone now? Not to mention that it's hot, and Mother Feldstein likes heavy dinners. Yet it seems simpler, really, to cook the dinner than to argue or to defer any longer. Sadie will come up with something, though at the moment she won't answer Bill: she dislikes his planning by fiat, and she will make sure the words *Syracuse* and *Police* are beautiful.

On Thursday Sadie roasts a brisket for her mother-in-law and her mother-in-law's fusty companion, Rose Teitelbaum. Bill is late from work, and Mother Feldstein arrives first, followed by an asphyxiating cloud of cologne and a squinting Mrs. Teitelbaum. Within minutes—four, actually, as Sadie's begun to time her mother-in-law—it's clear that Mother Feldstein does not like the aqua davenport, a color she finds alternately clownish and risqué; or the fresh lemonade which is apparently too *lemony*. She somehow manages a second glass after Bill arrives, which is when—twenty-one minutes into the visit—Sadie detects a smile. Mrs. Teitelbaum quietly demolishes the plate of hors d'oeuvres, and speaks to Sadie only when Mother Feldstein is focused on her son. The subject is the season, which is Rose Teitelbaum's second least favorite, the very least favorite being winter, the most favorite being not a season at all but the second week in September, which happens to coincide with Mrs. Teitelbaum's birthday. At the dinner table, Mrs. Teitelbaum accepts a large helping of brisket and then, in whispered tones, complains of excessive summer perspiration.

No one speaks about Goldie. No one. How is it possible? Sadie's not about to invite Mother Feldstein's speculations, but wouldn't her mother-in-law say something? True, Mother Feldstein lost her own sister years ago to influenza, which was tragic, terrible, but no one questions the whereabouts of dear Aunt Ida now. Maybe if Goldie's fate were known for sure, Mother Feldstein and Mrs. Teitelbaum would inquire. Maybe. Instead they frown, pointedly it seems. The third time Mother Feldstein frowns in the direction of the aqua davenport Sadie wonders—is she herself unbalanced to wonder?—if Mother Feldstein sees not a sofa but evidence of the Cohens' moral failings. Goldie's had the poor judgment to disappear, and Sadie is, after all, her sister. Just look at that davenport.

True, Sadie *is* on edge. She determinedly serves up the chocolate cake, which Mother Feldstein eats but does not criticize or praise, instead smiling at Bill and holding his hand and ignoring her. After coffee, Bill walks arm in arm with his mother to her taxicab—they're cozy together—and Mrs. Teitelbaum follows, leaning into Sadie. Both women offer Sadie perfunctory kisses on the cheek, and she resists the impulse to wipe her face.

The evening has apparently not dampened Bill's mood. In spite of everything, he's buoyant. Isn't that one of the reasons she married him, his buoyancy? Once in the bedroom, he seems interested in her shoes, now off her feet; he finds them adorably small. The interest travels to her feet, her stockinged legs. Her body pleases him and she likes her own shapeliness, the way dresses and suits fit her, but how she got this particular body is a matter she had nothing to do with. And it has an odd power she can't control. For example, the way the simple gesture of taking off stockings affects her husband: it makes him amorous, the dressing and undressing she does—just look at his eyes, the band's in full swing—though to her it feels no different from the dressing and undressing she has done since childhood. And how anyone can feel amorous after three hours with those women is a mystery. Sadie sits up and brushes off her dress and kisses her husband. He is the most familiar of strangers.

WHEN SADIE and Bill are called to Niagara Falls, she tells no one.

"I can go without you," Bill says. "No reason for you to go too." Sunlight through the window reflects off his glasses—it's hard to see his eyes—but his tone is commanding. This is a tone he sometimes takes, and Sadie often pretends to heed: he's stubborn and she finds ways around him. But she can be stubborn too. She climbs into the car and says nothing, and he drives. A herd of clouds covers the western sky, keyhole patches of blue emerging to the north and east. At the morgue they are led to the bloated body of a woman, drowned, found at the edge of the whirlpool rapids. Brunette, probably in her thirties. A suicide? No one can say. She has not been embalmed; from five yards away, the stench is overwhelming. Before Sadie even sees the face, she knows it is not Goldie. The body is too tall, the hair even now closer to dishwater blond. Still, Sadie forces herself to look. The face is swollen, disfigured, the hair matted, but you can see she's someone else, Irish maybe: an unclaimed Irish stranger. It's hard to breathe, hard to move. Sadie studies the woman-turned-grotesque as if mesmerized.

"Okay then, let's go," Bill says. "Come on, Sadie."

But her husband seems remote, as if he is calling from another room, as if in this room there is only Sadie and the drowned woman, a woman not Goldie.

"Sadie?"

And Sadie recognizes in herself the absurd desire to speak to the woman, to utter some mix of *What happened?* and *I'm sorry* and listen for a response. Before she turns away, impulsively she touches the woman's arm.

"YOU GET these ideas," Bill says. They're in the Ford again.

She isn't listening. The woman's anonymity is terrible, it's all putrid and terrible, the silence, the woman's state. Sadie doesn't even know how to think of her, except as the drowned woman, as a drowned not-Goldie, and this is unacceptable. Now that they know of her, they should not abandon her: she needs proper care, proper burial. These are Sadie's recurring thoughts, the ones she spoke aloud to Bill, who seems prepared to let the drowned woman drown.

"Sadie?" Bill says. "The answer is no. I can't pay for something like that."

"Sadie?" And now the tone is coaxing. "Darling, this person is not your sister. You can't even know how to bury her." And here he has a point: she's almost certainly Gentile. Maybe Catholic, maybe Lutheran, but not Jewish. "You can't go around claiming other people's dead," Bill says.

It's true, the stranger *is* someone else's dead, but she is unclaimed: is that why Sadie touched her? The woman seemed so enormously sad, or perhaps the sadness was the absence of the woman within the body. Sadie knows that touching doesn't comfort the dead, and how could it comfort Sadie herself? Was it, then, to confirm that the woman did not still live, the way children touch dead squirrels—to see what happens? Nothing happens except the contact itself, and now Sadie carries with her this touch, this absence, this awareness of the woman who is not. And even though Sadie's washed her hands, the morgue smell seems to be on her.

"This isn't like you," Bill says. "When we get home, why don't you sleep?"

. . .

SHE SLIPS OFF her shoes in the bedroom, but does not undress, rests in her suit dress and stockings, ready to answer the next call. Sadie does not put much stock in dreams, but she can't ignore the one in which her legs wither, and she does not want that dream again. It returned last week, in the August heat: she woke to the hazy sensation that her legs had given out altogether. As if she'd been walking interminably and finally could move her legs only by pushing them with her hands. She woke intact, slid out of bed and paced the room, testing each muscle; a creeping strangeness? No. They were ordinary capable legs. It's only the dream legs she has to watch out for, and perhaps keeping her clothes on will help remind her. Still, it would not surprise her to discover, one afternoon, that her legs are made of paper and disintegrate in rain.

"You have to be more sensible," Bill says. He's in his undershirt, impatient, frowning. "What are you doing?"

Apparently she's flexing her legs. There's a rhythm to the flexing and relaxing, something iambic. "It's an exercise," she says. "For ballet." Sadie's seen a few performances, hasn't she? She switches to pointing her toes. She does not tell Bill about the dream, or mention the waking impulse to fall, which arrives in dizzy irresistible waves.

Subsequent afternoons in the city, Sadie imagines she sees Goldie. One day she recognizes what might be the dead woman's sister: widely spaced blue eyes, dishwater hair going gray, Irish tilt to the nose. Visible without the water-mottling, freckles.

The freckled woman is not the last she and Bill are called to view. "Maybe you can identify this one," the shift officers say. "Maybe this one's yours." Women die all the time, it seems.

CHAPTER 5

Goldie

I.

1928

Hours flaking at the edges then cracking through, the bits flaking further and dissolving: during her mother's last days the names of the world seemed to slide away. Time and light and sound seemed to collide, and Goldie developed a deaf ear. Which seemed the sanest course, given the splintered orchestra of family sounds and the eerie chiming of spoons against medicine bottles, glasses of water ringing. In silence, Goldie bathed her mother and most afternoons held her mother's hand, sometimes talking, sometimes not, and her mother sweated and watched the changing light and slept, and the silence seemed a shared, more benevolent country. Then Sadie would arrive and take over, and Goldie would sleep. She didn't anticipate that the deafness would continue beyond her mother's death, yet if anything it deepened: Jo and Celia opened and closed their mouths and Goldie attached herself to the silences, the pauses and missed beats and long soundless stretches when the talking was done.

She was mired. The Lancaster house had mired her just as it

had mired her mother. She was not supposed to notice the mired-ness, the way the housekeeping had fallen to her, the cooking and marketing, the watch-guarding of Celia, just as she was not sup-posed to mention her father's cruelty, his philandering in plain view. In the mornings when Goldie combed Celia's hair, Celia squirmed and resisted the small hairbrush, the simple comb: *Don't let it touch my neck, it mustn't touch my neck.* Goldie moved her hands gingerly, considered the pink strips of light on the Bermans' roof. Sometimes her father spoke to her, sometimes Jo spoke. Most of what they said did not require a reply, and her father, shameless with Lillian Schumacher, did not deserve one. Still, there was never enough silence. Even when the house was empty of family, a low buzzing remained, a pervasive, staticky hum. Perhaps it em-anated from Celia. Perhaps Celia was just the one most affected; after the funeral, she'd taken to sleeping in their mother's sick-room, which now seemed coated with dissonance. Goldie tried to imagine the buzzing and family voices as water; in water she could hear the beginnings of silence.

It was better, of course, to leave the house. She resumed her job at the library, where no one squawked or tugged at her and si-lence was revered. Even in winter she walked the city, where si-lence flourished below the noise, both profound noise and its opposite occupying construction sites. She took a streetcar up to the Falls, to the obliterating sounds of Niagara, and the vast rapids and the ragged ice floes and the silence they contained. And there was Daniel, always there was Daniel.

Returning to the house, she withdrew into her body. Ignored the others, played the piano to drown them out, occasionally dropping the tempo and letting the notes hang. The snow finally melted. At the late edge of day she stepped out to the yard, at-tended to birdcalls. Clouds matted and fell into other clouds, pil-ing up across evening, briefly infused with violet and fuchsia before melting into an opaque low-slung night.

In the silence, she heard trains.

II. FIRST ARRIVAL

1901

At the pier the air smelled of illness and brine. She did not remember her father, though she could see he was waiting for her to speak: for too long she hesitated and a sourness crossed his face. He wore a suit finer than the suits she'd seen, gray wool with a vest and pocket watch; he spoke more English than Yiddish, words like hail, melting before she could know their shape. Her mother's face puckered in concentration and he shifted to Yiddish and lowered his voice. Then he stood between them, steering them through the crowd, and she tried to slip around to her mother, and he held her shoulder in place.

He smelled of tobacco and pencil shavings, laundry soap, sweat rinsed with spice, but the scent didn't match his expression. The sourness did not leave her father but in those first weeks solidified into a stern chill, and she later supposed he could not forgive her for the moment in New York when she gazed at him so blankly. Or perhaps for the fact that she remained a daughter and not a son, as if a fraud had been perpetrated; or because she was scrawny for a five-year-old, often taken for three; or because poor, ramshackle Dinivitz—and the whole, bleak Ukraine—had indelibly marked her; or because he could not find enough of himself in her face. At that first meeting, she had a smell: she'd been ill on the boat, both she and her mother, and they still stank like barnyard, with no chance to bathe before the long, feverish train ride to Buffalo.

Over a decade she found that slices of herself were missing, and she imagined her body to be a variegation of solid stripes and empty space, like a wrought-iron fence. There were the babies, that cycle of her mother's belly rising and the new squalling babies turned to toddlers and climbing and clinging; and sometimes miscarriages, and her mother sick; and more new babies, all of them it seemed eating her mother alive and starting in on Goldie.

Even then, the first desire was to be with her mother, the second to be invisible. It was difficult to hide completely, but she found ways. You could leave your body without the family noticing, as long as your hands were occupied. A hiding different from Russian hiding with her mother, which had been at once safer and more dangerous. Her uncles had doted on her mother and on Goldie but their village seemed now a gray blur against a chalk sky: still she wore plain dresses and braided her hair. In Buffalo she perfected her English and could speak without accent, as she had perfected phrases in Russian, another language of disguise.

For years she liked to hide in the storage closet and read in the puddle of light from the hallway. In the warm seasons she used the garden shed, but Jo and Celia followed her whenever they were not affixed to her mother, who was tending to a younger infant. And when Celia's tantrums began, Goldie would be left to watch the milder ones, or sent to the market or the neighbors', which meant giving up her mother altogether.

Eventually there was a piano, which her father approved of as long as she played florid romantic pieces without error. In summer vegetable gardening, though she had to supervise Celia, which meant always paying attention. Sleep seemed a reprieve, and as a young woman she wondered if there were a difference, really, between *dead* and *sleeping*. Of course her mother was here, this side of dead, and on rare occasions they took an afternoon, a couple of hours to sit and drink tea, or in fine weather stroll through Delaware Park, and once even visited the Falls, and were happy.

III. DANIEL

1929

Desire flared in Goldie when she was pouring water, lifting the white pitcher, one hand in the stream; her skin jumped the way it did when Daniel touched her, an all-day ache. Every week this desire and every week the waiting, interminable. Desire flared and she was no longer Goldie, a scrap of wood inside a dress, but instead a ribbon of light above the lake, a swimming in water and orange air and shadow. On Wednesdays she went to Daniel. He touched her, her skin jumped, that's all she wanted—for him to keep touching her. Three o'clock Wednesday his father left to practice with his string quartet: three o'clock Wednesday they had the house, Daniel's narrow bed, thickets of clouds out the second-floor window, three o'clock he undressed her, she arched toward him, three o'clock they'd couple, heat and tang of his skin, rhythmic thrust, Wednesday his mouth on her breasts and throat, Wednesday his walnut eyes. Two hours. A clear pocket of time before his father returned, before she left through the front door, as if from her piano lesson, into the stark evening.

Some days she was overcome by his voice alone—Daniel's voice uttering the most mundane of sentences, simply asking the time—as if she were breathing ether. He wanted to marry her, but what could he foresee? What he knew was the ecstasy of love-making, piano sonatas, the quiet of his father's house, not the chaos and chafing and illness delivered with infants, or the ways men wander.

"What about this autumn?" he said.

Her breathing took a fast plunge. "Where would we live?"

"Here." He kissed her, stroked her face. "There's plenty of room."

With his father, a sweet man, a widower who had raised him alone. Daniel would never leave his father's town, she knew this. Just as she would not have left her mother.

It was almost spring, a month before her mother's unveiling.

"Not just yet," she told him. "Soon."

CHAPTER 6

Sadie

SEPTEMBER 1929

Pearl Kaminsky buzzes around the dress rack where Sadie is idly sifting through the better pieces. A hot September Thursday, a day on which Sadie needs to move slowly, and Pearl—a saleswoman more often discreet than not—has apparently had too much coffee. Thin and nervous, her eyes overbright, eyelids stuck open, she circles Sadie, flashing handbags and accessories. The oblong clutch perfect for swatting.

"No thank you, Pearl."

"Is there something else I can help you with? How about hats, Sadie? Do you need a new hat?"

"Not just yet." Sadie flashes her *keep away* look, the closest to rude she's been to Pearl, who God knows has her own burdens—tubercular husband, reprobate son—and could be snapping beneath the weight of them. Who would have predicted these turns in Pearl's life, or the way they've dimmed her early glamour? Today, Pearl *has* held back for some time: Sadie's been floating through the store for a half-hour, trying to stave off a growing preoccupation with undergarments. She ought to buy a dress and sweater for Celia, whose clothes are an amalgam of hand-me-downs and bright ill-fitting dresses from sale racks. Yet she returns to the display discreetly tucked into the store's back corner, pulled by the absurd desire to replace the ragged underclothes in Goldie's bureau—as if *knickers* could bring Goldie back. And here Sadie is, considering white cotton. With a bit of lace? Lace can't hurt, really it's lovely, the pattern of flowering vines along the leg and waist bands. You can't help but admire the handiwork.

She's dodged Pearl's questions and wonders if Pearl guesses the direction of her thinking. Goldie's disappearance makes people nervous. Even Sadie's friends, who've stopped inquiring, have taken to a forced cheeriness, and this makes Goldie—or Goldie's imprint—all the more present, a kind of pet ghost trailing Sadie through the city, hovering invisibly in shops and weakening the floorboards. Which might explain beyond coffee and commissions Pearl's own obsession with handbags and evening gloves.

But the floorboards are solid. Maybe Sadie needs some lace-trimmed underwear of her own. Pearl tends to her other customers, and Sadie tries to distract herself with sweater sets, which are soft and finely made but too warm to contemplate in this weather. A dizziness passes through her, what might be the beginnings of a migraine; for an instant Sadie could crumple like a two-year-old. This Pearl Kaminsky does not seem to notice: she's advising a matronly woman who loves yellow and pink. Neither color suits the woman, and Pearl holds up a blue-gray linen suit. The woman gazes longingly at a pale rose debutante's gown on sale. Everyone is unhappy. "Pearl," Sadie says. "Could you help me find some things for Celia?" And the moment passes.

IT'S BEEN two months and Sadie feels herself becoming strange: the impulse to buy underclothes and lipsticks (they are everywhere, her lipsticks); smoking in public; absentmindedness (where are her keys? Her hat? Her umbrella?). Ordinary life seems to occur in islands of time divided by maverick currents. Jo is as moody and difficult as ever, though more pensive; Irving's hands won't stop moving—he's smoking, or habitually smoothing his hair, or rubbing a rabbit's foot on a metal clip (and must regularly be asked to put that thing away). Celia's sadness seems more intractable: she's taken to wearing Goldie's skirts and beads, as well as Sadie's lipstick—must she wear the same shade?—and spends long hours in Goldie's room. Bill's more hardheaded, and he seems increasingly in league with her father, who himself is unbearable, sterner, more strident than usual. He won't refer to Goldie by name and he regularly shouts at Celia, who he knows cannot bear shouting. He refuses to hire a housekeeper, despite Jo's avoidance of housework and Celia's spotty competence and Irving's refusal to wash anything other than himself. He persists in his affair with Lillian Schumacher, and all this Sadie has tolerated, making only the mildest of suggestions about the house. Instead, she concentrates on her own domestic routine, trying to extend the ordinary islands of time, though Goldie's absence keeps eroding them. Diligently, Sadie keeps the Sabbath, which seems a claim on permanence. And it's a relief when her father agrees to come to Shabbos dinner: maybe for an evening they can find normalcy.

His arrival at first seems indistinguishable from last year's Sabbath visits, when he was somber but self-possessed, and later wistful, more relaxed. This evening is quiet, Bill is deferential and kind, and though Sadie does not feel at *ease*, exactly, there's a formal calm, the sort she wishes would mark a permanent change. She serves a light meal and good wine, and her father speaks about his plans for the store, his buying trips to New York, the new bridge to Canada. Tonight his voice is smooth and low, the one she likes— no sign of disturbance or shouting—and it comforts her simply to hear him talk, even about construction. Throughout dinner she finds herself contemplating his elegance, a handsomeness enunciated by his beautiful suit. No doubt the suits also caught Lillian Schumacher's attention, and she wishes he would choose a more dignified woman, though it is, of course, not her place to say: he will not abide mention of other available women. She clears the dinner plates, and before she has brought the dessert he fills his pipe at the table and lights it, as if he's forgotten the order of things, or her general insistence on eating and smoking in separate rooms. She brews and pours tea, and Bill smokes too now, a cigar: plumes of smoke fan out along the ceiling.

"Your sister, she's gone," her father says. "We should sit."

She freezes. "What?" She's been lulled, despite his recent behavior, she's been lulled—and by talk of steel beams—into forgetting the shouting, the unkindness. When *did* he last speak Goldie's name? But this, to sit shivah, consigning Goldie to the dead? "What do you mean?"

"The calendar is where?"

And Bill's watching her now, concern in his face, but no surprise or distress: this is, she thinks, the face he uses with his patients before pulling their teeth. And her own face feels hot, her throat constricting and her whole body tensing, a momentary absence of breath. "You can't," she says. The dining room table seems wholly combustible. *Shameful,* she thinks, and the word slips out sotto voce, a hiss.

Bill, apparently unashamed, shakes his head slightly and coughs.

Her father's voice rises in the old pinching way. "This is how you speak to your father?"

"You don't know if Goldie's dead," Sadie says.

"To me, she is dead." Or has shamed the family and ought to be considered so. Her father, stone-faced behind his cloud of smoke, acknowledges no hypocrisy.

And Sadie can only think of her own limbs then, the pulling currents in her arms and legs, and she rises, a drumming in her head, the air in the room turning to a bilious warm fog, which finally clears when she reaches the kitchen porch door and opens it to a rush of cold. From here she can see past the dark fence line to the lights of other houses, starred patches of sky between clouds, oak leaves rustling on heavy branches and along the damp ground. Sadie's mother would not have chosen this way, her father has to know that, but he knows many things he ignores. He's never spoken of Russia, as if in not speaking he could cast off those years. Perhaps he's wanted a casting off of children as well; if so, starting with Goldie makes little sense. Cruel thoughts, but ones Sadie lets herself hold in her mind while she listens for the cats that prowl through her yard and the night birds cawing somewhere beyond the fence. She keeps the back door open and at the kitchen sink fills the pans to soak and soaps the china, while pipe smoke seeps into the kitchen. She will not bring out the dessert, and her father will not follow her here: unless they speak on his terms they will not speak. He'll smoke and finish his tea and explain his plans to Bill. This is his way. The continuing pipe smoke says enough. It trails Bill into the kitchen, and he takes the calendar from the wall and Sadie feigns absorption in the silver.

Once Bill retreats, she waits several minutes, closes the back door, and forces herself out to the dining room. Her father and Bill sit beside each other now, talking in low tones, teacups pushed aside for the calendar, her father sipping a new glass of sweet wine. Sadie leans through the doorway and fixes her gaze on the crown of her father's head. "Good Shabbos," she says, then hurries across the living room and up the stairs to the second floor, where she picks up a novel and locks herself in the guest room.

Here too she can breathe. There are only murmurs from the dining room, the rush of night air through the window screen. The novel is set in New York, a romance. *Margaret loved the bustle of the city*, Chapter 3 begins, but that one clear sentence seems to devolve into a pattern of ink she traces for pages without comprehending. Eventually she hears footsteps downstairs, the front door opening and closing, her father's Ford coughing on the street.

Bill's footsteps travel to the stairs, turn to a knock on the door. "Darling?" he says. His coaxing tone. "Sadie, it's your father's decision."

New York. A city that seems, like many places, lovely and unkind. Before her mother's later illness, before Bill, before she'd even finished high school, she'd wanted New York—the New York of theater and symphony and style. College at Barnard. Her father permitted only the University of Buffalo. And now that time was done, the desire to unravel it mediated by this: she'd had years with her mother. She'd met Bill. She'd moved to this house, away from Lancaster, and she planned for children. But what if she'd settled in New York? If Goldie had?

"Sadie?"

"I'm busy just now." She returns to *Margaret loved the bustle of the city* and begins the chapter again.

YOU CAN'T erase a person, though her father in his rage will try. But Goldie keeps becoming clearer to Sadie. Saturday afternoon the light is pale saffron, sometimes chalky, muted by low clouds, and through the shifting brightness, Goldie's body emerges in sharp detail. The body that is or is not: the narrow ankles, delicate feet, easily bruised—hence the solid shoes. Plump elbows, full breasts not unlike Sadie's, her whole body not unlike Sadie's, but for slight variations, and poor taste in clothes. A few more scars. Is Goldie less careful? Or *was* she? And there's the confusion again: which tense do you use, even in thought? Can you say she was more scarred without asserting her death? *When last seen*, Goldie had limber hands, a once-injured hip. In cold weather, there was the faint stiffness to her walk, and when she was surprised, a slight stutter peppered her speech. Of course the small details surface: Sadie has memorized Goldie, memorized all of them and now they are imprinted. And it's absurd of her father to believe otherwise.

This Sadie concedes: if Goldie is unharmed she's got herself into something her father would condemn. Which would mean what? A romance with a Catholic? Pregnancy? Not what you'd expect from Goldie but you wouldn't expect *dead* either. And if Goldie is dead? Which she is not. But if? Only *if*, Papa has a point: seal away the body, seal away uncertainty, end false hope. *If not*— and how can you believe her dead—what then?

The Sunday after her father's visit, Sadie's in bed, the thickness of sleep still on her and at its perimeter a sensation of dirt falling over her. In the half-dream her eyes are open. Paralysis has climbed from her legs to her torso and arms, and then she reminds herself to breathe. The bedroom comes into focus, and her perfectly movable limbs, and Bill beside her sleeping.

Forget dreams: edge the thought out a doorway, lock the door. Her panic abates, and she wraps her arms around Bill and pulls tight, as if he is the missing body. For two days they have been speaking in empty pleasantries, and she has not wanted him to touch her, the loneliness worsening. Awake, he will not budge from his support of her father, and she is appalled. Asleep, he is better company, comforting to touch—the husband she wants him to be.

. . .

FOR A WEEK her days seem slippery and uncertain: she tries to remedy this by cleaning. Her own housekeeping takes on a frenzied, hysterical quality—her manner not unlike Pearl Kaminsky's—though at Lancaster she is focused and methodical. If there is a clue she missed in Goldie's room—in the closet dust, on the rain-streaked windows—she will find it. She sweeps and scrubs the floor, bleaches the sheets, polishes the bureau, the rocking chair, washes the windows, the oval mirror. It isn't as much satisfying as trancelike. Sadie doesn't bother with the rest of the house, though it's in shambles: for a moment the flaw in her logic gapes at her, then she continues with the woodwork.

In mid-September, before the shivah starts, Sadie visits the Falls alone. Swarms of tourists gawk at the torrents, the mist. They mill in predictable patterns: the Falls is turning them all into sheep, stupid with the pleasures of the autumn, sun, mist, picnic lunch, the giant curtains of water. It's as if no one ever drowned here. There's pleasure in that forgetting, and the illusion that scanning the crowd will evoke Goldie herself. As if all this time she's been a tourist with a bag of peanuts, walking the paths of Goat Island, watching couples kiss near the Horseshoe Falls. Or maybe kissing someone herself? What could be so wrong with kissing? And why not imagine Goldie, here or elsewhere, with or without someone to kiss, with or without the bag of peanuts? Why shouldn't she see chunks of rainbow where the sun hits the mist? Far better than dead: why not pretend this? Which Sadie will do.

SO SADIE'S FATHER will mourn, and she will quietly disavow the shivah. This she cannot tell Bill. Craziness, he'd say. Wouldn't he tell her she was sick with loss—all the more reason to sit shivah? He might blame Goldie, and even if he doesn't, he's so much more pleasant when he's not enforcing a point. No, she won't tell Bill. She'll think of the Falls.

Still, Sadie is unprepared for the scene at Lancaster on the first day of mourning: the house in fact now clean but underlit, mirrors covered with sheets, a flat silence, her father in the parlor, sitting stiffly on a wooden chair, summoning all his stoniness. It's a mourning unlike any she's seen: no weeping, just a vast chill. Lillian Schumacher sits beside him, hair swept up, queenly in a soft black dress and blue silk scarf, and quietly coos. He does not seem to mind Lillian's pigeon sounds, though they interrupt his silence and rage. What is it you say to her?

"Hello, Lillian. Thank you for your kindness," Sadie manages.

Lillian nods and seems to contemplate the eternal via the floral wallpaper.

Irving is glassy-eyed, clearly drunk, propped up in a hard-backed chair. Today he seems to be palming a marble. Celia's in a dark blue dress—one of Goldie's—and she fumes from the window seat, apparently hoping to stare Lillian down, but Lillian holds to her affected piety and strokes Papa's hand.

All morning he rages silently and accepts condolences from reluctant visitors, neighbors who move slowly into the house, hover for a few minutes, leave food in the kitchen, and quickly depart. A handful stay longer: a few cousins and Moshe Schumacher, the lawyer; his dazed wife, Bertha; and Lillian, his regrettable sister. Nothing like the shivah for Sadie's mother, that week of bittersweet collapse and near-constant company.

Even in his wooden chair, her father seems massive, royal, though a royalty she does not understand. She cannot summon her love for him. And sitting in the parlor will not help her understand, will not remind her of love. You sit and time crawls. You sit and eventually your mind empties, doesn't it? And fills with the knowledge of absence? Of God? But what she hears is Lillian's cooing, which seems more and more like bedroom obscenity. By late morning, Celia is perfectly still, a furious stillness no one would mistake for peace.

Just before noon, Irving begins to snore, and it's Lillian who goes to him, nudges him awake. "You must be exhausted." She smiles at him and widens her eyes, as if in private understanding.

"I suppose we all are," Sadie says.

Lillian returns to their father, resumes stroking his hand. "Of course," she says. "And I'm so sorry."

At this Celia snorts, and then their father stamps his foot, and

Lillian turns her face back to the wallpaper—as if they have synchronized their movements, which in some peculiar way they have. But the quiet can't last much longer, the room's too stifling: Celia's bound to do something more provocative than snorting, and if she doesn't maybe Sadie herself should.

"Excuse us," Sadie tells Lillian. She turns to Celia. "Help me for a moment, would you?" and they leave the parlor for the kitchen. Out the kitchen window, a thin stream of smoke rises from the back porch. Jo, in her usual spot.

"It's Lillian's fault," Celia says. "Big Tit Lillian. She's a menace."

"I don't know what you mean," Sadie says.

"Yes you do."

"And I wish you wouldn't talk like that."

"I know," Celia says, pity in her voice.

Then Jo's in the doorway, cigarette in hand. Slim, wearily elegant. Behind her, jays disappear into the orange and red of a maple.

"Nice job on Goldie's room," Jo says. Of course she'd have recognized Sadie's work, but her tone is unreadable. You never know what Jo might say next, how deep it will cut.

"Jo, please. Let's not."

But Jo simply offers Sadie a cigarette. None of them return to the parlor.

WHEN THE SHIVAH is finished and the sheets come off the mirrors, Abe's anger persists, now more tempered but more inclusive: his daughters have not respected his wishes. Sadie quietly continues the out-of-town Missing Persons ads, checks in on the house, occasionally brings her father and Irving lunch at the store. It's a matter of time before her father starts in again. He waits until October, just before the High Holidays. He's at the jeweler's bench, sorting a group of tiny sapphires, blue dots on a black tray.

"Your sister's things, it's time to pack," he says. "Give them to a church," he says. Meaning *not to Jews.*

"Why?" Sadie says. "We keep Mama's things."

"Catholic or Protestant," he says. "I don't care." He pushes gems back and forth between small blue hills.

"I'm sorry I don't have time to help," Sadie says. "I've left sand-wiches and apples."

Her father does not raise the subject with Sadie again. Accord-ing to Irving and Jo, he wants *that* bedroom cleared and painted. He intends to buy a new bed. He will hire outside the family to do it, if he has to.

Jo capitulates, or so it seems. She's demure with him, and it's a strange thing to witness, all her "Yes, Papa"s, "Of course, Papa"s, and then her lonely smoking out in the yard. She packs for dona-tion to St. Vincent de Paul and hires the painter; she prices beds. And when the painter's done, she has him paint Celia's bedroom and her own. Goldie's bed is hauled away, a new mattress deliv-ered. After she's finished with the house and the visit to St. Vincent de Paul, she leads Sadie to the upstairs storage closet. Two new boxes are wedged into the back. "He doesn't know the difference, you know," Jo says. "My clothes from Celia's from Goldie's. Doesn't know Mama's."

IT'S A COLD rainy Thursday when Sadie enters the house to si-lence and Celia napping on the new bed, wearing Goldie's dun skirt and white blouse though they're too thin for autumn. Cream-white arms covered by goosebumps, no garish makeup today, Celia's prettiness surfacing in sleep. Sadie tucks a wool blanket around her and descends to the kitchen to start tea. After a time, Celia appears, the pale green sweater Sadie bought her covering the blouse.

"I suppose Goldie's in New York," Celia says. "Don't you think?"

New York. *Margaret loved the bustle of the city.* "You sure about that, Celia?"

"No. It could be somewhere else. Miami."

"You talk to Jo about this?"

Celia shakes her head. "Jo's in a mood."

"Why don't you sit down?" Sadie says. "You want a bite to eat?"

Celia complies. The orange cat saunters by and leaps into her lap, and she scratches its head and strokes the thick fur of its back, the purring radiating through the room, over the low rush of wind against the house, the round clock's ponderous ticks.

Sadie slices bread and cheese and apples, holds an apple slice on her tongue and lets the sugar melt. Did her father foresee this, Celia's devoted, embroidered waiting? Because what, short of formal mourning, would it take to end Celia's pining? Which will now continue nonetheless.

It's November. Through the city there's the shock and chaos of the crash, the markets dissolving overnight, her father and brother locking down the jewelry store *just in case,* Bill hiding cash in the cedar chest. But alone in her house, there are moments for Sadie when everything drops away. There's the sudden arrival of geese, a sound not immediately beautiful but compelling nonetheless, the squawks a wild yearning. Then they stop, and you can imagine yourself light, unencumbered. The sensation is temporary but seems permanent; you can't hear anything but birds' wings and the northern breeze and rustle of browning leaves. Angora clouds dip low and white and gray, and the geese pass south.

CHAPTER 7

Lillian

1927–29

It wasn't always the handsome men Lillian wanted: she liked a certain assurance, a scent, the way ordinary men were transformed by desire. How beautiful they became, their bodies shimmering, muscular legs stretching, broad backs and thick arms bending around her, cocks hard in the dimness of hotel rooms, balls delicate against her thighs. She chose men who only in private revealed their sweeter natures: all had unforgiving lives, all wanted forgiveness. Even, it seemed, begged for such a thing, not simply sex but the transcendence sex might confer, a wild impossible blessing. Was it delusion, seeing them this way? Imagining her fingers slipping past a man's ribs, palm cupping his heart. She wanted that and in certain moments, the men—their faces bathed in yearning— seemed to want it too. But for all their spur-of-the-moment appearances and near-desperate fucking and orgasmic proclamations *I love you Lillian I love you Lillian oh Lillian Lillian oh*—the men quickly vanished, never left their wives. It was a story she'd heard elsewhere. How it became hers she did not know.

But one way or another, your life unspools. Lillian saw the ways it could go. Take her parents, her father oafish and generous and dead; her mother fish-pale and morose, an ineffectual, complaining woman. Carp under river ice, nibbling ancient disappointments. The smallest pleasures—hot bath, tea, orange dusk through the bare elms—dissipated in Lillian's mother's house. Lillian could, at least, choose her own loneliness: at seventeen she took a tiny flat, a job as a shop clerk.

Years tick. You pass certain men in the street. Some you pull into your body, briefly, always too briefly, singular tastes and scents with you even when you're sure you have forgotten. And then, at a holiday party, a wedding reception, there's the quick peck on the cheek, close enough for you to catch the scent again. A sexual thrill rushes through you: you have to brace against it as the next in line, maybe his wife, maybe his daughter, also kisses your cheek, and other men you have known and their wives look on.

In 1927, the year she turned thirty-six, Lillian was plush. Zaftig. Dark lipstick, flowery perfumes, plunge-neckline blue satin and beautiful shoes. In a tiny shop off Main Street, Kaplan's, she sold stationery, fountain pens, account ledgers, dark leather diaries. When Abe Cohen appeared, she made no assumptions: for years he had lived on the outskirts of her thinking. Dull. Handsome. Relentlessly upstanding. A friend of her older brother's, respectable in ways Moshe was not. A family man, which is to say he slaved to bring his wife over from Russia, then kept her pregnant for a decade, his life increasingly obscured by that strange brood of daughters, one pleasure-loving son. There had once been rumors—a romance with a Polish girl before his wife arrived—dusty now, insignificant. He himself insignificant but for his jewelry store, display cases stocked with opals, rubies, diamond studs, pearls she could pull across her tongue.

"Hello." Abe Cohen smiled, removed his hat, and made a show of examining leather-bound account books and watermarked paper. He sorted through the ivory letter stock and asked, "Would you like tea?" his English accented but precise.

"Pardon?"

He gestured at the street. "Miss Schumacher, would you like a cup of tea?"

His thumb moved across the ivory paper in small deliberate

circles. Cultured pearls, she thought, *tea?* He dampened his lips with his tongue, and his gaze was direct, chestnut. She'd forgotten his eyes were chestnut, if she had ever known. Bits of white in his hair now, charcoal overcoat like an unbuttoned pelt and beneath it the three-piece suit. Trim for his age, trim for any age except boy and the thumb circling and circling, and when had he unbuttoned the coat? Fedora in his left hand, deeper charcoal. "May I take you to tea?" A soft grit in his voice—this was what sold jewelry to women, of course, that landscaped baritone, and the three-piece suit with all the buttons suggesting their opposite, a continued un-buttoning, and those thumbed circles on the notepaper saying what he meant by tea.

His wife was ill, she'd heard, *failing.* "That's kind of you," she said. This was the moment to decline, or at least steer their meeting to a public venue, sanctioned commiseration: *How is your wife today? Is she feverish? Walking? Eating? Can she take soup?* Tea and pastry. He had beautiful hands. She wanted to touch his mouth, the point on his lip he reached for with his tongue. "I would like that."

She closed the shop early, aware of him watching her hands as she locked the windowed oak door, pulled on her leather gloves, wrapped her blue scarf around her neck. He stood out on the side-walk a respectful distance, easily a chaperone sent by her brother. When did she decide? In a shopping bag, she carried a box of notepaper and a box of envelopes. The air smelled of snow, the daylight weak behind pillowing gray clouds. Wind pushed east from the lake. She hesitated. Paper in paper in snow, she thought. Wet scraps. He was pressing his tongue against his upper lip. "Would you mind if I stopped home?" She gestured at the shop-ping bag.

She didn't pause in the foyer of her building, even when he fell behind her, slowed, presumably readying to wait. He followed her up the stairs to the second floor and her apartment. And she was thinking then of the cold outside and the heat of her apartment, the charcoal coat and the buttons, forgetting already his larger life, almost forgetting the tearoom down the street. *Please come in,* she said and he removed his overshoes and followed her into the small parlor. A reserved breathiness to him. Lillian touched her palm to his right cheek, and he kissed her hand and then her mouth. There was no hesitation, only a brief awkwardness in the undressing: her fingers pulling open his shirt buttons, *Oh*, his checked step back, as if he'd always undressed himself. His face bore the near-drunk, desperate expression of men who have been fighting desire and have given over to it—men who might later soberly admit *I have broken a commandment*—tiresome as that was. Best to see him with this expression, beyond caring. In her bed he entered her and moved slowly and then rapidly, climaxing quickly. He touched her for an hour, then rose and washed and kissed her forehead and left.

Two weeks later he reappeared, plied her with cakes from a Polish bakery and good gin smuggled from Canada, moved his fingers over her face and kissed her on the mouth, all gratitude and lust, before running his hands over her breasts and belly and down between her legs, stroking then entering her: it was staggering and deeply pleasurable, bitter to relinquish.

IN THE FIRST MONTHS, Abe's courtship seemed to her a kind of truth, his attentions and her pleasure contradicting all absence. *Sheyna* he called her, beautiful one, and during their hours together she believed him. How easily she could forget all previous courtships, the fickle nature of men and romance, the impermanence of passion, the moment at which unalloyed sweetness begins to change. Abe liked ritual, and in the first months held to the rituals of cake and gin and tenderness, intense sex during which his desire seemed to meet her own. But in the spring Abe came to her restless and unhappy and without gifts. She offered him holiday wine, which he refused. What he wanted was hard and unsparing: he took her from behind, not kissing her, not looking her in the eye. It was something men did. *Oh*, she thought, *this*. She gave over to him and her body seemed a separate thing and she dissolved beneath him. He wanted her to say *Yes, I like it*. "Yes, I like it," she said, both lying and in some way meaning it. A strange release when he pinned her down, as if she had reached the end of fear. Her lungs refilled only after he'd left her apartment. He returned the next week with fruit and chocolate, kissed her, caressed her, and did not mention his previous visit.

No one seemed to notice the affair, Abe's biweekly visits to Lillian's apartment, although he was known in her neighborhood. Or perhaps no one would believe it of Abe, who after all was her brother's dear friend, a man suffering the burden and sorrow of his wife's illness. Lillian did not meet him in public or ask for more time. She did not want Rebecca Cohen's life: she wanted Abe as she had found him in her flat that first day, a man shaken loose from the world, immersed in the pleasures and wilder demands of his body and hers. For the first year, the trysts at her apartment were enough. For the first year she did not stop seeing other men.

AND THEN ANOTHER January. Rebecca Cohen collapsed on a streetcar and was confined to bed. This was the word from Lillian's sister-in-law Bertha, the word in the markets and beauty parlors. A brief note from Abe: *my wife is ill.* And nothing. Slow ticking days, desire accumulating, a honeyed thickness becoming ever more dense, the surface of each hour coated with the repeating question *where's Abe where's Abe where's Abe,* which did not stop when she drank or slept. And sleep was instead a drifting, the bed an ice floe, lake winds pushing her farther and farther into arctic realms. She tried the remedies she knew: bootleg gin, reefer, mechanical sex with other men, *not-Abe,* through which the thrumming persisted, without return or release. There seemed no end to her awareness of him in the world. Downtown, almost daily, she saw walking reminders: his daughters, a small army, everywhere. The sourest one, Jo, now worked in Moshe's law office; the strangest, Celia, wandered the city, regularly stopping at Kaplan's to touch and sometimes steal sheets of paper. The librarian, Goldie, was forever at the druggist buying syrups and pills for her mother; Sadie, the stylish one, appeared at dress shops Lillian preferred. American girls, really—deliberately American, their accents perfectly local. Two daughters had his eyes, the others his mouth and brow but favored Rebecca, whom Lillian now thought of only as *her.* This required effort. At the butcher shop, the fruit market, in department stores and tearooms, in the beauty parlor, the post office, on street-cars, in the lobby of the Hippodrome, women clucked and murmured *Poor Rebecca*, and *Rebecca's girls look pinched* (hadn't they always?) and *Rebecca's Abe is so pale, poor Abe.*

By mid-February Lillian was half-eaten with desire and mute grief. What reprieve she found came late at night when the arctic drifting deepened, and the night seemed a translucent haze, bits of other winters resurfacing as if new: a burgundy reading chair, air colored by men's voices—her father, his friends—boisterous and gravelly-sweet, tobacco smoke, hot tea. Peppermints. Her father's tone of hilarity, his off-key singing, his callused hand resting on the crown of her head. The chair and voices and smoke blurred into a single feeling pulled from that other decade, a feeling as immediate as the streetlight through her bedroom window or her white quilt or the freckles on her forearm. And yet it was intangible, a feeling yoked to empty space.

The hazy merging of *then* and *now* quietly leaked from a night into a morning, and then into a day, and another day, as Abe's absence solidified. On Main Street, Lillian would hear and immediately lose not Abe's baritone but a graveled laugh—perhaps the exact laugh she remembered, or a stranger's, or just a misinterpreted squeal of streetcar brakes. The burgundy chair would swim up at her while she restocked sheets of onionskin, as if it had been there all along, waiting for her; as if it might even restore the tea and tobacco smoke and peppermints, the gravelly voice, the hand on her head, all of what she could and could not name. Say the burgundy chair was waiting for her, say it was *that* chair—would the room and by extension the house it had occupied also wait for Lillian? There was a single Brunswick Boulevard address, a house her father had chosen and paid for, a house her mother inherited and from which Lillian had fled. Yet in her mind there seemed two separate houses, one she wanted to visit and one she did not. Was one hidden inside the other? Throughout the city, snow fell in thick flakes, day after day, and the wind came in off the lake, the air itself blurring, and on these, the blurriest of days, it seemed possible the Brunswick house was still her father's. On a Friday evening Lillian set out through the snow to the two-story wood-frame off Humboldt Parkway, the painted steps and snow-drifted porch and thick brass mezuzah in the doorway convincingly belonging to the house of memory.

Lillian's mother appeared in the doorway in a dark blue dress and glass beads, lipstick brightening her face, but the red mouth shifted between a flat pucker and a frown. She kissed Lillian on the cheek, an unfishy kiss. Lillian tried to decide what parts of her mother to believe: the kiss or the furrowed brow and intermittent frown. And what parts of the house to believe. The kitchen smelled of bread and roast chicken; in the dining room, the linen tablecloth was spread, the table set with her mother's wedding silver and white china and brass candlesticks. But the living room seemed eerie and hard to navigate: three card tables covered with jigsaw puzzles—half an Eiffel Tower and two scrambled landscapes—occupied the space between the sofas. Porcelain figurines of forest animals crowded the old bookshelf and mantel. And where was the chair? Had there ever been a burgundy chair?

Isabel lit the candles and murmured the Sabbath blessings, and the frown and furrowing vanished. She must have been beautiful, Lillian thought, and it seemed a new thought, though her mother had been called beautiful and still sometimes was. During Isabel's prayer, you could almost see her as someone else, someone gracious. The house as that peppermint house. Then the blessings ended and Isabel's mouth reverted to a carp's and she took the carving knife to the chicken. "Nice you decided to visit, Lillian," she said. "And for Shabbos. Who would have guessed."

"I wanted to see you," Lillian said, but the *you* wobbled.

"So you say. Good Shabbos," Isabel said. "You need money you go see your brother Moshe."

Lillian felt a sharp prickle in her temples. Already, the beginnings of headache, her beautiful forgetting unraveling. How fast the turn—had it always been this fast? Had the Brunswick house ever been anyone's but Isabel's? In the dining room's flat coolness, fishmouthed Isabel slapped potatoes onto wedding plates, and below the aromas of dinner lurked the house's trace scents of ammonia and talc and chicken fat. As always. The absence of deeper voices as always, a bitter, heart-stopping *always*. How could Lillian have thought otherwise? In her belly she felt a sharp pull, an impulse to hit. "I don't need money," she said, and reached for the sweet wine.

"You going to bring me more of that?" Isabel said. "I got that from Rabbi Greenberg."

"Moshe will. I brought you paper from the shop."

"Paper I can buy," Isabel said. "But thank you."

"If you don't want it, Ma, I'll take it with me."

"Did I say thank you? I like the paper. It's good what you bring."

And maybe *good* suggested another opening, slim, evanescent but still a crack in a door through which Lillian might see through her mother to her father. She waited, ate in silence. The chicken tasted of rosemary and onion and salt, there were roast carrots, and Isabel set out honey for the challah. Poppy seed cake. Strong tea, which Lillian cut with lemon.

"You met someone?" Isabel said.

"No."

"You going to tell me or not?"

"There's nothing to tell."

Isabel sipped her tea with exaggerated care. "He must be no good."

"Ma, what did I just say?"

"Your brother Moshe, he's a good man. A schemer but a good man. Bertha too, you should take a lesson from her. Stop with the nogoodnik."

Had her father's friends actually visited? Lillian couldn't have made them all up. Couldn't have made him up.

"Lillian? You hear what I'm telling you?"

"What else do you want, Ma?"

"You already got pearls."

"What?"

"You think I don't know you. I know you. You want more pearls, you ask your brother Moshe."

SHE HAD NOT invented Abe Cohen, his hands moving over her, had not invented their coupling: these remained clear. What seemed slippery and opaque was the life he occupied without her. Lillian could only imagine it as a shell around blank air, the reasons for his absence spurious. And so, in the late weeks of winter, Lillian deliberately circled Abe's life, choosing the streetcar stop nearest his store, visiting his favorite bakery, buying from the pharmacy near his house. Twice she borrowed her brother's Packard and drove it up and down Abe's street. House lights on the first floor and often the second, occasional fluttery movements at the windows. Snowdrifts against the side of the house, the front walk cleanly shoveled, ice sheen on porch rails and shingles, the interior impenetrable, a kind of shadow into which Abe had disappeared.

She waited until March before visiting the jewelry store. The son, Irving, minded the counter. Beautiful boy, spitting image of his father but still soft, irresolute, except for that glimmer, the same pleasure lust she saw in Abe's private moments. In Irving the lust was more public but more diffuse. "Can I help you, Miss Schumacher?" A light purr in the voice.

No sound from the back room, where Abe set stones, though the door was ajar. She asked to see bracelets, and Irving opened up the case, pulled out a velvet card with four, let her hold them to the light and try them on. For her sister-in-law Bertha, she said. She'd have to confer with her brother, she'd send him over to look. And would Irving please give regards to his family, all best wishes for good health?

Two nights later, Abe returned to Lillian's flat, defeated and sad, his hands redolent of illness. Complied when she asked him, first, to bathe.

ONE THING Lillian knew: open the door to risk and the room will widen and stretch. The work of caution—automatic at first—becomes over time onerous and boring, another chore in a too-long list of chores. You can't manage it all, defer whatever seems inessential. And this was how she explained Abe's about-face. Almost nightly he visited; seemed, in fact, oblivious to risk, foggy with exhaustion and despair. He wept when she touched him, wept when she did not. The weeping, she knew, was hidden from his family. Seeing Abe this way—shaken down to boy, neck-deep in bewilderment and sorrow—moved her. But she also preferred him careless. He'd appear at her flat, late, and collapse on her bed, and after a time they'd make love without speaking. For an hour he might sleep. And though she knew better, some nights she'd meet him on Delaware, a few blocks from his house. Once, at two a.m., Lillian parked the Packard across the street from his house and he slipped out the back door and through the neighboring yard, crossing the snow-crusted lawns to the curb, her borrowed car.

They carried on this way until Rebecca died. During shivah, Lillian joined her brother and his wife when they paid their respects to the family. Red buds studded adjacent trees, crocuses bloomed in the Cohens' front yard, the bright greens of the new grass mixed with the winter browns. For the first time, Lillian entered the house on Lancaster. In the foyer the dark wood shone, the wallpaper pattern of spray roses spilling down the hallway and into the parlor. There was a faint scent of cedar and baked sugar and tea, and in the parlor visiting relatives sat quietly with the daughters—the crazy one, the paper thief, Celia, perfectly still and paler than usual; Irving slumped beside her; Sadie elegant in black, whispering to Abe; her husband standing guard beside them, adjusting his spectacles and surveying the room. The other daughters were ragged and red-eyed, Goldie strangely ethereal, Jo meeting Lillian's condolences with a scouring stare. The pattern of roses dropped behind the upright piano; sheet music lay open, a sonata. Lillian retreated to the hall that led in one direction to the fragrant kitchen, the other to the front staircase, with its fat maple banister and Persian runner, silent invitations to push farther into the house. She passed the formal dining room (more roses) before two synagogue women arrived, arms loaded with platters and casseroles, a jumble of piety and whispers, noodles and fish. Lillian stole outside to the empty front porch, away from the windows, and waited for Moshe and Bertha to finish with their sympathy.

LILLIAN WOULD NOT have chosen that wallpaper: the clipped pink roses girlish, sentimental, falling in dainty lockstep. Still, the papered rooms felt like sugar bowls, and after she left that day the image of the spray roses returned to her. Davenport in dark wood, upholstery the color of biscuits and linen, Abe's reading chair a fine pale green. Upright piano, the scatter of black notes across the white pages of the open score. She pictured the parlor empty of visitors, the davenport clear of Celia and Irving, open, inviting, a place to let the day hush, to gaze up at roses, light patterned by budding trees, lazy piano softening the afternoon. That night, Lillian imagined her own bed as the davenport, lulled herself to sleep with the pretense of thick petals and buttery air and Abe's weight upon her.

That was the beginning of a more deliberate daydream, the trail of roses leading up and back to both glimpsed and unseen rooms: the wide white kitchen, the polished dining room table, and the tall glassed cabinets, company china and Passover dishes, thin-stemmed goblets, heavy brass candlesticks, silver Kiddush cup. And upstairs? The carpeted stairs led to an unlit pocket of space. And to pass through such space? Like passing through night, perhaps. Lillian knew about the windows, stout rectangles facing the street, a round moon of glass above them, smaller windows on the sides. She guessed at the floor plan: front and back stairways, the windows suggesting a division of rooms. In some of the rooms there would be beds, dressing tables, chairs. Cream walls? Some ought to be cream, a base that would hold the light but allow you to add color. And in the master bedroom, there ought to be violet and royal blue bedcovers and chairs, which would suit Abe. She imagined herself and Abe coupling in pale blue sheets, his broad back and thick arms wrapping her, intermittent dark freckles on the white skin, black eyelashes against the blue, and the steady rhythm and near ache of Abe moving inside her. Butterscotch and white for the front guest room, perhaps some fleurs-de-lis.

She considered colors for other rooms, tending toward blues and greens, inventing a complete house the shape and size of Abe's house on Lancaster. Downstairs, the rose wallpaper stayed, the piano stayed, the parlor furniture stayed, and at moments the invented house and the real one seemed indistinguishable. In the fantasy house, Abe's children did not appear; presumably they had moved to another invented house, or, better, another city. That could happen, in the mind. The arrangement seemed beyond Lillian's will, as if Abe's house had chosen to occupy her and she could not refuse it. The invented house hummed, waiting to be manifest in the physical world.

YOU BEGIN, of course, with where you are. Begin with the life you know, begin with sex. Try a simple request, and make the request late at night, after he has climaxed. A Thursday. Lillian and Abe were spooned together in her bed, Abe's hand still on her breast, when Lillian asked, "Shall we go to a restaurant next week?"

Simple and not simple, a meal in a restaurant. Or tea? Wasn't it what he had once proposed? A table, a waiter, a menu. Polite conversation. Nothing, compared to what they'd done. Tea, but tea in public and now: a signal of earnest courtship or of scandal. He closed his eyes, sighed. She had seen him respond this way to Celia's *Could we?* or *Will we?* before he answered no. But to Lillian he said, "I don't know." To Lillian he said, "Perhaps in time."

A week later, she cooked a dinner at her flat. Abe arrived harried and distracted, and she poured him gin, set the table with a blue-bordered cloth, carried out plates. Roast beef and sweet potatoes, glazed carrots, salty bread. Tea and linzer torte. By dessert he was back to the Abe she wanted: alert gaze, body tipped in her direction, his cheeks slightly pink. "Does this feel like home?" she asked, and he answered yes. She stroked the back of his hand. "You don't invite me to your home."

"Oh, but Lillian. You know why."

"Good reasons," she said. "Before."

"*This* is our place."

She hesitated. The blue-bordered tablecloth seemed part of a past life, and she thought of that other polished table, and the imagined linens and the glass bowls, a basket of pears. The invented house seemed wholly real and she did not know what this meant. "Not forever," she said. She loosened her fingers from his and rose, cleared the dinner plates and the empty serving platter and the used glassware. Then she offered him chocolate from the box he'd brought, square pieces decorated with waves of green.

. . .

"TELL ME," Lillian said to her brother, "how a person buys a house."

Moshe had always been a big man, but here at his law office he seemed even larger than usual. An enormous, round-bellied suit, sighing at her. "Lilly, would you like a cigarette?"

She took one from him, allowed him to light it, noted the resemblance of his fingers to the cigar he lit for himself. "A little house?" he said. "Just for you?"

"Maybe that."

"Or maybe you're thinking a bigger house?"

"I think all sorts of things. Let's say any house."

"Are you asking can I buy you a house?"

"No. I want to know how a person buys a house."

"First," Moshe said, "a person needs to have money. Lilly, sweetheart, you do not."

"But if I did?"

Moshe squinted, as if he were adding numbers in his head. Pursed his lips, not unlike a fish. "A very large if. You understand that? You be careful, Lillian."

YOU CANNOT rush fate, Lillian told herself, no matter how sure you are of your path. For now, she was in God's hands; she imagined a light touch on the top of her head and refrained from talk of houses. Surprisingly, this seemed to work. In the spring of 1929, Rebecca Cohen's gravestone was unveiled, and two weeks later Abe again asked Lillian to tea. A Wednesday afternoon. They took a table in Emma's Tea Room, surrounded by middle-aged women. Abe bought tea and sweet cakes, inquired about her mother's health. Asked about the stationery business, where the paper was shipped from, if the owner, Harry Kaplan, traveled to New York, as Abe often did. Mentioned that her brother's law firm was growing admirably. Lillian watched his lips as he talked. This was a strange game, Lillian thought, but a pleasant one. She sipped her tea and folded her hands in her lap and spoke about her fondness for, of all things, gardens; she imagined kissing him in the tea-room. After an hour he asked if he might secure a taxicab for her.

Among the gossips there was murmuring the next day, there always would be murmuring about Lillian, despite the propriety of tea with a widower. But Lillian's faith in God seemed justified. She felt a surge of hope: Why shouldn't she be happy? Why shouldn't Abe? On his next visit, he brought flowers to her apartment, and there seemed a new lightness to his mood. Now he wanted to make small but definite plans: tickets to the theater, an afternoon at the Falls. In May he suggested a restaurant dinner with Moshe and Bertha, followed by dessert and coffee at his house.

The evening they went to Little Paris, Lillian wore black silk and pearls, her hair cut that day in shoulder-length waves. Abe brought corsages for Lillian and Bertha. At Moshe's house they drank illicit champagne, then drove to the restaurant, Bertha carrying Moshe's gin in her handbag. A waiter arrived with savory tarts, then soup. Four courses. They drank the gin on ice. Through the dinner, Abe joked with Moshe and squeezed Lillian's hand and seemed purely happy; by mid-evening Lillian was awash in grand hope. The soft night air seemed a confirmation, and on the drive to Abe's house, she leaned her head out the side window—the elms and maples in full leaf, the breeze pushing her hair from her face, Abe holding her hand, kissing her on the cheek and pulling her back into the car. And when they reached Abe's house it was quiet, the lilacs swaying in the light wind, perfuming the parlor, which was as Lillian envisioned: falling roses, empty davenport, pale green chairs. There was a bakery cake, chocolate, and Bertha brewed tea. In the china cabinet, Lillian found dessert plates: gilt-edged, the inner pattern a ring of grapes on the vine, the fruit precise and dense and violet blue.

Would the evening have gone any differently if, instead, she'd taken down the everyday china, left the grapevines dutifully in place, stubborn tribute to the dead? Abe and Moshe lighted cigars and patted each other on the back, and Bertha—cheerfully drunk—concerned herself with cake, which she served in thick slices. Lillian sipped the milky tea, savored the chocolate. Abe sat beside her on the davenport, and it seemed that another life was beginning, that grief had fallen away and time had stopped, leaving them forever in this bright soft evening, this parlor, this house. Abe's fingers circled and circled Lillian's palm, sweet measured pressure he might later move to the rest of her body.

If the others sensed the presence of Abe's daughters in the house, they didn't think much of it. Why would they? Moshe and Bertha commonly entertained, their children and housekeeper discreetly migrating to the upper floors. Here on Lancaster, there had been little entertaining for years, but Abe—admittedly flushed with alcohol—seemed completely at ease, affectionate and unworried. It was after all Abe's own house, his parlor, his evening with Lillian and Moshe and Bertha. And the parlor seemed fully the parlor Lillian had imagined.

They were still eating cake when Lillian heard the steps on the back stairway, an uneven thudding, the steps approaching from the kitchen through the long hall to the parlor. A muttering. And then in the parlor doorway stood Jo and Celia—Jo in another of her mud-colored dresses, Celia puffy-eyed, her thick hair disheveled. They stared at Lillian, Lillian and Abe, Lillian again. Celia swung her left arm back and forth.

Jo snorted. "You seem pleased," she said to Lillian.

From across the room, Moshe cleared his throat, and Jo registered his presence and placed her hand on Celia's swinging arm. Moshe smiled his expansive, warning smile and gestured at the cake. "Would you girls care for some dessert?"

"Mr. Schumacher," Jo said. "Thank you, no. Hello, Mrs. Schumacher. We'll go upstairs. Celia?"

"Hello." Celia relaxed her arm, then fixed her gaze on the dessert plates, and in that moment the evening tipped. "Those aren't yours."

"No," Lillian said.

"Celia," Abe said.

Bertha traced the grape pattern with her index finger. "Beautiful," she said.

And Celia stepped into the parlor, her arm swinging again. "But not yours." She yanked Bertha's plate from her hand, then Lillian's from the table, bits of cake still on them.

Abe, white-faced, stood and lurched toward Celia. "Celia, leave the plates."

But Celia grabbed the other cake-stained plates, tucking them against her dress and retreating to the hall.

"Enough." Abe's voice was louder now and harsh, and Celia unblinking.

"They're not yours," she repeated, this time to her father.

Moshe licked his lips, a deliberately delicate gesture. Checked his watch, while Bertha glanced out at the swaying lilacs.

"You don't tell me," Abe said. "You do not tell me."

And now Celia turned back to Lillian. "You stay away from them."

"Celia, you will apologize," Abe said.

Celia backed up to the staircase, the plates crushed against her, chocolate crumbs falling over the parquet floor. "*You* apologize."

"Jo, take your sister upstairs," Abe said.

But Jo crossed her arms across her chest and studied Abe's shoes and did not answer.

Would knowledge have mattered? Lillian did not yet know that Celia slept in her late mother's sickroom (a second-floor room which faced the street and the tall elms, and from which a familiar Packard could be remarked); that Jo had suffered insomnia since her mother's collapse; that Goldie Cohen was listening from the top of the stairs; that Rebecca Cohen had not been an Isabel. These were things you tried not to know, truths that might starkly appear and pin you down anyway.

Neither Abe nor Jo nor Celia moved. There was the chugging of a car on Lancaster, and Moshe rose, smiling, stretching, as if nothing had transpired in the mood. "What about a nightspot?" he said. Ashed his cigar. "I think we should. Lillian? Bertha love?" He set a hand on Abe's shoulder. "Abe?"

"What?" Abe said.

"Let's." Moshe ushered the Schumacher women to the front door, nodding to Jo and Celia, "Good evening, ladies." And then Lillian was out on the lawn, stranded it felt, her sister-in-law murmuring *That Celia's a nasty one* and strolling past her to the Packard.

The upper reaches of the house appeared lightless, remote. Lillian's palms were damp with sweat, and the lilac-scented air seemed a strange trick. How could she forestall what had already passed? Lillian counted the windows. The ember of Moshe's cigar marked his progress down the front steps and the walkway, Abe and Celia and Jo now fragmented silhouettes through the open front door. *Lillian?* Moshe's hand a warm weight on her shoulder. *Lilly, come with me.* Cake still sweet in her mouth, thin breeze nosing a sycamore, the Packard sputtering awake. Then the puzzle of silhouettes shifted, lush grass spilling over Lancaster Avenue, her fingers not exactly her own, her body close to dissolving in the fragrant air, and the night sky unspeaking.

Three weeks later, Goldie Cohen disappeared.

CHAPTER 8

Goldie

1929

All year, to the east: construction of the Central Terminal, vast enough for eight train lines. Deafening, and yet the cacophony suggested its opposite: beyond the engine drones and shattering booms, the hammers, the grating of shovels, beyond the shouts and mud suck and raining dirt, an opening into silence. She could swim under the sound. It was a cathedral of noise, which seemed to solidify into an actual cathedral. And she began to be late to everything.

In June Central Terminal opened, marble and brick rising into grand arches, sweep of the high-ceilinged concourse, four-faced clock a gleaming sentinel, and around it the polished kiosk stocked with magazines, cigarettes, chocolates, *notions for travelers*. Beyond: the row of gilded ticket vendor windows, dozens, like portals to other lives.

When she walked into the terminal, indoors and outdoors blurred, the crowd purposeful and thick as shopping crowds on Main Street, and the sense of space barely diminished. The station's ceiling domelike, sky blue with painted stars. In the diner the walls were a pattern of beacons and flames, black and white, red and green; in the Ladies' Lounge marble tables flanked red leather divans; but what drew her most were the arched windows at the end of the long concourse, three stories high, daylight pressing into the station. Almost holy, they seemed. *Ark of the Covenant*, she thought, and weren't all holy things more or less that blast of light? If only you could rise into it.

She could not resist the new station. Visited quietly three days in a row, bought cigarettes there and sat in the elegant Ladies' Lounge or at the slick onyx tables of the coffee shop, reading books and newspapers, studying the timetables, drinking coffee with cream. It was, she knew, the waiting room for other lives, but she couldn't tell when the waiting would end. And her planning was the planning of a sleepwalker, half-conscious at best but progressing: money saved, clothes sorted, a small valise she bought secondhand. At Central Terminal, as in sleep, she was alone. And then in July, a quiet morning with a doorway in it: this time upon leaving the house on Lancaster she took the money and the valise. In the Ladies' Lounge she dressed for the occasion in new clothes: a cream-colored hat, cream-colored veil, tiny sprigs of lavender tumbling through the fabric of her pale green dress. A ring of her mother's. In her handbag she carried a small gold cross, the tiniest of disguises, just in case. She lined up at a ticket window and paid. Waited in view of the windows and the four-faced clock, and then in the balmy air out on the platform.

It couldn't be simpler, stepping onto the train. One foot on the narrow step, the other lifting from the platform and for a fraction of a second hanging in air and a porter offering her a hand. Then she was up to the next step and finding her way through a plush car of the Twentieth Century, the air, it seemed, propelling her to a seat upholstered in burgundy fabric, the window beside it open and the whistles and shouts from the platform seeping in. Passengers trundled in and rustled and adjusted, heaving bags onto overhead racks and hanging hats, accompanied by the smell of sweat, coffee, tobacco, hair oil, shaving soap, peppermints, face powder, mustard, apple tart, hand salve; and they opened more windows as the train jolted south and west.

. . .

EYES CLOSED, at first: there was the hypnotic motion and percussion of the train rocketing west. Eyes open and out the small
square window blue patches of sky and familiar cumulus billowing
and beside the tracks flatlands and fields and warehouses and rows
of stained brick buildings and ragged houses and then blue-gray
lake and steel plants and more empty flats, then fields: pastureland
and thick grass and low hills, farmland, the interruptions of towns.
The endless green was at first elating and then, for brief instants,
monstrous: it swelled up alarmingly, without end, and she was
seized by the cold panic that such green could swallow her. She
felt a choking and a wish for her mother. And then it passed, and
in its place the recognition of absurdity: she would not be eaten by
corn. More murk of industry and glimpses of lakeshore and green.
Heat rising.

   She slept fitfully in the heat of the afternoon, a day ever hotter
as the train crossed into the Midwest. Her body rocked with the
train, longing rising in sleep, a liquid opening and clenching and
rolling: Daniel's skin and muscle, the rhythm of sex. She woke for
the first time in years not in Buffalo or even in New York State but
moving over Ohio. Woke in motion, as she had on the crossing.
The train compartment had transformed into a momentary home,
replacing in her mind the house on Lancaster. She was altered.
There was the memory upon waking of Daniel's fingers like water
over her clavicle and breasts, mouth against her neck. The near
sense of him still with her as the elderly woman in the next seat
blew her nose and a redheaded boy sulked and his plump and elegant mother sighed. They didn't seem to notice the wild tumult in
Goldie, or if they noticed, it was too much to acknowledge. A
public train, after all.

   Pears, Goldie thought. What she'd give for a pear, sweet slices
on her tongue.

   She made her way to the dining car and settled at a table near
the back and ordered tea. A few tables away a potato-faced man
held forth about the future: he talked about beef, Midwestern cat-
tle and the heaviness of winter. His hands dwarfed his coffee cup.

He seemed inordinately pleased with himself, although his suit was the unfortunate color of crushed acorns. Goldie stirred sugar into her tea.

By Toledo, she found that pinches of sadness expanded into waves. At the train station, a skinny woman in a navy blue dress mumbled and kicked a carpetbag; on the platform for the south-bound local, a girl slumped on a bench, dark hair falling lank in the heat. They could hear Goldie if she called to them and she wanted to, for a moment the desire fervent, but what could she possibly say? It was ridiculous, the impulse to call. In her head there were loose phrases, fragments of songs. Because of the heat, she thought. Past the railway percussion and squeal of brakes the tunes accumulated and broke off, leaving a few notes adrift. She'd been cultivating silence but now this, a desire for the simplest music.

In Chicago she paused briefly but stayed in the train station. Then resumed, her train snaking west, Goldie deep in the center of it watching the fields and prairie unspool. The dust increased. After several stops she wanted to wash more thoroughly. She imagined swimming, ridding herself of clothes altogether. And though she could have disembarked in any city and taken a hotel room and bathed, she did not. Passed through the languorous heat of the plains, the great distance from water affecting her now. On the third day the landscape turned again: it made her thirsty simply to look at it. The midday sun was burning, sky relentlessly clear, and it seemed the earth could barely stand it, but in the evening as the train crossed farther west, the world turned peach, with streaks of magenta, and later a pure indigo.

PART TWO

Beyond Lancaster

Early 1930s

CHAPTER 9

Sadie

1931–32

The smell of fried eggs nauseates Sadie (though raw eggs aren't any better, it's best not to bake) and the air at Lancaster smells precisely of fried eggs. It's as if Jo senses her aversion and cooks eggs to spite her, waiting until Sadie's parked in the driveway, then slapping butter into the skillet. The problem isn't just Lancaster, of course, the nausea comes and goes, but you have to think ahead, choose your fastest exit, or else lose your breakfast of plain toast smack in the middle of the parlor.

Today Sadie's dropping off Celia's birthday present, a lamb's wool scarf and gloves, pale blue, very soft; but Celia is out, and Jo lurks, with her newspaper and the egg smell.

"How are you, Jo?" Sadie sets Celia's present on the piano bench. It's warm in the parlor, much too warm with her heavy coat, and before she can unbutton it the queasiness overwhelms Sadie— she feels as if she's been spun in fast circles and pummeled and dunked in vinegar. She rushes out the front door to the edge of the driveway, where she retches and wipes her mouth with a clean handkerchief and kicks new snow over her mess. The whole business is mortifying, her body having its way with her. She rummages through her pocketbook for a lipstick and crosses the snowy lawn to the front steps, the veranda, the door, where Jo stands peering out.

"How you feeling, Sadie?" Neither kind nor unkind: it's a scrim behind which another question lurks.

Sadie hasn't yet confessed her pregnancy to her family, though retching in the snow could be taken as a kind of admission. Of course she hasn't wanted to tell any of them—they harass her enough about other things, about nothing, about their unhappiness with the weather—and she wants privacy; she likes the thick protective band of her family's ignorance. The pregnancy is the most delicate of secrets, a gradually illuminating landscape only she and Bill perceive, a quiet euphoric alteration in the earth's tilt. And she would like to stay in this deep wonder with Bill, forget the city, forget the families—but already the secret's dispersing, the quiet interrupted. Unfair. Two nights ago, at dinner with Bill's mother, the chicken Mother Feldstein cooked repulsed her, and Sadie could barely stay in the dining room. Mother Feldstein studied her for several minutes before offering a predatory smile. She addressed herself to Bill. "Well?" she said, and he blurted, "Sadie's pregnant," and Mother congratulated him, and then Sadie, and began what Sadie could only think of as her advice diatribe. At the end of the evening, Mother Feldstein patted Sadie on the belly, as if Sadie were herself an infant or, worse, a dog.

Some of the other perceptual shifts unnerve her. She wonders if pregnancy makes you hallucinate. It's possible, isn't it? Last week at Lancaster, the stains on the kitchen floor and counter appeared to her as crawling insects. She tried to smash a spot of molasses dead with her shoe, and Celia asked if her feet were troubling her. Two days later she glimpsed through Lancaster's front window a man walking inside the parlor, but the image was fleeting. She opened the door with her key and called and heard nothing. Then Jo appeared, annoyed. There was no man in the house: what she saw must have been a coat and hat, or a melding of the coatrack with some other movement. She could only blink. And then Jo became unnaturally polite, and offered Sadie coffee. The hospitality seemed so anomalous Sadie wondered if, miraculously, a man—a beau or someone less respectable than a beau—had visited Jo and slipped out the back. But there were no other signs. She said yes to the coffee, and followed Jo to the kitchen and gazed out at the yard, which was empty but for blown brown leaves and unremarkable squirrels and a few wayward branches.

Today there are no fake insects, no elusive men. Only new snow, the neighborhood offering the reliable stasis of a photograph. The nausea has passed for now, and Sadie unbuttons her coat and reenters the foyer. Jo is waiting. "I'm fine," Sadie says. She'll tell the family soon, not today, but soon. "Thought I left the gift card in the Ford. I'll stay just a minute."

"Sit down," Jo says. "Relax." And despite the air's remaining whiff of egg, the suggestion has appeal. Sadie would like to sit quietly for a while; she wouldn't mind a nap. But once she's settled on the parlor sofa, it's clear that there's no sitting for the sake of sitting, and Celia's birthday present isn't quite enough in trade. Jo's agitating for a new icebox. Their father says he can't spare the money, but more than once the milk has spoiled. "You owe it to the family," Jo says.

Sadie owes the family quite a lot, it seems. She'd like to point out that Irving is the one who perpetually owes—he's courting trouble now and she's worried—but telling Jo will only magnify the trouble. "How often," she says, "is the milk left out?"

Jo narrows her eyes. "Never."

"I've seen it left out," Sadie says, but Jo will have none of it. And now Sadie's queasiness is rising again—even more unjust.

"Aren't you the Queen of Sheba," Jo says. Sadie might just retch again—but what of breakfast could be left? She stands to leave. "You won't even hear me out," Jo says, and then she too is up from her chair, moving between Sadie and the door.

"It's not just my decision," Sadie says.

Jo stations herself in the foyer, rallying the heat and egg smell, and doesn't budge.

Air, Sadie thinks, ice and air. "I'll talk to Bill."

Which is all it takes for Jo to step aside.

.   .   .

PREGNANCY IS NOT something to be shamed by, she tells her-self, though of course it's the evidence of what happens between a husband and wife, proof of those nighttime romps Bill is so fond of. What was private seems alarmingly public, one's body turning into a bright, expanding placard announcing Sex Was Here. And despite the certainty of public display, what sets it all in motion—the moment of conception—seems to her indistinguishable from many other moments. She wasn't prepared for that: she'd imag-ined, absurdly, that she would "know" at the exact moment, and had never determined *how*. As if chimes would strike or a chorus of cherubs would sing from the mantel. For weeks in the fall, Bill was especially amorous and Sadie did not stop him, though she didn't much drop into fever. Most of the time she was distracted by the messiness of sex, the unpleasant wet spots on the sheet, the liquid drip down her thighs, the routine reaching for towels or toilet tis-sue to clean up. She's always cleaning up one thing or another, isn't she? The inelegance of it—especially of cleaning *down there*—galls her, and thank God for long baths and for Bill's reaction to her pregnancy: gentle restraint.

It's a lovely thing, restraint. Bill's a man with a temper, not a violent temper but a temper of unfortunate and sometimes bellow-ing magnitude. Many men have such tempers, her father for in-stance, it's not surprising to her, but the bellowing really does suggest a distressed cow. Or, she supposes, a bull, the way he booms her name when he's upset, usually about her loans to Irving, or Celia wandering into his office, or inadequate attention to his mother. Too often she listens and makes soothing noises or no noise at all until he wears himself out. And his newfound—though temporary?—restraint is useful now, since Irving *is* in money trou-ble again. This time Moshe Schumacher's son Leo came to her, warning that Irving's gambling debt is too large, large enough that her father will soon hear of it, will be asked to pay on Irving's be-half. Business is off, of course, everyone's is, some jewelers have closed altogether. It's an idiotic time to gamble, Irving knows that. She stops short of naming Irving himself an idiot.

After dinner and dessert, after bathing, there's Bill's daily ritual of palming her belly—as if by his rubbing it, the baby will grow and emerge like a genie from a bottle. The gesture is oddly sweet. Bill's hand is warm, and the warmth moves through her and, she imagines, through the baby. It's soothing, as long as his fingers stay above her hips. Bill himself seems soothed and though she doesn't want to break the spell, this is the best time to ask him about Irving. She tells him about the call from Leo Schumacher. Bill sighs and gazes at the bedroom ceiling—does *he* see cherubs?—apparently counting to ten, and manages to control his temper, love and cunning and pity seeping into his expression.

"Darling," he says. "Your father might have to help Irving."

"I don't know if he can. And the fury."

"Mm-hmm," Bill says.

"Irving's young, you know that."

"Foolish, Sadie, he's foolish. I can't pay for his nonsense."

"Will you at least talk to him?"

"Sadie."

"Just talk."

He nods but his face is a deepening red. There will be no mention of iceboxes.

HER BODY SWELLS in places she anticipated and places she did not. Her feet, for example: what does a growing baby have to do with your feet? Also her behind, which seems oddly square. It's difficult to get a clear view, of course, and when she asks Bill he tells her she is beautiful and sometimes he waxes on about sons and mothers. She finds the "beautiful" sweet and mollifying, and the sons and mothers part a little enraging: Mother Feldstein? Is he thinking of Mother Feldstein, who does not after all like Sadie, and might be capable of stealing this baby away? Overfeeding it. Forcing it to breathe gardenia perfume and withstand Mother Feldstein herself, whose behind is overly prominent and definitely square, the collateral effect of four sons and a single unhappy daughter. And Sadie has a sudden wave of sympathy for her dour, insufferable sister-in-law, Nora.

"We might have a girl," Sadie says.

"Well of course," Bill says. And after a moment, "a beautiful girl."

And though she finds herself on the verge of tears—why tears? why now? she can't possibly be crying over the squaring off of her behind, can she?—she knows better than to pursue *boy or girl?* with Bill. It's no surprise that he's thinking of sons. He's already mentioned his father's name, Jacob, and his grandfather's name, Samuel, as possibilities. She's thinking of colors, of pastel pink and yellow. She's seen boy babies and their fountains of urine: Delia Lefkowitz's colicky Adam, her own brother. She loves Irving well enough, but she'd rather have a girl. A smart, good-natured, utterly sane girl, the sort she imagines her mother was. Is it odd not to want, first, a little Bill? But clearly Bill can do that kind of wanting for both of them.

Sadie's monthly calls to the police, the ads in out-of-town papers, have become routine, detached, it seems, from the Goldie she knew, and she isn't sure why the Goldie of childhood is so much with her now: Goldie who was often brusque, combing out Sadie's hair with hard tugs despite Sadie's objections and tears. But in other moments she was kinder and tended to stare out the window at stray light on the maples. The thought of the light and the trees and Goldie moved by light and trees—even a mean young Goldie moved by light and trees—is enough to push Sadie to the brink, she's sniffling and blowing her nose and a swarm of tears is blurring the bedroom. No word. No word. Sadie tries to train her mind on the image of Goldie as a tourist in New York or Chicago, but the image fragments and gives way to more bewilderment and blurriness. Pregnancy is one puddle after another, Sadie thinks. All you can do is follow doctor's orders, have the seamstress alter your clothes and purchase maternity dresses that billow like parachutes. Don't give up on lipstick.

"Samuel Jacob?" Bill says. "Jacob Samuel? Dear? Which?"

"I'm not sure." *Glen,* she thinks. *Douglas.*

"Rebecca?" he says.

Oh. There is tenderness in Bill's face, but why does such evocation feel like a punch? She swallows and counts to ten. Maybe he has read her mind—Rebecca *is* her first choice, of course they should name after her mother, but there should be no false Rebeccas. The child has to match the name, especially that name, and how can they know? Of course there's Goldie too, Golda really. Though you mustn't name after the living: Goldie could be alive, must be. And Sadie's back in the puddle again, suppressing a sob. Better, isn't it, to choose something modern, unmarked by family history?

PERHAPS TALL WOMEN or stout women carry less obviously, but Sadie is neither and by her seventh month her belly becomes a medicine ball everyone feels entitled to comment on. In department stores complete strangers—women—ask her when the baby is due. Men open doors with small flourishes and smile encouragingly as they size her up. She's an object of easy public discussion, like the weather. And like the weather unpredictable: on the Hengerer's Department Store staircase, halfway to the landing, she has to stop. She's huffing, dizzy and sweating, there's a small fire in her lower back and the baby seems to be wriggling inside her; she'd brave the embarrassment and sit down on the stairs if she could, but she's trapped in the streaming crowd, which makes the huffing worse. Sadie hugs the banister, and the baby's foot, or elbow, or *something*, presses hard into her side. She could easily be stomped, she thinks. The other shoppers all seem to be in full possession of their bodies, either staring or ignoring her, and the annoying tears begin. A woman in a blue raincoat says, "Let me help you dear," and two other women make a barrier around which the other shoppers have to walk. They cluck about pregnancy, and a man with pomaded hair nods and openly stares at her belly, and newcomers to the staircase pause to see what's going on. She's a huffing weepy spectacle. Can't this happen in private? Sadie is not the weather—but how is it that she even feels the need to clarify? The strangeness of the idea frightens her into collecting herself. She lets the woman in the blue raincoat lead her to a tearoom.

When Sadie is calm, when she has had her tea and a slice of cake—was that all it was? she needed lemon cake?—she notices the striped blue and white upholstery of the tearoom chairs, the bright bud vases and glass sugar bowls, and also notices what she has forgotten, how the comments and smiles form a warm mist of approbation, the sort she felt as an A student. Her pregnancy is good and right, she herself is good and right, this is how things are properly done. She is not, as she sometimes fears, walking a thin paper bridge over the paralyzing rapids of Celia's craziness and Goldie's absence. She will soon have silver baby spoons and knitted booties and rattles. When the panic strikes again, she wills it away by conjuring tiny hats.

AT HOME, the department store panic seems distant, incomprehensible, the mistaken intrusion of someone else's pregnancy and temperament onto hers. Like a party line: sometimes you pick up to the wrong conversation. Instead there's a pale slant of light against the bedroom sheers, more tea, quick shadows of sparrows skimming in and out of the maples. The baby is no longer jabbing her, and she feels more like she is captaining a boat. She wonders if the tiny hats she imagines are, in some inexplicable way, her mother. As the absence of Jo calling and the absence of Mother Feldstein and this present moment of June light and sparrows are her mother, or the closest she will come. And the need for tiny hats, for sparrows and light is infinite.

By summer it's more difficult to care for her own house, more difficult to pay attention to the house on Lancaster, or even to dress properly and put on shoes. In the last several weeks of her pregnancy, she hires a woman named Rosalie to help with the house, a Colored woman with a mild Southern twang; a woman in her twenties with a small son of her own and good references; a churchgoing woman who understands kosher and comes to Sadie's house in a white uniform. Rosalie uses hair oil, sweet and strong, which permeates the house. Sadie has not asked her to wear a uniform, but apparently this is what one wears. It would be rude, Sadie thinks, to comment on the hair oil.

Rosalie unfailingly refers to Sadie as Mrs. Feldstein. This is proper and propriety appeals to Sadie: a formal name is like a well-made coat. It is *odd* to wear a coat in one's own home, but unavoidable. Sadie is Mrs. Feldstein and Rosalie is Rosalie. And Colored.

And in the house for long hours, repeatedly, which of course she must be. Sadie has grown accustomed to silence and retreat, and it's strange to have someone else there, trailing that odd scent, a woman so vastly unfamiliar. A Colored woman with a Colored husband named Thomas and a Colored son named Thomas, humming what seem to be Colored church songs as she cleans the kitchen. And although Rosalie's presence is a shock unlike the shock of Sadie's husband on weekends, for the first few weeks Sadie feels the same impulse to hide in her bedroom. She tries to resist: it is, after all, her house, and she's happy not to worry about clean floors, isn't she? She's worried about floors and laundry since she was nine: it's a relief, if a fraught one. You have to pretend there's nothing odd about a stranger managing your underclothes and sheets.

THE FINAL WEEKS of her pregnancy offer reprieve: for a brief time outside demands drop. Sadie can in fact retreat to her bedroom and no one interrupts her, or expects dinner, or presumes she should manage the house on Lancaster. This in and of itself seems justification for pregnancy. Sadie would like to have her body back, but once that happens the air will change, the quiet will be torn open. Now at least she can read or sleep uninterrupted by anyone, the baby moving but not wailing. This pool of time is ephemeral, and beyond it waits the prospect of rarely being alone or at leisure in the house. Alone with a baby does not count, though she hopes for calm days, for a baby who will easily fall asleep, for that warm dumpling weight and sleep-breathing against her chest. But *alone with the baby* is also her unhinged neighbor, Delia Lefkowitz, who rhapsodizes about her son's toes, then weeps from fatigue. Delia's son *is* beautiful when he doesn't scream, Sadie held him herself, marveled at his smallness, the perfection of his mouth and ears and fists. And not all babies scream as he does, she knows this. Sadie will be fine: she reminds herself this before she naps, and again when she rises and washes. She will be fine. And in the afternoon, when she fixes a pot of tea and cuts thick slices of coffee cake for herself and for Rosalie, Rosalie tells her, "You'll be a good mother, Mrs. Feldstein," unprompted, and sets the cake aside for one of the Thomases and returns to dusting the cabinets. Has Sadie been sighing again? She does try not to.

As her due date approaches, Sadie's retreats to the bedroom seem altogether too lonely. She returns to reading in the living room, and when Rosalie is there—more and more Sadie is glad for Rosalie's presence—they listen to the radio. She keeps the front curtains closed, and when the telephone rings, Rosalie answers with "Feldstein residence." She tells everyone but Bill that Sadie is asleep. Some days, Sadie would like to be asleep for Bill too, but that seems improper, far more dubious than lying to the mahjongg group.

On weekdays after Rosalie leaves, Bill returns from the land of work and changes the radio from music to news, and kisses Sadie and kisses her belly, and then Sadie remains relentlessly cheerful. It's exhausting, being so cheerful. Her migraine headaches are not Bill's fault, she knows that, but it's peculiar how often they begin in his presence. The cheerfulness must lead to migraines. She does not get migraines around Rosalie. Of course she's paying Rosalie, paying her well, and that's the crux of the matter, isn't it? Rosalie is paid to be helpful and unobtrusive; helpful and unobtrusive, Rosalie will keep this job. And still Sadie feels a comfort and what she might consider a kinship with Rosalie, which seems neither entirely real nor entirely illusory.

WHAT SADIE EXPERIENCES when she goes into labor she would not call hysteria, but a seesawing between hope and fear. Mortification, yes, at the puddle spreading into the living room carpet when her water breaks, at the lack of privacy, the raw exposure in the hospital room, the sweating and moaning, the way ordinary respectable women—she herself—become sweat-soaked, bawling animals. And people who are themselves still ordinary and respectable, doctors, nurses, witnessing all of this; the desperation with which she tries to find them through the saw-toothed contractions; the sweat and murk replacing air. No shred of grace.

But not hysteria. There is the fear she will split apart before the baby gets out of her; the fear the baby will emerge damaged or dead; frustration that she's afraid. She cannot change the subject to something more pleasant. In a birthing room there is no way to change the subject. The doctor seems entirely and stupidly calm and she's grateful for his stupid calm. If only they had knocked her out. If only she could do this in her sleep, and the doctor and the nurses could, after birthing the baby, become amnesiacs and forget gazing up between her legs and handling her there. All that handling, which it turns out is the most appalling thing about pregnancy, worse than the weepiness, worse than the early nausea, the later ballooning.

But also this: a teary elation when the birthing's done and there's the baby, amazing and bloody, her face a little mashed, her cry thin and weird, a seven-pound girl with a cap of brown hair. There is a moment of wonder larger than Sadie had imagined herself capable of: stunning to hold the dark-haired mashed-face baby, whose toes are in fact even more perfect than Delia's son's. The nurses refer to her as Baby Feldstein, but her name is Margo, a new and not a family name, Rebecca for the second name: Bill accepts Sadie's decision because the baby is not a boy. He appears in the delivery room after they've cleaned up the baby but not Sadie, and kisses Sadie's sweaty face and rhapsodizes. When he holds the baby, he is not awkward. It's as if he has been practicing in secret.

Sadie feels a high-strung euphoria that skids off into exhaustion and overwrought tears and back again, and she finds herself drifting away and returning. Time becomes slippery and strange, she's disoriented, and the arrival of her relatives pushes her over the brink. She gets a glimpse of Mother Feldstein, and she feels herself still half-goat, ineffectually bleating. Isn't that her sister-in-law Nora in the hallway? And Bill's brothers, a parade of olive-skinned, balding dentists?

Sadie is huffing. "But I need to sleep," she says.

"Of course," Bill says. "You've slept only a little. Darling, they won't be here long."

He's right, she has slept, she's in another room now, not nearly so bloody—what *is* happening to time?—and now her father, *her father,* is dewy-eyed in the hospital room doorway. He walks in and kisses her on the cheek, wipes his eyes and pats her hand. And just behind him is Mother Feldstein, who has apparently informed the staff that Sadie's own mother is dead and tells a maternity nurse, "Sadie's like my own daughter." She also kisses Sadie: she's teary, exuding that gardenia perfume, and she wants to *hold the baby*. She asks Sadie about her breasts. Which has to be a tactic, to shock Sadie with talk about nipples and milk—and in front of her father!—so Sadie's distracted from *hold the baby*. Not even Sadie has gotten much holding-of-the-baby, the nurses swept Margo off to the nursery—how long ago? How long was she sleeping? And where is that nursery, where is Margo now: the panic spikes and Sadie bites her lip and calls Bill over and says, "Darling, get me the baby."

"She's in the nursery," he says. "We'll have her here soon."

"Now," Sadie says and makes bug eyes at Bill until he gets the nurse back.

This is not full-blown hysteria, though she is breathing rapidly, she's on the teary side, and she's stanching an impulse to harm her mother-in-law. The stanching is important. The nurse tells her twenty more minutes and they'll have the baby back with her, and by the way her sisters have arrived.

TOTAL STRANGERS—the round nurse named Patricia or the skinny one Doris—hold the baby and Sadie does not mind. But the pudgy, perfumed hands of her mother-in-law frighten her, as if they've been dipped in radium. "Like my own daughter," Mother Feldstein repeats. (And just look what's become of Nora, a perfectly nice-looking melancholic who has no friends and spends too much time with her mother and Rose Teitelbaum.)

And now Sadie feels herself falling into a rapid heaving for air, which hurts. Her whole body hurts. She's fallen into sick, useless, bleating goathood, and in the waiting room and peering into the nursery, somewhere far beyond her room, Jo and Celia skulk. Her father sits beside her patting her hand and murmuring *ssshhh* with a Yiddish inflection and some indecipherable word attached, her father in his vest and coat, gold pocket watch hanging, the stern mask of his face cracked open to reveal someone yearning and moved, someone she can't recall meeting, though her mother might have. Her mother who is not in the hallway and not on this earth. Her mother.

And if Celia touches the baby—then what? Will there be a mark?

"Darling? Darling?" Bill says. "The baby's fine, she'll be back soon."

What if Celia doesn't wash? Though perhaps she'll lose her way to the maternity ward, she and Jo both. And Sadie's father is standing now and Bill has taken his place with the hand patting, her father and Mother Feldstein conferring, drifting out to the hall. Sadie is crying. She is not speaking, she is crying, and hates crying around her family and cries anyway, and what about the baby? And the round nurse Patricia brings her in, a tiny howling thing in a fat blanket. Then Sadie's holding Margo, and the world begins to still. It's time, Patricia says, to nurse, they can be alone now, and even Bill leaves. And Sadie stops crying long enough to have a lesson in nursing. It's awkward and there are false starts, her milk not yet in, but at least no audience, just Round Patricia, who claims to have three children. Stunning little squash-faced Margo, such a tiny thing, now not howling at all.

Not long after they are finished and calm, the baby falling into sleep, Jo is at the door, austere and tight-lipped, and Celia, washed and combed and wearing a yellow dress less frumpy than usual. Celia's eyes seem to be wet. And then they're at the side of the bed, Celia smiling, saying "Oh she's pretty." Jo says, "What kind of name is Margo?" and Celia says, "A good name." The nurse Patricia stays. Sadie's arms do not feel like her own when she lets Celia sit to her left and hold the baby. On her right she clutches Round Patricia's hand. Celia herself is pretty in the yellow dress, bathed and combed and holding the newborn, Celia's face pink and open, as if she has never fallen apart, or tried to pull you with her, as if in this world no one falls apart.

CHAPTER 10

Goldie

VENICE BEACH, CALIFORNIA, 1932

Along the piers the air thickens with spun sugar, and you hear the intermittent sounds of dance bands from the halls and the tinnier music near the amusements; the town is awash in garish attractions, which do not trouble Goldie. She's surprised to be at ease here, but Venice so loudly announces itself that Goldie is unremarkable. At first glance no one belongs here, not permanently, and the temporary quality comforts her.

Permanence seems only to be within her body, and she has become denser, less porous, her skin somehow less permeable than it was when she was younger. She is more immutably herself, though she is not certain what this means, only that the town and the coast seem to wash over her instead of inhabit her, that she has been shaped in part by lake weather and eroding city pavement and a house on Lancaster, but only in part. There were the more distant, more porous, early years in the Pale, which was itself a false home but entered her skin nonetheless, a thick sky and days defined by cabbage and worry and ice, and also by family devotion. On her beach walks she is aware of her density as a reversal from those years, when she herself was almost air, her mother live granite. And now there is just Goldie and the sea air. She would like to be made of this California balminess, this salt, this weather; there is relief in it, a lifesaving but shallow relief. She does not know if it will ever deepen, if she will ever be *of* this coast, but it doesn't matter: Venice seems costumed and masked, a town acquired somewhere else.

She's done all she can to forget Buffalo, shrinking it so that the landscape seems tiny, a smear on the far periphery of ocean, the Lancaster house a fig-sized shadow. But in small ways it persists, her family floating in a netherworld like a souvenir globe from the Falls, white crystals drifting over the painted torrent, Daniel passing through dreams. She's most peaceful during the morning walks, after which she reads at the library: later she starts her shift at the restaurant, beyond the noise of the pier, a white-and-blue building with a black-stenciled fish over the entrance, a long patio outside, and inside a balmy airiness. The dining room windows look out on the water—large squares of ocean and sky—and the bar's heavy polished wood seems to be from a ship. (Yet a ship without crowding or turbulence, just broad tables with candles and the view beyond.)

A thin, rangy Southerner named Stan runs the kitchen, and when he is angry he is prone not to yelling but to excessive politeness; his assistant, Luca, is quick and sad and more likely to swear. The men in the kitchen have stories locked away in them, they are from Elsewhere, and don't speak much of it, and in this regard are no different from Goldie. They cook thick soups and serve up plates of fish and plates of beef, and drink soda water on ice through the night and pretend it is beer. If it's a good day, Stan will sing low to himself, songs from the radio, and what he calls campfire songs, which have a twangy yearning to them. On harder days the air seems to pop with the sounds of metal against metal and abrupt chopping and sizzling meat and impatient calls to the kitchen boy, Clark, for more onions or more butter or more minced greens. The cooks are not unkind to her, and when they are happy they flirt in the mildest way by calling her Goldilocks. The other waitresses, Marie and Jocelyn, and the manager Max just call her G or sometimes GeeGee and invite her to drink with them after the shift. In the early evening the tables fill, and the hours of travel between the tables and the kitchen seem to be a kind of train. There are brief moments during dinner service when Marie and Jocelyn, like Goldie, stop and watch the sea and sky from the windows: they too are from somewhere else. But the speed of the job resumes, and the evening busyness makes her forget time until closing, when time again slows, and she sits for a drink. Jocelyn waves her cigarettes as she talks about movie stars and their visits to Venice Beach and the broader subject of Hollywood gossip, and there's an ease and sense of play in this, a relief in the glitzy surface. Marie prefers to talk about weddings, especially grand ones.

One night a week, Goldie sells tickets at the ballroom on the pier, to hear the music, she tells herself, though there is a shiny allure to the couples, and from her ticket booth it's as if she is watching scenes from moving pictures. Occasionally she meets men. And it seems that she has shed her old life, or that the light and salt have burned it away; that her past is no more real than imaginary lives she invented as a girl—a dream life with her mother in Paris or Warsaw or Prague. Here, now, she stays conscious of the boardwalk at Venice, the persisting sunlight, the blues and greens and grays that sweep in and every day define the horizon, the sea-rubbed glass on her windowsill, the heat on her skin, and cold gin at night and Jocelyn's grit-and-honey voice describing her latest infatuation, an actor named Pete.

In California she can breathe. Still, there is an increasing slippage between the years on the calendar and the years as she feels them, and she's lost her bearings with the seasons. Summer seems constant and permanent, and chronology fades. Maybe this is why after three years her sisters begin to swim up out of the dark: she does not know. It's June, she's in the theater with Marie and Marie's sister, Paula, shiny Iowa girls in their twenties with wide blue eyes and amber hair, their wish to laugh shot through with longing. They are nothing like her sisters, but in the theater, after the feature has begun and as the screen romance is unfolding, the dark seems to shift for her, the way a room does when one blinks; and there is a rising sense of other places, of other theaters and other women, Sadie, Celia, Jo. For an instant she feels as if she could turn to her left and see not Marie but one of them. The feeling is palpable, the familiarity seductive; there is a comfort in the sensation, along with a startling craving. The silvery light pours through the dust motes in the theater. A wave of sadness rises, and then she turns; Marie is engrossed; it's California. She forces herself to focus on the picture, but the sensation remains with her. After that night she is aware of her sisters in odd moments on the street and in the earliest waking and late at night, Jo and Sadie and Celia like small spots of color flashing in the air and retreating.

Irving is not present with her in this way, nor does the image of him bring the same wave of sadness, and this makes him easier to contemplate. He is still in her mind a boy sulking in the high branches of the oak—as if the tree unexpectedly refused to take him farther from the house—but simply a boy, unable to harm her. She and her sisters would coax him down with sweets—and there the memory is more deeply etched, a weariness in Jo's face, Sadie calling his name, Celia standing at the base of the tree with a slice of cake. None of which should make her nervous now, years later, but it feels as if Sadie is still calling, Celia still standing beneath the tree. The nervousness comes on her several times a week, and sometimes a shortness of breath, and the old feeling of suffocation descends, and she sits on the beach until it passes. Her family has not come for her, no one has come for her, she has nothing to be frightened of, but the pattern repeats itself. To say she misses them would be too simple: there is an old piercing loneliness, but she does not trust them, not Sadie, not Jo. They would not understand her life. Irving might or might not; he is, at least, unlikely to judge her. With Celia it is not a matter of trust, but of worry: if you worry too much about Celia it will crush you.

Goldie tells herself this and yet it might be raining in Buffalo, a cold spring rain, and Celia might be standing beneath that oak, or beneath another tree somewhere in the city, after walking for hours. Her clothes will be soaked before she'll climb the front steps and cross the doorway into the foyer, where she'll become conscious, and then embarrassed, of the rainwater puddling from her dress, and will stay there until you bring her a towel, and tell you of the dogs that frighten her.

CHAPTER 11

Irving

1932

There is, somewhere beyond Delaware and Lancaster, a turning of chance, the arrival of fortune, and Irving awaits the signs: the approach of the streetcar just as he reaches the stop; a coincidence in numbers—the time, the streetcar number, the building address where he notices a beautiful girl. Tidings. Here is the swell of possibility, forever present, that today will offer good luck, that one day of good luck will lead to others, a string of such days, then a solid floor of them lifting him into a soft brilliance, into a life like Leo Schumacher's.

And maybe Sadie's daughter is a sign for Irving after all—Leo toasted him being an uncle, gave him scotch—just a sign requiring more interpretation. Bill is startlingly cheerful—he's stopped lecturing Irving about gambling—and Irving's father has gone into a sentimental phase, the hawk-eyed supervision loosening for now. This itself is auspicious. Today, a perfect August Tuesday, there's leniency when Irving asks for a few hours off to visit Sadie. It's a relief to be out in the mild air, and he does miss Sadie: she hasn't taken him to lunch for months. When he arrives at her house, she is wearing a loose pale green dress, and tendrils of hair have fallen out of her barrette, and though she is tired, there's a pink flush to her cheeks. He can't stop looking at her. She kisses him on the cheek and offers him a chair in the living room, and when he asks how she is, she recites the minutiae of Margo's sleeping habits. Sadie's also concerned with matters of feeding and diapering, the necessary singing, but she can't talk about these things forever, can she? He's there only ten minutes before two of Sadie's neighbors arrive—women with names that vanish after they're said—and then a nurse brings Margo down from the nursery, and the pretty Colored girl, Rosalie, comes in from the kitchen. Now the room is full of women, all of whom ignore him. The baby, who seems at first calm, is handed among them until she's howling, a shocked look on her squinchy little face, though she herself is what's alarming— a strange, incoherent, demanding thing who might just as well have dropped from the sky. When her shock dissipates and the crying stops, he can see Margo's a good-looking baby, thick dark hair and dark eyes and delicate features, but he's relieved when she quiets and the nurse takes her back upstairs to her bassinet, and the neighbors leave. Rosalie offers him coffee and cookies, a further relief: she has noticed him, and she's leading him back to the familiar country where men and women drink coffee. Sadie shows him the tiny knitted hat Celia made, and when she leans in close she smells of milk and sweat and flowery talc. She sighs about her mother-in-law, and finally asks him how he is. As he answers, her head's tilted toward the stairs, her eyes a little glazed, as if she's listening beyond him. There in her living room he's become translucent. An earthworm.

Irving clears his throat and says he's thinking of buying a new suit. Sadie nods distractedly.

"How much do you think I ought to pay for a suit these days?" He waits. "Sadie?"

"Sorry," she says. "Margo's been so fussy today, I thought I heard something."

After he repeats the question, he can see her coming into focus, considering. "What does Papa pay? He always looks good."

"His suits are expensive, I think."

"Mmm," she says. "More coffee?"

"Maybe if I get a few more dollars together."

She won't take the bait. "It's hard times, isn't it?" she says. But Margo's healthy and she and Bill are grateful—has Irving seen Bill with Margo? He's fallen in love again.

She offers Irving a chocolate from the ribboned box Bill brought her. She's a master at subject changing, steering talk only where she wants to go and away from Irving's needs and interruptions. Leo would marvel.

He'll have to wait a while. "She's beautiful, Margo," he says, and takes a chocolate. "Looks just like her mother."

This doesn't seem to charm Sadie as much as it ought to, which is disconcerting. Why can't he charm her? He needs money, sure, but there's another reason he wants her full, unrestrained smile, something connected to the dress and the loose strands of hair. He begins his imitations of movie stars, which usually send her into spasms of laughter, but she gives him the half-smile that means *Again?* There is apparently no other subject but the baby. And before he's found a way to reach her, more visitors arrive, a few Jewish girls like Sadie who've married up and started families. Their arms are loaded with casseroles and pink booties and dresses the size of handkerchiefs. They smile broadly at him and say *Mazel tov*, as if he's the father. What a lovely surprise it is to see him again, Delia Lefkowitz says, using the bright, flirtatious tone that means her sister is still single.

Enough. He kisses Sadie's cheek and makes his way to the Hertel streetcar and transfers to a downtown line. It's three o'clock, a mild breeze coming in from the west, and he counts the car stops. Exactly what sort of luck is the baby? Margo Rebecca, MR. M being the thirteenth letter of the alphabet, R the eighteenth; he's superstitious about 13, but combined the initials make 31, or 13 reversed—which ought to mean luck. He detours to a pharmacy on the East Side and finds his bookie, Murray, bets on the Saratoga fourth race for a horse with number 31 named Lightning Bolt and also in the sixth, on a long shot named Red Molly.

.   .   .

MARGO'S ARRIVAL has translated to a mix of dreaminess and deliberation in Celia: she bathes and dresses every day as if for temple, though Sadie lets her visit only once or twice a week. *Come over
with Jo,* Sadie tells her. *Wait until Jo's free. What about Saturday?* And in
her most respectable, Sadie-pleasing dress, Celia shows up at the
store instead, her handbag stuffed with crocheting projects and
bright rattles for the baby. Mind your sister, his father says, leaving
Irving to entertain her—which is not hard, she likes the attention,
likes to laugh—and he sets her up in the office reading chair, giving her tea, and cajoling her into crocheting and listening to the
radio while he helps customers. If she's too restless, Irving takes
change from the till and walks with her up Main Street, well beyond the Palace Burlesque, to the department stores. "Why not
get Margo a bib?" he says. "Don't babies need bibs?" Pacifiers? Toy
animals? He gives her the till change for a streetcar home and a
small treat for herself, and says good-bye to her in the doorway of
Adam, Meldrum and Anderson's, and hopes she does not wander.

Today he's missed Celia and his father only asks, "How is my
granddaughter?"

"She's a beauty," Irving says.

THAT FRIDAY there's a touch of Schumacher luck, Lillian stopping
by for his father, Lillian with her rich curves and seductive laugh.
His father isn't a fool. And it would be fine to take up with a girl
like her, younger but with her spark and taste for nightlife and
frank sex appeal—and Jewish, yet not the Jewish of Sadie's crowd.

Stay away from the shiksas, Irving's father says, but Buffalo is a city
of Gentile girls. All sorts. The Palace Burlesque's only two blocks
from the store and the girls there are nothing like the temple's
prim coterie of Idas and Mauras and Ruths, even less like his sisters. He'll take a flask and find a seat close to the stage, watch the
new fan dancer and the girl named Hula Lulu—sweet skin of her
thighs, sweetheart bottom and sweetheart tits with the tasseled
pasties any minute ready to drop from the nipples and scatter beyond the lights, and there you are waiting: any second her sweet-
cream body might offer itself into your hands. You swoon for
those girls and for that moment leave your life.

"How are you?" Lillian says. She reaches over the counter and straightens his collar, and his face flushes warm. "More handsome every day, aren't you?"

And then Irving's father appears with the bank deposit bag tucked under his arm, and Lillian moves to greet him with a kiss, which he allows. "Irving," he says, "the first drawer is off, twenty cents. You look. See if you dropped something."

But Lillian smiles at Irving, as if to say *It's nothing, don't worry*, then leans against his father, his father now smiling too, and they leave the store.

IRVING HAS a way with women, the proper Jewish girls and the winking burlesque girls, the girls in the speakeasies, even the ones at the dance hall on Main, where the Gentile girls are higher-class. They wear shimmery summer dresses and let you hold them firmly and spin them on the ballroom floor, and sometimes give you a little extra. He introduces himself as Thomas West. A name for a rich adventurer, the nickname, Tommy, conjuring up jazz horns. And maybe one of those blue-eyed brunettes or blondes could be his stroke of luck. You never know. Not for steady, not like Leo's girl Sofia, just a single stroke of luck that changes the days ahead. One encounter that alters the staleness of ordinary days, of returning the twenty cents he lifted from the drawer; the staleness of leaving Sadie's house, having failed again to capture her attention or to comprehend her life; the staleness of being Irving.

After lunch and his father's return, a few merchant sailors walk up from the docks to buy presents for their girlfriends, friendly, this group, trusting him to steer them right. The sky's a resonant blue, and when they've left, Irving takes the push broom outside to sweep the walk, the August air mild. He watches for more signs, this time finding a nickel on the street, a ticket stub from the Hippodrome, a cloud in the shape of a lion.

Later, when the mail arrives, his father glances through it and gives him the pile to sort. There's a typed business envelope addressed to him, the return Leo Schumacher. He pockets it and groups the bills and payments and his father's personal correspondence, delivering it to his father's office desk. And when his father is busy at the bench, he opens the letter, finding two folded sheets, the first a typed note:

> *Dear Irving,*
> *I hope this finds you well. I am in good health and*
> *sufficiently content. I hope you understand. Here's*
> *something for Celia. I hope she's all right.*
> > *Your sister,*
> > *Goldie*

The second sheet's a blank, folded around a twenty-dollar bill.

And at first he feels his own blankness: he rereads the typed note, examines the twenty, real enough, magnificent, but what does Leo have to do with Goldie? A prank? Irving does not understand, and then he does: Goldie's signature's as real as the twenty, the postmark on the envelope blurry but legible—Los Angeles, California. And now he is flushed, tingling: she ran off, just as he thought, she's not dead at all. That in itself is the luckiest of signs—Goldie not dead—and a twenty-dollar bill as if to prove it, as if to multiply the luck. In that instant he nearly calls his father, to tell him she's alive, no need to think of dead bodies, or to keep yourself from thinking of dead bodies, she's alive. *Healthy*, she says, *sufficiently content*. But of course she wouldn't pretend to be Leo if she wanted their father to know, would she? And she's right, the shivah was no invitation home.

She's a smart one, Goldie, you have to give her that. Very smart. He slips the bill into his wallet and tucks the letter in his inside suit pocket. It's true that Celia's situation is not promising, you have to admit that, even a fine stroke of luck—and isn't this a fine stroke of luck?—won't change her life the way it ought to. But she isn't so bad lately, summer is always her best season, what with all her gardening, and now Sadie's baby, a niece, you see the way Celia tries. But these things come and go. Goldie has a point. Goldie who is healthy and sufficiently content and clever enough to pretend to be Leo Schumacher. Clever enough to find her way, to find money, clever enough not to be dead, and good for her, he thinks. In Los Angeles or wherever. Though she might have said *where* a little more exactly. She might have wondered about Irving's prospects, which are brighter than Celia's of course but no sure thing. Does she wonder about him? She did choose him to write to. Chose him over Sadie. She always was fond of him, wasn't she?

The news melds into the late afternoon light, the high clouds streaked with pink, and Irving walks up several streetcar stops before deciding to ride. There's a rush of well-being, he's the one Goldie chose—*more handsome every day*. This is how fortune arrives, when you don't expect it, just as you don't expect the lawns on Lancaster to turn emerald green, but they have. And house after house the roses are blooming, even at his family's house, like floating bowls of red silk. Hadn't he noticed? Tonight, he decides, will be a dance hall night.

The foyer smells of cooked meat, and before he's hung up his jacket, his father calls, "Irving? Good. Come to the table."

The dining room is set for Sabbath—white tablecloth, the fancy china, the once-a-week wineglasses. Jo carries in plates of meat and vegetables, wiping her hands on her apron and only nodding hello: Celia's already seated next to her father, hands in her lap, eyes closed. Jo removes the apron and lights the Sabbath candles and Celia opens her eyes. Celia herself appears brighter than usual, like the lawn, like the underlit clouds, a little dreamy, a little like a girl in love. Did she hear from Goldie too? Not likely—he got the twenty. Is it simply that she'll see the baby tomorrow? Women are mysteries in this way. Their father says the Kiddush, the Hamotzi, still in his own cloud of sentiment, smiling at Celia tonight, happy to talk with her about *the baby the baby the baby*. Who looks like Sadie, don't you think? More like Sadie than like Bill? And all that dark hair, so much lovely hair for a baby. A lot of them are bald.

"Your head was peach fuzz," Jo tells Irving. A smirk. "Part of it, anyway. The rest like an egg."

He smiles and nods, as if she's told a fine joke. "It grew in," he says, preens a little, tells Celia her hair looks good today. Celia smiles, but Jo glares at him: she's warned him not to comment on Celia's hair. You don't want to jinx anything.

"Margo's a little thing, isn't she?" Jo says.

"Tiny," their father says. "You all were tiny. All new babies, tiny."

As he forks up his supper, Irving feels himself drift from the table, watching the conversation unfold as if from a neighboring house, or a back row seat at the theater. It's like this with his family: scene after mundane scene in which he has no part.

HE STARTS the evening at the dance hall, which tonight is filling with couples, a few single girls chaperoned by their married sisters and brothers-in-law, one slim young brunette who tells him her name is Donna. She looks like a Donna, clear-eyed and graceful, her skin warm through the yellow satin dress. A sweet face but just from the way she moves you can tell she's proper to the core, the kind who expects a man to escort her to dances and court her and some year kiss her on the lips. Tedious. He should know better, he's a quick judge of such things, but she's lovely, this little Donna, and she smells like warm leaves and rosewater. He introduces himself as Thomas West, and she believes in the name, believes in the neatly pressed suit, the Protestant pretense: see the way she looks at him, a man dressed as elegantly as his father, down to the gold cuff links he borrowed from the store. *More handsome every day.* "My best friends," he says, "call me Tommy." After three dances he bows and tells her he hopes to see her there again soon. Then he dances with less lovely, equally proper girls, one dance each, a Lucy and a Harriet and a June. Always, he is Thomas.

And why shouldn't he be Thomas? Tying his shoe, how easily he could be another man, the two-toned size ten from the Florsheim on Main easily purchased by another man with size ten. Plenty of men wearing tens move through the city and they have other names, all of them not Irving: other men meeting girls, other men visiting dance halls, other men sipping fast from gin flasks in dark back corridors, or leaving for other venues, the late clubs, a kind of brotherhood leaning down to tie their size ten shoes and in that moment loosened from their given names, each becoming a man with a shoe, call him whatever you want, call him Thomas West.

Later, the women at the speakeasy smell of perfume and cigarette smoke, they move languorously, smile at him less shyly and more often than any of the Donnas. He prefers the less forward ones though, buys a gin for a quiet girl with a beautiful mouth, a beautiful shape to her, Margaret she says her name is. She says she was born in Canada. "We've got a lot in common then," he says. "I wasn't born here either." Which she's willing to laugh at. He tells her he's from New York, in town to visit his sister; he's in business, he travels, he comes here quite a lot. New York City? she says and he asks if she's been. She hasn't, and here's his chance to talk about his life in New York, Thomas West's life in New York, and the marvelous hotels and the swell of people and the glamour of Broadway—his father is always talking about the glamour of Broadway—once he shook hands with the governor. A fine man, the governor, she would like him, he's the sort of man you respect. And would she like another gin? She would, that's generous of him, he's a generous man. She's a beautician, she tells him, she does good work, and if she's lucky she'll have a beauty parlor of her own someday.

"I believe in luck," he says. "Don't you?"

And she does, of course she believes in luck, you never know what can happen.

"For instance," he says, "I just came by here to get a nightcap and now I've met you. That seems lucky to me, if you don't mind my saying." And now he touches her hand, lightly touches her forearm and he can feel her warming, opening to him, can feel the gin confidence. He gives her a light kiss on the cheek and waits to see her expression, waits to see if she wants more, and she seems to, she squeezes his hand. "It's a lovely evening, don't you think?" he says.

"Lovely," she says, "yes it is."

He asks if she might like to go somewhere else, and a look of mild confusion crosses her face. "There's a lounge in the lobby of my hotel," he says, "not much to drink of course but it's quiet, elegant, you'd like it there. Or I can get you a taxi home, maybe you're tired." It's a gamble of course, but she smiles and lets him get a taxi for the two of them, and he directs the cabbie to the Statler Hotel.

The lobby of the Statler seems like velvet, thick carpets and fine chairs and divans in groupings, the light bright but soft. It's as if he's passed through the doorway into a world of warmth and light, leaving the other rooms of his life completely. He seats her on a plush green sofa and excuses himself for a moment, strolls to the desk. Luckily, the clerk is easy with him, and unerringly polite: there's a nice room on the fourth floor. He signs the register Thomas J. West II, opens his wallet, pulls out the twenty, and pays for a night, overtipping the clerk.

The elevator operator wishes them a good evening and they rise in the gold-trimmed elevator, which seems to lighten him, he can feel the lift in his belly. Then they are in Room 420, with the bed and the brocade wallpaper and thick curtains and dark wood furniture. Room 420, its own velvet-lined box. Room 420, where he is quick to put on a safety, where he kisses Margaret, undresses Margaret, who is beautiful, completely beautiful, her skin almost glowing in the light from the bedside table, breasts high and round, sweet hips and desire, you can feel her wanting. *Thomas*, she says, *Tommy*, sighing and pulling him to her. There's a slight burn in his throat, Thomas's throat, and in his body, his bones themselves a kind of hot syrup, he's touching her breasts and she calls the name again, *Thomas*, and in that moment he is no one but Thomas, with the velvet life, with the velvet Margaret, and then he is inside her and the moment shifts to a greater forgetting, the loss of names, as when the sky and lake merge into one silver blue plate. And you can call it neither sky nor lake nor not-sky, not-lake. The purest luck of all.

For a time they sleep in the jewel-box room, and he wakes now and then to see bits of city light patterning the window sheers, the room a deep dream, Margaret a deep dream, one slim arm flung over her head, a swath of auburn hair fallen over her cheek, the sheets pulled tight against her body. This is where he ought to stay, this hotel room on this night, which seems somehow his true home. He is spent from sex, happy, the yearnings quiet, and he pulls Margaret to him and presses his face to her hair and returns to sleep. And when he wakes again, early light is leaking through the sheers and Margaret is stirring; she kisses him on the cheek. Then she's gone from the bed, quickly dressing, he can see she's drawing into herself, moving away from desire, plain practicality in her gestures. There's the day to face, but she still whispers. *Thomas, I have to go now.*

I wish you didn't, he says.

Me too. She hurriedly washes and applies lipstick, and then the divide feels certain and solid: he's still in the bed, undressed, the hotel room his for hours to come, and she is a departing visitor. Not unlike a customer at the jewelry store, he thinks. He remembers to offer her cab fare. "Thank you, Tommy," she says. She takes the fare and kisses him with her lipsticked mouth, and leaves, and the room in her absence declares a budding impermanence he'll need to stave off.

He bathes and orders coffee delivered to the room. It's a delicate business, putting on his suit, the same one he donned yesterday at the Lancaster house, but he concentrates on the elevator ride and the moments in the lobby and the speakeasy, the Thomasness of it. And when he checks out of the hotel he finds a barbershop to get a shave, as if he were an out-of-towner, and a coffee shop near the hotel he's never been to. The day's a patchwork of cloud and blue, and there is still the sense of possibility he always feels downtown. He does not think about his name. The waitress brings his breakfast, eggs and toast and the bacon he orders only when he is alone. It's Saturday. Saturday, and his father will be expecting Irving at the store—those Saturday hours a necessity now—and with this thought he is Irving. He is Irving and his sisters Jo and Celia will be visiting his sister Sadie and her baby. He is Irving and his sister Goldie is alive, and maybe now the world will right itself. He doesn't quite have the money he had yesterday but still plenty, enough to stake him nicely at Leo Schumacher's Saturday night poker game. And perhaps the fact of Margaret stakes him too, marking the change in his luck, the night at the Statler a secret charm. The spending is worth it: *You have to invest to earn,* Leo says. It's the kind of thing Thomas would quote.

And when he leaves the coffee shop the air already seems thicker, and the streetcars harshly ordinary. He buys the *Courier* and reads the sports news while the car lurches west and north, the passengers all seemingly washed out and dull, even in the loveliness of late summer and the promise of baseball home games. It's inevitable, this trip to the house, he has to change his clothes, the shirt and undergarments but also the suit, which is wrinkled and smells of smoke. And as he walks up the steps to the house, Celia's there in the doorway, blue dress and matching shoes, pretty, pushing the screen door open. He could tell her about Goldie now, while she's alone—*I have a secret, Ceil, don't say a word*—but she starts waving him toward the staircase, mild warning on her face. He touches her shoulder and passes her quickly, and he's halfway to the second floor when he hears Jo's hard steps down the front hall, Jo calling, "What you been doing? Tomcatting? Papa's waiting at the store, opened without you."

"Don't get in a mood before we see the baby," Celia tells her.

"You're one to talk," Jo says, but then they both fall silent.

Irving hurries into his room, with its white walls and dark wood and white chenille bedspread, neckties hanging off the bedstead, the framed oval mirror in which he is always quizzical. Soiled shirts piled at the foot of the bed; two clean ones in the closet with his second summer suit, clean underclothes and socks in the bureau.

He changes quickly, flinging the wrinkled suit on his bed, and finally steps back into the two-tone shoes, taking the laces in his hands, pausing and closing his eyes, as if to feel himself back at the Statler, the same hands tying the same shoe, a small bubble of Thomas rising.

He remembers the gold cuff links, his watch, stuffs his wallet and carfare in his pocket and hurries down the hall and front stairs, out the door, before Jo starts in on him again. Really she could use a night at the Statler herself. From the lawn he waves back at the parlor windows, where Celia often sits.

"I STAYED at Leo's and overslept," he tells his father. "I'm sorry, Papa. It won't happen again."

"You make sure," his father says. "Irving? You understand me?"

"Yes, Papa."

"No foolishness."

"No. I understand," Irving says.

His father sighs and gestures toward the storefront, and from the storage closet Irving takes the push broom to sweep the front walk, and a bucket and rags, water and ammonia to clean the front windows, a work apron to cover his suit.

The afternoon seems beaten down but surprisingly busy, filled with sailors, men his age who started out somewhere else and for a few minutes find themselves in the jewelry store, musing over lockets and heart-shaped brooches, charm bracelets, occasionally the gems. A couple of men remind him of himself—the ones who go straight to the sapphires and diamond-studded cuff links, despite the sailor's uniform. And why not? Why shouldn't they too have luxury? His father tries to steer them to more likely buys, but Irving goes with their enthusiasms and sometimes it works, sometimes a man will spend a month's pay. Isn't it worth it? Just before closing Irving sells a sailor ruby earrings for his girl.

His father doesn't comment, doesn't praise, but as he locks up the store for the night, he tells Irving, "You want to stay at Leo's, you stay on Saturday night," the closest he'll come to relenting.

ON SATURDAY NIGHTS he is always free of his family: his father goes to Lillian's and doesn't ask Irving's plans. Tonight Irving stays downtown, buys himself dinner at Laube's Old Spain, as if he were again a traveler, the man who stayed at the Statler. He pours gin from his flask into a water glass and lets the warm flush of it take him as he eats the meal and contemplates the well-dressed women, the men in good suits. By the time he leaves, the sense of well-being has returned, and he takes the streetcar north to Leo's flat, to the poker game, still with plenty to stake him, the fine luck of Margaret, his array of smaller charms.

Leo deals him in. On the first and second hands he wins a little, on the third a little more. The cards are solid, not dramatic but good. And then luck shifts to Bernie, and then to Max, eroding Irving's gains. Leo takes a hand, and then Irving again, twice—he was right, there were signs, though the pot is not large. "You've got something going," Leo says, and in that instant he feels perfect. At the end of the night he comes out ahead by five dollars, a very nice gain, though he owes Leo two for staking him last week. And Max asks for a dollar loan, he's miserable, he played with household money and now he's stuck, he's covered Irving before. So Irving leaves two dollars ahead, still good, he doesn't owe Murray the bookie (thanks to Bill, who could have spared the lectures), and Max will pay him back. It's an auspicious night. He leaves Leo's flat with six dollars in his wallet, a fine amount, more than he'll need for the week, money for next week's game and maybe a bet or two on the horses.

And when he arrives at the house, only the hall lights are on. It's late, the doors to his sisters' rooms closed, his father's open and empty. And he can carry the flush of the night with him when it's like this, the deep quiet, no one calling his name or chastising him for the drinks—he's had plenty tonight, he knows he smells of it, though he can't smell it himself. In his room he turns on the bed-side lamp, which spreads a circle over the clean bed and thick rug, onto the wood floor. His wrinkled suit is hanging on the standing rack, neckties evenly distributed over the bedpost, no other soiled clothes: his sisters must have picked up the laundry.

He falls asleep immediately, content, sleep like a silver blur that carries him far into the morning. A thick, irrefutable sleep, broken by church bells and the clang of pans and the muted voices of his sisters. He did all right last night, didn't he? On the bureau top: his watch and housekey, over a dollar in change, his wallet holding five one-dollar bills. Not bad. But there's still the wrinkled suit hanging on the rack, like a half-man, waiting for him. He checks the inside pocket and finds the letter tucked away as he left it—exactly as he left it, isn't it?—the typed note and the blank page.

Goldie's worried about Celia but Celia looked good in her blue dress, didn't she? She did. And five dollars is enough to give her, it isn't twenty, but five is fine, substantial. Only if he hands it over this week, he'll be broke. He should wait at least until next week's game, add his next winnings. Of course he can't show the letter without the money: right away, Jo would ask for it, and even if he handed the five dollars over, they'd guess he'd been spending. Sadie would know, and then she'd shut him off for good. No. Next week is much better. He'll tell them about Goldie and show them the letter: he'll hand over, say, ten dollars for Celia then. They're wrapped up in the baby now, anyway. Goldie is just fine. After three years, a week will not matter.

For now, he slips the letter under his mattress and returns to bed.

It's lonely, the way he touches himself.

CHAPTER 12

Sadie

1932

Six weeks after she's brought the baby home, the world still has not become real in the old way. It's as if the days themselves have been attenuated and merged, the hours and minutes reconstituted into a pale blur of tired wakefulness and brief light sleep. She likes it best when Margo is quiet after nursing; and just as Margo slips into deeper drowsiness then falls asleep on Sadie's shoulder. The fact of Margo herself—the small, bewildered face and miniature fists, the full breathing weight of her, the way sleep overtakes her—remains astonishing. She *is* beautiful, Sadie thinks, and that Sadie herself has borne such a child stuns her. This is something she does not say aloud to anyone but Bill, a feeling so rare and private she cannot bear for others to intrude upon it.

But in the recent haziness and loosening order, Sadie's fears spike: intrusions seem especially dangerous. She knows new mothers can be a little demented—witness Delia Lefkowitz—but Delia has always been as flighty, her baby especially difficult. Margo is not colicky, you can tell what she needs, and Sadie's gradually more confident taking care of her. But Sadie's relatives still frighten her: she can't stop imagining little nightmarish scenes. Even in her mind, her sisters keep appalling her. She pictures Celia pushing a stroller down a too-busy thoroughfare, giving Margo costume jewelry she can easily choke on. Or trying to feed her solid food—herring, Sadie pictures herring. The actual Celia does nothing of the sort: she's quiet, shy when she visits, talks softly the way she does to kittens, lets Sadie supervise every gesture. And while Jo has never in her life seemed drawn to babies, her gaze is unnerving—the gaze one might find on a kidnapper. Jo might just lock the baby up at Lancaster, like Rapunzel. A herring-fed Rapunzel.

At least they don't visit without asking, unlike her mother-in-law, who, if she could, might nurse the baby herself. That alone seems shocking, worse to remember that Mother Feldstein has in her life nursed several children—five—including Sadie's husband. This is the sort of thing one should not think about. In truth, Mother Feldstein probably does not want to nurse the baby: rather she gazes at Margo as if she wants to eat her. Or take her home and give her to Nora, as she might give a doll to a toddler to cheer her up. Stop, Sadie thinks, but since the baby was born, runaway thoughts are harder to stop. And some of Mother Feldstein's comments do smack of possessiveness, don't they? *I'm her grandmother* in a way that sounds more important—well, grander—than ordinary mother, mere changer of diapers, mere wet nurse. And look at Bill, stunned by the baby, a little in love with Margo, a little annoyed by her, utterly pleased to be pleasing his mother—just look! he's made a grandchild! not quite a grandson, but a grandchild, good enough! A Feldstein baby.

In early September, after another of Mother Feldstein's day-long visits, Sadie tells Bill, "Margo isn't, you know, your mother's child. Your mother's already had her children."

Bill eyes her carefully. "I understand that, Sadie."

"Does she?"

"She's Margo's *grandmother,*" Bill says, with his mother's exact intonation.

"Exactly," Sadie says. "Babies need their *mothers.*"

Bill, turning red, offers, "It's an emotional time for you. I understand that."

"What?"

"You're very touchy. New mothers often are." Another Mother Feldstein quote.

"Your mother shouldn't visit every day. Tell her to stop visiting every day."

"Sadie, you need help here."

"I have help. I have a visiting nurse, for pity's sake. I have Rosalie."

"You miss your mother, I know."

"Don't bring my mother into this."

"You can't exactly rely on your sisters."

Which is true. "I miss my mother, not yours, darling. *Well-meaning* as she may be."

"Careful, Sadie."

"Do you see the way she looks at Margo? She wants to eat her up."

"That's enough."

"I think so. Tell her to stop coming here so much."

"I'll tell her what I tell her."

"I won't let her in the house."

And now Margo is awake and wailing again, and there's the pang of despair: Sadie hasn't slept. She's desperate for sleep. If only she could put a note on the door: *No solicitors. No family.* Though of course there are milder, easier family members, like Bill's older brothers and their wives, kind and unobtrusive, the middle brother bossy but quick to defend Sadie, quick to say, "Ma, it's time to go."

Bill himself is not mild or easy; is this why his sympathy for his mother seems boundless? While to Sadie it's as if a curtain has fallen, hiding Mother Feldstein's saving graces; Sadie can read only one voracious expression. Was it always this way, Bill defending his mother no matter what, Sadie suspecting every gesture? Mother Feldstein did, for example, inquire what colors Sadie was using for the nursery and made no critical remark. Brought Sadie a bottle of the perfume she prefers, as a baby gift, saying *You need something for yourself.* And in that moment there seemed a kind of loosening, almost an acknowledgment of difficulty. Mother Feldstein had raised four boys and a girl, after all, her husband working forever to get by and then too early dead. And Sadie finds herself relenting—

she should relent, she isn't heartless, Sadie *has* compassion—and she decides to simply limit the length of Mother Feldstein's visits. This seems fair, doesn't it? Yet in the night—the darker hours of the long blur—Sadie envisions Mother Feldstein's arms wrapped around Margo, a turning away, just out of reach, the smile at Sadie more triumphal than loving, the gaze unblinking and eerie as Mother takes a step further back, and another, distancing Sadie from the baby.

In the morning she's exhausted, and when Rosalie offers to walk Margo around so Sadie can get some rest, Sadie's more than relieved. *Take her, yes, for a while, thank you.* This Sadie cannot explain: she would never accept such an offer from Mother Feldstein, even when it seems that Margo will wear Sadie down to nothing. In the moments of greatest and most head-splitting demand, Mother Feldstein and Margo do seem linked: the horrifying thought recurs that Margo is Mother Feldstein's true heir, all ferocity and limitless need. But Rosalie intercedes, takes the baby and somehow in taking the baby returns her to Sadie.

When Sadie gets two good hours of sleep and awakens, Margo is her daughter and lovely. Mother Feldstein is simply Bill's mother, and Sadie sees no signs of conspiracy. Later in the morning, Sadie nurses Margo and rocks her, readies birth announcements and listens to the radio, and Rosalie brings her biscuits and glasses of milk.

IT'S A SATURDAY afternoon when Sadie's father drops by to see the baby, bringing Lillian Schumacher with him. He is no less conniving than Mother Feldstein, is he? Certainly if he'd asked to bring Lillian, Sadie would have found perfectly reasonable grounds to refuse him or at least delay the visit, but now Lillian is in Sadie's living room and so is Mother Feldstein. Sadie's bleary today, though capable of civility. Lillian offers up a box wrapped in white paper with a pink ribbon, which Sadie opens to find a tiny pink dress with roses embroidered across the skirt. Beautiful.

Sadie holds it in the air, like a flag strung with pink candies. "Stunning, Miss Schumacher, really. Thank you. You shouldn't have gone to such trouble," Sadie says, and makes a point of calling Rosalie to view the dress.

"Good afternoon, Miss Schumacher." Rosalie fingers the embroidery. "My. Isn't that something."

"She'll have to wear a bib with that, Sadie," Mother Feldstein says.

"Rosalie," Sadie says, "shall we have lemonade?"

And Rosalie disappears to the kitchen, then brings glasses for the women and a plate of shortbread, while the men retreat to Bill's study to smoke.

Lillian does not ask to hold the baby, instead knots her hands behind her back and looks into the bassinet, smiles, takes a seat in the reading chair a few steps away. And while Sadie's attention is still on Lillian's comfort, Mother Feldstein lifts the sleeping Margo out of the bassinet, makes a slightly choked crooning sound, and walks the baby in circles around the room. It's as if Sadie's late-night vision has manifested itself in her living room—and just after she's gotten Margo to sleep. She swallows a shriek, which continues to bubble in her chest, along with the impulse to steal Margo back and knock Mother to the floor. The wish shocks her, but the shock is clarifying: she's thrown from the sleep haze into her more assured social self. This is her house, her child: she is Mrs. William Feldstein.

Mrs. William Feldstein asks Miss Lillian Schumacher how Kaplan's stationery store is faring.

"It's a hard time for everyone," Lillian says. She admits she's working fewer hours but it's a good little business, she thinks Kaplan's will survive. "The shortbread," Lillian says, "is delicious." Lillian's delicate in her gestures, her fingers plump and silky. In spite of herself, Sadie imagines a majestic swan.

Mother Feldstein coos more loudly at Margo.

"Mother, perhaps Miss Schumacher would like to hold the baby," Sadie says. The words pop out of her mouth unplanned, but they are the right words.

Lillian's only sign of surprise is the shortbread held aloft for an extra second before she places it on her plate and dabs her fingers on a napkin and quietly says, "I would be honored." She is a woman Sadie does not understand, but she knows how to behave.

Mother Feldstein approaches Lillian's chair and reluctantly shifts Margo into Lillian's arms, and Margo does not fuss. Lillian smiles at her and sways just a little and asks about Sadie's health, and how long the baby sleeps, and if Sadie's friends have infants too.

Mother Feldstein paces and takes another piece of shortbread. "Of course it's a great adjustment," she says. "For husbands too."

"I would imagine," Lillian says.

"Of course you're right," Sadie says.

"Men, they're a different breed," Mother Feldstein says. "They're sensitive to changes, more sensitive than you'd think."

"Bill's quite devoted to her," Sadie says. "Don't you think?"

"To Margo. Of course, she's a beautiful child," Mother Feldstein says. "It's just that men sometimes, well, miss their wives. They miss their wives' attentions."

No question about the tone: a needle dipped in honey. But Lillian focuses only on Margo, a tenderness in her face, then on Sadie. She is utterly poised, as if Mother Feldstein is no longer in the room. "Mrs. Feldstein, I'm delighted to hold her," Lillian says, "but perhaps she needs her mother?"

"I'll take her whenever you're ready, Miss Schumacher," Sadie says, but Margo looks peaceful, and Sadie doesn't rush to take the baby back. "I think I had just a little light hair when I was born."

"Bill had thick dark hair. She looks exactly like him, you see?" Mother Feldstein says.

Mostly Sadie sees glimmers of her father, and of Goldie. "Bill would be happy to hear that."

"He seems happy, but I worry for him," Mother Feldstein says. "You know, a new father. You must be mindful, Sadie. Others could take advantage."

And now Sadie focuses only on Lillian and Margo, as if her mother-in-law is a small talking bird. "Miss Schumacher," Sadie says, "did you see Margo's feet?" She crosses the three paces to Lillian's chair, sits beside her on the footstool. "Here," Sadie says, unwrapping the baby blanket and pulling off a small pink bootie. "So tiny, aren't they? It's hard to imagine such smallness."

"I think so too," Lillian says.

Then Margo's restlessness begins, a small cry. "Here," Sadie says, "why don't I take her?" and lifts the baby and stands rocking her beside Lillian's chair, while her mother-in-law stands pressing her hands together, half-turned toward the dining room and the hall to Bill's study.

"Papa and Bill can't smoke forever," Sadie says. "If you don't mind, Mother, would you see what's keeping them?"

And for an instant Mother Feldstein seems stung, her eyes a little too shiny, a momentary frailty in her stance.

Lillian rises from the reading chair, and there it is again—*swan*—though Sadie does not want to think *swan*. Sadie does not want to think anything.

"We won't stay long," Lillian says. "You must be exhausted."

"It's surprising how tiring this time can be," Sadie says. Her mother-in-law retreats down the hallway to the study, and Margo begins to cry in earnest. "Rosalie?" Sadie calls. "Would you mind getting more lemonade for Miss Schumacher, and anything else she wants? I'm taking the baby upstairs."

"I'm fine," Lillian says. "Mrs. Feldstein, do you need help?"

Ordinarily, no; Sadie would automatically say no, simply because Lillian is Lillian. But her arms and legs feel rubbery, peculiar, and the fuzziness of late nights is resurfacing: what she wants more than anything else is quiet and sleep. "If you wouldn't mind," Sadie says, "tell Bill I'll need time alone with the baby?"

"Of course," Lillian says.

Sadie can hear Bill and her father approach from the study, Bill's response to the crying, "Oh, Margo," and more quietly, "good lungs."

"Thank you for the dress," Sadie says, and whisks Margo upstairs to the nursery. She closes the door and finds the rocker, Margo wailing until they're both settled into the chair and Margo's begun nursing—that quiet, insistent tug. Sadie doesn't lock the nursery door: with a baby in the house, one mustn't lock certain doors. It seems fewer and fewer doors even exist, fewer walls; her house has been thrown open, Sadie herself thrown open. From downstairs she can hear conversation, Lillian giving her message to Bill. There is more, Lillian talking to Abe now, telling him Sadie of course wants to see him soon, and he should telephone her. And what occurs next, Sadie never would predict: she hears Lillian's voice, firm and clear, suggesting they give the senior Mrs. Feldstein a ride home.

"It would be no trouble at all," Lillian says.

There is the murmur of Mother Feldstein's objection.

"I insist," Lillian says. "It would be our pleasure."

CHAPTER 13

Jo

1933

Lucia Mazzano is a loaf of bread. Black hair pinned into a tight rosette, black lashes, olive neck, olive fingers, tapered, small, her dress a long flute, yellow of forsythia, yellow of butter. The young lawyers fawn and loiter at her desk, the older ones wink, Moshe Schumacher grins: fat Moshe, fat boss, herring breath and stench of cigars.

"Good morning," Lucia says, and returns to her filing, while Moshe Schumacher lights up and watches her legs. She's young, at the job a month, Catholic in a firm that hires Jewish.

From her own desk, Jo watches the men parade, pretends she's alone in another building, concentrates on typing, *in such instance, the injured party shall be granted no less and no more than one-third the proceeds,* carbon paper the indigo sky after dusk.

And when Schumacher finally leaves, Lucia crosses the office from her desk to Jo's and holds out her hands. *Bread,* Jo thinks.

"Take a look." Lucia holds a pile of buttons, shiny black geometric hills. Her palms are pink. "For the jacket I'm making. Aren't they smart?"

Smart? Yet Jo reaches over, takes one, and there's a tightening low in her belly when she runs her finger over the ridges and polished planes.

"Sophisticated," Jo says.

Lucia's teeth: white against her carmine lipstick.

BREAD. A hard thing to refuse, if you are Jo, if you picture your life as filament tracking back and forth between your father's house and the lawyer's typewriter, between men obsessed with order: brown suits, black ledgers, tobacco clouds. Weekday hours partitioned by documents: wills, contracts, letters, motions, pleadings, orders of the court filed alphabetically by client, daily and chronologically so the story unfolds backward as you read from the top. Evening: dinner at the appointed hour, fish and potatoes, eggs and noodles, chicken for Friday night. A pot of tea at eight and the dishes washed, the dining table cleared and rubbed with linseed oil. Then pipe smoke seeps up from the parlor, the evenings her father stays in.

Even her body seems reduced to wire: sealed, unerring, monochrome. So unlike Sadie, spawning in her neighborhood off Hertel, or Celia, who will never keep her thoughts straight, who starts for the department store and ends up at the soup kitchen or the burlesque. *A half-step from vagrancy.* Celia would spawn if she could, *try to keep her from rutting in alleys.* Not the kind of thing you say aloud.

Goldie's stubbornly gone, now just air and trembling, it seems. Irving comes and goes as he pleases, and leaves his dirty clothes at the top of the stairs.

Pour the tea at eight, precisely; five minutes past and her father will begin to sniff and glance about, ten minutes and in an irritated tone he'll call her name. Pour tea and then he works in silence on his store ledgers. Celia listens to the radio. Jo reads the newspaper and bathes and retires early, so she can wake before dawn, when the others are asleep: then it's as if the house is hers. Nothing encroaches and she can fill the emptiness as she chooses. Lately she's allowed herself to pretend the rest of her family has vanished and the sleep belongs to someone else. A woman, young, with black lashes, her yellow dress hanging over a chair. Lucia Mazzano in the predawn light, asleep in the next room while the tea steeps and Jo considers breakfast. Jo curls into the sofa and drifts and does not rise. The furnace blows and ticks. Wet breeze against the house: the lake ice is almost melted. Late April, and the dampness has its own weight.

The light arrives. Her father stirs. He'll be downstairs soon, waiting for breakfast, and Irving will follow, and then Celia, loud and clinging.

And the house is again an alien thing.

IN THE FIFTH WEEK of Lucia Mazzano, Jo is called away from the office. It's Tuesday, early afternoon, she hasn't yet taken lunch. Celia again. This time, a coffee shop. It's Minnie Greenglass who calls, Minnie Greenglass from Hadassah, Minnie who even in high school didn't say much to Jo, she was mousy then, her last name Rabinowitz, but now she's married and plump and in the habit of hiring maids. When Jo steps through the doorway of Schroeder's Coffee & Lunch, Minnie's in a lush burgundy suit and new heels and pearls, talking with her hands. Celia really is a lovely woman, Minnie tells the owner, but she has troubles, has some terrible days and this is one. "We all know about troubles," Minnie says.

Celia is docile, sitting on a counter stool next to Minnie Green-glass and the skeptical owner, neck bent, lipstick reddening the corners of her mouth, purple jam on her fingertips. The counter in front of her is strewn with broken pie. At a nearby table a man thumbs a paper and glares at Jo. He's blue-eyed, German-handsome, slightly dissolute. Blotches of purple mar the right panel of his shirt.

Schroeder the owner sizes up Jo. His forehead is wide and meaty, his mouth a thin slit. "The lovely woman disturbed my customers," he tells Jo. "And wouldn't pay."

"Please accept our apologies," Jo says. She tries to be small, innocuous, but Schroeder frowns.

"Minnie, thank you," she says. Lays a hand on Celia's shoulder. "How much is the bill?"

"Mrs. Greenglass has taken care of it," Schroeder says.

"Minnie, what do I owe you?"

"It's nothing," Minnie says.

"No, really."

"I'm happy to help," Minnie says. "Celia and I go back a long way."

"That's kind of you," Jo says. Schroeder and Minnie Greenglass lean close together, a unified smugness, and Jo urges Celia by the elbow. "Very kind," Jo says.

"Very kind," Celia repeats, and after a pause, "Sorry. Thank you. Sorry."

The streetcar, the walk down Lancaster, the white frame house rising into pastel green—bursting elm buds, frilly maples. Celia doesn't explain. Won't. And Jo is left to puzzle out the incident using Minnie Greenglass's summary and the raw evidence: pie stains, the averted eyes of the female customers, the raised eyebrows of the men. Celia slumps and in the hazy light seems frailer than usual. Her hands are small and bony and she doesn't know what to do with them, and finally tucks them into her coat pockets. At the house, she heads directly to her bedroom, coat on, and lies down on the bed. Jo offers to help her with her shoes, which she allows.

"What were you doing?" Jo says.

"Nothing," Celia says. "Good-bye."

When Jo hesitates, Celia starts to hum. And it is safe to leave her now: she'll stay in her room for the rest of the afternoon. It's what she does after being humiliated.

Jo's been away from the office two hours: she'll have to work late. When she returns, she tells Lucia, "My sister is unwell."

"Oh no." Lucia's neck and face flush pink.

"Sorry to leave you alone here."

Lucia shakes her head. "I'll pray to St. Michael."

And then they are both typing, there is only the sound of typing and breathing, the occasional shuffling of paper, a suggestion of leaves.

IT'S NOT the first time Lucia has mentioned saints: the Blessed Virgin Mary, St. Francis, St. Luke, St. Vincent de Paul, St. Joseph, St. Agnes, St. Catherine, St. Nicholas, St. Michael, St. Stephen,

St. Mark, St. Antony, St. Jude. She's studied their lives and deaths, talks of them as if they lived next door. When Lucia describes their torments, Jo sees a chorus of macabre dolls, most of them missing parts.

But no, Lucia tells her, after death they are restored. After death they are beautiful and holy.

"St. Cecilia," Lucia says, "unsuccessfully beheaded."

THAT SUNDAY, Jo wakes early, thinking of Lucia's wrists, the point just below her palm where the veins branch, slim bones, delicate skin, imprint of cologne. Jo's walking up Delaware when the bells begin, stitching Sunday together. St. Everything, ringing in tandem. If you let yourself into the heart of the city and walk, the calls come from the neighborhoods.

Once, last year, the windows of her father's jewelry store were soaped with *CHRIST KILLERS* in Polish. Catholics, and not the first with their threats and profanity and soap. But imagine Lucia in her yellow dress, her hands extended, those sweet wrists, while the bells multiply, the chimes hovering over Lucia and her mother and their army of saints, Lucia praying to St. Michael for Celia's health, Lucia with her eyes closed, mouthing the Rosary, mouthing *Hail Mary Mother of Grace*. Picture her in the grass, *Mother of Grace*, she says, black hair loose against the green. Her saints descend and rise, miraculous, their eyes restored, their breasts intact, necks swan-like, uncorrupted. They are blessing the onions. They are feeding the birds.

Jo follows the bells. Thick clouds slide over St. Louis's elaborate spire, the door of the church opens into—what? A dark vestibule, beyond which Jo cannot see, only invent. Outside: pale husbands in tight suits, wives—brunette, earnest, fake flowers pinned to their hats—herding children who are scrubbed miniatures of the parents, all of them approaching the entry with careful steps. The door closes and the sounds of the pipe organ leak out into the street. Once Mass has begun, Jo ascends the stone stairs, touches the thick door, and sniffs the air, which smells like evaporating rain and wax and libraries. *Illumination*, Lucia says. *Miracles can happen anywhere.* As the organ bleats and Latin harmonies rise from the choir, Jo closes her eyes and leans into the door.

That night, when Jo is alone again, she conjures the thick wood and old rain and thinks yes, Lucia illuminated, floating in the yellow dress, holding out her hands, offering buttons and transcendence. Wind pulls at the dress, there's a dampness between Jo's legs. In the vision, Jo is wearing a brown fedora. She's near enough to touch Lucia's hem.

IN DAYLIGHT, Jo types pleadings and imagines the texture of Lucia's skin, while Lucia organizes files and takes letters for a jittery, myopic attorney named Feigenbaum. As usual, Feigenbaum leans too close to Lucia; Jo's impulse is to swat him away. She turns instead to the windows, imagines the neckline of Lucia's dress plunging, Jo herself sailing up to the highest branches of the elms. An unaccustomed lightness overtakes her.

Such pleasure feels new, addictive. *The elms,* Jo tells herself, *remember the elms,* and her fantasies multiply, deepen by the day: Lucia beneath the trees in Delaware Park, her dress gauzy and sheer; Lucia in repose, waking in a low-lit bedroom, her breasts exposed, repeating Jo's name in a voice laced with desire. The fantasies multiply despite Lucia's long hemlines and safe necklines and careful office behavior, intensify with the thrill of secrecy, a giddy ache that overcomes Jo at the typewriter. They multiply despite all signs that Lucia—with her talk of gabardine and linen, infant nephews, holiday cooking—is really no different from Minnie Greenglass before marriage, no different from Sadie, who comes around with her baby in a pram, who enters the house and sighs, tells Jo to see a dentist, a hairdresser, a tailor, who makes Celia wash her face and bribes her with cakes and leaves, back to her husband, her marital bed, her mah-jongg games and flower arrangements and charitable works. Jo pretends otherwise, imagines the dark thatch between Lucia's legs. Pretends the saints, in all their eccentricity, hold sway. Pretends that the ordinary is a disguise Lucia will shed in time.

For now, Jo adopts disguises of her own. Clothes are only clothes, but the ones she wears—heavy cotton dresses dulled from wash—will get her nowhere with Lucia. In early June she counts out her savings and shops downtown Main Street, acquires a pale blue suit, a cream-and-plum-striped dress, three blouses in pastel and white, a beige skirt, new leather pumps. Visits a beauty parlor on Hertel, where a plump, efficient woman named May cuts and curls her hair and insists on regular appointments.

"Beautiful," Lucia says, and fingers the sleeve of Jo's silk blouse. Wonders aloud if it's French. Offers Jo a lipstick. And Jo takes the tube, peers into Lucia's compact, and dabs the color on her mouth. Lucia hovers, waiting for the result.

"Pink Bouquet," Lucia says. "That's you."

For the moment, Jo accepts this: she is as much Pink Bouquet as anything else. A small price for Lucia's approval.

On Friday night, when Celia lights the candles, Jo silently prays to the candlesticks and the tin ceiling, *Blessed art Thou, O Lord our God, bless and keep Lucia and bring her to me.* But then her father barks the other blessings, his tone of accusation seeping into the food. Irving opens a second bottle of sugary wine, having drained the first: he's sloppy and loud, though harmless. The ceiling does not change, the table does not change, and Jo thinks, fleetingly, of shul—services? should she go?—and then, depressingly, of Minnie Greenglass.

HOW LONG will it take? How long before Lucia can see Jo as Jo cannot even see herself? Consecutive Sundays, Jo dresses simply, pins on a small blue hat, sits across from St. Gregory's, St. Michael's, St. Joseph's and watches the parishioners arrive. On a weekday afternoon she walks into St. Mary of Sorrows. There is a scattering of women, each alone, in separate church pews. A table of candles beside the Virgin Mary, a city of small flames, leaning and nodding in the slight draft. One of the women crosses herself and kneels to the Virgin, leaves a coin in the box and lights a candle. When she's gone, Jo leaves a coin and lights one of her own, as if she speaks the language of the Virgin. As if Mary might recognize her longing and dispense grace.

At home, Jo's father seems to recognize nothing. He does not mention the blue suit, the lipstick, the stylish sweep of her bangs. Not her new pumps or his missing fedora or the tobacco she has recently pinched from his tin. He does not look at her the way he looks at Sadie—appraising, pleased—despite the white silk. It's too late for that; how long has she deliberately made herself plain? He regards her as if she were a kitchen table. Reminds her to fix the loose porch rail.

Irving follows their father's lead, gives her suit a glance, shrugs. Only Celia remarks: she stands in doorways, holding the cat, sizing up Jo's clothes, assessing her face. *Pretty one*, Celia says. *You are the prettiest one.*

"JO, TAKE A LETTER," Moshe Schumacher says, flicking his eyes over the plum-and-cream dress. "Well. You got yourself a beau?" and she smiles at him the way Lucia smiles at him, calm, benign, follows him to his office, sits in the side chair taking shorthand while he paces and gestures with thick hands. Today she feels as if she's inhabiting someone else's skin, a body over her own. Only her fingers are recognizable. Worth it, she tells herself, and begins the second letter, her notes fast and fluid, and words imprinting themselves and drifting: *Dear, it is a pleasure, when we next meet, I remind you, please call, I look forward, most sincerely.*

At her desk, typing, she glances over to Lucia, who is explaining Attorney Levy's handwriting to Attorney Levy. Lucia rolls her eyes at Jo, smiles. In that moment, what else does Jo need? *most sincerely a pleasure. most sincerely, please join me. most sincerely, yes.* In the afternoon, Moshe Schumacher leaves for court. The other attorneys are burrowed in their offices, and Lucia stands beside Jo's desk, her dress a field of white dots over peach.

"What Mr. Schumacher asked," Lucia says, "about a beau?" Drops her voice to a near whisper. Her face is flushed, she's absently stroking a loose strand of hair. Smiles. And for an instant, Jo hovers at the edge of anticipated joy, up in the elms, Lucia floating, they are far from the office and the house on Lancaster, they are falling into the grass, Jo immersed in the green of the lawn, the black of Lucia's hair. There's a two-second delay before Jo registers the name *Anthony*, which Lucia embroiders with sighs. A city clerk, Lucia says, eyes the color of walnuts. On Wednesdays after work

Lucia does not go to Mass, but instead meets this clerk, who buys her cups of coffee and rides the streetcar with her back to her neighborhood.

Jo's throat dries and she's overcome by a choking sensation, like fishbones needling her esophagus. "That's lovely," she says. There's a slight distortion in the sounds from the street, a whining echo, and the light in the room splits into patches, which seem to swim away from each other.

"It's still a secret." There's a low thrill in Lucia's voice. "He hasn't met my father yet."

"You look happy." Jo searches for a handkerchief, then pretends she is backlogged with her work for the day. She squints at her own shorthand, coughs, leaves the room to fill a glass with water. Her slip clings to her thighs as she walks, the dress moving as her body moves, though it seems to be someone else's. In the ladies' room she splashes water on her face. It will not last, she tells herself. She ignores the water glass and drinks from her hands. Surely Lucia will not fall for the polite door-opening, for the cups of coffee and escorts home, transparent rituals that mean nothing. This Anthony will exit Lucia's life as quickly as he's entered it. Perhaps he will prove himself unworthy. Perhaps he will die. Jo regains control of her throat, slicks on the Pink Bouquet, crosses the hall to the office. "Your dress," she tells Lucia. "Lovely."

For a few hours, a numb calm descends, a state Jo associates with frostbite and emergencies. She stays late at the office, and after Lucia leaves, after the last client and even the attorneys leave, she crosses the room to the desk along the wall and opens Lucia's cabinet of active files. Her hands move over the folders, fingers pick at documents and pull them out, a simple shifting of rectangles. She takes a real estate agreement from the Saltzman file and slides it into the Schwartz file.

On the streetcar home, Jo's exhausted. She stumbles into the house and up to bed. Dusk: the afternoon's seeped away through the trees, which are black against a backdrop of indigo. The streetlight casts a yellow the color of bruises almost healed. New rain, honeysuckle blooming on the side of the house. It makes you yearn the way the radio symphony does, the way Lucia's wrists do. And then Celia's in the bedroom doorway calling, "Jo? What about dinner?"

In the morning, while the house is hers, Jo tries on her father's spare fedora, soft brown darkened by rain, slightly misshapen. For a while, her face assembles itself. For a while the desire to break out of her body abates.

IN SUMMER, Celia spends whole days in the garden: this seems to keep her out of trouble. But if it rains for too long, Celia's agitated, distraught; she paces, chews her hair. "What is it?" Jo asks her. "What now?" When Jo gets home from work, Celia demands to play gin rummy and checkers, games she quickly abandons. Bad signs, Jo knows, but who can keep track? It's enough to make dinner, brew the eight o'clock tea. Jo smokes her father's tobacco on the back porch while the rain falls and Celia rants: today the postman ignored her. But evening company is not enough for Celia, not if the rain persists, which it does. In the morning, she follows Jo to work. Not the first time: occasionally, Jo buys her coffee and sends her home. But now the streetcar lurches, the passengers lurch, the scents of lake water, soap, wet leather shoes mix with old smoke while Celia breathes into Jo's ear, "You hate me, don't you?"

"Not this," Jo says. "Why aren't you home?"

"I hate you too," Celia says.

"Don't be stupid," Jo says. "You hate the rain."

"Stupid," Celia says. "That's what you think."

"What is it you want? You want a Danish?"

"Hate," Celia says. "The truth is out." She points to a young man hunched over a newspaper. "He doesn't hate me."

It's the sort of maneuver that can escalate in seconds: harassment of strangers, angry conductors, annoyed police. The man wisely stays hunched. "Let's get off," Jo says.

"No. I'm riding. I paid."

What choice does Jo have? She takes the streetcar past her office stop and uptown again, rain pummeling the packed car, until Celia calms down and Jo can get her home. But it's a lost day. Jo persuades Celia to change into dry clothes—"I don't hate you. Try this dress"—brews tea, and, at Celia's request, rolls out pie dough, washes strawberries, measures sugar. When the pies are in the oven, Jo chews a finger of horseradish. Her body seems to flatten and gray until its lines are indistinguishable from the walls. It's only the horseradish, the daily tobacco, reminding her she is separate.

Celia sits on the porch and hums. Water draining from the roof ticks over garden tools and mud. Once the rain stops, she moves down to the flower beds. Yellow print cotton dress, thick apron, bare feet. She's pulling weeds from between wet calla lilies, damp patches spreading over her dress. The peonies are blooming, the grass is again thick, seductive. Watching Celia move through the yard, Jo can almost forget her wildness. She's almost a picture of holy.

Wine helps. After dinner, even when there is no rain, Jo pours herself the sugary kosher wine; a glass or two and the day's disturbances retreat. Trouble appears as if on the far shore of the river, tiny, increasingly remote: city clerks waving to Lucia, Celia's petty thefts. From the near shore you can sift through Lucia's stories, decide what to save, what to erase: the Archangel Gabriel, leading the Herald Angels; St. Agnes, the Virgin, accused of witchcraft; Anthony the clerk bringing snapdragons to Lucia's mother. When Lucia speaks, her face seems incandescent. Keep that. Keep Agnes's death sentence, the white and yellow snaps, the singing angels. Forget St. Cecilia's damaged neck. Let the rest blur and fall away.

IT'S JULY, a Sunday at Old St. Joseph's: Jo's across the street, beside a sycamore. Parishioners arrive, dark suits in the heat, long dresses and small hats, automobiles parking with slow deliberation. Jo no longer watches their faces, only their bodies moving through the heavy air, the fluttering arms of the women, the solemn gaits of the men. But her reverie is interrupted by the O of Lucia, today in deep blue, hair pinned beneath a matching hat with a tiny veil, a flock of family around her. Lucia does not look at the street or the sycamore, but ahead to the entrance of the church, increasing her pace. Follow her gaze and there he is, a handsome suit holding a hat, hair a cap of black, dark eyes and long lashes floating above a flash of teeth. A body bending toward her, and she toward him, he is bowing to the family at the door, he is taking her arm in their presence. The church entry swallows them and they do not reappear. The door closes. Jo waits for it to reopen, but of course it does not; the service begins and she paces. Her legs move independently, carrying her in circles around the church, up one block and down the next: up over down across, up over down across. The breeze increases and she is a thin vertical line moving over the horizontal of the sidewalk, the city is a scattering of rays, and the sky fills with its customary banks of clouds, occasional patches of blue among the bloated layers. She breaks into even finer lines—arms, fingers, legs—all in flat continuous motion down one side street, up another, now away from the church and onto broader avenues, until she's in front of a department store on Main Street. Only there does she notice her location and the blank interval that brought her from Old St. Joseph's. Think. Think. She can imagine the route as if to give directions, but not today's version, not the particulars of open windows and parked cars and broken curbstones. The sky seems half-familiar. Did she walk the whole way or was there, at some point, a streetcar? She cannot remember a streetcar. This isn't like her, she's never lost time this way; it's Celia who appears at unplanned destinations, forgetting how she got there, panic in her face when you ask what happened.

SUPPER AND COLLAPSE, sweat and collapse, bitter insomnia, stifled weeping, open weeping, sharpness in the belly: two days. Two days of moving from the bed only to relieve herself and make her way back, of pretending *Father, I am ill with flu. Best to stay away.* Celia hovers outside the door, disappears, returns with water Jo will not drink, toast she ignores, dense berry pie, cold tea, souring glasses of milk.

By Tuesday night Jo is empty, body slack, worn-out. No weeping, no tremors, no waves of nausea, just an awareness of indigo air and the outlines of curtains. Eventually she sleeps. Wednesday morning, when she sits at the edge of the bed, the room appears to have shifted, but how? The bureau, framed pictures, and rocking chair remain themselves. The glass cover of a bookshelf is open—

as she left it? Clock tick, faucet drip, barking dog, footsteps on the street, insect fizz. Ordinary, expected sounds. Where was she? Already a blank. She closes her eyes and sees blotches of light shaped like pits and fruit. Where? A vague, untouchable *there*, and didn't *there* include a woman? A line of color, white or perhaps blue? Pale blue or something deeper?

There is one person who loves her, and it is Celia.

WHEN JO ARRIVES back at work, the office appears unchanged; she approaches her desk the way she has for years—before Lucia Mazzano—barely glancing to the desk along the far wall, acknowledging nothing but the need for more light, the necessary adjustments to the blinds.

"How are you, Jo?" Lucia says. She's on her feet, listing in the direction of Jo's desk; Jo glances up long enough to register a blurred slim figure, green topped with black. She can't focus any longer than that, even if she wills herself to, not in that direction. She nods and bows her head over her desk of files. "Better, then," Lucia says, her voice filtered through air as dense as glass.

Jo remains silent. Isn't that all she has—insulating silence, the silence of retreat? She rolls paper into the typewriter and imagines the monotone percussives filling out into a chant. For an hour, two hours, she types beautifully, unthinkingly. Nods hello to Moshe Schumacher. Nods to Attorneys Feigenbaum and Levy. Takes her lunch in silence, the noise of downtown passing around her, the afternoon light glossy and peculiar. She waits until the end of the day, unaware that she is waiting. The office emptied, she returns to Lucia's files, which she has not touched since the first day of Anthony. This time, Jo rearranges the papers in the Markson file, ruining the chronology. Closes the cabinet. Closes the office. Cooks fish and noodles for dinner, pours her father's tea, sleeps the night without interruption.

By the end of the week, Jo's wearing the cream-and-plum dress to work, bringing Lucia breakfast rolls and coffee, regularly riffling Lucia's files. Lucia smiles her carmine-and-white smile. There's talk of Anthony, Lucia's family warming to him, the invitations to dinner, of the lingering good-byes and ecstatic hellos, kisses in the theater. Outside the office, a light rain has begun to fall, occasional plinks against the glass. Kisses in the theater, imagine, and his hands, where were his hands? "Delicious coffee," Lucia says, and the theater evaporates. "Thank you."

"Of course," Jo says. Nods. Sets her fingers on the keyboard.

She sticks to the easy misfiles, chooses the busiest and most distracted days. The attorneys appear at Lucia's desk, at first inquiring mildly, then demanding: *The cover letter for the Kahn agreement? Have you seen it? Brodsky case, Motion to Amend—don't you have it? Find it. Now.*

"It's in the file," Lucia repeats, checking her desk, the basket of documents to be filed, the floor, the wastebasket, the desktop again. "I'll have it for you in a few minutes" she says, and the attorneys wait, impatient. She's flushed, miserable-looking. "I'm sure I filed them," Lucia tells Jo. "I know I did."

The deadline on Brodsky arrives. Jo nods in the direction of the attorneys' offices. "One of them probably has it. I'll help you look." Together they search the files, trying different dates, searching out other Brodsky matters, checking under the client's first name, Jacob. Try the files on either side: Blumenthal, Broadman, Bryson.

It's in Broadman. The attorneys nod and retreat.

"Such stupid mistakes," Lucia says.

"Don't give it a second thought," Jo says. "These things happen."

Twice, Jo stays late retyping Lucia's work, this time with errors.

TWO WEEKS OF misfiles and Lucia does not smile at the attorneys, does not speak of Anthony, does not mention the saints. There is no talk of lipstick: there is almost no talk. As if she's absorbed Jo's silence. She stops objecting when the attorneys point out errors, turns beseechingly to Jo. *Let me help,* Jo says. *I can proofread. I'll take the Lipsky pleadings. Why don't I file that last group of letters?* Once, Jo asks Moshe Schumacher to wait while she helps Lucia correct an error.

He stares at Lucia, his mouth a flat pout. "Miss Mazzano will have to do that herself," he says.

"I understand," Jo says, and then, more quietly, "Give her time." To which he makes no answer.

JO CAN'T REMEMBER her dreams, but that is familiar, the old way. She does not consider the grass, observing instead the space between trees, the neighboring yards. Continues to smoke tobacco in the evenings behind the house, while Celia watches without comment, the orange cat rumbling, its eyes pressed shut. There is no pleasure in smoking, no pleasure in anything. But also no tremors, no bitter cramps or ragged breathing.

It's a Monday morning in early August when Lucia is called to Moshe Schumacher's office. She leaves her desk for no more than five minutes, returning tight-lipped. Pale blue dress, hair pulled back tightly, head bent, her gestures jagged and fast. From her desk drawer she grabs up a compact, a handkerchief, a palm-sized print of the Virgin.

"What happened?" Jo says.

Lucia's lashes are wet spikes against her face. She chews on a fingernail, clearly forgetting herself.

"What is it?" And Jo crosses to Lucia's desk, shocked: in that instant she does not remember the sabotage. She touches Lucia's shoulder. "What can I do?" Jo is sincere, she could even save Lucia, earn her gratitude. It's a chance, isn't it? To prove, finally, that though Lucia has been foolish she can still be forgiven, that with Jo she can be redeemed.

"He's got another girl lined up," Lucia says. She steps away and organizes her desktop into rectangles and squares—files, stationery, message slips—and beyond it the parquet floor extends to the sharp lines of the windows. Lucia herself is blue curves. She hands Jo a lipstick. "It's a new one," she says. "Why don't you keep it?" she says. And then she's at the door.

Jo mumbles *Oh,* and *Thank you* and *Oh,* but already Lucia is fleeing, an echo of footsteps in the hall.

At her desk, Jo completes a letter in the matter of *Brodsky* v. *Ludwig.*

.   .   .

CELIA WEEDS and waters and the zinnias bloom. Delphinium, snapdragons, honeysuckle, common daisies, roses in yellow and red and white. Some of these Celia cuts and brings into the house; others she won't dare touch. Peas blossom and mature, green tomatoes fatten. It's best to think only of the colors, to be empty except for yellow against green against red. The back porch is the only place Jo can breathe, at least for a while; she can't cook dinner unless the porch door is open, and she won't sit at the dining room table, despite her father's complaints.

At summer's end, Moshe Schumacher's cousin Gert, a terse, stout woman in her forties, takes up Lucia Mazzano's desk. Daily, Jo falls into the percussive hum of the typewriter, works precisely and without thought. She walks instead of taking the streetcar, and her body seems as light as a lifted fever. Still, the cooling nights are marred by poor sleep, which seems connected to no one but Celia: Jo imagines Celia humming through wounds in her throat; imagines the roses in the yard blooming over Celia's body until she falls beneath their weight, until she is buried in roses. Their malignant proliferation speeds on, obliterating the house. Even when Jo is awake, the humming persists, mixed with patternless ticking and faint sporadic bells.

CHAPTER 14

Lillian

1934

Moshe's voice on the telephone is unhappiness itself, potent enough to change the air and seep through Lillian's skin. He's been calling to remind her to visit their mother, and for months she has ignored his reminders. Now he says, "Lilly, we need to talk, you and I. When will you come talk to me? Tomorrow? Come to the house to dinner. You will be here, Lilly?"

She pours rose oil into her bath and drinks a gin over ice. The unhappiness of men so easily chafes. You have to be watchful, let the weight slide off your shoulders and neck, keep your hands hidden or they will at once be burdened. Lillian has her daily rituals of lotions: face cream in the morning and at night, hand cream three times a day, once a day lotion for her legs and arms and neck. The rose oil she drops in her bath twice a week, as if this will keep unhappiness from sticking to her skin.

Of course you need more than bath oil: be careful, decide when to listen and when to feign listening, daydream when you can. Lillian pretends she does not see the deepening worry in her boss Harry Kaplan, an old friend of her father's, who now slumps in the stationer's back office recalculating numbers, closes the store on Tuesdays and sends her home early on Fridays; Harry who is so mired in his worries he doesn't notice Lillian speaking to him. "Have a good evening," she says, day after day. She locks the store entrance, returns through the already dark afternoon to her flat, and smoothes on hand cream.

Abe's unhappiness seems constant, though now more than usual his unhappiness is tied to his store. Jewelry sales have stayed flat; some of his competitors have gone under. Worry makes Abe efficient and unsentimental. He stocks simpler pieces—more garnets, more diamond chips—offers payment plans, expects less from walk-in business, and more, it seems, from Lillian. More patience with his moods, more cooking at her flat instead of dining out, more fast unromantic sex, while he offers fewer endearments, fewer gifts, less affection. One day he is obsessed by the loss of a fedora, convinced it is at her flat, and the next visit he mentions nothing about it, brings a bottle of wine and gives her a perfunctory kiss. She has seen these phases arrive and depart, fluctuations within a larger too-familiar stasis, but she has learned to keep to her own rituals and turn him down when he is most harsh. She has her gin, her baths, her own quiet pleasures.

But Moshe's unhappiness she cannot shrug off: his voice swims in her blood. She should not ignore her mother—there is always a price to ignoring her mother—and perhaps the scales have tipped, the price of ignoring higher than the price of visiting. Now his unhappiness is a man's reinforced by a mother's, by their mother's— sharp-toothed, daubed with lavender. Even though you know better, the lavender will fool you, so fragrant, so promising, you lose yourself in burgeoning hope and find yourself bleeding from the ankles and wrists. The longer you visit Isabel, the greater the chance you will be afflicted, all the while you are stunned by lavender. You leave her house gasping. She's an old woman: how does this happen? Even now, Lillian isn't sure. She pictures her mother as a middle-aged woman, a woman the age Lillian herself is now, a morose beauty confounding her husband. From Isabel's pink mouth there's a steady murmur of dissatisfaction, dour music, which hangs in the air when she is silent. *So clumsy you are, so childish, no good,* she says, and how do you forget your shame, your father's shame in the face of such unhappiness? No one could stop the murmur, not even Moshe, the one she loved. But Isabel is not middle-aged, and Lillian is not a child, and Sol has been dead for decades. In recent years Isabel has weakened, but she's also soured down to essence, a bitter extract lavender does not mask. Does anything? Sleep? Perhaps in sleep she is satisfied; perhaps in sleep she forgets them all.

Still, even now small specks of hope survive, like spores adrift for years, announcing themselves in liminal moments. You steel yourself but then you're lulled by a small unexpected kindness—a birthday note—and you're stupidly, irresistibly drawn to her. For a moment Isabel seems open, she kisses you, and then she's murmuring her discontent, and before you've steeled yourself again, there's the insult, the snuffing out, and in the place of hope a flush of shame. Go home. As quickly as you can, go home to your bath, to your gin on ice, remembering your own small life, beyond your mother's reach.

And without those specks of hope? Hard to say, just as it is hard to decipher which fragments of memory will serve you and which will do you in. Once Isabel called Lillian *nafka*, under her breath but loud enough to be heard, with the knowledge of Lillian's perfect comprehension: whore. Years have passed. If you choose to forget, the word might rise up at you again, or another word, another kind of insult, *fat* perhaps, she likes to call Lillian fat, and wrap the insult in an ordinary sentence Lillian cannot refute (Still fat Lilly, but healthy, you can thank God for your health). Scowls at Lillian's clothes, though Lillian is wearing a dress she bought at Joseph's, where the mayor's wife shops. If you choose to remember every insult, you cannot bear to be in Isabel's company.

The only alternative is to dodge the question, which Lillian has been doing. Dodging her mother. After each conversation with Moshe, there is a shallowness to her breathing, a tightening in her belly, a blue-black dread. She has on this earth one mother, a mother she wishes to forget, whose love is the color of bruises and who will, if you ignore her, haunt you into the next world.

Lillian breathes and sucks at the gin and feels a slow remove from her own body. Fat but not a whore. Fat but no fatter than Bertha, who is accused of nothing but goodness. Or Moshe, dear God, she loves him, but the man is a house. She rubs lotion on her hands, her elbows. Fat in whose eyes? Who cares about fat? Her father never insulted her, or anyone for that matter, not even in reply to Isabel's taunts. He deserved better, deserved to outlive Isabel, to retire in the house he bought, where Lillian would have visited him daily. Instead her mother claimed it all, her mother, who deserves *what*? Lillian thinks, and there's another sharp pull of breath, the gradual blurring of the living room into watery shapes, cream, violet, the fine penumbra of oblivion. No. Lillian's an imperfect woman but she is not a monster: she's neglected commandments, but she has paid the price of transgression. Hasn't she? She does not honor her mother, but that other wish—*dead*, she's said it—does not belong. The gin is very cold. *Not honoring* is the best she can do, with this mother, in this life.

MOSHE'S HOUSE is a large red-brick on Nottingham, a street of gracious houses, wide lawns, spreading trees, and from his living room window there's a view of Delaware Park, snow-covered, the snow blue under streetlamps and the early rising moon. At the door, Moshe kisses Lillian and sets a hand behind her elbow and guides her into the house, all one smooth movement, as if she might slip away. "I'm glad you're here, Lilly," he says, and hangs up her coat and offers her a gin with lime.

In the living room's blue damask reading chair sits Isabel, though not the Isabel of Lillian's imagination or even of her visit four months ago: this Isabel's a wren, tiny in the Moshe-size chair, blinking at Lillian. Her chestnut wool dress bunches around her hips, fine bony hands drop from her sleeves. It's hard not to stare. Lillian at least has the presence of mind to set down her gin and take her mother's hand and kiss her on the cheek.

"Hello Mama, how are you?"

Isabel frowns at Lillian's dress. "The same," she says, though she clearly isn't the same, or, rather, the same has become different. "I don't know about your brother," Isabel tells Lillian. "You look well."

"What about me?" Moshe says. "Never been better, Ma. Did Bertha get your tea?"

"She's an angel, your Bertha," Isabel says.

"Lilly, see if there's some tea for her, would you?" Moshe waves toward the long hallway, the casual wave that always accompanies his orders.

"Of course," Lillian says, and in fact it's a relief to have a moment in the reliable company of the parquet floor and hallway chandelier. She glances into the dining room—table set with wedding china, a couple of bottles of French wine on the sideboard—and makes her way to the kitchen.

The air smells of good meat and rosemary and cooked fruit, and heat fills the kitchen: Bertha is roasting lamb. She's pumpkin round in her blue apron, hair swept back in a bun, wisps clinging to her temples, face pink from exertion. Bertha squints at roast potatoes.

It's easier here. Lillian would not mind squinting in the kitchen with Bertha. True, Bertha can be an angel of sorts—and angels are tiresome—but you'd have to be one to live with Moshe, to ignore his dalliances and raise his children and be kind to his prune-hearted mother. A dopey angel, Lillian thinks, one who closes her eyes when she needs to. And maybe it's a fair bargain: she's a rich woman, a woman whose husband loves her even if his way of loving is wildly flawed, a woman whose loyalty is returned with affection and security and fur coats. She has made her compromises, and she has been good to Lillian (who is not fat and not a whore). She deserves, if not Lillian's love, then her kindness and respect.

"It smells wonderful in here," Lillian says.

"Oh, Lilly." Bertha leans over to kiss her on the cheek. "I'm glad you could make it. Moshe's been wanting to see you."

"He asked about tea for Mama."

"I took her a cup and she sent it away. But there's the tray: you might try again."

The tray appears untouched. Perhaps she did bring Isabel tea, or perhaps this is a way to make Lillian serve Isabel, who likes to be served and softens toward those who serve her. "I see," Lillian says.

Bertha forks the potatoes onto the serving dish, blows at the tendril of hair falling over her right eye. Lillian stanches the impulse to tuck the loose hair behind Bertha's ear. "Do you need any help?"

"No. Just take the tea to Mama, thanks, Lilly."

"She's changed," Lillian says.

Bertha hesitates over the roast carrots, sighs. "Poor thing. Did Moshe get you a drink?"

"In the living room." Lillian picks up the tea tray, leaves the fragrant kitchen and recrosses the long hall out to the living room and Moshe and her mother, the wren.

"Here you are, Mama," Lillian says. "Here's your tea."

"Thank you, Lilly." Pleasant. And holding her teacup, Isabel has the mild expression of sleep. It's true she doesn't look good, but her expression belongs to someone else's mother. Lillian sits on the sofa beside Isabel's chair, picks up the gin, and over the top of her glass watches Moshe, who seems both anxious and deliberate. He's expert at hiding his moods, but not expert enough for Lilly: he's rattled, and he wants something.

Headlights slide over the snow of Delaware Park, a few flakes beginning to drift down again, the trees' dark silhouettes layered with blue. "I love that view," Lillian says, and Moshe says, "Nice, isn't it?" and Isabel sips at her tea. Her silence seems a kind of vacuum, anomalous to Lillian. No one yet leads the conversation: always it has been Isabel, with Lillian defending herself and Moshe clowning to distract them.

"You've gone to the doctor, Mama?" Lillian says.

"Bertha drives me to the doctor."

"What does he say?"

"He's a fool," Isabel says, and there's a warning look from Moshe. "A nice fool, but a fool."

WHEN EXACTLY did Isabel become a wren? The last time Lillian saw her, here, in September, Lillian arrived late. Isabel was already seated at the dining room table, and she chastised Lillian, and did not relent: was she wrenlike then? Lillian spent the evening deliberately blind, evading her.

Moshe seats Lillian across from Isabel and uncorks the Bordeaux, and Bertha dishes up thick slices of lamb. Isabel slowly eats and smiles at Bertha and then at Lillian, her sweetness as peculiar as her tiny body. And here, again, is the hope, appearing and dissolving in the air between them, like some odd reflection from the candles. Stupid hope, fat hope, there and gone and there. And Lillian senses something else in the air, a stickiness despite the dry heat of the dining room, something webby and troublesome and linked to Moshe. Lillian holds out her glass for the Bordeaux. Whatever it is, she thinks, will require more than lamb and wine.

It's hard to stay vigilant at Moshe's table, in this house. The house has always seemed to her a plush and spacious cocoon; she's wondered what it's like to stay in the house alone, even for a day, to have as your own the several bedrooms, the living room, study, summer porch, the enclosed garden. Carpets thick enough to sleep on: Lillian studies the pattern in the dining room's Persian, even as she tells Moshe and Bertha about a Garbo picture, *Queen Christina*, and Isabel quietly picks at her lamb.

"You just want to look at her face," Lillian says. "You could spend a whole day looking."

"Mm-hmm," Moshe says. "No kidding. A real knockout."

Bertha presses her lips together, smoothes the unwrinkled tablecloth.

Isabel should not be drinking wine, but already the glass Moshe poured her is empty. Though she barely eats the lamb and simply rearranges her potatoes, the wine she's pleased with; she would like more. "Moshe," she says, "you can just refill the glass, don't be stingy. There. Thank you."

Even wren-sized, Isabel will have her way: she also has a sweet tooth, and knows that Bertha's made pudding, chocolate. She doesn't care that it's dairy. Isabel would like pudding—forget kosher—and she would like that pudding now. So before the table has been cleared of dinner plates, Bertha retrieves four small white bowls of pudding and a separate bowl of whipped cream.

And Moshe, subdued for most of the dinner, pours Bertha and Lillian brandies, Scotch for himself.

Isabel spoons up her pudding, animated now, talking in the old way. "Bertha will teach Lillian how to make this. This is something Lillian can learn."

"Sure she can," Moshe says.

"Bertha will make it again, won't you Bertha?" Lillian says.

"I make it all the time," Bertha says, but Isabel frowns at Lillian.

"That's you," Isabel says. "I thought so. A lazy cook."

"Mama," Bertha says.

And Lillian takes a long sip of her brandy and asks Isabel, "Why do you care?"

It's as if she's thrown a switch: Isabel's face pinches up and you can see her shrink into her seat, into her wrenness, stung. How small she can make herself—awful—but the pinched look reddens, as if she might cry. She drops her spoon to the table and then she *is* crying, her mouth quivering, tears leaking down her face. She turns to Moshe, addresses him only now, her voice choked: "She's ungrateful, I told you. Ungrateful. May you never know such a thing from your children."

"What's going on?" Lillian says.

And her mother turns back to her, still choked but stern. "When you live with me, Lilly, you will have to cook."

Lillian swishes the brandy in circles around her glass and breathes it in like sweet ether, and narrows her eyes at Moshe and smiles at Bertha. A gauze veil has fallen between them. She tells her mother, "Mama, no one makes pudding like Bertha."

"That's right," Isabel says. "You're right."

Why she did not see this coming she does not know. Or does know: it's unimaginable, to live again with Isabel, even a less virulent Isabel, it is enough to be in the same room for an evening. But she is the daughter, the unmarried one, the one without children, without money, naturally she'd take care of her mother, naturally she'd be grateful, wouldn't she? Strangers would think so, but Moshe? Yet it's exactly what he's thinking, what he implies when he pauses over his pudding and says, "We think it would be better for Mama not to be alone. This I believe is the simplest solution. No more rent for you, Lilly, it will help you both out."

"You understand, Moshe, I'm not asking for help," Lillian says.

"So proud," Isabel says. "Too proud to ask."

"No," Moshe says. "I'm asking."

There's a slight catch in his voice, and she feels the catch in her own throat, a welling dismay at the specter of herself: if she were a better woman, she would say yes. If she were a better woman she'd embrace Isabel, ferry her mother to the doctor, bathe her, keep watch at night, stock the house with Bertha's pudding. If Lillian were a better woman, she would have known months ago of her mother's decline.

And look, her tiny mother droops in the dining room chair, smaller than a mother ought to be, even a mother like Isabel, whose diminishment Lillian has wished for. And Moshe, for whom she would pledge almost anything, Moshe without whom Lillian would have done herself in long ago, really she would have, the loneliness unbearable. Her eyes fill from the thought of Moshe's kindness, and from the brandy and the wine and the gin. Yes, she wants to help him, how can she not help him, her older brother, her truest friend? He's middle-aged now and so big, you can't see his eyes as well as you once could, those beautiful eyes. But it's impossible, what he's asking, the plan he's designed, and he knows this, and he asks nonetheless, and in that way she wonders what hidden desperation he must suffer.

"There is no greater mitzvah," Moshe says, but the catch has gone, he speaks in his attorney's voice, and Lillian blinks. He is smooth and distant, not desperate at all. For an instant she can't breathe. The word *mitzvah* hangs above the table, hollow promise of redemption, though even the gossips will know better: instead Lillian will have her comeuppance. The good is only that Moshe will rest easy. Look at him, big and smug and drunk, pushing the bitter little mother into her lap.

Lillian feels a heat move from her belly to her face, a sweat, a passing desire to break the glassware, and then a calm comes over her. She turns to Bertha. "But we'll have to find another arrangement," she says. "I'm engaged to Abe Cohen."

"Abe Cohen?" Isabel says. "He'll never marry you."

"We're engaged," Lillian repeats.

"Congratulations, Lilly." Bertha smiles and glances at Moshe and does not change her expression.

"I was not aware," Moshe says.

"You're a fool," Isabel says to Lillian. "Abe Cohen."

"Why would you want to live with a fool?" Lillian says.

"You know what that man thinks of you," Isabel says. "I am your mother."

"He loves me," Lillian says.

"I am your mother," Isabel repeats and the tears begin again, she's frail enough that the whole of her trembles. Moshe shakes his head at Lillian, he's trying for his disapproving stare but there's a waver in that too: what choice has he given her?

"Mama," he says. "We should be happy for Lilly."

"I will not live with Abe Cohen," Isabel says. "I will not."

Lillian feels her eyes widening, feels the desire for more air, any air, the cold blue of Delaware Park.

"Of course you mustn't," Bertha says. She's cooing now, she's moved to Isabel's side, she's holding Isabel's right hand. She is too kind for this family, Lillian thinks. She'll be suckered by all of us, eaten alive. Moshe holds a hand over his eyes; he knows what's coming next.

"You must stay with us," Bertha says. "That lovely room with the camellias on the walls?"

It takes a moment for Isabel to hear: she's lost in her pique, still trembling, a few loose tears dropping from her chin.

"I know you love this house," Bertha says. "There's more than enough room," she says, and enumerates—the guest rooms, the bathrooms, the housekeeper who can mend anything. "Would you like to see it again? The camellias?"

Moshe sighs in defeat. "Mama, why don't you take a look?"

And the weeping subsides, and Isabel allows Bertha to help her out of the chair—pausing to wipe pudding from her lips—and lead her down the hallway, footsteps quieting as they retreat to a second hall, and the room with the camellias and the adjoining bathroom with the white claw-foot tub.

"You could quit your job," Moshe says to Lillian. "I would pay you."

"I don't want to quit my job."

"Harry Kaplan's going under, Lilly. You must see that."

He's right, Harry Kaplan *is* going under, she would not have phrased it that way, *going under*, but Harry's already living below the waterline. You go under and likely do not come up, at least not in this life. How much resilience can one expect from a man in his seventies, the scrupulous and increasingly sad Harry? Harry will not fire her, but he's whittling down her hours and soon the money won't cover her rent. Her job will last for a few more months, perhaps. Harry will not say.

And when the stationer's goes under completely she'll have to find another job, though there's not much to be had. What could she tolerate? Moshe's law firm? Even if Moshe offered her a job— and he won't, not now—how could she work with Jo Cohen or the unlovely Gert? Just the thought of that office depletes the oxygen in Moshe's dining room: the water is already rising. No, Harry Kaplan is going under and Moshe is making use of this, Moshe who will defend Lillian to the world but feed her to their mother.

"I'll find something else," Lillian says.

"You think Abe can support you?"

"That isn't your concern."

"I see," Moshe says. "Well I suppose not. Though we'll be happy to host your wedding reception. You just tell me when."

She cannot look at him. Allowing his mean streak to surface, trumping the lie: this is his worst mistake. Smug Moshe, Moshe with his law practice and side deals, the expensive house, the de-votion of Bertha, the cadre of sons, Moshe with his string of mis-tresses and his beautiful suits in ever-increasing sizes, Moshe fat in every way. Moshe whom Lillian has revered and defended and loved, truly loved, though he is not a lovable man. *You just tell me when.* A coldness comes over her. She would have done herself in without him? That would have made her a fool. But she is not a fool (not a whore, not fat) and there is good brandy here and she will drink it. She will not clear the dishes for Bertha, she will not rush out the door, and she will not converse with Moshe. She will have her brandy, and a bit more of that pudding. Perhaps she will turn on the radio. Perhaps she will sit in silence, and consider the color of the brandy. Moshe can do what he likes.

From the hallway leading to the guest room, Lillian can hear

Bertha murmuring, a bubbling sound reverberating off the main hall chandelier. Does anyone really need a hall chandelier? The bubbling is a kind of talk Bertha used with her children, who are now too old for it, but it seems to come in handy with Isabel and perhaps, in the bedroom, with Moshe. There are other sounds: sniffling, a brief mutter, perhaps about Lillian, but then the note shifts to a major key, a "Bertha, dear," a quiet "Oh." They have apparently found the camellias: picture them, Isabel and Bertha, bubbling, murmuring, holding hands within walls raining pink and white blossoms. It is a picture Lillian cannot enter: she does not belong, and Isabel has left her, which was what Lillian wanted, wasn't it? This separateness? But it feels like blank space, and for a moment the blankness seems ominous, perhaps fatal. Lillian feels the urge to call back her mother—*Wait, don't go*—even as she knows the calling will do nothing, will at best reopen a door to a room not of camellias but of old unhappiness. Bertha's guest room will never contain what Lillian has been missing. Just as Lillian could not call her father back from death, though she'd been possessed by the wish—*Wait here, in this world, with me.*

And so as Isabel fails, it is not Lillian but Bertha holding Isabel's hand in the hallway, Bertha leading Isabel to the room with the camellias, Bertha soothing and making puddings and preparing to share her house with her mother-in-law. Bertha's voice echoing off that chandelier, "It's the best tub." The white bathtub *is* beautiful, though four or five Isabels would fit in it now, a nest of wrens.

Apparently Bertha loves Isabel in spite of Isabel, loves Moshe in spite of Moshe, scheming, boorish, unkind Moshe. Perhaps it's just the gesture of loving that Bertha's after, Lillian thinks. Maybe Isabel has become a substitute: Bertha's first devotion is to her own mother, her aunts, her Warsaw grandmother, Polish wrens. The beloved dead. Yet here in Buffalo there's only shrunken Isabel, hard-hearted but still of this world, still a mother. Moshe's mother. Bertha has devoted herself to Moshe and so by extension to Isabel, because that is how Bertha loves. And because when you lose someone from the deep of your life, and you find an echo in another—a stranger, a relative—you give to the other what you'd give to the lost one. Just to hear the echo.

"There you go." Words floating down the hall, Bertha's voice. Presumably Isabel is on the guest room bed, having had too much wine, having cried twice at dinner—something Isabel herself abhors—in need of such a bed. Lillian takes her brandy to the living room and Moshe follows. There again, the expanse of snow in the dark, which she wishes she could dissolve into. She returns to the blue chair and closes her eyes and sips at the brandy, which is warming. She'll need the warmth. The blueness outside has shifted to a dark blurry gray, falling snow slanting east. There's a match strike, the sound of inhalation, pipe smoke wafting from the direction of the sofa. Moshe will meet her silence with silence: he has a gift for waiting. That is not her gift, but when she must she can vanish from a room into herself even as she leans against the thick upholstery of a chair and sips at her drink. And so she vanishes, and the snow falls, and Bertha's murmuring becomes indistinguishable from the sounds of the house, and pipe smoke drifts. And after ten minutes, when her brandy is gone and she has finished vanishing, Lillian sets her glass on the coffee table and silently passes the damask sofa and Moshe and his pipe, collects her coat and laces up her heavy boots. If she stays quiet enough, the cold will not disturb her.

"Let me drive you home, Lilly," Moshe says. He taps his pipe against an ashtray and pushes himself up from the sofa.

"Thank you, no," Lillian says. "Please thank Bertha for the dinner."

"Don't be stubborn," Moshe says.

And the snow keeps falling. Flakes the size of camellias, she thinks. She does not kiss her brother, or say good-bye; she's careful to close the door softly, because her mother might be sleeping, because Lillian needs silence. She walks along the park to Delaware and catches a bus, and transfers, resisting the pull of the downtown nightspots. She's oddly sober for all she's had to drink tonight.

Once in her flat, Lillian craves only more quiet, as the city beyond, even in snowfall, seems now a roaring, the voices of her family and even Abe a roaring. She fills her bathtub and takes a second hot bath of the day. The flat fills with steam. She's warm again, wrapped in her robe when the telephone begins to ring:

perhaps Moshe, perhaps Abe. She does not answer. Before she turns off the light, Lillian brushes her hair, smoothes skin cream on her forearms and hands.

IN A DAY, when the roaring subsides, this much is clear: the lie itself is more bitter than she'd known. It's been years since Abe hinted at marriage, and stopped hinting at marriage, years since Lillian turned her mind from the question. Yet here, resurfacing, is the old hope, still raw: there seems no end to her own naïveté. Except now she is tired, and the baths and the gin do not restore her. Her brother is not her brother. Isabel's a wren, and the vitriol has worn her down.

Lillian cultivates silence. For a week she ignores the telephone, and then emissaries begin to arrive at Kaplan's Stationers. The first is a courier from Moshe's office, delivering another lunch invitation, which she glances at and returns. The second is Abe himself, arriving during a midmorning lull: when he enters the store there is always the echo of the first time he approached her, it's unavoidable, but Tuesday morning she is strangely unmoved. It is as if she's wearing gloves; as if her entire body is gloved.

"Why don't we have dinner at your flat?" Abe says.

"No," she tells him. "I think I'm getting a cold."

Abe does not want her to be tired or ill, or perhaps he doesn't believe her. Her answer seems to agitate him; he paces in front of the counter, and suggests he visit her flat anyway, though he rarely looks after her during illness.

"Better not," she says.

Finally he stops pacing and leans in close. "Your brother, he came to my store," he says. His eyebrows lift as he says this, and he gazes at her as if she's a child in need of correction.

"Yes?"

"Lillian, I would like to speak with you privately."

"Not now," she says.

He scans the empty store. Huffs. "You know we will not marry," he says.

And she is glad then for the gloved feeling, the sense that her body is not her body; the lie she told at dinner becomes ephemeral, a dead leaf swept into a dustbin. "Please go now."

"Lillian."

"You should go."

ON WEDNESDAY, Lillian's nephew Leo stops by the store in his beautiful overcoat and calfskin gloves, kisses Lillian on the cheek and delivers gin and small cakes from Bertha. His voice is deep and smooth, and he smells of barbershop aftershave and sweet to-bacco. He hugs Harry Kaplan—"Uncle Harry, how are you?"— says he's just in the neighborhood and needs a few things. He chooses expensive items—a hand-stitched ledger and a leather portfolio—and while Lillian rings them up, he mentions that Bertha and her housekeeper are cleaning Isabel's house.

"Nana doesn't look so good," Leo says. "She sits in Ma's living room with the radio loud. Hours. Size of a chicken, Nana."

Wren. "I know." Lillian packages the ledger and portfolio and hands them to Leo, who says "thank you" and stands at the counter, waiting, at ease, like his father. The store refills with quiet, and Harry retreats to the office, and still Leo waits.

"What else can I get you, Leo?" Lillian says.

"It's peaceful here," Leo says.

"Um-hmm."

"I could just stay all afternoon."

"You could."

"You want to see her today, I'll go with you," Leo says. "Aunt Lilly?"

"Don't get mixed up with Moshe's plans," Lillian says. "I can't do what he wants."

"I know."

"Leo?"

"Aunt Lilly, I know."

He assures her that Moshe is in court, Moshe whose calls she will not answer, whose invitations deserve no reply. Leo is, it seems, Bertha's emissary.

The snow in Delaware Park is crisscrossed with footprints,

snowbanks along Delaware and Nottingham collecting dirt. Lillian enters the house to the sound of a symphony pouring from the radio. Isabel's dwarfed by the blue chair again. She's wearing a green wool dress and sweater, a blanket pads her lap, and the bulk of the wool exaggerates her smallness. No glaring, no crying, no spite. A young uniformed nurse sits straight-backed on the sofa and reads the *Saturday Evening Post.* When Lillian gives Isabel a kiss on the cheek, Isabel says, "Lilly," and offers her the newspaper. Isabel doesn't seem to want conversation: she too is retreating into silence, or at least music, Lillian thinks, and how strange that she and Lillian should do anything alike. Leo brings cups of tea and more of Bertha's cakes, and they sit together with the radio symphony and the newspaper, and Leo holds Isabel's hand. There is no apparent bitterness in Isabel's face. Don't be fooled, Lillian thinks, and her own body is tense, as if to deflect a blow, but her mother is merely a tired woman in a chair.

The orchestra completes one movement and begins another; the paper reports snow in Cleveland, in Chicago, in Canada; Leo finishes the cakes. "Today," the nurse says, "isn't one of her better days," but it's peaceful with Isabel in the living room, the bad day oddly good. And Lillian stays a bit longer watching the park beyond the windows, women in heavy coats walking, flying bits of snow.

THE LATEST ISABEL is a paradox, in the face of which Lillian is disarmed and melancholy and strangely tender. On other weekday afternoons, she returns to Bertha's living room, to the radio and small cakes, to the day nurse and to Isabel in her chair—occasionally dozing, often gazing out the windows while the radio orchestra plays another movement. Sometimes Leo stops by, sometimes Bertha is home, and Lillian finds the same peculiar peace. There will be more nurses, Bertha says, a second bed in the room with the camellias. Beside Isabel, Bertha herself seems a large pink blossom. She offers Lillian a drink, drops olives and ice into her gin.

They do not discuss the men, or how it is that Lillian can visit during work hours (as is, Harry can barely pay her; at least she can choose her own schedule). At the store, Lillian treats Harry gingerly: he too sits in a chair for hours, listening, but to some inner music—maybe a requiem, maybe an anxious march. It's good, isn't it, that her father can't witness these disassemblings? Yet more than ever she misses him. Her father would be appalled at Moshe. Her father would insist Abe treat her with more care.

But the fury and insistence are hers, must be. She will not see either Moshe or Abe, despite their constant messages and notes. Moshe has declared himself not-family. Abe has made a similar declaration. If she were younger, her rage would drive her to other men, but who needs another man? More trouble, more demands, more humiliating ways of being pinned down. Though in her bed she is too much alone; and the separateness of days exacerbates the loneliness, which is increasingly stark: craving mixed with exile. Each night in the bath, Lillian reminds herself, *Don't give in, don't give in, it will only lead to greater unhappiness.*

But she is running out of money. In March she searches for another job, though there is little; and she scans the classifieds for efficiencies and decent rooming houses—they can't all be grim, can they? She is losing weight, and it occurs to her that she and Isabel are more and more alike, silent, shrinking women, though Lillian can speak and by April Isabel cannot.

ABE AND MOSHE, Moshe and Abe: she has never known what transpires in the closed sanctuary of their friendship. The business of men. And it will do her no good to speculate. But in April, after Lillian has interviewed for a part-time job at Berman's Shoes, Harry Kaplan surprises her. He's alert, smiling, almost the man she remembers from childhood. He's sold the store, and at a fair price, a generous price, at a time when there are no buyers. "Today," he says, "I signed the papers." The new owner is Moshe, who wants her to manage the store.

A bribe? An offering? How can she know? She kisses Harry on the cheek. "That's wonderful," she says. She promises—what else can she do?—that she'll go through the details with Moshe.

And it is only a matter of days before Abe again appears at Kaplan's, somber, formal, though he carries a bouquet of daffodils. The sight of him brings an instant rogue wave of desire speckled with grief. "Lillian," he says. "Would you care to join me for lunch?"

Do not give in. "What you said about marriage?" she says.

"You think that would make you happy?" Abe shakes his head. "You are wrong." He sets the daffodils on the counter, but beside them his hands seem uncertain. "May I take you to lunch?"

How she has missed touching him. The scent of him in an ordinary room, the burnished depths of his voice. Her life is better with him than without him, isn't it? Though there was the hope, that sweet, dumb hope. It is not so easy.

"Abe," she says. "Abraham." She thanks him for the flowers. The room is a spill of yellow and olive and pearl gray. She tells him, "Please ask me again next week."

CHAPTER 15

Goldie

1935

And the day begins bright and cool, the sky overhead determining itself and uncoupling from the stars. Tuesday. Today she visits her friend Emily and Emily's two small sons: they will all paint pictures, and during between-time snippets Emily will teach Goldie about line and form and shadow. These are mornings Goldie looks forward to, when it seems she's a part of a larger life and what counts the most are colors and shapes, small games and snacks. She dresses; she thinks about the color orange; and she remembers a moment in a room painted dark cream, looking out over the span of yards behind the house, the trees dense with color. There seemed no end to the intensity of color, or the wish for such intensity: she'd wanted to press her face into the leaves. The air held a touch of chill, the wild reds and oranges and the still-green grass darkened and brightened with the movement of clouds in a variegated sky, blue patches, white and blue-gray clouds clumped in patterns difficult to discern; still, she searched out half-formed arrangements, emerging signs. And there was a tremulous quality to the day, the possibility of bursting into tears at the orange blaze of maple or the house cat in the window across the street, a slight calico who seemed somehow on the other side of the world. She'd needed to untie everything that bound her to that life, and did. Yet here years later is that moment's imprint, an image hovering, permanently, just out of reach.

Now the world trembles less. October arrives as a warm fair month, that other October out of view. The days of being on the second floor of an old house seem distilled into a remembered moment, the ache for that moment unanswerable, even if she were again to find the room, an identical October day. This is the trick of memory. She has not heard from her sisters; there are rare scribbled postcards from Irving but nothing from her sisters, not even Celia. It's shocking, really, that she would hear nothing. She cannot know the intricacies of this silence but it seems her sisters have chosen; to ask them directly would be humiliating. Every few months she still writes to Irving, the notes and occasional dollars at first like pennies dropped in a fountain, though she is beginning to see that this will soothe her conscience and no more. Outside the trolley clangs, the gulls call, the breeze carries the scent of brine and old fish and sweets from the pier. She brews herself a cup of coffee and opens the box of sugar. And then she knows: the darkened cream room was a bedroom in Daniel's father's house, where one day she rested while Daniel played the piano. She could hear the music and she went to the window to watch the leaves, her body languorous after sex. For the briefest instant she'd imagined her life might always feel this way, raw and delicate at once: exquisitely perched at the edge of such color; and then there was the merest shift in perception—was it the patterning of clouds? A change in Daniel's playing?—the day becoming rare and finite.

In California, the first man she brought home was a trumpet player named Albert she met while selling tickets at the Sunset Ballroom. He was in Venice for one week and she learned then that she could take pleasure without love but also without wonder, a diminished pleasure circumscribed by harsh shadowy forgetting. Still, his vocabulary altered her own: he's long since disappeared but she finds herself holding one corner of a sugar cube to her coffee and watching the coffee run upward into the cube, defying gravity it seems, until the cube is coffee-soaked. As Albert taught her.

PART THREE

Winter Stars

1943–45

CHAPTER 16

Sadie

1943

Early mornings remain tender for Sadie: in the bluish light Bill kisses her good-bye, and the neighborhood is still, her daughters' movements dream-inflected. At this hour the girls rarely fight: they are quiet and affectionate, staying close to Sadie in the kitchen. Both girls are dark-haired, dark-eyed, curious—Elaine more skittish, Margo headstrong—their presences solid and irrevocable. They can't imagine the world existing before their consciousness of it, and sometimes Sadie can't either. Her own girlhood seems simultaneously closer and farther, but isn't it easier to begin history with them? She pours milk, cooks oatmeal with fruit, and Margo and Elaine slowly come awake at the table. Sadie would like to think the morning closeness has nothing to do with the war's inescapable anxiety, though it well might.

She would like to replace history with oatmeal and fruit, saving only the best bits, starting again: Poland would mean Chopin, pastry with cinnamon, the ivory tablecloth Delia Lefkowitz inherited. But there are whole centuries to manage, and even her daughters' brief lifetimes: when war broke out, Elaine was mastering socks and shoes. It had been a relief to discuss socks, shoes after socks, the matching up of shoes and feet, finessing knots and bows. To teach the rudiments of footwear and take her daughter to the park. For a time, Sadie tried to acknowledge Europe only after the girls were asleep, but even the attempt seemed absurd. There were temple meetings, committees for fund-raising, committees for refugees; and the weekly arrival of worsening news she learned to hold in her mind, silently, while drawing the alphabet in huge blue letters and slicing apples to demonstrate fractions.

She's better at balancing the extremes now, and the city is strangely vibrant, infused with money and unified purpose. The early mornings help, but after the girls have left for school, the phone begins to ring, and Sadie must snap into her more worldly self. She dreads the telephone but cannot ignore its sharp insistence—like a mischievous child pressing the doorbell. And often the call is a prank, or nearly: Jo with her usual litany of complaints. But it could be Bill, or Sadie's friend Anna—she loves talking to Anna— or the plumber who needs to check the basement pipes. And a true emergency could be wedged in among Jo's gratuitous calls. With the war, emergencies are rampant.

When Sadie isn't in and sometimes when she's home, Rosalie will answer and then there's a long interlude before the next call. A kind of respite. If it seemed proper to have Rosalie answer all calls, Sadie would, but Jo does not like Rosalie, and when it comes to Coloreds Jo veers fast to insult. So Sadie tries to pick up first, to Jo's *Sadie, when you going to bring those kids over here?* Or the occasional, ugly *Sadie, that schvartze still in your house?* It isn't just mornings, of course, Jo will call randomly through the day, her timing never good: she'll call when Sadie is serving lunch to her card club and complain about the neighbor Ruby Berman. Fat Ruby, she says (though Sadie pictures the average-sized Ruby who would joke with their mother on the porch, and lately Jo herself is stout). Cats fighting in the yard upset *Celia* today—Jo herself pays no attention, but *Celia*. Who seems to have adopted yet another kitten, but forgets to look after it from time to time, that's the way she is you know, it's all *kitty kitty kitty*, and then for days silence. It's a good thing Jo's taken to those cats, a good thing Jo will feed them, but you know cats bring other cats. You know what all that howling in the yard is about, don't you? You know about the howling, Sadie, course you do, you've got kids. When are you going to bring those kids over here?

Jo doesn't call much when she's working at the jewelry store, or when their father is home at Lancaster, but that doesn't rule out some nights, or occasional early mornings. In the evenings Bill answers and the call ends before Sadie picks up, and sometimes her daughters answer and stand listening to God knows what before Sadie gets to the receiver.

But emergencies exist. And with Irving in the army and her father frailer, slowly unraveling, really, and the war seeping into the smallest corners of life, you can't ignore the phone. True, for now Irving's safe in Georgia—an uncouth wilderness, she thinks, but at least an American one—though who knows where he'll be sent, to the bloody mess of Europe (a continent alternately glamorous and murderous) or the incomprehensible Pacific. She sends Irving care packages to the base. She volunteers at the Red Cross. She can hardly bring herself to read the *Jewish Review*, the reports inconceivable; now and then Bill hides it from her. The radio seems to broadcast from Mars. On bad days she worries about the anti-Semites in Buffalo, who are of course everywhere and include children who sometimes yell slurs at her daughters on their way home from school. Though it's been a few months. What good will it do to dwell, unless the yelling starts again, or someone soaps the store windows?

It's a January Wednesday, the girls are at school, Sadie's hands are wet, and the phone is ringing again. Rosalie answers, "Feldstein residence," and says, "I'll surely tell her, Miss Cohen. I'll surely tell her right away. Yes ma'am, Miss Cohen." There's silence, and in a harder voice Rosalie says, "Miss Cohen, I will relay your message. Good day." And when Sadie enters the living room Rosalie is taking a deep breath.

"Miss Cohen called," Rosalie says. "She said to tell you it's important. She said to tell you to please call her immediately."

"Thank you," Sadie says.

Rosalie returns to the kitchen and begins to scrub down the stovetop, humming one of her church songs. Her fixed concentration on burned gravy barely hints at how far Jo's gone this time. Sadie ought to call back; there's likely to be an hour of quiet now, perhaps an uninterrupted hour to read—but she ought to call back. If nothing else, Jo will blame Rosalie for not convey- ing the message fast enough. But now the telephone is ringing again, and Rosalie hums a little more fervently, and Sadie picks up to Jo saying, "You've got to come over here, Sadie." An urgency in her voice, but also a wavering, as if the sentence itself is push- ing through radio static. "Celia is fine," she says. "Celia's at the Red Cross. You've got to come here, Sadie."

"I can't bring the girls to visit," Sadie says.

"Not them," Jo says. "Just you come. I've got something here."

Sadie drives down Hertel and over to Delaware, Lancaster, the bare trees partitioning a gray mottled sky. Perhaps she should ask Rosalie not to bother with the telephone at all. They should both pretend no one is home, muffle the thing with a blanket. It's tempt- ing. But of course a mother should not do that. A wife should not do that. You cannot ignore your life because your sister has bad habits.

For example, the front walk at Lancaster is in need of shovel- ing: Sadie would not change her daily routine because of Jo's fail- ure to clear the walk. The house itself needs a coat of paint, and when she enters it, a threadbare patch gleams up from the foyer carpet. "Jo?"

"Parlor," Jo says, and there Sadie finds a pot of tea and teacups set out and a little tray with cigarettes, and beside them an enve- lope. Jo's in their father's reading chair, his carved walnut pipe in her hand. She's dressed for the store, matronly in a dark wool skirt suit. "There's tea," Jo says. "I found cigarettes."

"What do you need, Jo?"

Jo shrugs and hands her the envelope. Lights her father's pipe.

The handwriting is vaguely like Sadie's but looser, addressed to Irving at the store (what sort of debt *now?*). A cold wave runs through her, and in its wake the parlor seems less solid and famil- iar. The letter itself is just a note, dated a week ago, tucked around a ten-dollar bill.

Dear I,
All fine here. Does Celia need boots? Deposit the rest.
                                                    G

The postmark Los Angeles, last Monday, but no return address. What is this, what? She examines the handwriting again. Unmistakable. There's a quick wash of confusion, as if the day has dropped away to reveal behind it another, more densely constructed, blinding day. G. The whole of her: just these lines and the letter G. Sadie squints. This should be a relief, shouldn't it? But instead there's a hard slam, as if Goldie's just gone missing again, a raw, new grief.

Goldie's alive, she's alive but did not tell them; why didn't she say? What did they do that kept her so far she'd pass for dead? The classifieds: they were simple worried classifieds, nothing harsh or recriminating. Years of them, but of course not in California—Sadie never thought of California. Why didn't she think of California? A better climate: why wouldn't Goldie try to find more summer?

And Irving knew, and without telling her, and for how long? She feels her lungs contract; the surface of the day seems patchy and unreliable, as if it might open and spill its contents—the parlor, the note, Sadie—into space.

"There's sugar for the tea," Jo says. And here is the teacup, the sofa, here is her father's chair, Jo, a pipe.

"Did Celia see this?" Sadie says.

Jo shakes her head.

"Papa?"

"No."

Jo is puffy-faced and cracking, and if the light in the room were brighter Sadie would have seen it at first glance. Jo says, "I am not myself today." She makes no move to get up from the chair. She sucks at the lit pipe and in truth she does not look herself. How could she? Sadie waits to see if the day will in fact spill, her own not-oneself feeling taking full control. She drinks her tea, rereads the note. *All fine here,* the phrase an opaque pond that becomes for a moment translucent, long enough for you to catch a glittering below the surface before the water clouds again. The day is not the same one she started with: the earth spun more than she knew. She has been a sleepwalker.

But Irving has not been a sleepwalker, he's been wide awake and for how long? Goldie has sent money before, that much is clear, but with money Irving is a sieve. Sadie's breathing speeds. She notices the cigarettes, lights one because it is there. Irving is boyish, not cruel, or so she's always believed, but maybe she's been wrong, or maybe the two states are less distinct than she'd imagined. What was he thinking? Of course he is untouchable now, safely in Georgia, safe but not safe, there is a war and he is a soldier but she will not think about that today: he is in Georgia where she cannot confront him.

All fine here, but nobody told her. "Was there anything else?" Sadie says.

"No."

And no return address. "I'll write to Irving."

And the air in the room seems thin despite the smoke. It's nearly time for the girls to return home from school—though Rosalie is there waiting—but Sadie should be home now, shouldn't she, with Margo and Elaine? She stubs out the cigarette: she must see Margo and Elaine. She will be calmer when she sees them, certain the world still contains them and remains familiar. How she will protect them, she does not know. "I'll write to Irving," she repeats.

"If you wouldn't mind," Jo says. "I'm not myself at all."

DRIVING HOME she feels a shakiness unreflected in the orderly traffic and clear silhouettes of the trees and the brightening sky. She would like to telephone Georgia immediately, find Irving at boot camp, but how would she begin? Emergency? No one has died—that's exactly the point. She can send him a telegram, though even that seems extreme: it's wartime. And what could she squeeze into a telegram? It will have to be a letter. She will need to calm herself and write a letter.

Sadie knows she's a different woman now than she was when Goldie disappeared—she is not, she reminds herself, a woman who falls down on sofas. There is no time in life for falling down on sofas. In her neighborhood, the shakiness abates: it is the same neighborhood she left this morning, her house the same house. Still, after she drives on and parks the Ford at the grammar school, a glance at Goldie's handwriting brings on another spasm, a mix of muscle cramp and mosquito bite, something you rub and scratch until you're mesmerized by scratching. Where you are falls away and time evaporates, and then you awake to a blood smear, the embarrassing need to cover broken skin, and the waiting school.

The school day is not quite over, but Sadie walks in and asks for her daughters, and in a few minutes they appear. How simple it is to find them.

"We need treats today," she says, "don't you think?" They watch her closely, Margo more skeptically than Elaine: Sadie doesn't allow them to miss class unless they are plainly ill, and she does not tolerate faking. And she doesn't explain why they need treats today, but that is not necessary. She drives them to Parkside Candies, where the air is sugary-thick, and the displays of chocolates and the soda fountain and the small round tables suggest a separate universe. The girls are distracted by ice cream but they still hover close; and Sadie is partly distracted by the girls, who do not know they have an aunt named Goldie. Finally the day approaches normal. Outside the pillowy afternoon clouds accumulate into a solid block, darker and less sculpted in the west, but there are still buttonholes of blue when Sadie begins to drive home.

Rosalie has finished for the day and left a note in careful script:

> *Miss Cohen called 1:00 pm, Wednesday. Miss Cohen called 1:10 pm Wednesday. Miss Cohen called 1:15 pm Wednesday. Miss Celia Cohen called from Red Cross 2:30 pm Wednesday, Would you like to meet her at the Red Cross Monday? Please kiss the girls. 3 pm Dr. Feldstein called and wishes to remind you of his sister's birthday. He requested biscuits, if I had enough time. Plate of biscuits under wax paper on the counter. I will wash the bed linens tomorrow. Have a nice evening.*

Jo. Sadie's neglected to speak to her about Rosalie: she ought to call Jo now. And say what, exactly? *Please be polite to Rosalie,* the kind of request Jo deliberately thumbs her nose at. *If you cannot say some-thing nice don't say anything at all,* Sadie tells her daughters, but it's schoolmarmish even to Sadie, and to Jo—whether or not Jo is her-self—it's simply a dare. Sadie will tell Rosalie to ignore the phone.

The kitchen smells of warm biscuits. From the icebox Sadie re-moves lake fish wrapped in paper, eggs, cold noodle pudding, car-rots to boil and butter; from the cold pantry a half dozen apples, cinnamon and sugar, flour. She cores one, then another apple, tucking them into a glass pan and sprinkling cinnamon and the smallest bit of sugar: an ordinary gesture, followed by the ordinary gesture of peeling carrots while Elaine leans over the kitchen table and draws flowers the same size as houses.

There's the question of what to say to Bill. Irving's silence is stunning, unforgivable, but all Sadie actually knows is that Jo opened Irving's mail—which Jo of course should not have done, Bill will jump on that—to discover a note and money she should not have seen (more jumping), the note and cash from a liv-ing Goldie. Sadie's temples pinch at the prospect of maneuvering through Bill's objections and unanswerable questions: it's like steer-ing a rowboat in high seas. She does not want to be in a rowboat, or in high seas. She can only admit her bewilderment and what will he do then? Comfort her or try to argue her out of bewilderment, into a rational state, which is what she's trying to maintain. Wait then, until she knows more? This is not, she supposes, the way one ought to behave with a husband. You keep your secrets—those little five-dollar loans to Irving—but certain things you ought to tell, for ex-ample that your disappeared sister is not dead.

Isn't the shivah alone reason to speak? In her throat there's a welling: this secret, lodged there and expanding, may soon be-come an outburst. But Bill might answer as he has before: it was her father's right. He repeated this just months ago, the last time they argued over what to tell the girls about Goldie.

"And would you disown our girls?" she asked.

His gaze became stony, the look of a man she didn't know; for an instant she wondered if he was capable of striking her. His face reddened, and then he took off his glasses and rubbed his eyes. After a moment he was again familiar. "Of course not," he said. "Don't ever speak to me like that."

"Promise you never will," she said, and kept silent until he replied coldly, "Never, I will never disown them. But how could you think such a thing?"

She did not know how, or why the promise did not seem to her implicit in her children's conceptions and births. Her demand did seem mixed up: Bill's a devoted father, if stern. But who would have predicted her father's call for shivah, even with Celia to consider?

She's pan-frying the whitefish, and above a sea of wax-pencil poppies and one small house, Elaine wrinkles her nose. "Not a word," Sadie says. "You *like* fish."

"What else?" Elaine says.

"Noodle pudding," which seems to satisfy Elaine. She returns to her poppies and the intricacies of a brick chimney.

Wait until you know what to make of the letter. Wait until the facts become clearer. No need to argue with yourself. Do not burn the fish.

And when Bill returns she hangs up her apron and kisses him hello; today he's brought flowers, as if he sensed something. Red and white carnations for the table. He's jovial, kissing Margo and Elaine, he's had a good day. "We went to Parkside Candies," Margo says.

"Did you have chocolate?"

"Ice cream," she says.

"An impulse," Sadie says. "It seemed a good day for a treat."

He studies her face for a moment, then asks the girls if they brought home any almond bark, which in fact they have, a small white bag Margo has labeled *Daddy*.

"The flowers," Sadie says, "are beautiful."

In the evening, Bill plants himself in his reading chair and sorts through temple board memos, and the girls take their homework to their rooms. Sadie listens to the radio and writes letters; to Ruby Berman's son Jacob, eighteen and now in the Pacific; to her second cousin Melvin in the army, last she heard in England; to Irving in

Georgia. Three or four times a week she writes to Irving, long chatty letters, but tonight she writes simply:

> *Dearest Irving,*
> *I hope you are well. A letter arrived at the store and Jo opened it before realizing it was for you, not Papa. A note from California with ten dollars enclosed. Here is the note. Please explain this. If it is from Goldie, you must tell us where we can reach her. Do you understand me? You must explain.*
> > *Your loving sister,*
> > *Sadie*

Before she seals the envelope, she slips in one of Elaine's poppy drawings, which doubles the thickness. She places the small stack of letters on the table in the front foyer, for Bill to mail on his way to the office.

IT DOES NOT occur to Sadie to hand over the money to Celia—who would surely spend it all on trash—and she will not shop with Celia. It's too *trying*, she tells herself, though the prospect of being seen in department stores with Celia—even a compliant Celia—unnerves her most. Twice last fall she offered to shop *for* Celia, and just last week bought a deep green dress Celia accepted without comment. Celia has new boots. In the morning, Sadie decides to put the money toward a new coat for Celia: surely Celia won't argue with a coat?

Rosalie has stripped the beds and begun to launder the sheets when Sadie remembers to thank her for making the biscuits and to tell her she might as well ignore the telephone. "It's a nuisance," Sadie says, "but use it of course if you need to call Thomas."

Rosalie nods and pulls out the box of laundry soap. "All right, Mrs. Feldstein."

At Hengerer's Sadie finds a coat in soft gray with red piping, and when she delivers it to the Lancaster house, Celia touches the sleeve, runs her finger along the piping, and squints at Sadie. "You just bought me a dress," she says. "I *have* a coat, you know."

"I thought you might like a new one."

"Why?"

"You've had your coat a while. But if you don't like this I'll return it."

"Buy coats for the girls," Celia says. "Don't *they* need coats?"

"They do. I'm taking them downtown on Saturday."

"You shouldn't show off your money," Celia says. "It's irritating."

Sadie hesitates, and in the pause can hear her own pulse, then wind gusts pushing a sycamore branch against the side of the house, the low clanking of the furnace.

"It's Goldie's money," she says.

"Is it?"

"I'm fairly sure," Sadie says. "If you don't want the coat I'll return it. We can put the money in the bank."

Celia lifts the gray coat, tries it on, checks the depth of the pockets. "All right," she says. "I'll keep it."

"Papa doesn't know."

"He wouldn't," Celia says. There's no agitation, no sign of shock.

"You don't seem surprised," Sadie says.

"You don't always listen," Celia says.

"Does Irving know?"

"He ought to." Celia lifts the coat and hangs it in the front closet. "Did you bring groceries too? I ran out of jam."

IRVING IS HIDING in Georgia but there is no need to dwell: she will be patient. After sending him the note with the drawing of poppies, Sadie returns to the chattiness of her regular letters: Margo's in her fifth-grade play, the lead in *Cinderella*, she practices with sorrowful looks when Sadie makes her do her math; there's a new junior rabbi at the temple, not that Irving is much for temple, but he seems a nice man, more popular with the children at least, etc. Toward the end a simple *I await your reply to my note. Your loving sister.*

Each day she checks the mailbox, and clearly he is busy, clearly mail to and from Georgia takes time, but with each day Sadie's irritation increases. Even the early mornings are moody and askew, though Jo's calls have briefly diminished. Irving seems in no hurry to write back and how much difference will a few days make after thirteen years? But thirteen years. Sadie wakes too early with a slight panic and the impulse to check her legs—why is she checking her legs? A dream? She often doesn't remember them now, but there's a feeling, a worry, a leg worry. She used to have those, didn't she? Bill walks in from shaving, he's in an undershirt and suit pants, his belly swelling outward. She's got both hands clamped around her left thigh. "Are you all right?" he says.

"Of course." She drops her hands and hurries to her closet for a robe.

But he follows her, his hands suddenly on her shoulders, rubbing, he leans in and kisses her on the cheek. She does not want to be kissed. She does not want to kiss him back: she wants a moment to disguise the leg worry.

"Sadie?" Bill says.

"The war gives me nightmares," she says, and it's probably true, how can it not give one nightmares? Aren't they all more irritable? The jitteriness she's felt—don't they all feel it?

"I know," Bill says, though he doesn't know at all, not about Goldie, and wouldn't this be the time to tell him? Or maybe he knows something Sadie does not, not about Goldie but about war and what might happen. Men seem to know about such things; it seems to go with shaving and heavy tobacco and father's rights. She's bewildered though, too fragile; she cannot risk his bellowing.

"Sadie?"

"Sometimes I miss my mother," she says. It deflects his scrutiny from her leg worry and Goldie worry, but it's true, isn't it? Every day, really, she misses her mother. As if missing were stitched into her clothes.

"I'm sorry," Bill says. "You do seem nervous. Make an appointment with Dr. Rosen, would you?"

"Dr. Rosen," Sadie says, as if remembering the family doctor exists.

"Have lunch with my mother," Bill says.

"Darling, of course I'd like to see her, but it isn't quite what I was saying."

"It's a frightening time," he says. "She loves you."

How would lunch with Mother be a comfort? And an appointment with Dr. Rosen? All for holding back about Goldie, which she can't do forever but certainly can't confess now. When she does confess Bill might be livid, which seems wrong, unfair—isn't it her turn to be livid? She has not heard a thing from Irving, and cannot find her robe. Or her reading glasses: in the last week, objects have begun to walk off.

"I'd better get dressed," she tells Bill. "I'm sure the girls are awake."

LUNCH WITH Mother Feldstein. Lunch with Mother Feldstein— tomorrow, she'll say. Or next week, she'll simply call and say next week, and though Mother Feldstein will try to keep her on the telephone, she will not allow it. She will not answer the phone this morning: perhaps Rosalie can. No, Rosalie shouldn't, she's told Rosalie not to, because of Jo. Which is ridiculous, to ignore the phone, it's Sadie's phone, not Jo's, not Mother Feldstein's, nor is her house their house, but they make themselves known nonetheless, they sprawl in the living room and often the kitchen and dining room as well—once their voices are in the house they spread out and inflate. All by asking the telephone operator to open the door. How can you stop them? You leave the door ajar for other people, for your daughters, for your friends, for Goldie—who has never telephoned but certainly could, now that she's alive. Not that she was dead. Why has she never called? What did Sadie do, that she would never write or call? Sadie's house keys have disappeared this morning, and when she checks her lipstick in the mirror she finds a coffee stain on the lapel of her blouse, a stain not there when she dressed, when Bill was making all his helpful suggestions and finally had to desist and get himself to work. Where he can tell other people what to do. And Rosalie's in the kitchen ironing, eyeing Sadie as Sadie searches the table and her pocketbook and the kitchen counter for her house keys. "Don't bother with the phone today, Rosalie," Sadie says.

Rosalie nods, "All right then," and presses the sleeve of Bill's dress shirt, but she's still eyeing Sadie while Sadie combs the kitchen for those deceitful keys. Rosalie sets down the iron. "Mrs. Feldstein," she says. "Is there something else you need today?"

Which means what? Rosalie knows perfectly well what's needed in the house, knows the house better than Sadie does.

"I'm just *fine*, Rosalie," Sadie says. "Have you seen my house keys?" The sharpness in her tone verges on uncivil.

"No, Mrs. Feldstein. I'm sorry."

"But they were right here," Sadie says, "So was the package for Bill's sister. Are you sure?" It seems another, ruder Sadie has taken charge, which is unfortunate but sometimes you can't mince words, there's been altogether too much word mincing and evasion, too much fuzziness and inexactitude, too many things slipping out of reach, house keys and birthday gifts the least of them.

"Yes, ma'am." Rosalie sets the iron to cool.

"They were here," Sadie repeats.

"Yes ma'am. I did not see them," Rosalie says. She quietly takes a rack of shirts upstairs, and does not reappear before Sadie remembers that Bill wanted to deliver the gift himself; before Sadie finds her keys on the telephone table, and leaves the house for no reason she is sure of. She does not see Mother Feldstein. She does not see Dr. Rosen. She misses her volunteer shift at the Red Cross. Instead she slips into the public library and browses the shelves, and for an hour thumbs through *Life*. She has taken to doing this now and then, hiding in the library: it's rare that she sees anyone she knows, except a woman named Sylvia who works there, and used to work with Goldie, and knows to leave Sadie in peace. You can see why Goldie liked it here, the reverence for books and quiet and being alone.

In the afternoon, at the house, Sadie reads another romance novel, which distracts her from the world. She ignores the ringing phone until the girls get home from school. Rosalie moves through the house quietly, saying little, though she calls Margo Cinderella and gives the girls oatmeal cookies.

And when Bill arrives home, Sadie forces cheeriness and later even makes love with him (ending talk of Dr. Rosen). She won't allow herself to be unhinged.

After two more days she receives a letter from Irving.

Dear Sadie,
I don't recommend Georgia, but at least it's still warm
here. If you want to reach Goldie you can write in
care of General Delivery, Venice, California. That's
all I know.

Love,
Irving

p.s. if Celia's boots don't cost too much, I could use
some pocket money here.

So there is the address and no more than the address. Is
Goldie's last name the same? It's difficult to imagine her married,
though Sadie can't pinpoint why. Before Goldie disappeared,
Sadie sometimes thought of her as a kind of mole, burrowing and
plain, despite her prettiness in photos: in her absence she's seemed
more consistently beautiful. Why is that? Is it simply the late
knowledge of her romance with the piano teacher? Something less
tangible? Or a flaw in Sadie that allows her to see the beauty only
when Goldie is absent?

It's true that as children, Goldie did not like Sadie, did not like
any of them it seemed, except maybe Irving. But later this shifted,
and for a time when Sadie was in high school she and Goldie
shared novels, passing them back and forth with the briefest of
comments—*I think you'll like this, the last one was lovely*—each of them
then off to separate rooms to read, to the separate private realms
of books, ignoring their father's identical warnings: *you read too
much, you'll ruin your eyes.* And there was the care of their mother,
and with it a kind of melding. During their mother's illness, perhaps they'd been too close: Goldie and Sadie taking care of their
mother, Goldie and Sadie bathing her, feeding her, alternating
sleep and watchfulness. It was an intimacy of worry and strain, a
closeness defying perspective. As when you cannot tell the difference between your body and your husband's in coupling, the moment in all that fever when the tangle of bodies seems a melting.
Or when what you feel and see don't match, when you are so close
to his shoulder you cannot see the whole man, just edge and curve;

so it might have been with Goldie. All you could see was the line
of sadness, or the ferocity, or the stinginess with love.

Goldie's edginess was likely a sadness, wasn't it? But some days
more than Sadie could bear; nor could she bear Goldie's undis-
guised sadness, just brimming at the surface. Giving in to grief
seemed to Sadie an unaffordable luxury. During those years she
did not acknowledge it, and maybe for that reason also could not
see beauty. You had to put the hard things aside and keep on,
Goldie had told Sadie, and then did not live by her own words. Or
did she? Why wouldn't she marry? Stubborn, it seemed they all
were. She'd had prospects, decent men, even in the year after her
mother's death, the lovesick piano player but also other respectable
men—a teacher, a shoe store owner—who tried unsuccessfully to
court her.

Sadie cannot picture California: she pictures Goldie only as
Goldie appears in photographs from Sadie's own wedding, the
simple sleeveless dress, a rose pinned in her dark bobbed hair, a
wry, slightly quizzical smile. At her writing table, Sadie begins:
Dearest Goldie, How are you? abandons the note card and begins
again. The letter emerges like a child's primer, in short graceless
sentences.

> *Dearest Goldie,*
> *How strange to imagine you reading this letter. For*
> *reasons I cannot explain, I have not known how to*
> *reach you. Irving is in boot camp—did he tell you?*
> *Jo works at the store. I have two daughters. We are*
> *grateful that you are fine and grateful for your help*
> *for Celia. You are welcome to visit any time. Please*
> *write when you are able.*
>
> > *Your loving sister,*
> > *Sadie*

She seals the envelope and adds a stamp and walks through
light snow to the letter box on the corner. After she drops the letter
into the box, the cold air seems more breathable. And when she

returns to the house, it's as if reentering a moment from a lighter season. She's hungry and chilled, considering hot coffee, wondering if the cookies for the girls are all gone. Rosalie sits at the kitchen table, polishing the silver for Friday night, Rosalie whom she was practically uncivil to. Practically but not actually, she thinks, she said nothing wrong, this is her home and in her home things happen, difficulties, moods. She's Rosalie's employer: there is no need to explain.

Rosalie glances up and back to the silver candlesticks. "Will you be needing the kitchen, Mrs. Feldstein?"

"Oh, no," Sadie says. "I'm going to brew a pot of coffee. Would you care for some coffee?"

"No, thank you," Rosalie says.

"The silver," Sadie says, "looks very fine."

"I'm glad. Thank you."

"You sure you wouldn't like some coffee?"

"I'm sure."

"Rosalie." She pauses, not knowing what to say, how to soften the sharp edges of the conversation. She's got one hand on the coffee tin, the other propped on the counter: her body feels airy and strange, like loose wool. The moment slips and she finds herself staring at floor tiles, blue hexagons interspersed with white. "It's a hard time, isn't it?"

"Yes, Mrs. Feldstein, it is."

Sadie scoops out the ground coffee, sets the water to boil. "Take some later if you change your mind."

"Yes, ma'am," Rosalie says, and it's a sting, the ma'am. Sadie opens her mouth to say something more, something else, but can't locate herself in words, finding instead an altered bewilderment, not a sea this time but a bog. And the question forming *Did I . . . ?* and before it's complete, the answer there in her mind again, *No, I've said nothing wrong*, and then the firmer reiteration, *It's a hard time*, yes, there's a war going on, and strain and moods, which everyone has, surely Rosalie has them, surely Rosalie knows, but Sadie's right not to make her answer the phone, Jo can be more than difficult, she's suspicious of Italians too, worse now that the war's on. *A hard time,* and Rosalie knows, her son Thomas a young man now, her son Thomas just the right age to go to murderous Europe, where glamour has died, and young men, and entire towns.

Sadie brews the coffee on the stove and the snow beyond the window seems a dry bleached sand. Rosalie remains silent while she polishes the candlesticks, she's not humming today, and not drinking coffee. And wouldn't it be better if she changed her mind? Because the coffee is good. Because Sadie does not know what else to offer.

CHAPTER 17

Lillian

1943

Friday evening at Sabbath services no one looks askance at Abe and Lillian: years of fresh scandals have replaced the scandal of their relationship, of Lillian herself. And now there is the war. Women who used to shun Lillian are strangely mild and kind, and Lillian finds the temple surprisingly comforting. Who would have predicted she'd attend by choice? At times she gives over to the hushed separate realm of the synagogue, and feels in some way protected. Abe is calmest in synagogues, and now visits daily, but outside the temple he's anxious and obsessed, burying himself in newspapers, constantly listening to war broadcasts—even tinkering with shortwave. He falls asleep to late news coming in from overseas. And with Irving enlisted, Abe's ever more fervent.

Bertha too attends services now—earnest, subdued, but fragile. Calm, too, for the moment. Lillian kisses her and brings her packages of writing paper, asks after the toddler grandchildren, steers conversation away from news reports and speculation about her Polish cousins. Lillian would like to speak with Bertha directly about them, but Moshe would certainly shush her. Lately he's secretive—as is Abe. Before services, the two of them consult in

the corridor outside the chapel, clamming up when Lillian and
Bertha appear, or when Abe's daughter Sadie arrives with her husband and daughters. Then they sit together, all of them sharing a
pew. The rabbi begins. Hebrew comes back to Lillian in bits,
though mostly she listens to the rhythms and phrases and waits for
the cantor's heart-strung tenor to pull emotion from the stream of
sounds. Perhaps it's better not to understand: in the melodic chant,
there's a swell of hope, a release of grief. Lillian invents her own
meanings, her own way to pray.

These days, there's a mild trembling in Abe, a weariness,
prayer absorbing his bluster. He does not speak about the past in
the ways men of his age tend to do—or at least not in ways she expects. He never mentions his parents; he does not speak of Rebecca. Instead a childhood neighbor's goat. A writing tablet. A
winter of no shoes. He will mention these things in a sentence and
say no more about them, but in the silence surrounding them they
take on weight and resonance, like small bells echoing *goat goat goat*
before the silence swallows them again.

Beyond the synagogue, the city bustles and hums, livelier than
it's been in years. How strange that business is good, Lillian's store
more trafficked than ever, filling up with women. They buy writing
paper and pens and envelopes. Some of them are determinedly
cheerful, some very quiet; a few of them cry. Lillian has come to
prepare herself for this, the occasional woman breaking down over
thin blue sheets and linen stock and plain envelopes in packets of
twenty. Unlike Abe, she does not keep the news on in her store:
she tunes the radio to music broadcasts or turns it off. She's taken
to keeping a pitcher of water and a small bowl of fruit drops on the
counter, facial tissue by the register. In the back office, a bottle of
sherry, and after five, when the worried and crying women are
gone, she pours herself a glass. Lillian herself does not cry. Hasn't
for years, though she remembers plenty of crying, a decade or two
stained by crying, now far away, like a faded star, still identifiable
but so remote you cannot dream of touching it. Perhaps if she'd
had children she would cry. If she'd married? Certainly if her father
had lived. Even now she feels a weakening at the thought of him, a
hot blurriness. He would have admired the shop, wouldn't he? De-

spite the chipped paint on the east wall, which she's covered with a calendar from the insurance company.

She does write letters, a few to Irving in Georgia, brief notes, with listings from the theaters and nightclubs and bits of Hollywood gossip. He would not have been drafted, at least not yet— too old—and he is not a patriotic man. He's a charming truant, and the military might squash him, Lillian thinks. He'll run his games and he'll be squashed by the army or, worse, by someone else's army. But he did volunteer.

Stupidly, Leo told her. Irving signed up when he was drunk and panicked about a gambling debt. He signed up knowing he would be whisked away not only from his creditor but also from some woman he was trying to shake off: for six inebriated hours Irving repeated to Leo that this was the perfect solution. Then there was the inevitable sobering, the inevitable awareness of transport to the Pacific or to Europe, the many opportunities to be killed. And Abe oblivious, patting him on the back, believing Irving was off to defend his family, to save Jews, his relatives and Bertha's and everyone else's. "Irving surprises me," Abe said. The sisters were more skeptical, but plainly worried.

Take Jo. Yesterday at the jewelry store Lillian tried to talk with her—"How have you been, Jo?"—and instead of answering with a curmudgeonly "Fine" Jo seemed rattled by the question. She emitted something like a squeak and excused herself. A squeak, the last response Lillian would expect from Jo, whose tongue has remained sharp as she's become an overstuffed matron. Maybe it was about Irving; maybe Jo actually loves her brother, fears for him. His absence *is* unnerving—it seems any minute he ought to stroll into Abe's store, but he does not. And Jo is hardly a replacement—she must know that—Irving so handsome and lighthearted, Jo plain as shaved wood, nothing sensuous about her. That she sells anything amazes Lillian, although Jo could pass for a soldier's suffering mother, and some people like that sort of thing.

Celia is faring better, and in Lillian's rare company she has not squeaked. She's been volunteering at the Red Cross. Keeping herself well, Abe says, which means she's clean and presentable and not wandering. The war is good for her. She has, now, a place and purpose: the Red Cross, where she writes letters with beautiful penmanship or rolls bandages or does whatever else the Red Cross will give her to do.

Lillian does not volunteer at the Red Cross. Comforting the crying women seems enough, though her own family—Bertha— she does not know how to comfort. The better moments at temple fade quickly, and Bertha is otherwise skittish and reclusive, as obsessed as Abe. It's unlike any state Lillian has seen her in, unlike her difficult pregnancies, unlike Isabel's death, when Bertha was subdued and spoke little. After the mourning she returned to herself, helped Lillian find a house. Now, with the war, her fragility seems degenerative and permanent. A few times a week she mails letters to her cousins in Poland, from whom she has not heard in four years. She sends letters to home addresses in Warsaw and Cracow, to the children's schools, the pharmacy where her cousin Max last worked. She mails the letters from the post office downtown, where one particular clerk takes them without warning her they won't get through. A balding man named MacKenzie. She patiently stands in MacKenzie's line, and he accepts the letters like any other foreign-bound mail and sells her more stamps. A few letters have been returned. And the rest? Moshe can't say. "It's terrible to watch," he tells Lillian. "But who knows? What if something gets through?" The writing seems a kind of prayer, a wishing on stars. How can you ask someone not to pray?

ON WEDNESDAY, when Sadie Feldstein shows up at Lillian's shop, it's nearly closing time. A young woman buys a notebook and bundles up and braces herself for the street. Often Lillian has a last-minute rush, women and sometimes men on their way home from work, but the cold today is sharp, Main Street already icy and dark. Below Sadie's fur hat there's worry in her face: Abe?

A tentative, almost plaintive "Hello, Lillian"—Lillian, not the "Miss Schumacher" Sadie still upholds in public situations. Sadie's hat matches her fur-collared coat, she's wearing sleek boots, careful makeup and under the heavy coat a knit suit, and yet in the store entrance she appears a blown leaf, distracted and unaccountably ragged.

"Come in," Lillian says. "I was just going to lock up and have a sherry. Sadie, would you like a sherry?"

"Sherry? Oh. Yes, please. That would be nice."

So. If there's an emergency, it isn't one Lillian can do anything about, at least right away. Abe is at his store, Irving in Georgia. For a moment she lets herself feel the weariness: it's exhausting, isn't it, to perch on the brink of emergency? You need the sherry and the fruit drops and the radio orchestras. Some days Lillian wonders if they've all been swimming through emergency itself, and for so long they can't distinguish it from ordinary life. But no. Perched. Europe is the emergency, leaking incomprehensible news. At night before sleep you check the walls of your bedroom, the ceiling, the floor: solid and there. Solid. The city is thriving, steel plants in full production, all day and night, money flowing downtown.

In the office Lillian pours sherry into glasses like inverted bells, offers Sadie a seat at the oak table from the house on Brunswick. Sadie's face is too-white, pinched, perhaps from the cold, perhaps from all the perching.

"This should warm you up," Lillian says. "Can I get you anything else?"

"Thank you, no." Sadie takes a sip and sits quietly for a moment. The gusts of wind against the building remind Lillian of trains, of travel motion, though it's the world that keeps moving, and just now Sadie and Lillian are sheltered in the solid office with their sherry, obliged to go nowhere. It is not unpleasant, and Lillian has become better at tolerating silence and waiting patiently, instead of rushing to fill the space with talk. *There is beauty in patience,* Abe used to say, a motto he often did not live by.

"Something's come up," Sadie says.

Lillian nods, lets the sherry warm her throat. It's good sherry, not the best, but nice and dry.

"My eldest sister lives in California," Sadie says. "Goldie. This is something I've just learned." She's the model of poise, Sadie, but still there's a frantic undertone, an incredulity that might explain the paleness. As if for her a ghost has risen.

"I see."

"You don't seem surprised," Sadie says.

And Lillian isn't, not really. For a time she'd thought Goldie might be dead, victim of something bizarre and random, but she couldn't hold to that story, not without proof. Why believe such a thing? Even from a distance you could see how smart Goldie was, and how estranged. "I remember her as a capable woman," Lillian says. "The type to get herself to California."

And now Sadie is peering into her sherry glass, as if it might illuminate a mystery, and her voice is like a young girl's. "Did Irving tell you?"

"No," Lillian says. "Irving's very private about the family." Which is one way of putting it. But there was something once, wasn't there? A curious phrase? Some mention of *the money my sister sent* instead of his previous, relieved *money from Sadie*. He'd been betting on the horses. "I suppose he knew?"

Sadie nods and for an instant her jaw tightens. "My father?" she says.

"He never mentions her."

"Today I told him I wanted to speak with him about Goldie. 'She's alive,' I said. 'The dead are dead,' he told me, and walked away."

Lillian nods. "That sounds about right. That's what he'd say."

"Will you talk to him?"

All that effort to steady himself, all that fervent prayer, the reservoir of things he does not say slowly burning in him. The unspeakable daily reports. *Goat goat goat.* Another man would accept news of Goldie as a gift, even after all this time, but another man would not have declared her dead. Abe himself is perched on the brink and wobbling. Could he embrace Goldie even if he wanted to? Lillian cannot imagine it. More likely he'll dismiss anyone who forces the matter, though more estrangement is untenable.

"She's his daughter," Sadie says, an open plea.

"Sadie, you want me to interfere. This matter is too private."

"But for Goldie," Sadie says.

"Has Goldie asked you this?"

"No."

"So this is what you wish."

"Shouldn't he know?"

Of course he should, but does *should* matter? He's chosen, more than once, and is it Sadie's place to decide now? "It won't do any good," Lillian says.

"How do you know?"

"I know."

"Have you tried?"

And she did try, in another lifetime it seems, when Goldie disappeared: first coaxing Abe to wait a while, Moshe too telling him, *There's no need to hurry this, let the police investigate.* Nor did she believe in the shivah, only that he had to go through with it. Beforehand, he'd been unreachable, a stone body, and after the shivah he reemerged, without lightness but at least himself. And years later, when he had grandchildren, she asked what if his eldest ever returned, and without anger he said, *The dead are dead, Lillian. Rebecca I mourn.* Rebecca's name, as ever, a warning not to go further.

"I'm not as bad as you think," Lillian says.

"I've insulted you." There's a quaver in Sadie's voice. "I'm sorry." She's tearing up now, but it's hard to know what she's sorry for: this minor trespass with Lillian, or Goldie's absence, the deep cold of January and the deeper cold abroad, the blank envelopes in the next room, or the way duress distorts her social grace. When she's possessed of herself, Sadie will not want to remember this moment, this vulnerability with Lillian; as the women who cry in the store may later be standoffish, needing the shield of formality, perhaps resenting Lillian for witnessing what they would choose to forget. Or as men act after making love and returning to the world, distant, denying intimacy. Lillian has learned to behave as if nothing has transpired. And with Sadie there is, too, the element of refusal: it's possible she'd have Lillian revert to Miss Schumacher. But now she is Lillian, and Sadie is bereft.

"Sadie, you have to understand. I have no influence here," Lillian says. She offers Sadie a handkerchief, pours her a glass of water, and refills the sherry.

"I suppose I shouldn't have asked," Sadie says.

"I would have done the same." It's true; in loyalty you ask for all you can. Rudeness does not count. And Sadie is, if nothing else, loyal to Goldie, though hers is a loyalty mixed with other, veiled impulses. "The sherry's not bad," Lillian says. "I only keep it here in winter. A treat at the end of the day."

"It's very good." Sadie's gathering herself now, the teariness subsiding. "Bill would like it."

"How is Bill? And your girls? "

"Fine," Sadie says. "They're all fine. Your brother? Bertha?"

What does one say about Bertha? Here are the worries, here the bewilderment: unimaginable, how she—or anyone else—will ever be unburdened. But Sadie can do nothing about it.

"All right," Lillian says. "Moshe and Bertha are fine."

There is the slightest hesitation in Sadie. "I'm glad." She gathers her hat and gloves. "We'll see you at temple on Friday?" Her car is just outside, and although there's snow, the streets aren't bad yet. She wishes Lillian a good evening. And then she is gone.

Patience, Lillian thinks, *goat*. She pictures her house undisturbed and the cats sleeping, unaware of anything beyond the furnace heat and heavy sofa, the bowls of water, the bowls of food. *The dead are dead*. Tonight, Abe will stay with her. Their time is not infinite.

CHAPTER 18

Goldie

1943

The Japanese seamstress with the sandpiper walk has disappeared and in her wake there is a strange chattering rush: though no one speaks of her, it is as if her movements, that quick flightiness, have reshaped the town. Everyone walks and speaks more quickly, speeding versions of themselves. Or maybe it is simply the town filtered through Goldie's own hurry, her pinched sense of nowhere to flee. The cities her mother desired, Warsaw and Paris, are impossible. All of Europe is impossible and worse. "Where can we go?" she asks Ted, the man she sometimes dates. He's fifty-five and has fled only a marriage. "What are you talking about?" he says. "What's wrong with here?"

In Venice Beach a carnival persists, patriotic, hysterical in its enthusiasms. The sailors show up days before their tours, the dance halls are filled with young girls kissing and even marrying new soldiers. She always prefers the more deserted hours and stretches of beach. She should not walk alone at night—Ted warns her, her friends tell her not to—but she likes the deepest dark, the black-outs, the starriness and the night's accompanying clarities. Even the jagged-edged clarity that she's afraid to ask about the seamstress.

And then there is a letter from Sadie, who is not the seamstress and knows nothing of the seamstress, but somehow the two
moments link in Goldie's mind, a seamstress has disappeared and
Sadie—the real Sadie—has stepped out of the shadows after more
than a decade. The envelope has the handwriting of formal invitation, the paper is dark cream. She recognizes the writing before
she reads the return address, the beautiful script Sadie labored
over when she was young. Nothing like Irving's scrawl, which
twice a year arrives on cards that are like glass, slick surfaces that
offer only that everyone is fine, disaster has not struck. Goldie sits
at the kitchen table and opens the letter with a butter knife. In it
is a single page on which Sadie writes that she thinks of Goldie
often and hopes she is well. Irving is in boot camp. It is kind of
her to think of Celia. Sadie has two daughters (and here Goldie's
imagination fails, she can picture only two small Sadies). Goldie is
of course welcome to visit any time, Sadie says, and includes the
same unfamiliar return address.

Goldie has become a woman who rarely cries. It's as if crying
were finite, and she has completed that part of her life. But something is loosened by Sadie's handwriting. There is the clear shape
of Sadie's life, suddenly real despite the vagueness and brevity of
the letter. *For reasons I cannot explain*, Sadie said, but what does that
mean? Perhaps the shock of Irving's service convinced her to write.
It's never occurred to Goldie that Irving (the boy in the oak, the
scrawler of cards) would serve, though she can find no reason beyond her own blindness and terror. He is still of fighting age, and
as far as she knows a man without children, unmarried. But he is
Irving, and he should not be in a war zone, none of them should.
For an instant the idea of Irving at war merges with lost cities, as if
at this moment Irving is pinned in occupied Paris. *Irving is in boot
camp*, she reads again. There is a Georgia address.

You are welcome to visit any time. Is this what it takes then, a war, for
Sadie to write? And now, when their lives are irrevocably separate.
She pictures Sadie's life as a tea service, china or silver; Sadie has
no doubt become a woman of means, you can see it in the fineness
of the notepaper, the confidence of the words. Goldie's own life
seems littered with driftwood and half-read books, and what

would Sadie comprehend? But Sadie has written. It is far too late for Goldie to cross back, it is all far too late, but Sadie has written. Once they were sisters: it is something, to have a sister.

She will write back to Sadie, a brief, careful note. *Thank you,* she'll say, *I live near the beach. Thank you, I am fine.* But she would like to ask Sadie what has happened to the Japanese seamstress. She would like to ask where else there is to flee, if one should need another place. And also if Sadie is happy, if *happy* is a relevant word—just look at the girls and the soldiers at the pier—or if Sadie is not happy, what she thinks she is.

CHAPTER 19

Jo

1943

In winter Jo walks all the way to the jewelry store, just to walk, though the city is frozen: clear sky appears only during the deepest cold. Now she's drawn by the blue, cold but compelling, a color to fly into. Since the air show last summer she's been watching the sky more than usual, the shifts in the clouds, these rare open spans of blue; since the air show last summer she has imagined herself a pilot. She would choose this exact sky for flight, and the clothing to go with it: trousers, a short jacket, a cap like Amelia Earhart's. Amelia is not dead, Jo's sure, though her plane has been missing for years. Jo has worried for her but no, she's not dead, she's got herself to an island, the Pacific is loaded with islands. Amelia changed her plans and secluded herself. People do such things: Goldie did such a thing. But does Amelia know about the war? Which is no better-looking in the Pacific than it is in Europe.

Jo's insomnia is back, maybe because of the war and the way it unnerves her father, the risks of Irving's service; or maybe because in California, Goldie's risen from the dead. Celia sleeps—even knowing about Goldie, Celia sleeps beautifully. But Jo cannot, she paces and frets; after the first shock came relief, and even gratitude, but they have given way to more angry shock. When the sky opens up like this, it's better to be outside, the cold air a clearing. For a brief time nothing's in your way; for that moment, imagine flight.

Jo arrives at the store half-frozen at eight, long before opening. And Eli Abramowitz is waiting outside, thick-bodied in his overcoat, hat pulled down low over his ears, work gloves covering his hands. Deep brown beard, brown eyes casting about. Eli the grocer. Eli who was once a quiet boy in a fifth-grade classroom, pudgy, dreaming, a boy with a secret skill for drawing birds; you'd know it only if you sat at the next desk, which Jo did. The grocer's son, now a stocky balding grocer himself, his father a few years dead. Eli who lives with his mother and has never married, nor shown signs of wanting to marry, even during the brief period in high school when he politely escorted Delia Lefkowitz to Sunday concerts and never kissed her on the lips. Eli, the man Jo asks about potatoes. A harmless man—and most of them aren't—a man who looks after his mother and does not frequent jewelry stores. He belongs in his market, not here on the blue cold street, waiting—isn't he?—to choose a gift some woman will find persuasive.

"Good morning, Eli," she says, and the cold stings her teeth. She unlocks the security gate over the door and then the door itself, and walks into a flood of heat, waving him in after her. "What can I do for you?"

"I wonder," Eli says, "if I might speak to your father."

"He's at shul. He should be here by noon."

At this Eli bows slightly and excuses himself and leaves, back out into the cold.

Which is just as well. She's got inventory ahead, and bills to send out, and for one hour she will gather herself. Her father is always at temple now, all his fury and fear poured into prayer. And the radio is going night and day, and during the news broadcast's mention of Hitler, her father's hands will palpitate with anger, and he has to stop work until they calm themselves. But in other moments the rage abates, and he is not unkind to Jo; though he insists she wear skirt suits and visit the beauty shop, he talks to her. They have things to talk about now: the keeping of the store, the pricing of bracelets, the likelihood that Mr. Friedman will buy a sapphire for his wife, the terrible behavior of competitors. True, she isn't Irving, with Irving's good looks and smooth charm, but precisely so: she isn't Irving. Now the paperwork is prompt and accurate, free of discrepancies, the cash balance exact. Her father lets her work on the books, trusts her not to pilfer, and in rare moments now he calls her *Jo Jo* or *Josephina*, endearments from her childhood. There's a small but palpable comfort in being at the store with him, though when he is out for too long and business is off, the emptiness unnerves her. Once or twice a day, there's a moment when the store seems like the molted skin of an animal, abandoned and frail, a hairsbreadth from disintegrating in the January wind.

All fine here, Goldie wrote. It's a sentence Jo could not write, but now knowing of this sentence, Jo feels clammy and unwashed, her body itself a kind of squalor. Alive and all fine here, the *here* that should have been Jo's, and Goldie, snatching it, sealed Jo's fate, apparently without regret. It's true, if she had said good-bye, Jo would have demanded she stay, but that excuses nothing. There was a hidden doorway, and Goldie found it first, walked through and shut the door, leaving Jo behind with the specter of another death. And no other doorways have appeared to Jo. *All fine here.* It's likely Goldie has always been fine, has never felt a moment of not-fineness: *all fine* for thirteen years. *All fine* though each year for Jo the moodiness of birthdays descends, including Goldie's, on which the sky always seems threatening, whether or not a storm is due. Goldie's birthday, the day that seems more somber and strange than any other; the day when you do not want to go anywhere, when you want to huddle in the house and seal the doors tight, as if a bad wind might carry you off. On Goldie's birthday this is what Jo and Celia in silent accord do. It is not deliberate. The day is washed out, every December 5 a day of paralysis Jo does not remember until the next December, but today, in January, each one seems perfectly clear to her laid end to end, a string of onyx beads. Days stolen—some apparently by Irving—just as the earlier shocked months were stolen, and all the time she's stood in for Goldie: time Jo deserves to have back.

Goldie betrayed her. Irving betrayed her (though it's true he has no will, Goldie could have roped him into it). *All fine* but not here, not today: blue skies but increasing wind the newspaper calls *lashing*. The store by eleven o'clock seems an abandoned outpost, the clamminess all through her now. And there is no remedy but to call Sadie, just to hear Sadie pick up the phone and speak to Jo from a house, with her arrogant belief in the solidity of the world. "Heard anything?" Jo says.

"Jo. Good morning." Sadie confirms that she has heard nothing from Goldie, and asks what it is that Jo needs just now. And for the moment the wind seems an ordinary wind, the store perfectly itself.

Just after noon, her father arrives, melancholy, immaculate, and turns on the radio news. "Shame," he says, but he is not speaking to her, he is speaking to the broadcaster. "A quiet morning, Jo?" he says, returning to the room. He smoothes his jacket sleeves and checks his pocket watch.

"A few customers." She shows him the receipts. He tells her to take a break if she'd like, have something to eat, though he's the one who looks exhausted. It takes effort not to ask him about Goldie: Sadie tried but got nowhere, and just look at him, how thin and papery he is. You have to be careful.

At one o'clock Eli Abramowitz returns, asking again for her father, who is at his bench. Eli waits silently, gazing at the display cases the way he used to stare out the windows at school. She pictures birds perched on top of math problems, flying through his notebook margins. "How's your mother, Eli?" she says.

"She's well, thank you."

"I'm glad."

"Yeah, she's well."

"Can I get you anything?"

"No. Thanks, no. I'll just wait for Mr. Cohen."

"He won't be long."

"That's fine."

Her father emerges, his melancholy more hidden. "Eli, hello. How are you?" he says. "Come talk with me. How is your mother?"

He ushers Eli into the back office and closes the door. She can hear murmurs, but two older ladies come into the store, one in a fur-trimmed coat and lipstick the color of day-old meat, the other in deep gray wool, trailing a chokingly sweet perfume. They want to look at pearl sets.

There is the sound of a door opening and closing, a second, heavier door—the back—echoing.

"Of course." Jo leads the ladies to the center display case. "What would you like to see?"

The perfumed lady points to a short string, luminous white. "Just how much are those?"

Jo unlocks the case and leans down to check the tag, and her father appears at the counter beside her, telling the woman, "You have a good eye. Those on the right, they are very fine, I was lucky to get them in New York." And Jo excuses herself and recedes to the counter space near the register, while her father talks to the women about pearls and how to choose the best ones, how elegantly they fall, beautiful with simple things. He shows them four necklace and earring sets, and you can see the women warm up to him, simple and elegant was exactly what they were thinking, the lipstick lady's daughter is engaged. Still young you understand, this is a gift.

"Ah. A gift from a mother to a daughter." He nods slightly while he looks the mother in the eye, smiles. Then gives them time to consider, busying himself with a nearby display. Jo absents herself altogether, hovering in the short back hall. Sometimes it's better when she isn't visible, the very fact of her dampening customers' enthusiasm, as if they sense her clamminess and squalor. Her father does not say this directly, but when he's there he always shows the higher-priced pieces. It takes only a few more minutes for him to make the sale. Then there's a brief flurry of customers, men on lunch break looking for watches and small gifts for their girlfriends and wives, before the store quiets.

"Jo," her father says. "You know Eli Abramowitz?"

"Eli who was just here."

"Eli has asked my permission to court you."

"What?"

"Eli has asked my permission to take you on a date," Abe says, his expression inscrutable, a careful mask. "I have given him my permission."

"I see," Jo says, though she doesn't see at all. In the navy blue suit she looks like a stuffed, aging seal. Too old for children. Why would Eli Abramowitz or anyone else court her? If he needs a housekeeper, he can hire one. What else could he possibly want? No, she doesn't see. She hasn't since high school hoped for men to see anything in her: she is bored by their company, alarmed by their proximity. They gradually learned to stay away, her last few dates all in the years before her mother's illness. And she is not seeking this attention—adamantly not—from Eli the grocer or any other man.

"You mind the store," her father says. "I've got to finish the Rosenblum ring."

He moves slowly and in the doorway appears to her an old man; she glances away. Automobiles skid along Main Street, one lurching into a snowbank. What *does* she seek? The question draws a dizzy blank. Nothing? How can the answer be nothing? She wants years back. But here and now? She wanted an automobile and she got one, and in the warmer weather there's pleasure in driving it. Often she wants candy, pastry, pie. She wants the store to remain solid and intact. She wants her father to stop listening to the war, it's doing him no good, just look at him. She wants Celia to stay calm. But none of this seems exactly right. What then? There's the other kind of seeking, of course, private, beyond the divide of daily life, the kind you don't tell Eli Abramowitz or anyone else about. Seeking, say, a plane. Amelia and her plane and her island. Imagining yourself in the cockpit of a plane flying over a vast ocean and bearing down on a string of islands, choosing one island for no other reason than the feeling it gives you, as if it in particular is watching you, waiting for you, and the feeling turns out to be right. Amelia's there alone, glad for the company. She's relieved that it's Jo, gratified and a little amazed that of all people, Jo's the one to find her. Jo whom Amelia has heard of, has wondered about. It could have been a navy pilot finding her, or worse. The navy has some real buffoons. Isn't, for example, Jo's brother in the navy?

Army, Jo confesses.

Army then, Amelia says. *Would you count on him to rescue you? To rescue anyone?*

He hasn't been helpful so far, Jo says.

Precisely my point. But here you are, Amelia says. *We have plans to make.*

And in haste too—they can't stay on this island long, the Enemy will find them. Jo's exhausted, but Amelia is rested and ready to fly. They set out for Hawaii. And the world drops away, it's just the two of them in the sky, and then the two of them on the famous shores of Hawaii, where they have meals of sweet fish and fruit, and rest in the sun the way Jo and her sisters used to at Crystal Beach.

It has been a long time since Jo lay in the sun anywhere. Once, months after Goldie disappeared, she drove east alone, to the meadows and farms just after harvest, the stripped-down cornstalks gold stubble in the fields, the grasses still high. An autumn warm spell. And she lay in the grass and slept there and awakened for a brief few minutes to another life, made of grass and sun and crickets and the warm melting feeling of her body after sleep, a pure contentment. And she paid attention for once to the grass itself, its lightness and height, the way the red-and-gold-flecked green seemed to hold all possibilities within it, all in arm's reach, there for the taking. The meadow seemed open to her as no place and no person was; and Jo herself had never felt such unlonely openness, one miraculous instant of knowing, before it seemed intolerable. Before she had to close her eyes, trying to fix it in her mind, though it could not be fixed. Perhaps it had moved to another point in the meadow; or to a nearby grove of trees; and so she rose and looked beyond the meadow to the roads and farmhouses, the tractors, the masses of clouds moving fast from the west and north; and then noticed the thin cloth of her shoes, the surprising smallness of her wrists—which have since thickened as all of her has thickened—and the moment had already dispersed. In a nearby pasture, cows grazed careless of her, simply standing and grazing, cows for the moment free of the farmers and the barn and the drudgery of milk.

BY MIDAFTERNOON the sky has clouded again. More snow. When the mailman arrives, her father glances through the stack of envelopes and hands it over to Jo to sort, as is his habit. Today, there is nothing personal or hastily handwritten, nothing from out of state. She opens and dates the invoices, prepares a bank deposit, calls the travel agent with dates for her father's next buying trip. And just as she's readying to leave, to find a bus home and start dinner, he tells her, "Jo, stay to closing today. Celia can fix the supper, yes?" Which in fact she can, Celia's a better cook than she lets on, she just doesn't stay with it long enough: the problem is planning and cooking consecutive meals. It's hard to know if this is deliberate or not, but you can't blame Celia for dodging the chore.

"Fine, then." Jo takes off her coat and begins to plan the February display: rubies, garnets, diamonds, pearls arranged on red and white satin hearts.

Just before closing, Eli Abramowitz returns. The same overcoat, the same hat, but different gloves now, gentlemen's gloves, and below his coat a suit. Jo is counting garnet earrings, marking down the number and size on her notepad while Eli hovers on the far side of the display case. She would like to hide beneath the case, in the storage area for gift boxes and wrapping and register receipts, though only a small child would fit, and of course there's no avoiding Eli now. She is lumpy and awkward, her face hot. Eli waits in his good clothes, holding his hat, finally saying, "Hi, Jo."

And Jo says, stupidly, "Hi."

"Would you like to go to the pictures with me?" One earnest, baritone sentence.

And when she hesitates, he says, "I asked your father's permission," as if to reassure her. Eli Abramowitz, who is pink-cheeked from the cold and standing by the garnets, breathes like an ordinary person, but maybe an intent ordinary person. Her own breathing seems to have a different rhythm, faster, unsyncopated, it's hard to keep track of both rhythms at once, but she listens, closes a fist around an earring, smooth and sharp against her palm. She pictures the interior of Shea's Theatre, the gilded boxes and gold-framed murals, the vast dome and the velvet curtains, and the way the darkness comes upon you gradually, and the screen fills with the exquisite faces of women.

"All right." The words coming to her of their own accord, altering this strange breathing moment.

Eli smiles and allows his hand to rest on top of the jewelry case. "Tomorrow?"

"SO YOU TALKED to Eli," her father says. They are in his Ford, navigating the uneven, snow-slick street. Traffic noise surrounds them but he has turned off the radio, freeing them for the moment from the war.

And Jo feels the heat in her face again, the wish to disappear. "Yes," she says, but nothing more, and he glances at her and back at the street. Beyond the windshield the air is dense with new snow, and the wipers scrape against the glass, where a line of ice accumulates and frames Ferry Street, then Delaware. He does not turn the radio back on, and instead drives with her in a silence that is neither hostile nor revealing, a plain silence spread over the fact of Eli.

When they enter the house, before he has hung up his overcoat, her father turns on the radio in the parlor, and stands listening to the hourly broadcast and asks nothing more.

Celia's at the kitchen table reading the funnies. She's still dressed for the Red Cross—a wool skirt and sweater, her hair pinned back with barrettes. "Busy today, I guess," Celia says. She's warmed the cold brisket, roasted potatoes, boiled red cabbage. Nothing in the kitchen is amiss: if only you could count on her every day. But she cooks only on a lark, or as a favor granted when the mood strikes.

"Busy, yes," Jo says and stirs the cabbage for the sake of stirring.

"You all right?"

"Fine," Jo says. *All fine here.* "A little distracted."

And Celia draws close, confiding, pulling her blue sweater tight and tapping Jo on the shoulder. "When Irving comes back you won't have to work at the store," she whispers.

The air pops with bits of a radio report from London, there's a sweet-savory smell to the meat, and Jo rubs her hands together: it's impossible to keep her hands warm. She's hardly thought of Irving today, except as a betrayer. Not the Irving Celia's invoking—Irving at boot camp, soon to cross one or another violent ocean. "You're right," Jo says. And Celia returns to the funnies.

She'll talk about Eli Abramowitz later, Jo decides. After supper, when their father has finished his tea and left for his room or Lillian the Tart's. Later would be best. Jo will be nonchalant. *By the way*, she'll say, as Sadie would. *By the way, I'll be out tomorrow evening. Eli—you know Eli from the market? Eli asked me to the pictures with him, so I'll be out a while.*

Jo silently practices the phrasing while she rinses a water pitcher, and then the silence gives way—some mumbling leaks out—and Celia says, "You seem odd today."

"A little distracted."

"You said."

"By the way," Jo says.

"What?"

"I'll be out tomorrow."

"Uh-huh."

"Eli Abramowitz asked me to the pictures."

"Eli?"

"You know, from the market."

"I know Eli." Celia turns back to the funnies, and after a moment rises and carries them to the parlor, where their father dozes in his armchair in his overcoat. Celia curls up on the sofa and fixes her gaze on him.

Jo follows only as far as the parlor door. "Don't you want dinner?"

"No," Celia says.

Jo shrugs, takes her dinner in the kitchen, and slips away to her room without saying good night to anyone.

In the morning there's an unsigned note on the kitchen table in Celia's hand: *Unfortunately, I will be unavailable for dinner this evening.*

THE IDEA of going to the pictures with Eli is separate from Eli the grocer. An anxious thing, an absurd thing. At work, Jo can't decide what she'll wear. Perhaps the green wool dress, though with all the snow, there's no avoiding her heavy, graceless boots. Sadie's are sleeker: everything about Sadie is sleeker, even the way she thinks, no doubt she married to keep up that sleekness. No, Jo's boots are clunky and solid and unmarried, and don't match the green dress. They ought to. But Jo can't feign sleekness; everyone knows that. Surely Eli the grocer knows that. And what if he finds her boots absurd? She's aware of the strangeness of feet: she doesn't want Eli thinking about her feet, and she doesn't want to consider his man's feet, the broadness or narrowness of his toes, the smoothness or sprinkling of hair. No. Forget about feet. Forget about boots. Amelia wouldn't worry about boots. It's winter: one must wear boots. Jo is ridiculous, and she hates being ridiculous, how irritating to find oneself in this state. She has no wish for a man. She is no good at soothing, particularly the soothing of men, she has never wanted a husband, has never understood those women who want husbands, and give themselves over to husbands, like Sadie, like Lucia Mazzano.

Just before the war, Jo glimpsed Lucia Mazzano on the street, pregnant, no longer Lucia Mazzano but instead Lucia Santora, married to that Anthony. Lucia at first alone on Main Street, and then holding the hand of a three- or four-year-old girl, and walking with her own mother, the keeper of the saints. A picture unraveling out in the street in which you witness dry-eyed what your life is not. A scene of the mother attending to the daughter who attends to the daughter. Jo could envision herself nowhere. Jo would never be pregnant, not a chance, but if she were a man she would marry and make her wife pregnant. She'd do it, she would. And there on Main Street she felt a wild fluttering at the thought of taking her wife in such a way, a thrill sustainable for the briefest moment before Lucia and her mother and the girl stopped at a shoe store and Lucia pushed open the door. Lucia, who was fat with Anthony's child, had let herself be touched in that way by Anthony, which was too much to bear. More little Anthonys running around Buffalo, little *dagos*, Jo thought, the word surfacing as Lucia disappeared from view, and Jo stared across Main Street, willing Lucia both to return and to vanish forever. After a moment

Jo's list of errands reasserted itself and she moved on with her morning. And now she rarely thinks of Lucia Mazzano, though that word sometimes hovers, two steps from *dog*. Once Jo said it on the phone to Sadie, and Sadie cut her off, saying "Hush," a rough, commanding "Hush," nothing like the soothing one Sadie offers other people.

Did Jo ever shop with her mother? She had only the smallest part in her mother's life, can hardly remember the two of them alone, though some mornings, even now, she has the fleeting impression that she might walk down to the kitchen and find her mother awake, drinking tea at the table, as she had once done. A slight smile. Her mother could put her finger to her lips and motion for Jo to pour herself a cup from the white-and-blue teapot. They could sip the hot tea while light fills the yard—the sky rimmed with pink and yellow, snow turning from blue to white. This must have occurred, but mostly Jo remembers the chaos of breakfast, her mother speaking with exaggerated patience to Celia.

FOR HALF the morning Jo works on the store's Valentine's Day advertisement, which this year will have hearts but not cupids. Idiotic, cupids. She tells the ad man at the *Courier*, no cupids. Because of the war, she says, hearts but not cupids.

Business is light. She checks and rechecks her father's ledgers, staving off the moment when the building molts and the walls thin. But the black ink numbers seem to sink into the ledger pages, a corrosive patterning, and the wind gusts whip fallen snow upward outside the store, and the radio's bright piano music mocks the day. At ten-thirty Jo calls Sadie, but it isn't Sadie who answers the phone, it's that Rosalie, and Jo hangs up.

Unfortunately, I will be unavailable for dinner. Celia and her note, taking a lesson from Goldie. An unwitting conspiracy—or perhaps more deliberate? *Unfortunately, I will be in California.* Where all is fine. Where Jo is smaller than an afterthought, so distant as to be invisible. Is that what Celia wants today? What Goldie chose: to make Jo invisible, to keep her invisible, Goldie never once writing to say *I am not dead.* Never offering an explanation or apology, never asking forgiveness, as if there is nothing to explain or forgive, as if Jo's forgiveness is dust, Jo herself dust. Jo can see no recourse with Goldie (the thief). From Celia she deserves better. Celia with her Red Cross and her clean clothes and her combed hair: for now she is washing, for now she is *fine* and Jo gets to be dust.

BUT ELI, the real Eli, does not treat her like dust. He picks her up at the house in a Chevrolet much newer than his truck, and he is dressed in a jacket and tie, just for the pictures a jacket and tie. He leads her through the snow, opens doors for her. He suggests *The Palm Beach Story*, which takes place in Florida. With all the snow wouldn't it be nice to be in Florida? Eli says.

"Much better than California." Jo tells him she often daydreams about beaches.

In the dark theater Eli sits beside her, straight-backed and attentive, and halfway through the film she is startled to discover his hand on hers, his shy glance. His hand is large and warm and doughy, not unpleasant really, and she does not pull away. Through the rest of the film they hold hands, which is partly pleasurable and partly unnerving. They are still holding hands at the end of the film, when the house lights come up: how does one stop such a thing? Isn't the man supposed to stop? She's relieved to put on her coat. And then Eli drives her home. "Thank you, Eli," she says. "Thank you for the evening." He makes a gesture to walk her to the door, leans slightly in her direction, but she wishes him good night and hurries out of the Chevy and up to the quiet house.

Her father's Ford is gone, which means he's with the Tart. The kitchen is clean, and there is no additional note. Upstairs, Celia's asleep. Jo washes and changes into her nightgown and climbs into bed, where she stays awake to the hush of falling snow, something palpable, that hush, like sound being drained from the city. The flannel of her nightgown rubs against her skin when she moves, there are low electric sparks along her belly and legs, and she thinks of yachts from the movie and Eli Abramowitz's hand, that warm hand running along her arm and under her nightgown. But then there's a wave of queasiness, his hand—its irrefutable fleshiness—too much to imagine, and she tries to banish the image from her mind, wrapping the gown closer around herself, pulling the pile of blankets up, so the bed is its usual warm cocoon. She thinks of the woman in the movie traveling to Florida to change her life, and the preponderance of men in Florida. Perhaps it is different in Hawaii; perhaps the men are all on battleships, readying for combat. Pacific islands will be shelled, though not Amelia's, and not any island Irving is on, he's in Georgia, not on an island, at least not now. In Georgia it may be snowing tonight—there's enough snow here to drift southward on the map, to pile up in Georgia as well, isn't there?—endless snow, January is like this. Eli wanted to walk her to the door. Held her hand again in his car, before she left without kissing him—was she supposed to kiss him? Or let him kiss her. The oddness of kissing through a beard she cannot imagine, but his hands she can imagine, they are real and what if those hands were to touch her, to move over her, those grocer's hands, if she let him do *that*, then what? She does not know, but imagines his hand moving over her, moving down between her legs, and the feeling is a wild open blueness and a kind of racing, and there's the snow hush and the hotness of the bed, the heat of a summer sky, heat of a blue sky, and a swaying dampness, as if she herself were in the Pacific. A kind of flight, and the face of Amelia, in close-up like Claudette Colbert, but it's not Claudette, it's Amelia, and you have to take her when she is so close, take her before she fades out, before the swooning ends, such swooning and heat, dizzy circles blurring and blurring and blurring, a drop into pure cloud.

And still she cannot sleep. The image of Eli's hand is again alternately tender and grubby; she recoils, but not every moment, as if the tenderness distracts her from recoiling, or perhaps she is lured in just enough to make recoiling possible. He is luring her with his hands. She does not want to be lured. After the hands other things follow. After the hands, he would expect to press himself against her, into her, maybe taking her apart—which is what men do, even Eli would. It's three o'clock in the morning. Why he'd expect such things from Jo she cannot fathom.

CELIA IS neatly dressed for the third day in a row, unusually concerned with the morning headlines. Their father eats a slice of toast and pores over the Jewish papers. It's as if they're both searching through the black-and-white pages for something essential. Her father is mild today, careful in the way he asks Celia for the jam. "Here, Papa." Celia smiles at him, then goes back to her paper, pointedly ignoring Jo. It's not a stance Celia can maintain without great effort, can she? All this cleanliness and calm and getting along.

Nobody says anything about the date with Eli, but Eli Abramowitz, tender or not, grubby or not, may be Jo's last chance for a life beyond Lancaster. A chance she did not expect. Marriage, the kind of chance she'd never seek, but with Eli would it be so bad? Here is her father in his freshly pressed suit, clean shaven, his breathing labored as he scours the *Forward*, and Celia pretending to be fine. And what is happening at Eli's house? Is his mother also scouring the *Forward*? And Eli? Drinking coffee, drawing sparrows? Jo, teacup in hand, imagines herself in some liminal space between houses, parachuting down through the snow, glimpsing her father and Celia through one window, Eli and Mrs. Abramowitz through another, the white ground dotted with canned vegetables and sacks of sugar and pearls on satin hearts.

IT'S AFTERNOON when Eli drops by the store. "I would like to take you to dinner," he says. "Saturday. How about Saturday?"

She's watching his hands. "Lookit," she says, "I'm no prize."

"What are you doing Saturday, Jo?"

"I'm not the type for this, you know?"

He is silent for a moment. "Would you like to have dinner Saturday?"

"I don't know," Jo says.

And Eli nods, his face reddening. "Okay. I'll call you tomorrow." He quickly leaves, the bells on the outer door jingling as he closes it.

And then she feels herself at the edge of things, a sickly haze in the room. If the snow would stop she'd leave now, she ought to leave now anyway, drive to the snow-filled farms and orchards and find a diner. Lockport maybe. Where she could drink coffee and eat a slice of cake and speak to no one, and not think, just breathe in the anonymity, the small pretend life of a woman at a diner. Which is how far from any other life? A life in California, say, or the life of a man at a diner, or the life of a pilot. A thick dizziness passes over her, a wavering, as if she's had liquor and is now buried in lostness, the edges of the world collapsing, right here behind the cuff links, the steel cash register could slide away and the room fragment as the city's swept bit by bit over the lake ice to open water, then into the mouth of the Niagara and down the icy rapids and over the Falls, to flow north unseen beneath the ice bridge into Ontario and toward the sea. A vast watery maw even larger than the lake, in which people drown and are lost, bones never retrieved. From the back room her father's radio reports new rationing, and bombs falling on London. If Goldie hadn't disappeared, Jo would know what to seek, wouldn't she? She would know.

She calls Sadie, even with her father at the store Jo calls Sadie, who answers exasperated. But Jo's voice is pinched, Jo herself pinched inside the layers of stuffing, and she asks if Sadie is thinking of coming by the store.

"What's wrong?" Sadie says.

"Nothing. Come take a look at the rubies."

"What's going on, Jo? I've got to get the girls. What's this about rubies?"

Jo doesn't know: it must be like this for Celia sometimes.

"Make sense, Jo. What is it?"

And Jo gathers herself. "Just thought your husband might buy you some," she says.

"Really Jo." And there's Sadie's habitual sigh. "I'm sure they're beautiful. Papa always picks good ones." There's a pause on the line, faint voices of strangers popping up and dispersing. "Did you sleep?" Sadie says.

"A little."

"I know you're upset about Goldie. But you can't go without sleep." Sadie's talking the way she would talk to her daughters, the way she would talk to Celia, Jo can hear the sureness and slight condescension. A tone that usually makes Jo balk, but not today, when the room is so fragile.

"Maybe I'll go home early," Jo says. "Maybe I'll sleep then."

She'll wait until four, she tells herself, she'll keep to the usual time, because further breaking the routine could break other things. She fidgets. She paces. Her father takes more pearls from the safe and restocks the display case, carefully arranging the strands. The postal delivery arrives, and he glances through the mail—there he is again, glancing through the mail. For how many years has he done this?

The words spill out of her as if someone else is speaking them. "Know anyone in California, Papa?"

He pauses and studies her for what seems a long time. Tilts his head. There's a slight trembling in his hands, from the question or the radio news or his age. "No," he says firmly. "You dreaming about pictures, Josephina? Hollywood?"

Jo feels the clamminess again, the room fragile as blown glass, and she imagines the movie yachts in Florida set loose from their docks, drifting in the sea toward Mexico. Nothing today is anchored.

"Maybe I'll take Celia to a show," she says.

For a moment he seems a frozen image of himself, his lips pressed together, the slightest sag in his shoulders. Anchor, Jo thinks, be an anchor. Say *Josephina* again. But he's motionless: it's terrible, the way he leaves like this.

She should not have mentioned California. How stupid—but now she's done it and he is traveling away. And she must find the right thing to make him return, to make the day stop tilting so wildly.

"Maybe Saturday," she tells him. There is no thought of Eli. "We can go Saturday night."

Finally her father summons himself, straightens his jacket, and offers the briefest of smiles. "Yes," he says. "Find a picture you like." If his face reveals regret (could that be it? Regret? The expression passes too quickly to be sure), she does not know the source.

"Have a good time," he says. He draws his wallet from his jacket pocket and offers her a dollar for the show.

CHAPTER 20

Irving

1943–45

He tried to follow Leo's advice, which arrived in frequent letters, and he did not know whether his assignment in Somerset was Schumacher luck or his own. After his unit shipped out he was transferred—it seemed at first the worst of luck, to be separated from the unit on arriving in Europe, everyone said so—but Rogers drove him to Yeovil and he got his assignment stocking a PX and driving in supplies. There were orchards in Somerset, and moors and hill country, and when he was driving the war itself would recede. He had a steady flow of cigarettes and beer and after a time he met a brunette named Meg. Maybe, he thought, Schumacher influence reached into the war itself.

During air raids he would fall into a panic that seemed a cold lagoon, and he would sweat through his shirts and carry a sourness with him until he could change: he had managed to requisition extra underclothes because of the sweating, but even so he could not always keep up. Driving past a bomb crater near Bristol he stopped and surveyed the damage and tried from then on to take other routes. This was easiest when he was alone and didn't have to explain circuitous detours, but when he couldn't detour he would sweat (humiliating that a hole in the ground made him sweat) and pretend the crater was from a different era, a loose, anomalous event that had jimmied itself free and smacked awkwardly into the English countryside.

At boot camp there had been the hard shock of being always Irving, and an Irving whittled down to bone, suspended in barren space: Private Cohen. *Keep your head down,* Leo told him. *Head down.* There were the deadly boring drills and exhaustion, the moments when adrenaline flared and the moments when he felt too tired to be afraid. *Pay attention,* Leo told him. *Listen.* In the barracks with the other men—kids, really, some barely eighteen—Irving said he was from Buffalo, he'd had a few girlfriends, and his family owned a jewelry business. Then he said he was the buyer for the store and took occasional trips to New York City. This did not seem so much of a stretch: in time he would be a buyer. But Leo's instructions echoed—*Don't talk big*—as if Leo were in the room; Irving would make himself stop and shrug. He didn't know the city very well, only a few hotels, a few ordinary restaurants. Really it was all business. The recruits who did know New York would jump in then and take the spotlight, and describe the city in technicolor details which he memorized.

In the early mornings when his bunk was still warm he felt a hazy sense of his bed at Lancaster—the air outside cool, the light beginning, the sensation of burrowing deeper—and he could imagine a different day ahead. First would be the necessity of washing and finding his suit, but the disruption of rising would be ameliorated by his walk in the city: here was the vast pendulous sky, buildings rising high above the broadest street, shops readying to open, legions of cars, the traces of the night still fading. A coffee shop for breakfast, which made him feel again like a city man, a traveler. Alone, he could relax with his coffee, his paper, and a fleeting royal feeling would come over him the moment the waitress set down his plate of eggs and smiled. By the time he finished his breakfast and paid, he felt prepared to open the store. He walked to lower Main Street, the weather easy—it would be May—and opened the metal gates over the windows, and the front door, and entered the silent shop, its thick rug and gleaming cases of necklaces, cuff links, rings, all intimating grand hotels and romance. For part of each morning, Irving could be the distinguished proprietor. This role sustained him for an hour (though its appeal ebbed and he grew bored); then there would be the relief of his father's arrival, the relinquishing of responsibility.

Mornings in his bunk he could conjure the waitress (more beautiful now, the smile more inviting), the plates of toast and eggs, the moment of unlocking the shop, but at night there was only blankness. On the dullest days his life felt tinny and airless, and he found relief in physical exhaustion. There were no women, no one touched him, and this seemed almost impossible to withstand. He found himself missing even the women who arrived at the store perfumed and smiled at him indulgently and left. In the mail he received occasional letters from Lillian Schumacher, which made him happy and unaccountably wistful; and frequent letters from Sadie, elegantly written and chatty. He paid little attention to the content of Sadie's correspondence but felt soothed by it nonetheless, the way he did when he sat in her living room and listened not to her actual words but to the music of her voice. And then she made the fuss about Goldie, and for a few days he wished she would stop writing and leave him be. All that polite fury, which came as a surprise, a shock, really—his feet were blistered from marching and he'd bruised his elbow, and the brief pleasure of holding the envelope was canceled by Sadie's slap. The fact of Goldie's life seemed to him indisputable: Sadie could hardly have thought Goldie was dead. She'd known better from the start, hadn't she? True, his awareness of her ignorance had slipped into a kind of nether space: years ago he'd stopped thinking about it. He had wrestled for a brief time with the matter, but then there were reasons, weren't there? Goldie's privacy to protect. Goldie could have written to Sadie anytime she wanted. This was not his fault.

Still, when there was a brief interruption in mail delivery, he missed Sadie's letters and was glad when they resumed, at first with a cool tone and later warmer though always without money. Goldie sent him a postcard with a picture of a carousel near the ocean, and Celia wrote two letters in careful script, one describing the latest pictures she'd seen, the other about her walks and her cat. And his father wrote to him, elliptical letters that seemed to be about Russian and Polish villages in a time before Irving existed.

Always there were the letters from Leo, with regular advice, some of it repeated for emphasis. *Do not establish a reputation,* Leo said. *Watch the cards.* And Irving was managing to keep his head above water in the barracks' poker games. He joined games but did not sponsor them and never stayed in until the very end, though he wanted to. *Stick to low stakes and get out early,* Leo had said. *You can't afford more trouble.*

The moment he was reassigned felt like tumbling down an endless flight of stairs. *Bad luck, sorry, Cohen,* the others said, real worry in their faces. Sweat leaked through his shirt. *Luck of the draw,* the sergeant said, but Irving did not know if this was true. He was older than the other men, and nowhere near the most agile. He was Jewish. Had he ticked off a superior? He had kept his head down, held to Leo's advice. For a few hours the falling continued—it seemed even his borrowed luck had run out, and then he was driven to a storybook town in the country, and introduced to his commander, a straight arrow named Leyton, and to a beautiful, roughly built PX.

At first he did not comprehend the locals, though their accents appealed to him, and he worked to understand and privately to imitate the sounds. He was grateful for pubs. He was grateful for the predictable routines of stocking shelves, of selling tobacco and beer and soap and tallying accounts. Often Somerset was startlingly quiet, and he braced himself for disruption: he knew he could be reassigned again at any time.

Most of the units coming through were new troops on their way to combat, and often they seemed like neighborhood kids; for a time Irving would strike up conversations and join their card games, but as soon as the unit was ordered to mobilize, he'd make himself scarce. There were other men convalescing before returning to action, and these men he tended to avoid, as they seemed haunted or naïvely patriotic. Occasionally they would talk to him anyway. The most likable of them, a Midwesterner named Graham, was worried about his buddies and spoke urgently of getting back to them. It was idiocy to return only to be wounded again or killed, and Irving said nothing. You could give only so much for men you'd just met, none of whom were Leo: Graham was a well-intentioned fool. Irving offered him a cigarette, and Graham accepted with a serious nod, and as Irving held out the lit match, he was nonetheless jolted by a quick, stinging wish for Graham's loyalty.

He followed Leo's advice to avoid the prostitutes—*Half the army has the clap, Irving, you have to watch it*—but the isolation in his own body seemed a kind of punishment, a flintiness just beneath his skin. After two months he met Meg: she was in her early twenties and soft-hearted, a little shy, with a small round face that reminded him of opals and budding leaves. He took her to a dance and brought her cigarettes and sweets from the PX. And then he began to break curfew to be with her in the evening, which was not what Leo would have recommended—but Leo shared a bed every night with his wife, and had been born lucky. Irving went to Meg's tiny flat and she undressed and touched him—it almost made him cry, Meg touching him—and she seemed to him remarkable, her body, her pale skin astonishing. And when he was inside her the flintiness dissolved, he felt immersed in syrupy hot light, and nothing was painful, and the world seemed defined by this liquid sensation he now called Meg.

FOR MONTHS Leyton gave no sign of a transfer order, and Irving began to relax. It seemed strange that Irving's luck would arrive with the war but he did not question it: his life had shifted, and he had become a lucky man. The men at the front were not so lucky, and when their stories drifted his way he paid no attention. Men were wounded; men were killed, including some of the men in the unit he trained with, but their stories were not his story. It was a matter of what you accepted and what you refused, he thought, a matter of what you allowed yourself to believe. You had to resist the unlucky stories. The rumors of atrocity—often involving Jews—he tried to shrink to small dark points held at a great distance, like the inverse of stars, but he would feel the sweat begin. A drink would smooth out the moment, a trip to Meg's would put the rumors out of mind. Here was her body, her bed, his streak of luck, safe and irrefutable. *Careful*, Leo wrote. *Don't get too involved.* But when there was a spell with clean shirts and no bombings and plenty of nights with Meg, Irving tended to believe himself.

His father's letters continued to arrive and Irving would open them with anticipation, only to find more details of Russia and the Ukraine: descriptions of a samovar, a meadow, a street in Kiev, all in beautiful archaic script. They were in English but seemed more like a secret code he grew frustrated trying to decipher, and he tucked them into his duffle and did not look at them again. Buffalo seemed increasingly miniature and fragmentary: he thought of Leo, and his numbers man, Murray, and the theaters on Main Street; of reading the racing forms and picking horses with smart, sprightly names. He did not have to think of Sadie, who seemed present enough in her letters, Bill shadowing her, the apparatus of her life spinning like a distant filigree ball. The Somerset orchards reminded him of western New York, and now and then he would walk in them alone, as he had been instructed not to do; but they seemed to him oddly serene, even when stripped of leaves in the winter damp. He thought then not of Buffalo but of the countryside he would drive through on the way to other towns, to the Falls, road trips on which he was not forced to be anyone in particular and could choose. There were days when he wanted to get lost in the orchards, or to drive his truck not to port towns but farther away, perhaps to Scotland. On the map there seemed to be plenty of places where one could get lost, though he knew better.

Even with the sweating and the threat of bombs, it seemed easier to be Irving in England than it was in the States. Purely Irving, he thought. Here he was more expansive, he felt more linked to New York City's grandeur, which could as easily belong to Irving as to anyone else. He imagined a life in New York after the war, imagined himself in Times Square theaters, in jazz clubs and posh hotels. He was relieved, he told Leyton, that his family was safe in America.

"God yes," Leyton said. "It's hell for the Brits."

· · ·

IN THE WINTER of '44 Leyton told him transfer orders would be coming through soon, but offered no details, and Irving waited. More and more troops arrived, the streets and pubs overflowing with them, and Irving found he did not want to be near them: this more than anything kept him silent and listening. Sometimes men assumed he had been to the front and returned, and asked him, and he would wave a hand and shake his head, suggesting he'd rather not talk about it and ruin a perfectly good pint.

But there were moments during the day when he would inexplicably break into a sweat, and the panic would come over him, and a coldness, and then it would pass and he would return to whatever he'd been doing. He wondered if epileptics felt this way, the day speckled with instants when the body took control. He sweated until his orders finally came through: he was to move to southeast England to help set up an evacuation hospital. He would not be sent to France, not yet anyway. It seemed his luck was holding.

Don't get into the medicine cabinet, Leo had said, though now it seemed a joke, another way of thinking about the nurses. Meg was teary about him leaving, though he'd still be in England. She carried on as if he were going to the front—he wasn't, was he? This was just sentiment, he told himself, her attachment overdramatized. But she was passionate and in passion they returned to her bed. He would miss her, he said, and he felt he would: a wave of sadness came over him and he buried his face in her hair and made fervent promises of letters and fidelity and a speedy return.

IN THE SOUTHEAST, he quickly learned to avoid conversation about his assignment, as it spooked the troops stationed nearby: they did not want to hear about preparations for predicted casualties. The troops were everywhere and you could see in their eyes an unsettledness, and he thought of the racehorses, how dramatically they could register panic. He carried a lucky charm in his pocket, a polished amethyst Lillian Schumacher had given him, and several times a day he held it in his fist.

In June when the first wave of troops went out, there was an odd quiet. He'd begun talking up a nurse named Laura—he was no officer, but why shouldn't he try? On the seventh he had been close enough to her to kiss her, and her mouth was slightly open, smiling, as if she wanted to be kissed. He considered asking her to take a walk. She was from Chicago, she told him. She was only twenty-four. He was talking about visiting New York, and a passing nurse called Laura's name, and then a general call went up: the casualties were arriving. Irving's sweating began, and Laura matter-of-factly gathered herself, her mouth now sealed, her attention elsewhere. In a minute she was halfway to a hospital tent.

He hurried to the harbor to help carry men in: there were dozens of soldiers half gone but still alive and he felt then a dizziness and a roaring in his ears, the light splintering. Even now the litters were slick with blood, and between trips to the hospital tents he ran behind a truck and was sick. Then he felt a sour distance, and continued carrying the men who were missing parts. It seemed not to stop, this carrying of men. Many of them had been given morphine, but sometimes the morphine had worn off. A bloody, brown-eyed kid who seemed torn up in the middle tried to talk to Irving, his sounds a muddled begging—maybe for water, though it sounded like *wa*, or *war*. Irving felt the glassiness of motion and the man's begging as if it were far away, a persistent call Irving could not answer. He wanted the voice to stop, but the man continued, and Irving could feel a jolt in his arm, a muscular twitch, as if he might strike this man who was bleeding and wanting something and watching Irving. The watching terrified Irving the most. His father would not have been terrified: his father would have found a way to quiet the man, the right word or gesture. Perhaps it was a question of will. But it seemed the most Irving could do was get the man's gurney into the ward and avoid hitting him. Irving could see the man's eyes widening as he left the gurney in the ward and drew back, more eyes on him—a nurse, a young one named Maxwell, watching as he turned away. And in his peripheral vision he saw Nurse Maxwell shift fast between patients, leaning toward the man and reaching for a tray with syringes and cups of ice chips.

Irving felt in himself the same splintering he'd seen in the light, and was sick again. Then the twitching in his arm finally ceased. The man's wounds were not Irving's fault: none of it was Irving's fault. The world seemed far away, like a staticky late-night radio broadcast. A faint breeze passed, and he noticed again that it was June, but June through a telescope.

HE WOULD GO AWOL rather than go to France, risk court-martial. He would feign mental defect. Anything. For a few weeks the casualties arrived, though sometimes he transported hospital supplies instead of men. He felt himself no longer Irving, simply a body in motion. But after a few weeks, when the evacuation hospital decamped and crossed the Channel, he was ordered back to Somerset. It had become July. Here was Meg who at first seemed a dream of Meg, and whose body seemed a lifeline; her attic apartment, with its slanted ceilings and drafts and bad plumbing an oasis. And yet even with Meg, the nightmares took hold—ghastly scenes of dismemberment—and from then on he kept a flask with him always, regardless of regulations. For a time he seemed far from the ground, and everything but sex seemed an imitation of itself. At first he did not gamble, his luck surely having ebbed. The prospect of losing money melded with a possible transfer to France: anything could happen. Anything. By August the days evened out, though his luck seemed provisional, a matter of the moment. Sadie wrote him letters about her trips to Crystal Beach: Crystal Beach still existed, the dance hall and the girls in bathing suits and the cool water under hot sun still existed, somewhere. He thought of Sadie's living room, and the guest room in her house, where he would like to sleep for weeks, where Sadie could bring him trays of pastry and hot coffee and soup while Bill and the girls lived their lives elsewhere. At the PX, recuperating men would appear, and Irving tried to think of them as customers without histories connected to his, simply customers.

Meg told him they needed to remember the good in their lives. "It's still there," she said. "You just have to look." She could imagine being with him forever, and during sex *forever* was exactly the word for his desire: this exact immersion *forever*. She said she could imagine his children, and though he did not picture children at all, he smiled at her and returned to the sensation of *forever.* He could stay in her body forever and never return to hospitals and never wash other men's blood off and never feel himself splintering. He told Meg he loved her, and he meant it as much as he had meant anything.

"I can picture you in New York City," he said, though what he pictured were women he sometimes watched on the street in downtown Buffalo, slightly altered. "But maybe you'd prefer London, after the war?"

"I've always thought about America." But Meg doubted her parents would approve, given the distance and, she admitted, her mother's views on religion. "She'll have worries," Meg said.

"Sure," Irving said. "Why wouldn't she?" There had been uneasiness in his family too, he told her, what with his late mother being a Lutheran.

"She doesn't mind Lutherans."

And so when he met her parents—her mother plump, with the same oval face, a deeper air of worry, Meg's thin, downcast father—they made no mention of religion. The dress uniform helped him, the gifts from the PX. He was careful to drink only one beer before meeting them, and he talked expansively about his prospects in New York City, which would be a good place for Meg, after they were married.

The meeting left him with a euphoric hope that lasted a day and then gave way to the more immediate problems of liquor and card money, and the persistent nightmares, and the need to sell a few things from the PX on the black market. There was no thinking, really, beyond immediate need.

Don't go crazy, Leo wrote, *I've got a girl in mind for you.* It seemed a voice from a different life. What could Leo know? Irving did not write back for a long while, though Leo persisted. It was Leo who met him at the port when he reached the States again, and Leo at the harbor, the city rising up, the war dropping away: all seemed like proof of grace. For that day in New York, Leo watched over him, almost carrying him. Leo paid for a hotel and dinner and Irving's ticket to Buffalo, and traveled with him home, all the while telling Irving he looked good, that Buffalo hadn't been the same without him. Leo felt very, very lucky, to have Irving home. "Buffalo is hopping now," Leo said. "You'll see. We'll go out on the town. Wear the uniform; girls love the uniforms."

Leo did not ask much about England, or anyone there, or about Normandy, which seemed to Irving a personal tornado. Irving could only offer an occasional solemn nod and murmur about the high price of liberty, a phrase he'd picked up from Leyton. Leyton, who toward the end of Irving's tour noticed PX stock was missing, and wearily told Irving he'd need to investigate soon. The sky that day had been a sheet of pale gray above a pinkish horizon. Irving offered Leyton a cigarette, and they stood quietly smoking and watching the narrow band of light, and Leyton gave him his transport papers. It had seemed to Irving that Normandy hovered beside them, ubiquitous still, despite all his efforts; and when Leyton walked away, Normandy remained, almost incarnate. He suspected it would follow him to Buffalo. Better to tell Leo nothing, let Normandy stand for victory without dwelling on the price. France had been liberated; Europe had been liberated; the war was over. And yet, if it hadn't been for Normandy, Irving never would have lifted so much from the PX, or barely avoided court-martial; never would have promised so much to Meg; never would have told her he'd be gone for a day in Bristol, and left for home so stealthily.

PART FOUR

Harbor Walks

Late 1940s

CHAPTER 21

Jo

1945–47

And then the war ended, and Irving reappeared and played the returning hero for months. For a time he seemed to have his own money, he avoided the store, and her father said nothing. In spring he began to show up for work, to stay the better part of the day. This was, Jo realized, no relief: the office was too small, and when she handled money Irving would hover, and when Lillian Schumacher visited he'd station himself at the counter and tell jokes. In summer he took long lunch hours, leaving her to mind the store while their father sat in temple or dozed in the back office. And Irving would return, stupidly cheerful, and pretend to be attentive.

The second October after Irving's return, her father called Jo into the parlor to talk. A Sunday evening. He stirred sugar into his tea, poured a cup for Jo, lit his pipe and asked her if she would care to smoke one of her cigarettes.

"You work hard at the store," he said. "You're a good worker. Thank you." He spoke quietly: he had not raised his voice, it seemed, for years. "Thank God," he said, "the war is over. Thank God we have Irving home." He would be grateful if she would go through the accounts once a month, something she could easily do right here, in the parlor. There was no need for her to continue to come to the store. He used no endearments, but he said this kindly, as if he were releasing her from pain.

"It's a relief Irving's safe," she said, though Irving had been safe for over a year now.

Her father smiled briefly. There would be, of course, the regular household money and then some, he said. He took up the Sunday paper, and Jo excused herself and went to her room and undressed and lay in bed leafing through the Sears catalogue.

She'd wanted Irving to be safe, she'd been afraid for him, but it was too bad that death had to be permanent; she'd prefer to will him dead, then resurrect him for her father's sake, as the occasion required. When he'd first returned from Europe she'd confronted him about Goldie: he'd offered her whiskey, shrugged at her refusal, and said, "You think she forgot the address? She didn't write to you—that's not my fault."

"But you said nothing." Her voice was sharp, rising. "We didn't know what happened."

And Irving remained calm, faraway though he stood beside her in the parlor. "Now you know."

She called him a liar. She wanted to smack him.

"What do you hear from her lately?" he said. And she left the parlor and did not speak to him until a day later, when he brought home a half-pound of chocolate.

She could tell her father none of this; and either way she would lose her job. The morning after her father's announcement, Jo did not return to the store, even though Irving overslept—further proof that the war had done little to change him. He had been spending most of his evenings downtown, the city now more brilliantly lit, exuding a fast energy she did not recognize. He went to hear club acts, he'd told her. He'd imitated a trumpeter and sung into his spoon a song she'd heard on the radio. Despite her outrage that he'd kept Goldie secret, she found it hard to resist the tunefulness of his voice, hard not to laugh when he'd puffed out his cheeks. And yet she'd seen these waves of enthusiasm before and did not trust them: they were built on guile and air. He was bound to be lying about something. Whether her father could recognize the underlying faultiness, she could not say, but his recent, preferred view of Irving—an honorable Irving—was no secret. When the insurance man, Marvin Brodsky, came to the store, she'd seen her father introduce Irving as *my dear son, back from the war in Europe.*

Marvin Brodsky grasped Irving's hand and shook it and patted him on the shoulder. "It's good to have you back," Marvin Brodsky said.

"Thank you."

Her father and Marvin shared then a solemn nodding: Irving had saved Marvin from Hitler. The fact that he had done so from a PX in England was a matter left unexplored.

The first Monday of Jo's unemployment, Irving eventually rose and shaved and left for the store carrying a small bowl of coffee, and Celia continued to sleep, and the house was quiet and cold. Jo brewed more coffee and baked a quick bread, then dusted the parlor and the dining room and the light fixtures in the hallway, and noon still seemed a distant shore.

Celia woke late, pleased to find Jo home, pleased to find the sweet bread waiting, the hot coffee. Light snow fell, just enough to cover the lawn, and Celia turned on the radio and brought her coffee from room to room, as she watched Jo clean the house. This seemed a continuation of the weekend, of Jo's ordinary Saturdays and Sundays, Celia's mood easygoing and mild. Celia even suggested a matinee. The week unfurled with the same pattern: housecleaning in the mornings, a film or a trip to a shop in the afternoon. Not once did Jo wear her stiff wool suits or tight heels; not once did the house threaten to collapse. The first week seemed, if anything, pleasant. Yet when the next weekend arrived, Jo's housekeeping was already done, and a sharp cold front came through, the wind too strong for walking. And it seemed every time she glanced up, there was Celia; and when she did not glance up, there was Celia. Jo had watched over Celia for years, but she now understood that the work week—despite its drudgeries and resentments—had offered a narrow respite. By Sunday it seemed that she had no moments without Celia, except those in which she bathed or slept.

The following days felt like glue, but Jo herself felt less cohesive, as if what held her together was the thick air between her and Celia and nothing else, and she could be disassembled simply by listening to the radio in Celia's company, day after day. She laundered all of Celia's clothes, as Celia's aversion to bathing flared again: Celia feared drowning, feared the water would infect her. She was especially skittish about washing her hair; Jo gave her headscarves, which Celia some days wore and some days did not.

When the novelty of Jo's presence wore off, Celia's winter self—more quarrelsome, more agitated—began to emerge. Jo could not tell if her own agitation was because of Celia or because of winter and the shapelessness of their days. Reprieve would be in sleep, and she found herself in the morning staying in bed, burrowing, hiding from Celia and from the day, until Celia or Irving or her father called to her, and then she let the day begin. She could feel herself fading, the fear of dissolution coming in on her at random hours.

In late December, in a fit of panic, Jo dressed in a wool skirt suit and pumps, picked her way across the icy streets to the bus stop and caught a bus downtown to Moshe Schumacher's office. The law offices were in the same building as they had been for years, but they had been expanded and recently painted. You could still smell the residue of the creamy paint; the floors had been covered with soft gray carpet, and the secretarial pool was twice the size she remembered. A nicer place to work. She had forgotten little, had learned more accounting. In the gold-stenciled letters of Schumacher, Stein, Dobkin & Feigenbaum there seemed a glimmer of hope, though beside the secretarial pool's one window she could see Schumacher's cousin Gert, iron-haired, unsmiling and strange. Closer to the reception desk sat a cluster of young Lucia-like secretaries, four or five of them in modest, stylish dresses and swept-up hair, red lipstick and tiny pearl earrings, a kind of secretarial chorus line. Gert typed assiduously, as if she did not see Jo.

A dark-haired young woman said, "May I help you?"

"I wonder," Jo said, "if Attorney Schumacher is in."

"Have you got an appointment?"

"No," Jo told her. "No appointment." But then she stopped, a fizzing seeming to wash through her, a pressure wave beginning behind her eyes. She looked at Gert, prehistoric in the corner. The five Lucias. It seemed that the old office, the one she had worked in, had never existed, that such an office could not exist. "My father is a client, a friend. Abe Cohen?" Jo said.

"Yes, of course," the woman said. She kept her face blank. She was not as beautiful as the real Lucia.

The fizzing insisted itself on Jo's throat, dropped through her chest and lungs. "I was on the block," Jo said. "Perhaps I should speak to Mr. Schumacher another time?"

The woman thumbed the heavy desk calendar, and Jo said, "I think that would be best, another time. I'll call him at home. Good afternoon."

"Good afternoon."

The fizzing propelled Jo into the hallway, and she did not look back; the office seemed to lock and crumble behind her.

THERE SEEMED no end to the fizzing and pressure; some mornings she could barely speak, and Celia would sit quietly and wait for her to return to herself, as if this were the ordinary course of things. It was a slow drowsy winter, and she kept the house meticulously clean, and hid herself in dime-store novels, in which the florid descriptions of bodies titillated and alarmed her. She teared up at odd, unpredictable moments: the sight of an unfamiliar car passing the house, or the thinning tips of tree branches, the thud of the newspaper's daily delivery. There were of course the daily walks with Celia, daily meals with Celia, the laundering for Celia, but occasionally Celia went out alone, and Jo went into the city by herself, and it seemed a moment from a separate life. Nothing fizzed. The sky seemed the same cloud-rich sky she'd watched all her life. And yet it seemed there was no separation from Celia: in March, months after she'd stopped working at the store, she was for the first time mistaken for Celia. This by a woman older than her father, a woman who had known her since childhood and had for those many years run a small bakery on Jefferson. Jo walked in out of the windy afternoon, and the old woman, Rachel Levy, said, "What will it be for you, Celia?"

There was a moment, like a skipped beat, of turning and checking to see if Celia had in fact followed her, but no one else was
in the shop. Clearly Mrs. Levy was speaking to Jo. Jo removed her
hat and scarf then. "I'm Jo," she said.

"Yes you are, aren't you? My mistake. What'll it be today, Jo?"

And the day righted itself, the transaction proceeding as every
other transaction she'd had at the bakery: Rachel Levy's careful
wrapping of the bread, slow notation of the sale on the small paper
tablet, lopsided smile as she handed over the package and accepted the money and sent good wishes to the family. She was
close to eighty now, a tiny woman, her spectacle lenses as thick as
oven glass. She had known Jo's mother, had probably held both Jo
and Celia as newborns. She was simply confused. She might have
as easily called Jo Sadie, or Irving, or Rebecca.

But later Jo wondered. She did not believe she looked like
Celia beyond a general family resemblance: a similar shape to the
mouth, the same eye color, a shifting hazel. Their bodies had
both, it seemed, widened more than Sadie's, and now had a similar
pearness, which was why Celia could so easily borrow her dresses.
But this was all. Rachel Levy knew them as sisters, had made an old
woman's mistake. When Jo glanced into windows and mirrors, she
saw not a bit of Celia, only Jo, though a Jo grown plain with time.
A bit wrinkled but clean, always clean. She bathed daily, washed
her hair often, combed and pinned it up. Twice a month she
treated herself to the beauty parlor for a wash and set, the pleasure
of the careful hands on her head: one girl, Ruth, was especially
good, gentle and not rushed, always remembering to check the
water temperature. There was a pink-and-white calm to the beauty
parlor, the air flowery and warm. In those moments she felt no
panic, the world seemed solid and whole, and afterward she'd
stretch the time by lingering at the reception desk, slowly choosing her next appointment, and in the perfumed ladies' room, trying
out lipstick. Yet these moments were brief, and she knew she was
not a favorite customer.

And Celia, Celia was not clean. Her aversion to bathing, down-
right refusals, increased over the winter to what Sadie called "abomi-
nable." A crisis, Jo admitted. Nothing, it seemed, would convince

Celia to do much beyond washing her hands and brushing a damp cloth over her face. Every day became a battle to persuade Celia that she would not drown by bathing, that warm soapy water would not infect her. Jo changed Celia's linens two or three times a week, endlessly laundered her clothes in an attempt to compensate, checked Celia's hair for lice, bought her new scarves to wear, daily laundered the scarves.

Once in midwinter, Sadie stopped in and lambasted them both for Celia's state. She tried to bully Celia into washing: "You're filthy, Celia, your hair is just filthy. What on earth are you thinking?"

Celia shrank into herself.

"You get her to wash then," Jo said. "She says she'll get infected. She's afraid she'll drown."

"That's ridiculous," Sadie said. "That's perfectly ridiculous. Celia?" But Celia was gone. Sadie returned the next day with expensive soap that Celia left on the shelf and a box of chocolate she absconded with. Later, when Jo in her own panic dialed Sadie's number, Sadie answered by saying, "Jo? Again? Well, did Celia take a bath?"

Both her father and Irving delicately avoided them—Irving was out of the house in the morning before she woke, and home late after his time in the clubs or tomcatting, whatever it was he was doing, no longer telling stories or singing radio songs in the kitchen, shrugging off her questions about Goldie. Her father seemed translucent, pale from winter and the preceding years, pale, she thought, from too many visits to shul. On the nights he stayed home, he would take his supper alone, with his newspaper and his Hebrew books, and then retire to bed. And it seemed that she would be forever yoked to Celia, with no escape and no other company.

In late March she was again taken for Celia, this time by a pharmacist who said, "You know you can't stay here, I told you that. You buy what you need and then leave." The other customers stared and she rushed away without her mineral salts. It was then she began to wake in the morning feeling murderous, suffocating in Celia and more Celia, and wanting nothing less than obliteration. Jo heard her father rise and leave for work, heard Irving rise and leave, and there was in her fists a smashing energy, the wish to smash unbearable. She was herself an anger, an ugliness, untouchable, and it seemed she'd been that way forever, and whatever she touched was corrupted, and whatever sweetness she might have claimed went to Celia, who wasted it. Whatever work Celia could not finish became Jo's. Celia's mind was touched, and now Jo was touched, and she was never to make Celia stop, or to leave Celia; there would be a slow dissolution until nothing remained of Jo, there would only be Celia, grown fatter on chocolate and Jo, crying because she couldn't find Jo, shocked to discover Jo's bones scattered about the house. Celia did not intend any of it, and yet sit in a room with her and her vast need, and she would take all that you were, until you were emptiness. Life seemed to leak away through her. And she was yours nonetheless. And when she was peaceable and sweet you were supposed to forget the horrible nights, the days you yourself had lost calming her down and coaxing her out of her room, cleaning up the stink of her when she let it go too far. And she remained devoted to you, would do anything for you, because you were her hold on the world. And if you refused her? If you let her drown? One way or another you would drown with her. There was no way out. There were only small reprieves, a morning, a cigarette, an hour. Pinches of reprieve.

The smashing rage surged again. It was still early. Jo wrapped herself in her coat. As she left the house she sensed Celia treading the staircase, heard her call, "Where are you going? Jo? Where are you going?" But she hurried away, the smashing feeling too strong, and she walked the muddy, iced streets off Richmond and up Elmwood, through the park, through the cemetery, hours it seemed, until the rage abated and she felt a tame emptiness. And she returned to the house to find Celia in the bathtub. Celia sat weeping, shivering, pale in the white porcelain tub, her hair soapy, the cool bathwater two inches deep.

"I'll help you," Jo said.

"Where were you?"

"I had to go out for a while." Jo rolled up her sleeves, added an inch of warm water to the tub. Carried in another basin for warm water, filled it, dipped a washcloth in and began by wiping Celia's shoulders and arms, so she wouldn't be frightened of the wash-cloth closer to her face. Jo ripped a towel into strips to make a headband for Celia, to keep the soap from her eyes and the water from her face as Jo rinsed her hair. Celia closed her eyes and leaned her neck back against Jo's left hand, bit her lip while cup after cup of clean water poured through her hair. When that was done, Jo wrapped her head in a towel, turbanlike, and helped Celia wash the rest of her body, insisting she soap beneath her arms and between her legs, pouring her more hot water and periodically draining the tub to keep the water level reassuringly low. And after Celia dried off and dressed in clean clothes, Celia herself changed her bedsheets and Jo's, as if to prove her good intentions. In the kitchen, Jo smoked a cigarette and then another, and made hot chocolate for the two of them, slipping a little bit of brandy into her own. The afternoon was a peaceful one, of listening to the radio and drinking more chocolate and smoking cigarettes.

Jo began to get up early again, before everyone, to leave the house for long walks alone, so the rage would not surge, and the impulse to smash was siphoned off onto muddy streets and the days would take their muted course. When she returned, Celia was often awake, and if it was a good day she was in the kitchen with the orange cat, and would say, "Better now?"

"Yes." Then it was time for breakfast and the radio and a quiet mapping out of the day. If it was not a good day, Celia was in bed, or rocking herself in the parlor, or gone, and Jo left again to find her. Luckily, the fine weather suited Celia, and the fine weather was increasing. Luckily there was the garden to plan, the cat to look after, the afternoons of radio.

IT WAS in late May, in Delaware Park, Jo and Celia on an after-noon walk, when they saw near the small lake their father walking arm in arm with Bertha Schumacher, escorting her as if she were a dignitary. And behind them, Moshe and Lillian Schumacher strolled and sometimes Lillian touched her brother's shoulder or pointed to the lake's edge or the sky. Their father's head tilted at-tentively toward Bertha, and once he reached over as if to hold her left hand in both of his. It was known now that the better part of

Bertha Schumacher's family had disappeared in Poland, some of them certainly had perished in the camps; and it was rumored that Bertha had gone into seclusion, that she was no longer the familiar Mrs. Schumacher, instead an expressionless woman who resembled her. And yet here she was on the lake path in Delaware Park, walking with sure steps and a touch of royalty, in her pale blue spring coat and beauty parlor hair, and their father, strolling the park with her, as he had never done with Jo or Celia. Nor had he walked in the park with their mother: he'd taken no time for such things. Yet Bertha and her father seemed to be a respectable couple, strolling the familiar paths in familiar ways, and the four—Bertha, Moshe, Lillian, their father—were clearly a family of sorts. There was something about the easy pace and easy distance between the two pairs, the casual turning to consult, the continued pointing at birds and jonquils, that spoke of long-established ritual, a private world of four in which Jo and Celia did not even appear as thoughts. And Jo wanted in that moment to be all of them and also to be what passed among them, to breathe the air of that small world, to be made of such air. The longing was as sharp as a craving for sweets, and she began to walk in their direction, thoughtless, following the craving. Her father and Bertha were several paces on now; she'd have to hurry to catch them, perhaps she'd have to shout. And then she felt a tug on her arm and Celia's liquid gaze. "You can't," Celia said.

"What?" The question as much to herself as to Celia. Moshe's heavy backside and legs were shrinking in the distance, the foursome appearing more like decorative figures in a painting of a lake, but the craving persisted.

"I know you want to but you can't." Celia pulled Jo's arm in the direction of the avenue, toward the cars and buildings and bus route. "Wouldn't you like a coffee?" Celia's voice a perfect imitation of Sadie's lovely hostess voice. "Let's find some coffee."

The lake began to blur, and hot tears sprang up. "Coffee helps," Celia said. "You'll see." And when they had reached the avenue, and the four figures had vanished altogether, Celia murmured, "That isn't us."

They did not discuss that moment again, and it became one in a universe of things they did not discuss but that nested in the trees around the house and occasionally popped into view. Love and falling in love and the other ways their lives might have gone: the closest they came to this was in reference to Sadie's daughters, now in their teens, more than usually beautiful in the way of teenaged girls. It was a shock to see them, these girls, and a greater shock to recognize how far Jo and Celia were from girlhood. There would be courting, Celia said. Dances and corsages and boys kissing them. Sadie would have her hands full, Jo said, and nothing more. She did not want to think about the actual kissing of boys and men—it was something else in novels—and there was that piercing longing she'd felt years ago, now resurfacing, as if for an instant, the young Lucia or the dream Amelia touched her face, then evaporated. And just as the piercing shot through her, Celia patted her hand. Celia was silent, as if to give the sadness time to make itself known, and leave. Then she said, "They're nice girls," bringing Jo back to Sadie's daughters. Celia speculated about dresses she'd seen in department store windows, satiny gowns, pastel summer shifts. Then she changed the subject to lilacs. They did not talk about other teenagers or children, or what it might have been like to have daughters or sons.

On good days, Celia seemed to possess this precise awareness of exactly what they would not mention. The universe of unmentioned things solidified after the moment in Delaware Park, and as the summer—Celia's best time—took hold, they spent bright days in the garden, listened to the radio, and slept in the hottest afternoons, waking to drink lemonade and sit in the shade and smoke, and there seemed an increasing oneness of thought between them.

For most of July, Jo felt no pressure, no fizzing, little need to call Sadie. Celia tended the marigolds and roses and zinnias, the tomatoes and peppers and beans, lounged with the cat, ignored their father, ignored Irving. She bathed in shallow tubs of water every other day and allowed Jo to wash her hair twice a week, such was her calm. Once Jo drove them both to the Falls, and they walked along the rapids, blue green and frothy in sunlight, the water like a live thing. And for a few minutes Celia sat on the grassy bank and Jo walked alone, and the river—vast and rushing—seemed surprisingly intimate. Exposed. Jo had not visited the Falls for years; standing beside the river, she missed it terribly and did not want to leave. Up the hill, Celia waited. And if Jo did not leave, and stood there indefinitely? Sooner or later she'd fall, or the rain would wash her into the river, the water melting her down to bone and then nothing; and yet she imagined herself for a moment complete, her own muscle part of the river's. How green the water seemed, its white froth unending. Yet Celia was there: from the grass, Celia watched her. Jo turned and strode uphill, and the two of them found a flat, sunny stretch of grass, and spread a picnic blanket, and watched the rising plumes of mist.

IN EARLY AUGUST, the sunflowers fattened on thick stalks, the nights remained warm. A month to let yourself drift in, to stay in the yard and smoke and allow yourself to forget anything beyond the flower bed's bright palette and the breeze from the lake, and at night the movement of low clouds, the intermittent moonlight. Jo had been staying up late and waking early, and sometimes dozed in the afternoons. The colder months seemed far off and any other way of living seemed farther.

August 3, less than a week into the month. Irving left the house before eight o'clock, with plenty of time to open the store. Now it was ten-thirty and her father had not risen and would not rise: she wanted to pretend she had not seen him on the bed, that she had not pushed the door open and called him and found him there un-breathing. Already his body, his hand was strangely cool in the swelling heat of the day, and after she touched his wrist the skin on her own fingers seemed to crawl. From the window she could see Celia in the yard, sitting in a wrought-iron chair, her back turned to the house. Also motionless, though a breeze lifted the corner of Celia's scarf and made the leaves flap against each other, and a bird called, a high trilling call. A cardinal? And Jo imagined but did not see a flash of red pass through the maples.

From the parlor telephone she dialed Sadie, who did not an-swer. Instead it was the Colored girl saying Mrs. Feldstein had taken her daughter to an appointment. The jewelry store's line was also busy, and Jo felt fizzy and breathless. She dialed Bill's office, where the receptionist did not like her and tended to hang up abruptly, but Jo insisted in a hoarse bark, *You have to get him,* and bit into her lip, and then he came on the line. Celia was still in the yard and Jo said, "My father is dead." The parlor air seemed overrun with dust motes, the walls thinning into imitation walls. Celia had not heard her though, Celia was in the yard, at the little table, perhaps with a cat—Jo had seen only the pink summer dress and the matching headscarf pulled over the hair she would not comb.

"Jo," Bill said. "Tell me more."

"He's in his bed. Just there in bed."

And then there was an empty while, with Celia in the yard and their father in the bed and Jo in the kitchen stirring sugar into undrinkable tea, and a bird trilled again, and another bird answered with a complex unintelligible call. Jo walked into the yard. Celia did not turn around, and when Jo said Celia's name, Celia did not answer, though she unlike their father was breathing, you could see the movement of the dress. Jo approached and gazed into her face and Celia seemed far away and blank. The cat lay on the nearby grass and Jo lifted it and placed it in Celia's lap, where it stood for a moment, ignored, and leaped back to the grass. And it seemed unbearable to be out in the yard with Celia not bothering to speak to her, and her father dead upstairs, and she walked back into the kitchen and stirred the tea until time seemed to break down into hot vague stillness. Bill arrived and went upstairs and came back down to the parlor, and on that same telephone dialed and hung up and dialed: she could hear the professional murmur, which meant doctors or funeral homes. Sadie arrived, and Jo could hear them talking in the parlor, and then Sadie appeared in the kitchen. Jo recounted her morning.

"Does Celia know?" Sadie said, which seemed an insipid thing to ask, given Celia in the yard. But the truth was Jo didn't know. Celia might have been in the yard since dawn, might not have looked in their father's room.

"You didn't tell her?" Sadie said.

"No," Jo said. "I guess not."

And various men began to arrive at the house: first thin, tidy Dr. Moscowitz, whose kindness Jo found suspect and detestable.

And then the Lipsky brothers, Seymour and Ira, and their ominous elongated car. Sadie was in the yard, touching Celia's shoulders and talking into her ear and kissing her cheek, as if Celia were a child, kissing her and leaning close that way. And Celia seemed to lean her head back against Sadie's for a moment. Then Sadie patted her and turned and reentered the house. She glanced at Jo but did not stop in the kitchen, did not also sit with Jo but went straight to the parlor, where the doctor was waiting, and then to the telephone, and made some calls of her own. Then she walked upstairs, and Bill went out to stay with Celia, and put his arm around her, and Celia leaned her pink-scarfed head against his shoulder.

The air thickened with strangeness: the Lipsky brothers waited in the parlor, breathing parlor air and probably smudging the furniture with their fingertips. There was the sound of a car, a woman's fast solid heels: Lillian Schumacher. You could hear her feet on the stairs and then through the upper hall and then not. Jo sat with cold tea, and the foot traffic out to the yard passed her—now Sadie out to Celia, Bill back to the parlor and the Lipsky brothers, and no Irving anywhere—and the same pair of birds called even in the rising heat, and the skin on her fingers crawled and she went to the sink to wash again. Lillian Schumacher was upstairs, no one had questioned her, no one had stopped her, not even Jo, it had happened so quickly. Jo roused herself to walk up the back stairs, to the hallway. She could see into her father's bedroom and Lillian was there, at her father's bedside, holding his dead hand and stroking his dead forehead and talking to him, saying *This too you had to do alone? How stubborn you are, Abe.* She hadn't wanted him to be alone, at the end, didn't he know that? *You can make peace now, can't you?* She used the word *love*. It was dizzying, nauseating to watch, and why this moment of Lillian talking to Jo's father struck Jo as the portal into grief and the surer knowledge of his death, she could not say.

IN THE PARLOR the Lipsky brothers went over arrangements with Bill, and Sadie stood on the front porch with Dr. Moscowitz.

"Please accept our condolences, Miss Cohen," Seymour Lipsky said. His face was a mask of exaggerated sympathy. "We're so sorry about your father. He was a wonderful man," Ira Lipsky said. Seymour moved toward Jo and placed a hand lightly on her shoulder. "Perhaps we can sit together for a while and go over some things with the Feldsteins." She thought then of his unsavory hand, the hand of the mortician, this hand that washed and repaired the dead for burial, that also touched, she supposed, his wife, because there were Lipsky sons now also in the business, imitating but not matching their father's bedside manner.

And then Sadie returned without the doctor, and said, "Oh Bill."

"I'll put on tea," Jo said. There was Celia to retrieve from the backyard, and Irving?

"Do you know," Ira Lipsky said, "how soon the young Mr. Cohen will arrive?"

Sadie vanished in the direction of the yard, and the Lipskys repeated their question about Irving, also saying that Jo would have a chance to view her father again if she wished, but of course not at the house: did she want to see him here again before they removed him from the house? Because they did need to go ahead with that quite soon. "Mrs. Feldstein will speak to your sister," Ira Lipsky said, and waved at the dense air where Sadie had previously stood.

Jo pictured Celia leaning her scarf-covered head against Sadie. "Excuse me."

AND THEN she was in motion, her body taking her away from the room, from the house itself. She glimpsed the foyer, the green of the lawn, the shining black panel of the Lipskys' hearse, and then a wheel of trees, which dropped behind her as the Lipsky brothers and the house dropped behind her, and her body moved of its own accord through the blanching sun and hard shadows while the city clung to outmoded faith in solidity. Nothing seemed to be itself: the street signs reverted to slices of metal, patterns of black on white, the cars on the block remarkable for their residual carness in the face of this division of light and shadow, the inevitable breakdown to blue rectangle and black circle and distorted glassy reflection. The moments seemed both to stall and to accumulate, as if the new order consisted of blue rectangles followed by mustard ones and cream ones and gray ones, the reflections shifting to the sides of the street, the flat sides of buildings and the static objects and moving figures on the far side of glass, and the brilliant lists of numbers and the wheedling ponderous letters—SALE—calling but not trilling, the doorways insisting on their own rectangular shapes. Then she too was on the other side of window glass, in shade, and her skin prickled, her face and neck gone damp, sweat like a living thing rolling down her back.

It's the sweat that startles her into more awareness. There's a basket in her hand: she has taken a basket. In front of her a pile of papery yellow globes, and she picks one up. An onion. And she is Jo. A woman holding an onion. Around her there are other women, picking up other objects. Vegetables. Fruit. The onion curves against her palm and there's a small noisy breeze, an electric fan. The market believes it is a market. The purpose of onions eludes her, and then she remembers, but does not know the purpose of this onion. She has no onion things in mind. But the market believes in itself, and perhaps she should believe in the market: perhaps she has marketing to do. She stands in the small aisle and other women move past her, past the bin of onions, and she turns her head. At the end of the aisle, watching her, is Eli Abramowitz. And now the onion seems heavy, droppable. With effort she sets it down on top of the other onions, and Eli says, "Jo? Something you need?" And the onion rolls and settles lower in the bin.

Eli too is roundness on top of sweating roundness: belly and spectacles and bald head. She would like to sit on the empty crate beside the stacked cabbages, pale green and purple cabbages leaning into each other. "I forgot my list." She takes a step toward the crate, finds her knees bending and Eli says, "You want to sit, Jo? I'll get you a chair." Then there is a kind of gliding, vegetables and stacked cans and loaves of bread gliding past her, women's dresses and pin curlers glide past, and she is in a chair by the window, near a sign that says BEANS and another that says COFFEE. A younger woman's face appears, its own set of roundnesses: big eyes behind wire-rimmed glasses, the light reflecting off the lenses and color from the street passing across them, the eyes like green fish moving in and out of view below the surface of a pond.

"Miss Cohen?" It's Sasha, the youngest Goldbaum, Sasha Abramowitz now and for a couple of years. The skittish girl Eli married, the girl who is no longer skittish and no longer a girl. Her green eyes swim like fish; her belly is a swollen moon. "Miss Cohen?"

She offers Jo a glass of water. Small patches of sweat spread over Sasha's white blouse, below the armpits, at the top of her belly. Jo takes the glass and drinks and imagines the water moving down her throat, trickling quietly through her ribs. She is exhausted. She thinks of cabbages. Women move slowly in the heat, singly or in small knots, and the market seems hushed, though it could be that she is hushed and the store is itself. The world seems to exist between the wooden chair and COFFEE sign and the cabbages, between the whirring electric fan and the sunlight wavering over the glass, patterning the linoleum floor. And Sasha says, "Sit as long as you need, Miss Cohen," and for a brief time Jo's life is Sasha and water and wavering light. For a moment she feels no longing. Then longing returns, and she cannot distinguish between longing and the memory of longing: they seem a single trembling.

"Mrs. Feldstein is on her way," Sasha says, the green eyes swimming.

"I'm so sorry," Eli says.

And there is the moon of Sasha's belly, and the sign reading COFFEE. Beyond the window, Elmwood Avenue, sun reflecting off a string of cars.

CHAPTER 22

Goldie

1947

Even after the war, letters arrived regularly from Sadie—the graceful script itself a constant thread—faithfully reciting the news of the family and of her weekly activities, some temple women's luncheon, some fund-raiser for refugees. There was pleasure in receiving the letters—they made a kind of light, serialized story—and Goldie would put aside her other tasks and pour a cup of coffee and read them slowly. But for all their charm, Sadie's letters revealed little: at first she did not even mention their father directly, only "the family" or "the store." And while this didn't surprise Goldie, neither did it stop her from looking for clues. In truth, if Sadie conveyed any greeting from him—a hint of apology—Goldie would have made some kind of effort. But Sadie conveyed nothing, once mentioning that *the war has taken its toll on all of us, Papa is tired,* and nothing more. Goldie did not ask.

It wasn't simply her own stubbornness or pride, but something deeper and more difficult to name: she was fairly sure there'd been a shivah. Irving once said as much, a glib remark on a postcard of the Peace Bridge. And it occurred to her that other than occasional childhood birthday cakes, this had been the only family ceremony marking her life. The thought of it left a harsh metallic taste in her mouth. And so Goldie did not mention their father in her letters back to Sadie, and did not ask leading questions—instead describing the shorebirds and the light on the water and the ways in which the sea differed from the lake. She enjoyed painting; she missed playing the piano; over time her cooking had improved. There were, of course, worlds of things Goldie did not mention: her relationship with Ted (a twice-a-week arrangement that suited her), her tendency to wear shoes only when absolutely necessary, her job waiting tables. But between Goldie and Sadie, among all the delicate noncommunication there resumed the occasional suggestion of a book one or the other had read and liked, and they took up the old habit of talking through books. Their preferences were more marked now and in some ways predictable: Sadie liked sagas and grand romances, Goldie preferred serious plays and poetry, but there was a care with this as well. Occasionally Sadie sent a small package of books, and once she included poems.

This was more than Goldie had expected, really, and also less, because of the silence beyond Sadie: it was as if Sadie herself was combating silence, making her small persistent noise to prevent the silence from taking hold everywhere. Goldie was not ungrateful, but she rarely heard from Irving and never from Jo or Celia. Their lives she knew only through Sadie's bright sketchy summaries, with rare after-the-fact exceptions. *Celia seems better now* (but what had she been like before?) . . . *I was worried but she is better . . . I cannot tell you much about Jo and Celia of late except that they are here at Lancaster and nothing has changed* (since when?).

She'd wanted something else, had vaguely imagined another gesture of care emanating from that house, more than Irving's annual scrawled postcards. But could you expect anything from Celia beyond Sadie's *p.s. Celia sends her love?* Celia and Irving had been irresponsible children; what were the chances they'd become utterly different adults? And Jo? She'd been quarrelsome, ungenerous. A troublemaker: from the time she'd learned to walk, Jo had tried to separate Goldie from their mother and yoke her to Celia, and sometimes it had worked. More often Goldie had looked after Jo, both of them unhappy. Years ago, all years ago, yet Jo's was not a loving nature, and how much did anyone's nature change? Sadie's letters would have to be enough.

GOLDIE HAS the morning free, she's cleared the kitchen table and set up her watercolors—trickier to use than they seem; she's working on a small beachscape, including a house and suggestions of sailboats offshore. And when Sadie's telegram arrives the typed form seems to Goldie like a shell on the beach, something small on the vastness of the coast, then larger as you reach for it and hold it close to your face, vast as you nearly spiral into its color and line. ABE COHEN DIED PEACEFULLY, as if *Papa* or *Father* might be confused with someone else. Then: SHOULD DELAY FUNERAL FOR YR ARRIVAL?

In the case of her father, the difference between dead and not dead is confusing. There is finality, an end to the smallest hope, but that hope was gone years ago, wasn't it? Perhaps not. Yet the loss is now confirmed, and public, and she is not alone in surviving him. She doesn't even know who he is anymore, or was, only who he seemed to be years ago: a man perpetually turning away. Now a blankness.

The kitchen table is covered with paper, her brushes lean in a jar of water, daubs of paint drying on a saucer. The beachscape recedes to a sheet of paper marked with color. It occurs to Goldie that Sadie is requesting her presence, something Sadie has not done before: she's not asked anything of Goldie, really. And Goldie must respond. A fear comes on then: she pictures the lake just before ice, gray black and unyielding. There is a heavy dropping sensation in her legs and belly and chest. She cannot imagine leaving town limits—her body will not have it. The cold wave goes through her, and a faint droning begins, a panic not unlike the panic from the war. For that moment it seems as if by leaving Venice Beach, she'll cause the town to wither and vanish, and she'll be unable to find it again. In fact, she does not even want to leave her apartment. It will be difficult to go to work today; she'll have to coax herself. But first there is the question, and she must answer the question. She does not know what to say to Sadie, and not knowing, she slices an orange. And now the air in the apartment smells more like orange and less like fear. For a moment she sits in the kitchen with the telegram and the watercolors and the sliced fruit, waiting for the presence of mind to call Sadie. This she has never done, though she cannot say why: it isn't just the money. Finally, she lifts the telephone receiver and asks for a long-distance operator.

The woman who answers the telephone is not Sadie. She is Southern maybe, Negro maybe. She speaks through the operator's line, saying *Mrs. Feldstein is not at home,* but Goldie puts the call through anyway. *I am her sister,* Goldie says, *in California.*

"Miss Cohen?" the woman says.

"I can't be there for the funeral. Would you tell her that?"

"Yes, Miss Cohen. I'll tell her that."

"Don't delay the funeral on my account," Goldie says. "I'm Goldie." But her own voice seems flat and remote. Then the woman on the phone asks if there's anything else, and the question's confusing: Goldie can't imagine anything else, even what *anything else* might include. "No," she says to the woman. "I don't think so. No."

And the woman on the phone at Sadie's house tells her, "I'm sorry about your father." The woman says, "You're all in my prayers."

CHAPTER 23

Lillian

SEPTEMBER 1947

After six weeks, only six weeks, there are moments when the voice that intrudes has the huskiness not of age but of desire, containing in it flirtation, a low, quiet _Do you?_ The full conversations have dropped away, and remaining is this question with its suggestion of pleasure and anticipated pleasure. A strange bittersweet echo. Two weeks ago she heard a man buy a newspaper, a young man whose voice had a pitch similar to Abe's—_Thank you,_ he told the paperboy—and the old phrase flooded back, rooted itself in the present. Echoing when she butters toast in the morning, as she unlocks the cash register, as she pauses to cross Elmwood, the phrase sometimes paired with a flash of Abe's face. Like a photograph surfacing from another decade, the face younger than the recent familiar Abe. _Do you?_ he says, nothing more. Just a fragment, but perhaps it's the fragment that lay at the heart of their relationship. Perhaps the exact center of her life with Abe was a moment in her flat, one day when Abe was happy and amorous and asked _Do you?_ after whatever intimate comment she'd made. What had she said? She liked some way he touched her? She wanted him to stay?

Mostly what she conjures is the sound of his breathing, thick at night, or his exasperation about Irving (*My Irving loves cards too much. Whiskey also*) or his daughters (*Celia*, sotto voce. Then a quick shake of his head. And later, perhaps by an hour, *Jo*. A sigh). Lillian can easily recall the recent pleasure of a mild evening, a walk, their early desire partly but not wholly eclipsed. But now this, passion-soaked, unwilled, present though the man is not. Had he spoken those words in that tone since the war began? She thinks not. The Abe of fifteen years ago, saying *Do you?* in that particular way, will likely be with her for some time. She ought to prepare herself for the recurring shock of him appearing—handsome, still middle-aged—and speaking one small phrase, for the single glimpse of him before he vanishes.

The recent Abe was more contemplative and sad. "Do not think you are free of the Old World," he'd told her. "You are not free of the Old World." He was thinking of Russia, Poland, a litany of other countries. And he may have been right: because she did not know those countries, she thought of her life as separate. At times they seemed mythic planets, though here was Abe, and here was Bertha, grief-stricken by the war and all that preceded it. Abe did not refer to her personal world, and yet that was here too, her own small history, her own small regrets, much of it connected to him—who, though dead, nonetheless continued to seduce. *Do you?* Perhaps—this is the part she cannot remember, the shifting part—after the question he reached to kiss her, or smirked and held back until she could not bear the waiting, for the kiss or for him to enter her. She can picture the scene unfolding: the younger Abe addresses some other, younger Lillian. It was *that* Lillian he kissed, a vanished Lillian she cannot pretend to be. And the coy Abe does not acknowledge the Lillian she is now. He can neither kiss her nor acknowledge that he won't. He simply repeats *Do you?* without self-knowledge, ready to proceed with the already vanished seduction. And as she buys her own morning paper and counts her bus fare, Lillian cannot stop him, can only wait for him to briefly fade out. As when the recording ends and the needle lifts.

Since early August she's been watching the days unfold as if from a great height, feeling clearheaded but knowing something would eventually give. She's waited, imagined an obvious fall—say, an actual collapse at his gravesite, or an unrelenting impulse to speak with a rabbi. She's waited and now Moshe has summoned her to his office for the reading of the will, and a younger Abe summons her from her old flat, and her skin feels strangely electric.

It was Sadie who summoned her in August. Lillian was wrapping a box of party invitations, silver writing on pale pink paper, and Sadie called and said her father had died in his sleep. He didn't suffer, the doctor had told her. His death was peaceful.

August. Her hands seemed pink and silver. The words had been uttered and could not be taken back. Lillian told the customer she would deliver the invitations later, and ushered the woman out of the store and took a taxi to Lancaster. A hot, bright, breezy day. A few fat white clouds sailed east over the city. The taxi smelled of tobacco, and in the backseat she held her own unlit cigarette and felt herself suspended between worlds. There persisted the sense that she could talk Abe out of such a thing, the way she might talk him out of bad weather travel to New York. She knew he kept secrets about his health; the previous winter had been especially hard. But he'd seemed better since May, and now it was summer, it was August, the clouds were sailing east.

When the taxi pulled up in front of the house, her fantasy of persuading him back dissipated. The maple leaves seemed unusually large and green, a kind of audience. The lawn was recently mown, the roses profuse. A silhouette appeared in the doorway—Jo? Celia? Sadie?—and vanished as Lillian approached. He was still in his bed, Sadie had told her, and Lillian walked without stopping through the foyer and up those stairs she had never ascended and followed the hallway to the doorway from which Sadie herself was emerging. For a moment, Sadie took hold of Lillian's hands. There was a slight quivering in Sadie, her eyes liquid, bewildered, her mouth a pinched bud. Then she released Lillian's hands and was gone. Abe lay on a large brass-frame bed, *as if asleep*, she wanted to tell herself, but there was an unnameable difference, even from the doorway. She walked to the bedside and touched his hands and face and sat with him for a time. Perhaps he had known this might happen: he had stayed at her house less and less in July. The doctor said he did not suffer, but the doctor was not there. Perhaps he was frightened. She had not wanted him to be alone, had not wanted him to be frightened, but he was a stubborn man, more stubborn, perhaps, than anyone else she'd known.

Below she could hear footsteps, the opening and closing of the front door, murmurs. The light made a shadow pattern of leaves against the windowpane and the sheers and the far side of the bed. She did not want to see how the hours to follow would change him, and draw his body further and further from himself, nor did she want to leave this room, with the pattern of light and leaves, the brass bed and Abe. For a short while she remained, in the state of not-wanting, touching Abe's hand, and then it was time to leave: she could not say why, but it was time. She kissed him on the forehead and left the room, and took the staircase down to where the Lipsky brothers were talking with Bill Feldstein, and passed them with a nod. It was all a matter of footsteps, she told herself, footsteps down the front walk, and the sidewalk, and up the street to Delaware, where she found a taxi.

There was a funeral, which she attended, and a graveside service, which she did not. She sent flowers and fruit to the house on Lancaster and did not sit with his family, but instead closed her store and stayed home for a week. There were condolence notes and visitors—she'd apparently become a respectable widow. Most days Moshe and Bertha visited her, and Bertha, still fragile but stronger, brought her dinner. And then she returned to the store and began to wait for the death to be real. Even now, in mid-September, there's the small daily shock that he has not come to her house these many weeks, that the death was not incidental and temporary, a buying trip to New York irritatingly extended. That he has not returned with the usual set of apologies for absence, the larger box of chocolates, the better bottle of gin, his favorite ways of touching her.

If she travels or moves away, it will not matter to him. He will not miss her, because he does not exist. He will not look for her, because there is no "he" to look. And this Lillian finds oddly difficult to comprehend, though she knows it to be true. There is each day the smallest grain of doubt, and the incremental relearning of her current state of affairs.

Lillian has not seen Abe's children since the funeral, when all of them, even Sadie and Irving, maintained a peculiar quiet, as if mute. And the image of them mute has stayed with her: she pictures them, lips buttoned, glassy-eyed, staring at the ground, the distant trees, each other, like dolls whose angle of vision occasionally shifts. But they must by now have returned to themselves, Lillian thinks, there are businesses and children to attend to. Though Celia might stay mute as long as she likes.

And when Lillian arrives at the law office—the same-as-always law office, richer than twenty years ago, carpets and furniture replaced, but the same stolid look—Abe's children are in fact speaking. Squabbling.

They're in the conference room with the long oak table, Sadie and Jo and Irving, and Moshe's partner Solly Feigenbaum, Solly at the head of the table and Irving to his right, Sadie two chairs down on the left. There's a file and a notepad in front of an empty chair toward the middle of the table, a scrawl of writing. Jo is severe in her navy blue suit, pacing the carpet between the table and the tall windows overlooking the city square.

"Jo, would you sit down?" Sadie says. "If she decides to come up, she'll come up."

"She said she would," Jo says. "This morning she was calm and she said she would."

"She doesn't like this sort of thing," Sadie says.

"Do you?"

"Of course not. Hello, Lillian."

"Hello, Sadie," Lillian says. "Hello, Jo. Solly, Irving." Irving too is in a suit, a new one, his face strikingly serious, an uncanny imitation of Abe's.

"We can't start without Celia," Jo says.

Feigenbaum busies himself with his file of papers, which attorneys confronted with families seem to do. He glances up, as if awakening from his reading, and checks his watch. "Moshe will be back in a minute."

"I gave her money for pastry," Irving says to Jo. "She'll be fine." There's a note of authority in his voice, recognizable if wobbly at the edges. He folds his hands on the table in front of him, another of his father's gestures, and it seems for an instant as if he might bloom into Abe. He is the spitting image—she's always known this but never has it struck her this way. She can't help but look at him, marvel. There's a curdling in her belly. As if something of Abe is physically alive, present, and it's true of course: this is Abe's son, and these his daughters (another one seems to be lurking in the coffee shop down the street). She glances away and then back at him: across the conference table in his suit—one identical, she realizes, to Abe's beige linen suit—the expression on his face is so somber and attentive, so un-Irving, he does not seem to be Irving at all. At a glance he is *Abe?* then Irving. She wonders—she does not remember, does not know, but it suddenly seems important— if he has his father's scent, a light musk mixed with tobacco and shaving lotion. The chair beside him is empty.

"Good morning, Lillian," Irving says. Somber, yes, though his voice is higher and less textured than his father's. "How have you been?"

And there's the strange electric sense and a tightness beginning in her throat. "Not bad. You?"

He shrugs, gestures vaguely toward the room, the way Abe might, the way Moshe might, the demeanor of a burdened, determined man. The merest flicker of fear crosses Irving's face before the good suit reasserts itself.

She could take the seat behind Irving (he used to borrow Abe's shaving lotion, didn't he?), but from the far side of the table she'd be more likely to see his young-Abe face. Behind her she hears heavy steps, Moshe's, and then Moshe is beside her. "Good morning, Lilly." He kisses her cheek. He is surprisingly pale (could it be that he, too, is disconcerted by Irving?). He takes the seat in front of the notepad, Sadie to his left, and pats the empty chair to his right. It occurs to her that the others have also been instructed where to sit, as if at a formal dinner, and for good reasons, though what Irving smells like may not be one of them—she sizes up her brother—or perhaps it is.

"Shall we, then?" Moshe says to Solly Feigenbaum.

"Celia isn't here," Jo repeats. She's jittery. Rattled, Lillian thinks. And of course she's rattled, her father is dead, anyone would be, but with Jo you can't predict.

"That isn't a problem," Solly says.

"Well, she should be here for this."

"Of course," Solly says. "We hoped Celia, as well as Golda"— eyebrows lift—"would join us today, but it isn't necessary. If you'd care to take a seat, here, I can show you the text of the will as I read."

Jo purses her lips, but acquiesces.

From her seat at the table Lillian can see the dropping curve of Moshe's cheek and chin against his gray suit jacket, the set of Sadie's white linen shoulders, Jo's face as she leans in to read with Solly Feigenbaum, Solly himself, Irving. Unlike Jo, Irving does not lean forward, though he is not relaxed. He sits the way Abe did at business meetings, straight-backed and attentive. He's a good actor, persuasive. She has known this about him for some time— has learned, for example, not to approach him in public—but knowing it does not seem to matter now.

Hardly a year ago, Lillian went to an Italian bakery on the West Side to buy cannoli for Bertha, and in the adjoining coffee shop she glimpsed a man she took at first glance for Abe, a startling, too young Abe, though of course it was Irving. He sat with a petite brunette, pretty, overly made-up. Perhaps Irving glanced her way—it seemed he had, but he hadn't caught her eye. As she was leaving the bakery, Lillian walked over to say hello. He was half turned away, though the woman gazed at Lillian directly.

"Irving?" Lillian said, and the woman touched his shoulder and gestured at Lillian.

He turned, greeted her with a look of incomprehension. "Madam? Is there something you need?" The woman glanced back and forth between them, assessing, but he seemed utterly innocent, baffled.

Lillian quickly apologized and pretended to fish inside her bag for her reading glasses. "You'll have to excuse me, I should wear my glasses, forgive me for interrupting. I mistook you for a navy friend of my brother's."

"I'm an army man," Irving said. "Is your brother's friend handsome?" He winked at the woman, who relaxed then, smiled at him, reached for his hand.

Lillian left for the street and the rest of her errands, and when she saw him again at the jewelry store, he greeted her as he did in the law office—"Hello, Lillian, how have you been?"—neither then nor later making any allusion to the coffee shop or the West Side or the woman.

And now she needs to be careful, with Irving consciously imitating Abe, and the younger Abe popping into her head, saying <u>Do</u> <u>you?</u> and Abe's will, his wishes transmuted to this other form and read in the voice of Solly Feigenbaum: all traces and echoes and illusion, seductive ephemera. She rubs her thumb and index finger together to calm herself.

Feigenbaum reads with lackluster precision, and there's a lulling effect, a counterweight to the strange thrumming that seems to swim through the room. The words do not sound like Abe's, though the logic does. He's left most of the jewelry business to Irving, with the intention that Irving manage it, but 30 percent goes to Jo. There's the matter of the house on Lancaster, ownership of which is to be equally divided among his children, Golda, Celia, Josephine and Irving Cohen and Sadie Cohen Feldstein. The Ford to be shared by Josephine and Irving Cohen. A small trust has been set up for Celia Cohen. Stock set aside for Josephine Cohen, Sadie, Margo and Elaine Feldstein and Lillian Schumacher, as well as $3,000 to Miss Schumacher. The wedding ring of Rebecca Cohen to go to Golda Cohen (at this Sadie inhales noticeably); Rebecca Cohen's pearls to Sadie Cohen Feldstein; Rebecca Cohen's other jewelry to remain with Josephine Cohen, with the understanding that she and Celia Cohen equally share ownership of this jewelry. A pocket watch, two particular pairs of cuff links to Moshe Schumacher (Irving nods. Jo bites her lip). Abraham Cohen's pipe collection to go to Moshe Schumacher.

"One of them is mine," Jo says.

"One?" Solly says.

"Pipe. Cherrywood."

"If you own a pipe then by definition it would not be part of Abraham's collection," Solly tells her.

"Well, it is," Jo says. "But he said I could have it."

"I see," Solly says. "Do you intend to contest this bequest?"

"Jo," Moshe says. "Why don't we talk about this later?"

"He did say I could have it."

"It's a pipe," Sadie says. "Why would you want a pipe?"

"It's my pipe," Jo says.

And Lillian pictures his pipes, the casual intimacy of Abe's smoking, some imprint of his lips still on the mouthpiece. Perhaps Lillian herself should have a pipe: how much closer can one get, now, to Abe's body? Which is gone, Lillian thinks, the man's gone, though perhaps Jo will try to extract him from the pipe. As if the pipe will confer what her father, or her life, has not. How can you blame her? Pretend there's a chance—tiny, but real—that a pipe could grant you your father's legacy, or any of your hopes: wouldn't you take it? Carry that pipe everywhere? Yet it's a dangerous impulse; what's the difference between the wish to have that pipe and to smell Abe's shaving lotion on his son? Imagine _Do you?_ expanding to a morass of Abe memorabilia (the house? the store?), Abe's shadow solidifying, then smothering her, smothering all of them.

Jo, don't, Lillian thinks. _Just don't._

"I'll buy you a pipe," Sadie says.

"I would be happy to buy you a pipe," Irving says.

"I'm sure," Moshe says, "we could work out a trade." There's an underlying tone of command, which seems to bring Jo back to herself.

"Go on," she mumbles to Solly.

And Solly returns to the monotone apportioning of the contents of the house and personal effects among Abe's children, most objects—the glassware and fine china and silver—intended for one or another version of shared use and joint ownership. And then he is done reading the list, and still that electric sensation is with Lillian and still she is waiting for something more profound, some deeper knowledge gleaned from the will. Jo's dogged concentration persists. Irving's brow furrows, though he remains still and mute. Sadie turns to glance at Moshe and Lillian, then back to Solly—all of them, it seems, waiting, though Solly has read to the end, they can see that. The room itself is silent, but for Solly Feigenbaum's shuffling of papers, and Lillian understands then that she is waiting for a personal message from Abe, something like a love letter, something like a kiss. And there is the startled recognition of her own childish confusion—a will is not a love letter. He has been generous in his provisions but money and stock are not the point, or, in truth, are not enough. She wants whatever lay at the center of her relationship with Abe revealed at last, named and offered to her safekeeping, the pure thing tangible as stone.

It takes a moment for her to collect herself. Moshe is watching her. Moshe himself is unmistakable, he seems utterly permanent—though today he is too pale. She cannot imagine Moshe's death, but she also cannot imagine his absence sparking this kind of bewilderment. He is her brother. He loves her. He has always loved her. He has never disappeared. Abe, alive, often disappeared, and what compensations are there for the ways the living vanish?

Jo is peering out the windows again. She leaves the room without a good-bye, and Irving shakes hands with Solly Feigenbaum. Lillian, stunned, remains intent on carrying herself through this moment, this leave-taking: the polite good-bye to Sadie, who hurries after Jo, the polite good-bye to Irving (Abe's lotion? She can't tell when he gives her a peck on the cheek) as he and Solly walk to Solly's office. She does not yet notice what has occurred, or failed to occur: that she hasn't once imagined the house on Lancaster. It is, for her, empty of desire, a house for strangers. And when she later envisions the house, it seems to her peeled into stiff wooden segments, the way you might peel the bark off a branch and idly split the inner green fibers.

Lillian crosses to the windows: along the street, a miniature Sadie waits outside the coffee shop and then a small Jo emerges through the door, and Sadie takes Jo's arm and walks her north up the block. Lillian's aware of her detachment, of watching without longing, but the distance, the sense of being outside other lives, is the old familiar one. Perhaps she has always missed the center of things. It's the periphery she knows, the periphery she moves through most easily, but with the assumption of some center, somewhere. And perhaps Abe recognized something beyond the loneliness of peripheries, or something about what the center is and is not. The time with him already feels like dandelion weeds blown, the small floating bits leaving a skeletal awareness. Of course you cannot save moments, but she thought they would have accumulated anyway into something more solid. Or that, at the very heart of her time with Abe she would have known—this is the center, the depth, the point of greatest immersion—and that knowledge would be a homecoming from which she could not be exiled. And if such a thing did occur with him, she was not aware, except for the intensity of their lovemaking at particular moments: was it then? Always something seemed withheld, the immersion so brief and fleeting that even then she remained on the peripheries. And he was too soon dead. And she had forgotten what is now evident: she is a woman with a home and a business, a life distinct. She is not in fact a widow: he has spared her widowhood, he has spared her the morass of his house and children, the financial squabbling that would have ensued, has spared her maddening years.

What had she wanted? Another city? Another world? Another life, certainly. All those dinners, and Abe with his gentlemanly Saturday evening routines of dining in the better restaurants and visiting her apartment, or in later years her house, making love with her and departing on Sunday to return to that other life of his, the one she would visit the public spheres of, the one linked to hers but untouchable. That was her bargain all along, and she's become a woman nearing sixty. And if she leaves the city now, so much later, it is not to leave behind the house on Lancaster. And if she stays, it is not to stay in its orbit.

"I have a client waiting," Moshe tells her. The room is empty. He stands beside her now, beside the tall windows, a large, wilting man. "Have dinner with us tonight?" He offers to pick her up at her shop or her house, wherever she likes.

Her mouth seems dry and she has to think the words before saying them. And then she speaks as if she's a self-possessed woman, as if everything is fine. "Yes, good," she says. She pictures her store, a checkerboard of light and shadow on the street beyond, Moshe's Chrysler pulling up before the plate glass window, imagines Bertha and Moshe in the front seat, peering out for her. And in this moment, if she wants anything, she wants the waiting Chrysler. "The store at five-thirty? Don't let Bertha cook. We'll go somewhere nice."

He nods and gestures toward the door of the conference room, and for an instant she does not want to leave this room, this moment, this spot by the window, as if leaving the room—and not an implausible moment in August—marks Abe's death. But the smaller, intangible deaths have taken hold: the world has changed. It is September, a day more August than October. In a moment she will be out on the street, passing department stores and bakeries and simmering crowds; and here is Moshe taking her arm and walking her, leisurely, into the hallway, and kissing her on the cheek. She is telling him to have a good afternoon, to give her love to Bertha, to choose a favorite restaurant, the words issuing as they always have, as if Lillian is in charge of saying them.

CHAPTER 24

Irving

1948

Irving's hand rests three inches from Esther Rosen's: for a moment the world seems reduced to the proximity of hands and the white linen tablecloth of the Hour Glass Restaurant, the small distance he does not know how to span. Sweat beads on his forehead, a cresting wave of sweat he associates with the war, and Esther—queenly Esther—smiles at him and sips her wine and asks him if he and Sadie were close as children. Because of course it's Sadie they have in common, Sadie who convinced him to call Esther Rosen, the crème de la crème of marriageable women, elegant and German-Jewish and, at twenty-eight, a war widow. Even in her long-sleeved dress, even with her war widow sadness, Esther shimmers.

She is waiting for him to answer and he forces his gaze away from the hands on the table—his own like dumb clay—to her eyes, chestnut and long-lashed, and what is it she wants to know? Sadie in childhood? A fine sister, sure, but his sisters had sometimes blurred together, a pervasive cloud of girl.

"My favorite sister," Irving says. "What would I do without her?" He winks. It's involuntary, this wink, and Esther Rosen glances away. She tells him she feels the same about her oldest brother. Brothers then, more than one: dicey, isn't it, with brothers around? He prefers sisters, though his own make a nasty hobby of his business.

In January, when Sadie repeated the usual advice, *It's time,* meaning marriage, he finally wondered if she might be right. He was lonely, the loneliness hardly bearable since their father's death, though he wasn't sure why. It seemed that for years his father had invisibly sheltered him from the deepest loneliness, and now that his father was himself invisible, the loneliness rose up stark and indisputable.

"Papa would want it," Sadie said, as if Irving's mind were transparent. In spite of everything, his father had believed in marriage, hadn't he? He'd wanted Irving to marry Rachel Brownstein, velvety Rachel, now the mother of four, living with her doctor husband in the suburbs.

Shouldn't Irving have listened? He's thirty-eight, he should be married—even Leo, once-wild Leo, has been married for years, he's got sons of his own and not much time for Irving. Twice a month Irving sees him at poker games, but then Leo is distracted by cards. In February, over drinks, Irving asked him, "You think I should get married?"

Leo smiled and slapped him on the shoulder. "Who is she?" he said. "She must be something to get you talking like that."

The smile and the slap bolstered him. After his second drink Irving was flooded by a peculiar, fervent hope.

SADIE INTRODUCED him to two Sarahs and a Rachel and an Edith; once she set him up with brainy, skittish Hannah Farber; once with Ida Levine, who had money and solid goodwill and no sense of humor; she set him up with Lora Goldberg, thirty-two and sweet, very sweet, doubtless a virgin, which was not in his view a selling point. Leah Berman he liked; she was earthy and funny and sexier than she knew. Just last week he took Leah to the pictures and thought about kissing her. This seemed to be progress. But in the presence of Esther Rosen, the other dates all seem somehow the same long date, the girls all blending into one Jewish girl, attractive enough, relentlessly nice, getting a little older, eager to please him without knowing what that actually required: they wanted to bake cakes for him. Or at least so it seemed. Perhaps they too were acting, perhaps they too were speaking in code and had hidden themselves away. It was impossible to tell. They seemed so wholly, convincingly good, so wholly, convincingly earnest and pious, not asexual—they were curvy, sometimes zaftig, sometimes sleek—but so wrapped in niceness could they know what sexual climax was?

It had taken months to get a date with Esther, though she was the first one he called. In '44 her husband had been killed in the Pacific, but even now no one expected her to date: Jacob Rosen had been her high school sweetheart, and this part of the story was always accompanied by a sigh, meaning *incomparable romance*. He'd been a medical student from a high-class family but at least he didn't die in France, in Irving's war: no one could say he died in place of Irving. And at least Esther would know a thing or two about marital relations.

Here at the Hour Glass—a place his father had frequented— Irving would like to discover just what Esther knows, to unpeel her navy silk dress; he would like to be inside her right now. If she were a free and easy woman in someone else's town, they might leave the table and find a room, even a bathroom, and do it right there, but you don't try that sort of thing with Sadie's set. He can't even bring himself to touch Esther's hand.

"Family's so important," Irving says. He speaks with all the gravity he can muster. "These last few years must have been difficult for you."

Esther blinks and sets down her wineglass. Her eyes are wet, shining, and he thinks they must look the same in passion. She's working on her composure, you can see that, he's rattled her a little, which is not a bad thing.

She nods. "For you too. The war, your father."

And at the mention of his father, his own eyes well, it's perfectly genuine, a quick piercing jab he didn't expect. He moves his hand the three inches over the linen tablecloth and covers her hand, which is warm, the warm sensation moving fast to his spine and groin. He strokes the back of her hand with his thumb, and a quote comes to him, perfect for the moment. "We have to remember the good in our lives."

"You're right to say that," Esther says. "We do."

She glances at their hands—he shouldn't overplay this, slow is best—and he moves his hand away and raises his wineglass. "To the good in our lives." They drink the Bordeaux, which tastes like thick velvet. Esther Rosen is beautiful, by any standard she is beautiful, and here she is with him: she could just be his luck. He feels a warm flush as the waiter brings their plates. Chicken in fragrant sauce, rice.

"Have you met Sadie's daughters?" he says.

Esther is smiling, smiling. "They're quite something."

"Sadie's got her hands full," he says, because this is what you say about teenagers, about all children, isn't it?

Esther nods and laughs. "I was trouble at that age too," she says.

"I suppose we all were." He pictures himself, and Leo. "Though not Sadie. That wasn't her style."

Esther's smile—the one he's been working for—fades out. "Your mother was sick then, wasn't she?"

And the image rises not of his mother, but of the house during snowmelt, a dripping from the eaves, crocus tips in a sunlit patch of ground, an earth smell. It's unnerving, how direct Esther is, but her look, too, is open, as if this were a normal thing to say. He would like to get off the subject of dead people. True, he started it, but only because it was a way in. How else was he going to get past the dead husband?

"She was a great lady," Irving says.

"That's exactly what Sadie says."

"Didn't I tell you about Sadie? My favorite sister."

For the moment they have recovered; for the moment they can eat their chicken and he can steer the subject to pleasure, starting with small pleasures, maybe the pleasures of summer. Long evenings, boats on the lake, Crystal Beach. Dinner with Esther is not so different from an ordinary date, is it? Not so different, for example, from meeting a woman in another town on one of his road trips. Take the club in Niagara Falls, the woman from last summer—Susanne. In July there had been a few uncertain, anticipatory weeks when he wondered what Susanne was capable of, a teetering, hopeful space he occupied until his father died in August and his road trips stopped. With Esther, Irving must work harder; he has to choose pleasantries that are in fact true, to behave at all times properly. But there's the off chance that Esther prefers improper behavior. That would be something.

They are finishing their meal when the waiter comes by with two glasses of champagne, compliments of the party in the far corner. It's the Schumachers, Moshe and Bertha, there with Lillian. They are putting on their coats: have they been here the whole time? Watching Irving try to hold hands with Esther?

He hasn't seen Lillian in months, and she looks majestic, the lush grandeur undiminished.

"I'd forgotten about your father and Miss Schumacher," Esther says.

And though Esther wouldn't know to say so, it does seem odd, the three of them without his father. They stop by the table to greet him, and Irving kisses the women, shakes hands with Moshe, introduces Esther, who apparently needs no introduction.

"Hello, dear," Moshe says. "How is your family?"

It seems that Lillian and Bertha are about to leave town for vacation. Florida, Lillian says. She's taking Bertha.

"The women are leaving me behind to work," Moshe says. And he's smiling, he kisses Bertha on the cheek, but Irving is struck: yes, they are leaving Moshe and everyone else behind. He has missed Lillian, he realizes. Now he will miss her more.

"Miami," Bertha says.

"Have a wonderful time," Esther says.

"Yes," Irving says. "Have a wonderful, wonderful time."

LATER, WHEN THEY LEAVE the restaurant, Esther seems more fully relaxed. Or perhaps it's Irving relaxing? She touches his arm and together they cross the street, the city block to his car; he opens the passenger door for her with a flourish and then they are in the private realm of the Ford, driving to her house in Kenmore, the spring air sharp with melted snow and new grass.

Does she desire him? He cannot tell. He does not know how to ask her, or even if one can ask Esther Rosen something like this: there are different rules here. You can tell she knows about pleasure, that shimmer she has, she's probably a woman who likes sex, who no doubt misses it. And as he pilots the car across Colvin the street seems reduced to a series of lights—lit windows and streetlamps, occasional red or blue signs—and the interior of the Ford expands. Now the world is here, in the front seat of the Ford, the radio dial pouring jazz through yellow numbers, Esther Rosen's face shifting with the passing lights. If he keeps driving, this space will hold, he is certain, they'll remain suspended in the motion and dark and light, in the scent of wet bark and turned earth and budding forsythia, in the warm apple scent of Esther, which seems to be filling the car. They can stay here and still drive south and east, to the sea, to New York or to Atlantic City; they could travel as far as Florida, Miami, a hotel on the beach, a wide blue pool, and hot sun. He and Esther could slip into the pool, float with their drinks, warm water around them and the smell of oranges, the smell of coconuts, he and Esther then kissing in the pool—how smooth her skin, there in the pool, his hands on her, easing off her bathing suit, his hands then on her breasts and between her legs, all of him pressed against her, then inside her, inside the blue pool, in the warmth and blue and Esther.

He pulls up in front of her house and stops the car. He does not want to break the spell of the silence, to leave the space of the car, but she is picking up her handbag, turning to the passenger door. It is terrible not to be touching her now. "Please," he says, getting her to stay in the Ford just a few more seconds, while he walks around the car and opens the door for her.

"Thank you, Irving." She's smiling again, maybe a little amused, but it's nothing bad: she is indulging him, which is a good sign. Perhaps she will invite him in. Perhaps she is ready for the pleasure he can give her. It seems to him as if she too might have imagined Florida, but he can't be sure, he can't read her face. She glances away toward her house, which like the others has a few lights on. Then the nearby houses also come into focus, the lights receding into their indicator of house-ness, of occupancy. The houses swell. The neighborhood, he realizes, is quiet but watchful, alive. He follows Esther up the brick front walk, and in an instant it is as if the car no longer exists, and the plush languid feel of the drive has been replaced with numbness.

Esther waves at some green shoots near the front steps. "The daffodils have started."

"Wonderful," he says. He is dismayed: they are nowhere near Miami, where they should be. Here is the Esther Rosen Sadie knows, and now he imagines Sadie shadowing him, peering out of an unlit window somewhere along the street. He does not know how to wish Esther good night. A kiss? He doesn't know how to kiss her, or rather, to do it in some acceptable way, pleasurable but not too pleasurable, not inviting passion. It would be too much for her, wouldn't it? The neighborhood *is* crawling with her friends, her family, her temple congregation.

This he knows: he cannot sleep with Esther without marrying her. Maybe he was wrong, maybe Sadie and even his father were wrong, and marriage isn't for him, that sharp loneliness just part of the long winter. But it's spring. And he cannot kiss Esther Rosen without his hands starting to move over her; he cannot touch her without trying to sleep with her, and if he tries to sleep with her, something will crack open, maybe the whole of his life. Her refusal would be crushing, but if she consents and he doesn't marry her, disaster will strike.

He walks her to her door and she thanks him for the evening. She seems sincere. She hesitates and for an instant he freezes, but finally manages to give her a peck on the cheek and step back, like a teenager, like a boy drowning in the smell of melting snow. He's afraid he might cry. He folds his hands behind his back, waiting for her to cross into her house and lock the door behind her, leaving him to drive to Lancaster.

The door opens. "It was lovely," Esther says, and moves into the shadow of the hallway.

"My pleasure." Irving bows slightly, a gesture of his father's, and hears her say, "Good night." Then the door closes and he's aware of the lighted windows of the nearby houses and the empty street.

On his way home he allows himself to drive to the park, and for a quarter-hour there in the car to imagine it is Esther Rosen touching him, Esther Rosen making him come; then to sit quietly watching a square of night sliced by branches, and sip from his flask and smoke. And he returns to Lancaster, with its strange blend of desolation and claustrophobia, the dining room table covered by Celia's latest jigsaw puzzle, which she has only just started. Three corners, two sides. In the dark the puzzle appears as shadows and pale shapes, the table itself part of the jigsaw, like a sea flooding a skinny chain of islands, though tomorrow Celia might tell him it is Paris, or a carnival scene, or bowls of fruit.

SUNDAY MORNING Sadie calls him: she often calls after he's met one or another of the marriageable girls, but the telephone still takes him by surprise. He's drinking coffee in the kitchen, and Jo picks up, says *Hello* and *Sadie*, then starts in about trouble with one of the rain gutters. She is loud: it's her habit to speak to Sadie in a half-shout, as if Sadie is deaf or culpable. Even when she asks Sadie about the nieces, she uses this loud, accusatory manner. "When you gonna bring them over? Haven't seen them for a while." (Jo does not speak this way to the nieces themselves, she likes them, you can hear her trying to be kind.) Quarreling with Sadie seems to sustain her, she'll stay on the phone as long as she can, so it isn't the best of luck to hear her say, "Yeah, Irving's home," and call his name. When he picks up the phone in the parlor, Jo's interest shifts to Celia's puzzle. He's holding his coffee cup but no saucer, and no coaster for the table. From the dining room, Jo eyes him, eyes the cup, daring him to set it down on bare wood.

"How are you?" Sadie says. "How was your dinner?"

"Good," Irving says. "Nice dinner." He turns his back to the dining room, but it's difficult to hold the phone and the coffee cup and in some way cover his mouth to thwart Jo's eavesdropping.

"Well, good. I'm glad."

"Um-hmm."

"So you're going to take her out again?"

And here he tries to cover his mouth with the cup itself, saying "Maybe so," but Sadie can't hear him and chastises him for mumbling. He swishes some of the sugary coffee around his mouth, a sensation he likes, and tries again. "Maybe."

Jo slips away down the hall, perhaps recognizing he'll say nothing revealing, perhaps already bored. There's a squeaking of hinges, the loud slam of the back porch door.

"You do like Esther," Sadie says.

"Sure I do."

"Well anyway, she had a good time."

"How do you know?"

"Her mother. We spoke this morning."

"Already? God, Sadie."

"Please don't take that tone."

"You talked to her mother?"

"Didn't I say that? I said that."

There's the passing image of Esther in the car, the blue pool feeling rising but quickly occluded. The porch door hinges squeak again, and a moment disappears, as if he has slept and awakened to find the clock advanced.

IT WOULD DO him good to talk with Lillian: he used to talk to Lillian all the time, didn't he? It seems that way. He pictures her in luncheonettes and at high-class clubs and on the far side of the jewelry counter, smiling at him and asking about his life while she waits for his father. She was the one who told his father, there in the store, to drop the idea of Irving courting Rachel Brownstein— as if recognizing in Irving qualities his father did not. Lillian would understand, but Lillian is going to Florida. And she's been more distant since his father's death. Maybe even before? It must have put her off, seeing him on the West Side, though you'd think she'd be the first to understand. But that was years ago. She seemed friendly enough at the Hour Glass.

Of anyone, Lillian might know why he so resembles his father—on occasional, bleary days, in the shop's window he glimpses his father's reflection in place of his own—yet he cannot learn how to *be* his father. As if a secret key has been permanently hidden from him, and lacking the key he lacks command and the good fortune that must follow in its wake. There is only the knowledge of suits: he's learned to choose good suits and he is careful in his grooming. He holds to his father's routines of opening the jewelry store and polishing the cabinets. He greets the customers deferentially. And perhaps the accumulated days worked in the style of his father will finally reveal to him what he needs to know. This is a thought he returns to, even as he is more and more stunned by uncertainties. He's gone as far as trying on his father's suits, in case his father somehow still inhabits them. But the suits literally do not fit him: they are tight in the shoulders, the pants loose and too long. They seem to move around the closet independently, rearranging themselves according to season, as if sentient. Though it must be Celia's doing, this feels like a sharp pinch from the other side, an edgy reminder of departure and refusal.

Yes, loss of shelter, Irving thinks, though the idea confuses him. The house is standing and paid for, the store the same store it was ten years ago, the bank account solid enough. And often he has taken shelter in women—the most profound (if temporary) shelter in sex. He's never really free of the lust, which is inextricable from need: they call and you answer. He hasn't found another way to fully quell the panic, though he calms when he walks alone in the city, and when he visits new dance halls, and when he stops at the main post office to visit box 764, which he acquired last summer.

MONDAY, the mild spring weather helps him stay buoyant. Sunlight falls in bright bands over the downtown streets, high cottony clouds move east from the lake, which seems bluer than usual. A new start seems more possible—exactly, in fact, what he needs. He sweeps the sidewalk in front of the store and polishes the glass cases before he opens for the day; he arranges a display of freshwater pearls; he is purposeful and resolute. He is wearing his father's brand of aftershave.

Maybe it's this, the aftershave, which allows him a momentary pleasure in the thought of Esther: she had a nice evening, she told her mother, and perhaps felt more than she admitted. Perhaps she felt desire. He has a small window of time now, a few days: he can't wait too long before calling her again, she'll be expecting to hear from him. A call or maybe a note, though what follows next is not clear. He's only considered a first date and the vaporous distant country of marriage, not what a whole courtship might involve. What happens on a second date, or a third, in the world of Esther and Leah, the Rachels and Sarahs? There are bound to be hidden traps, and the key is to keep his wits about him. But a nice evening is propitious, he thinks, and it is the season of new beginnings; it's Monday; the good weather will bring in business. He has a window, it's small, but a window. A good day, he thinks, to play the numbers.

At noon Jo arrives, Celia with her. You can tell the way they walk in the door what the afternoon will be like. The prospects of the morning always shrink in the afternoon, but at the store Jo's less aggressive than she is at home. Maybe it's the presence of customers, or those reflections of his father in the window. Today Jo is quiet and uncomplaining, which passes for cheerful, and Celia clearly has bathed. They're both wearing spring dresses, new ones, Celia's yellow and white, Jo's a pale green. They look almost ordinary.

Of course he'd rather they left the store to him—Jo at her worst is snappish and mean—but whenever he decides to bar them from it, he falters. Inevitably, he'll have a bad morning, a terrible morning, on which it seems his body has lost substance and might dissolve altogether in the next trembling wave. Jo and Celia arrive for the afternoon, and the feeling recedes, and he is safe again. And so he relents: he can see no other way.

And at least Celia does not pin him to himself the way Jo does. Most days, Celia sits in the back with a card table set up and builds her jigsaw puzzles, which hold her concentration the way almost nothing else can. She causes no trouble, and most of the time she's more peaceable than Jo. She turns on the radio and opens up a bakery box of cookies and quietly reconstructs panoramas, her puzzles of cityscapes and seaside towns, or the duller, static flowers and cats. She does not bring her actual cats with her to the store, but there is often a rank catlike odor on her. She keeps her hair wrapped in scarves and works the puzzles and seems to him a theatrical, prematurely aging babushka. He has taken to buying her bottles of perfume shaped like inverted tulips, which help with the smell. Some days, after closing, after his sisters have left, he finds himself working on the puzzles. They comfort him, though he cannot say why.

He does not know how long their good moods will last. The weather helps; their trip to the department store helps. Celia's hair is clean today, which is a kind of triumph. These are good signs, better signs than he'd expected, and he leaves the store quickly, before they evaporate.

On his lunch hour he strolls. There's a watery scent in the air, a lake smell overlaid with the fragrance of soup and bread and cooked meat from the restaurants; the city's thick with noise, with buses and voices. On his walks, he's grateful to be in Buffalo, grateful, still, the war is over and receding: he allows himself to dwell only on the orchards in Somerset. They were beautiful to walk in, those orchards.

It's been a long road since England, long and not happy, but Esther Rosen had a nice evening. He will have to find a way to explain his life to Esther Rosen, and this will take ingenuity, not only because parts should stay hidden but also because he is unsure about what exactly has happened. His other lives seem unthinkably far away. As if there was a before and now there is an after, or, rather, a series of befores, a series of afters. And once the afters accumulate, certain befores seem nonexistent. Maybe this life began with a day in New York with Leo, a fancy dinner, though the memory has the patchiness of a dim room, the eye adjusted to a few details, the restaurant's red-and-black carpet with fleurs-de-lis made bold and large, steak with onions. Whiskey from a glass with paneled sides, like small windows that caught the light and spread prisms over the drink. Leo paid, and the coat-check girl had one dimple. The rest is oddly blank to him, though loose pieces occasionally swim up, as in dreams, Meg's face flashing into view and gone: someone else's story he's been told.

Returning to Buffalo he felt exhilaration in the city, the victory overshadowing the war. There was plenty worth forgetting and he had a gift, he thought, for moving on. He worked with his father again: he felt less a boy. So there was that before, that after. Irving's father seemed older, sure—Irving hadn't kept watch and he'd become old—but he still lavished appreciation on Irving for being a returning soldier. It seemed all past wrongs had been washed away, and even Irving's late, wild nights in the city were forgiven because the war was over, the war was over. Still, it was hard to ignore altogether his father's somberness, the endless clippings from the dailies and the *Jewish Review* and sometimes from the New York Yiddish paper, the way he and Bertha Schumacher would huddle with their files and dictionaries and write letters of inquiry in English and Yiddish and Polish and Russian.

The day Jo found their father unbreathing in his bed, Irving was hung over at the store, no eggs that morning, just toast and coffee and the prospect of a beautiful day spent inside. The first hours seem covered by a scrim, now a play of silhouettes: his own figure turned the CLOSED FOR THE DAY sign and covered the store windows while the sky outside was at its August brightness. His shadow figure walked to a small bar open early in the day, just for one drink before walking to the house, which was by then empty of his father.

What is sharp and clear from that day is Celia sitting in the yard with Bill, one of the odder sights he'd seen—Bill in his summer suit and tie, quietly swelling in the heat beside Celia, the two of them gazing at the grass and the plain summer air. Jo was not there, nor Sadie. Irving stood on the porch and said Bill's name and Bill turned his head and nodded and then Irving walked down to the wrought-iron chairs and the wrought-iron table, aware of his own smell, his drink, the cigarette he'd smoked. Bill's left hand rested on Celia's forearm, which seemed distinctly strange for Bill and distinctly strange for Celia.

"Sadie's gone to pick up Jo," Bill said.

And then Celia turned to Irving, Celia who had been so absolutely still. "I'm tired," she said. "Aren't you tired?" She made no move to get up.

Bill stood and offered Irving his chair and Irving sat and then seemed for a long time to be simply a floating body in the green and heat, he and Celia floating in the green and heat. She was wearing a pale blue headscarf. There was dirt on her hands from gardening, and the yard seemed lush, blooming, the zinnias and snapdragons and roses all blooming, tomatoes forming on the vines in the sunniest part of the yard and the marigolds almost winking, and he drank from his flask and sat next to Celia. And later Sadie returned with Jo and brought them cold drinks, lemonade in fact, which seemed perfectly reasonable, in the heat. He stayed in the chair, and Celia stayed in her chair, and after a while Sadie carried wet sheets into the yard and pinned them to the line, enormous white flags. The windows of his father's room were open, as if his father had escaped that way, crossing the rooftops the way an East Side boy might. One of the funeral home brothers appeared on the porch, wanting to know if Irving needed a viewing of the body. Irving's answer was definitely no, though he couldn't say why. Was this the right answer? If he could have moved from his chair, he would have called Leo, Leo would have known.

IT'S ALWAYS the Schumachers who know, isn't it? He should also talk to Leo now, about the Esther question, and how to handle it, and what he can tell her, and how to behave—maybe for once Leo will have lunch hour free—but when he calls Leo from a pay telephone, Leo says, "You okay?" and cuts in too soon with "Buddy, let me call you in a few days. I'm swamped."

He'll have to write a note then, some flowery thank-you, a way to buy some time. And anyway, it's a reason to go to Lillian's shop: maybe she hasn't left yet for Florida. The city seems alive today; it's spring; he can do this, he can sort out the marriage question. It's a matter of patience. He catches a bus up Main, and Lillian's shop is open—there's a little leap of hope—but a hired clerk is arranging notebooks on the counter. A snappy dresser in his twenties, a Mr. Green. He says he will pass on Irving's regards to Miss Schumacher, though he can't say for sure when she'll be back.

"I'm Abe Cohen's son," Irving says. "Maybe I'd better leave her a note."

"A note would be fine, Mr. Cohen."

But when he steps to the side counter to write, he realizes he cannot explain what is happening, that the matter of Esther is a thread linked to other threads he could untangle over drinks, given enough time, given enough drinks and Lillian's willingness to listen, but in a note he can only scribble: *Dear Lillian, How are you? Would you like to have lunch sometime? Fondly, Irving.*

AT A COFFEE SHOP, he orders a grilled cheese sandwich and works on the note to Esther Rosen. The first two sentences come easily, and then there's the vexing question of whether to allude to seeing her again. He does not know. He does not know. Finally, he settles on: *Dear Esther, Thank you for the marvelous evening. I hope this finds you well and enjoying the spring weather. Sincerely, Irving Cohen.*

He carries the note in his jacket pocket through the afternoon, and after closing, when Jo and Celia have again left the store, he places a stamp on it and drops it in the letter box on Main. He decides then that he deserves a small reward, a quick drink at a bar down the block, where he has taught the bartender to stop calling him Irving in favor of "TJ," claiming TJ was his nickname during the war. Now he is known in the bar as TJ, and he is immediately happier, with his whiskey and beer and improved name. And once he is feeling solidly TJ, he has no interest in going home. There is nothing to do but buy a ticket to the burlesque, which is featuring a new fan dancer and a lineup with a redhead named Dannora.

THE WINDOW of time is beautiful, free of worry. For two days he moves with ease, and a vague, giddy hope takes hold. Soon he'll talk to Leo, soon Lillian will write to him: it's spring, she'll be back soon. They will know what to do next, they will tell him, and meanwhile he will relax.

It's Thursday when Sadie calls, her "Hello" today decisive, smacking of mission. Thursday, still window-time, a point she has failed to understand. She wants to talk about the state of the store, and at first he thinks she means the carpets. He thinks she means the paint. These seem to him worthy of discussion, details his father insisted they attend to. The paint should be more cream than

white, the carpet does need cleaning. Maybe he should have fresh
flowers now and then, something Celia could take charge of.

"You could move north." Sadie mentions a location on Hertel
Avenue and another north on Delaware. "Get a pencil," she says.
"I'll give you the realtor's number."

For a moment he does not know what she means: it is as if she's
suggesting relocating an entire building from South Main Street—
in fact, an entire block, and the next block, and perhaps the lake.
The store has always been here, a snug shop in a busy commercial
district, gold lettering on the plate glass, *Abraham Cohen Jewelers*, just
as their father chose.

"I don't want a pencil," he says.

"Oh, Irving, it's only an idea."

"I don't care for your idea."

"Fine."

"Jo wouldn't like it either."

"Maybe not," Sadie says. "It would probably make her unhappy."

This sounds conclusive to him: it seems he has prevailed, and
they can return to something easy, like commiserating. "*More* unhappy," he says.

Sadie half-laughs, agreeing with him, yes, this is how they
measure Jo's moods, in degrees of unhappiness. "How's the store
for her these days?"

"I wouldn't say she likes it. Who knows what she likes."

"Well, you don't really need her there, do you? Business is
good, isn't it? You could hire a clerk."

He does not know what to say. It occurs to him that she's re-
making the world and teaching him how to marry Esther Rosen:
open a store in a genteel neighborhood, give his little profit to a
smooth, good-looking salesclerk—another Mr. Green—keep Jo
and Celia out of sight. And isn't she right? It's what he would need
for Esther, or for Leah, or for most of those girls. What he would
need to be the brother Sadie expects. Sadie doesn't understand at
all; how could she? She's not like Jo and Celia, not like him. She's
luckier, she has always been luckier, and now she's substantial,

marrying the way she did. There's even still a sexiness to her, which she wraps in suits and perfume and motherliness, and uses for persuasion. All part of the luck.

But she has ruined his window of time. Ruined it. "I have a customer," he says. "I have to go."

He hangs up the phone but his calm has vanished: his agitation spikes and soon the splintery vulnerable feeling returns. He closes the store for an hour and paces and smokes in the back. Where is the shelter? Where is the shelter? The store is his father's and not his father. He's confused, and Sadie's taking advantage—using Esther Rosen to take advantage. This he feels with increasing conviction, though he can't say he was forced into an evening with Esther. He phoned her, didn't he? He drove the car, paid for the meal, brought her home again. But this is not the point. The loneliness is not his fault, it's terrible and not his fault, and no one should take advantage.

By noon, his mood is so foul it's all he can do to keep himself from snapping at Celia when she arrives with Jo, smelling of cat. She gazes at him for a long moment, then asks if maybe he'd like to go for a walk now. She's talking to him the way people talk to her, as if he is a bomb sheathed in glass. He *does* want to go for a walk, that's exactly what he wants to do, to get out of the store, away from this place that is and is not his father, away from the cat smell and Jo's cold gaze—but that's none of Celia's business, is it? Still, he manages to quickly say yes, and to leave without exploding.

After two blocks of fast walking he stops to light a cigarette, and then he notices the city again. Despite the agitation, he is not impervious to the day, bright and breezy, to the liveliness of the streets, the women in lighter skirts and snug dresses with small jackets, no overcoats, their mouths lipsticked in pinks and reds, boys selling newspapers, lunch carts selling hot dogs and soda, yellow cabs easing their way through traffic, intermittent bursts of sun over sidewalks dense with suits and hats rushing to lunch. A beer? He will take himself out for a beer, but first to the post office, which does not take long to reach. He avoids the line of customers and heads for the boxes, to 764, which is brass-plated with black numbers. 764, the numbers that have in some way claimed him, the numbers he's started to play and that feel in this moment like deliverance. He turns the lock—more magic—and opens the box to a postcard which has been there for two weeks, a postcard he himself has mailed. It is addressed to TJ Gordon. He loves the moment of turning the lock, as any man might, and finding the card marked TJ Gordon, and taking the card as if it belonged to him, which in fact it does. On the front is a cartoonish map of New York State. On the reverse is a rhyming poem about sea battles he copied from a book in the parlor. It calms him to read the poem and turn the postcard over in his hand, and it seems enough for now, but he would like another letter, one from a woman. Maybe Susanne from the Falls. Last summer at the club, he took her phone number and address, and gave her the number of the post office box. He had liked the way she talked to him, with a chumminess that wasn't too coy, and the way she'd touched him. Why hadn't he been back there? August, yes, with its hard shock and impenetrable fog.

He is holding the postcard and the mailbox is empty. A small space but one in the real world marked TJ. It's a start, a foothold, but the size of it is a problem: you can't exactly live there. You can't bring a woman there. He feels good standing in front of the box, but he would feel better standing *in* the box, were the box on another scale, say the size of a room, or an apartment. A place with a good bed, a fine sofa, a nice oak table, an icebox. A tiled bathroom with a large white tub. You wouldn't need more than that.

And it is this he thinks of—the image of an efficiency taking shape in his mind—while he exits the wide doors of the post office, back into the day, having spoken to no one. In this moment he is a man who has checked his post office box and is now considering his apartment. The women on the street, all of them, seem lit up now, as if they have shed a final chrysalis, especially the young secretaries. Free for a while, they are marvelous, the slender one with the pink skirt and yellow waved hair, the coal-eyed one with the snappy walk. He can't take them all in, their bodies and voices:

there on the street, a hundred possibilities. The world could be that open, he thinks. And he stops at a bar and grill and drinks a cold beer, eats a sandwich, and watches the street scene through the screen door. For a time it seems anything could happen.

On his return to the store, a quiet elation stays with him: he senses an inevitability to the expansion of the post office box. This other space and the life it contains are fated. He does not know how it will occur, only that it will, it must. So he was not so wrong, this week, to hope: he just couldn't see the true source. There's a perfumed lightness then to the air, a sharp pleasure in observing women, the warm breeze itself a promise, and he is swept by a sense of generosity, which leads him to buy a bag of bakery cookies for Celia and Jo.

Through the afternoon it remains easy to be kind to his sisters, who are at first watchful, then seem to give in to the fact of spring, to the sugary cookies, to the new way of seeing the world. It is that simple to set the mood, isn't it? At the end of the day, after they leave, he takes his newspaper to the bar down the block and orders another beer. The bartender calls him TJ again, and he writes one more note, this one to Susanne in Niagara Falls. He's been traveling but now he's back, he says. He'll try to stop by the club one of these weekends.

IT IS BEST not to question a lucky streak: you ride it as long as you can, avoid diversion. If you stay focused, it just might carry you into a charmed life. It requires patience and faith, a heightened lucidity, attention to signs; also, avoidance of contradiction and doubt and anyone who closes windows of time. The elation is worth every attempt to sustain it, and Irving begins to visit the post office twice a day, once before he opens the store, once at lunch; has his daily beer at the corner bar; scans the classifieds every day for the right ad, the right efficiency. He will know when he sees it. He spends as little time as possible at the house, ignoring laundry, ignoring mail and chores, the rain gutter problem, the newsboy's bill. At the store, he does not answer the phone in the mornings—it's a risk for business, he knows, but worth it. He tells Jo to take messages from Sadie: he'd rather not speak to her right now.

Jo observes him but there's nothing disapproving in her manner. In fact, she smiles. "Sure thing," she says. Maybe she understands more than he gives her credit for: maybe she does in fact wish him well. He could use a sister wishing him well, but what matters is the way ahead, his own mission.

A week passes, and there is a brief note back from Susanne. *I'll be at the club Saturday night. How are you?* So she is still there: she is waiting. Saturday evening he drives out of the city to the Falls. The weather has brought people out, and there's a swing band with horns, a smooth-voiced tenor. Here is Susanne, just as she said, just as he remembers her: she's sweet-looking, with curly amber hair and a quick smile, a good dancer, an unfussy way about her. But she's cautious at first: it has been ten months, after all.

"I want to talk to you about what happened," he says. "I want to apologize for not writing to let you know." And he tells her the truth, or at least the important part: his father died.

She squeezes his hand, her face filled with sympathy. She's sorry, she tells him, she's glad to see him again. It's beautiful, the way she stays close to him in the crowded club, the way the name TJ sounds when she says it, a little amused. At a corner table she lets him kiss her, long deep kisses. He wants to sleep with her tonight—it takes an effort not to push her—but there is the promise of another date, and she's eager, he can tell she's eager. He has time ahead. Later, when he checks into a motel, it does not bother him to be alone. He signs in as Thomas Gordon, the name itself a kind of elixir, the room plain but still a confirmation of this life.

Sunday there is of course the dampening effect of return, there is always that, but he does not hurry back to the house; he buys a newspaper and reads in the closed store. Jo's hawk-eyed about the store accounts, but she won't fuss long about a missing twenty, and a few good bets should give him what he needs for an efficiency.

MONDAY EVENING at Lancaster, in the upstairs bathroom, he finds two small envelopes set atop his shaving kit, one on pale pink stationery, one on white. Neither has Lillian Schumacher's return address: the first says E. Rosen, the other Mrs. David Markowitz. His sisters are downstairs, listening to the radio in the parlor, and he carries the envelopes with him to his bedroom.

The room is dusty and sour, his dirty clothes scattered over the bed and chair. It does not comfort him to be here, and he is looking now for comfort: the envelopes make him uneasy. The paper is very fine, the handwriting like elaborate bakery confections—all too delicate to handle. His name is on the envelopes, but they do not seem to belong to him: the pink one in particular seems a taunt he can't defend himself against. E. Rosen. E. Rosen, whose hand he touched two weeks ago. E. Rosen, who must think Irving lives in a different kind of room, a clean, distinguished room, one more like his father's down the hall. Polished, aired, uncluttered. And maybe in his father's room he can be that man. He tries. He carries the envelopes down the hall—also clean and polished—to his father's room, which his sisters tend like a shrine. He sits on the bed and waits, tries to feel the glimmer of that night with Esther, but it keeps swimming away from him. He is squinting to see it, and it won't swim back. As if a blue-black sheet has fallen, blocking light, blocking the glimmer from returning and Irving from retrieving it. Is there anything he knows how to retrieve? A word from Lillian would help—even a postcard. Or some letter he could open, maybe a letter from Niagara Falls.

He abandons the envelopes and leaves the house without a word to his sisters. A light rain is falling and he drives the Ford to a pay phone, where he counts out his change and gives an operator Susanne's number. She picks up on the third ring, her voice sweet—had he not noticed that, how sweet Susanne's voice is? He lights a cigarette as he talks, introduces himself again on the phone, and she laughs. "I know who this is," she says. "How are you, TJ?" She's making it easy, and he is remembering himself now, the bad moment is over. He's done exactly the right thing. He asks to see her again on Friday, and she says yes, and he arranges to meet her at the club, he'll be there at eight, he says. If he gets to the Falls early, he'll call before.

How simple it is. After the call, he stops at the liquor store on Delaware for a fifth of whiskey: he likes the bars but they're expensive. If he's going to spend money at the Falls, he'll need to economize—and he *will* spend money at the Falls, maybe this time reserve a hotel room in advance, something with a bit more style. He might need cash for a new suit, or at least a pair of shoes.

He samples the whiskey in the parked car before he drives home; it's warming, a little smoky. When he enters the house, Celia's working on her puzzle, Jo's in their father's reading chair with a dime-store novel. "Hi, Irving," Celia says, her voice kind and unmuddy, and he stops to see the puzzle.

"It looks like ships," he says, and she tells him yes, a fleet of ships. "I like ships," he says, which is true. Also a way to be nice, and he wants to be nice, doesn't he? "Do you want a drink?" He holds up the bag. She shakes her head and he turns to Jo. "You? A drink?"

It surprises him that Jo accepts. It surprises him that she says, "Thank you," like a normal person, but he's relieved, and pours himself a drink too. They aren't so bad, Jo and Celia, there's something they understand, he's certain of it. It's as if they sense the rightness of what's happening to him. "Jo," he says, "you think you could help me out with my room?"

She pauses, considering. "Put your dirty clothes in the laundry," she says. "I'll do the rest next time I clean." It is clear from her tone he'll owe her something. But it doesn't matter, does it? He'll always owe her something: this time he'll know why.

FOR THREE more days, telephone messages accumulate, all in Jo's neat script, with the date and time of the call, Sadie's messages with exact phrasing: "Call me today," "Are you going or not?" and "For Pete's sake, what is going on?" There are two from a Mrs. Markowitz, who Jo tells him sounds nothing like Lillian Schumacher. He drops the messages in a drawer. There is too much else to think about.

Friday afternoon, when Sadie shows up at the store in person, it seems only he is unprepared. Jo, unruffled, says hello and compliments Sadie on her new hat: she's suspiciously friendly, as if she's enjoying a private joke. In the work room, Celia offers chocolate cookies, then returns to her puzzle, farmland dotted with cows.

But Irving is stunned by Sadie's presence, her peach suit and flow-ery perfume, her purposefulness and solidity, the clarity of her voice, the Sadieness of her. It's as if she's appeared, suddenly, from China. "We need to talk," she says.

"Of course." In the small office he offers her a chair but she does not want to sit. Instead she paces in front of the desk.

"Exactly what's going on?" she says.

"Nothing," he tells her. "Nothing." And it seems that nothing is going on: it is an ordinary Friday afternoon. He has sold a bracelet, accepted a deposit for some pearls. Celia is quiet, Jo is quiet, the bills are paid up. "Would you sit down?"

"I'm not sitting down. You haven't been taking my calls."

"It's a busy time," he tries, but you can see she'll have none of this. She's pale, possessed by a quivery rage, the sort she rarely shows. Too worked up: he'll have to be careful.

"You should have gotten back to Esther. Or at least to her mother."

Esther. Her mother. Sadie seems to be talking about people he knew years ago, or not at all. "Her mother?" No, he does not know her mother.

"The dinner invitation, Irving. I know you got it."

And he does not know what to say to Sadie now. It seems he has entered a dark, unfamiliar house—so many conversations with her are like this—and he'll have to find his way nonetheless. "That's not your business, Sadie."

"It is when I have to make excuses for you. Do you want my help or not? I thought you wanted my help."

"I know. I appreciate it, I really do."

"No, you don't. You don't, Irving." And now the rage is mixed with something else—anguish? Why is she anguished? It's as if he has broken a momentous promise, betrayed her; as if he'd pledged to marry Sadie herself, then refused. She is on the verge of tears and he himself is trembly: the verge of tears always frightens him.

"I appreciate it," he says, and again it seems a bald lie, though it isn't really, he doesn't appreciate everything but most things yes, Sadie herself, yes. If only she didn't expect so much. And now there's a curdling to her expression, she's disgusted—that's even worse, isn't it? She won't look at him, as if he repulses her, it's unbearable, the moment she turns away like that. And the loneliness seems to well larger again, he can feel himself adrift, splintering and drifting at once. In a moment he'll be falling, swept by vertigo. "Please sit down," he says, and she waits until he repeats it. "Please sit down." Finally she takes a chair.

"You don't understand," he says. "Really you don't."

"Explain it then," Sadie says.

She is gazing at him now, and he notices he has started to cry, which is terrible, the way of small boys. But he has to gaze back at her: she must not leave the office.

"It has to do with the war," he says.

She's wan but composed, waiting.

"You know the war was hard," he says. "It really was. But something else happened too." And then the story comes to him, his story, the story of England, how he fell in love with a woman and wanted to marry her. "Sarah," he says. Sarah broke his heart. And as he tells Sadie about this woman, this Sarah, he pictures walking with a woman in an orchard, and the heartbreak is immense, as if his body cannot contain it. Sarah left him for another man, he says, a refugee. What could he do? He didn't know if he would recover, or how, but he returned, pretended to be done with it. He thought he was over it, he really did, but there have been so many changes. He's been struggling. Sadie's right, he hasn't been fair, he hasn't been honest with her, but he's been struggling. And Esther Rosen's been through too much already, hasn't she? She has, Sadie knows she has.

Sadie scrutinizes him. She says nothing for a long time, and then, finally, "This is true?"

If she believes him, he knows she will relent. She will continue to gaze at him, and he will be her brother. There is nothing else he can explain: this is the truest story he can tell. He looks her in the eye and nods.

"I wish you had told me before," she says. She is calm and unhappy. "I'll call you later." She rises to leave and does not kiss him on the cheek, the way she usually does, and he feels a strange pang, not having the kiss on the cheek. He needs to have that back, and the need itself shocks him. She crosses from the office to the workroom, to the card table, the puzzle, and murmurs to Celia, something about meadows and red cows and spring hats. And for a brief moment, before Sadie's gone, before Friday resumes as Friday and then as Friday evening, before he's had a whiskey or phoned a Hotel St. George or left for a night in Niagara Falls, he's sure he'll vanish without her.

CHAPTER 25

Sadie

1949

Sadie's life seems to be the one she wanted: there are dinner parties with music, evenings with Bill at the theater, weekly luncheons with her card club. Her daughters are lovely if confounding. Yet it's all less solid than she expected. Days seem rife with loosely woven spots and frayed bits, and she's discovered that *wanting* itself is slippery. What she once wanted is not necessarily what she wants now, but desire often slides to the periphery, or beyond, into murk. She does not like murk and would rather avoid the matter than venture into unknowing. It seems she once felt more certain—even during the war—but perhaps she's confused her younger self with the past's more definite shape. Still, tonight she *had* hoped to put up her feet and hide in a novel while Bill read his newspaper, and while the girls finished their homework like calm and reasonable young women: she had a real and certain wish for *Dinner at Antoine's*. It was not an impossible wish, but today Elaine is teary, fighting with her best friend over something Sadie cannot comprehend. Elaine's face is pink and blotchy, her wavy chestnut hair wild with alarm. Her words sound gluey and choked, and even if they were clear, Sadie might not understand the cause of the rift, the day's particular slight. *Don't think about it*, she wants to tell Elaine, *read a book*, but Elaine is entirely and convincingly thirteen, and Sadie might as well say *Don't breathe*.

Elaine has tucked herself into the blue reading chair, her legs curled under her, as if making herself as small and inconspicuous as possible, though her sniffling is loud. She's finished the hot chocolate Sadie made, accepted the handkerchief, the mint-green afghan. Her mood will last as long as it lasts: no one can predict, though it's unlikely that Elaine, shy Elaine, will make the first call to her friend Daphne. The chair she has chosen—Bill's favorite—is the one closest to the telephone, and from time to time she gazes at the black dial with puffy-eyed longing. Sadie closes the living room curtains, beyond which the sky is a dim quilt of cloud. Four blocks away little Daphne is no doubt sulking with equal fervor.

Bill has taken his second favorite chair—a distant second— where for five minutes he riffles through the evening paper and rises again, gazing around the living room as if he has become a guest. He has nothing to say, and this appears to confound him. It's not the usual thing, this living room display of tears: Elaine prefers to go to her room when she's upset, but the telephone is here, the possibility of Daphne is here, next to her father's favorite chair, and here she waits. Bill stands. He takes a step in Elaine's direction and frowns. She is a little afraid of him, both the girls are—Elaine freezes in place—but he shakes his head and turns away, now hurrying out toward his study.

Sadie does pick up *Dinner at Antoine's*, takes the chair Bill's abandoned, and tries to read despite Elaine's sniffling, but now the book itself seems more melodramatic (weepier?) than it did yesterday— or is she just seeing it clearly now?—in any case unsatisfying. *Dinner at Antoine's* is not what she wants at all. She does have other books, one that Goldie mentioned in a letter, a few classics she returns to. She could dig out something by Austen, or a Brontë. But they do not seem right either. She starts again from the beginning and reads with half-attention, nearly ten pages, before Margo intrudes. *"Mother?"* A call from the kitchen in a voice both plaintive and demanding. It is not the voice of math homework, which Margo has agreed to spend a full hour on.

The call is followed by footsteps, and Margo's own appearance in the living room. At the sight of Elaine, Margo huffs but stops short of calling Elaine a baby. Margo has a lead in her high school's production of *Anything Goes*, which opens in three weeks—her world, and apparently Sadie's, must this instant revolve around the accuracy of the costume Sadie is sewing for her. Margo has requested blue spangles for the bodice and sleeves. Sadie has procured blue spangles, and they are on the kitchen counter, and it is time, Margo believes, to discuss them. Otherwise she cannot concentrate properly on her math.

Sadie does not remember demanding spangles as a girl, but she was young in a different life. In this life—the life she wanted—teenagers desire precise glitter. She follows Margo to the kitchen and takes up the cards of spangles, blue, shiny disks that catch the light and will no doubt increase the costume's glamour.

Margo flicks a hand at them. "Not these."

"What do you mean?" Sadie says. "Blue spangles. You wrote that on your list. Here they are."

"Smaller ones," she says. "They should be elegant." Margo wants more subtle spangles, the kind, it seems, an actual heiress rather than a stage one might wear. True, Margo is looking more and more like an Italian starlet, she's a striking girl, but this is high school, this is *Anything Goes*.

"No one will know the difference," Sadie says.

"Of course they will," Margo says, and more to the point, she herself will. How is she to be convincing if she herself is unconvinced?

Margo is sixteen.

"Math," Sadie says. "Finish your homework."

The telephone rings and Sadie starts, as she always starts, bracing herself for Jo. There is a long pause, and then muffled talk in the living room, and Elaine's more audible, emphatic "I'm sorry too." In the kitchen Margo rolls her eyes. Ignoring her homework, she begins to sketch her character, Hope, lounging on an ocean liner.

Would boys have been easier? Sadie can't imagine: she pictures a herd of goats climbing over the furniture and chewing up her rugs, though Irving was sweet enough as a boy. She wishes her daughters would befriend each other, but Margo and Elaine are happiest apart, off with their separate friends. They seem in these matters unteachable, but perhaps Sadie does not know how to teach them. Her relationship to her own sisters is no example. And isn't she herself plainly happy when alone with her friend Anna?

"Tomorrow . . . ," Elaine says in the living room. "Let's not." Margo draws the ideal spangle to scale. " 'Bye, Daphne." Elaine shuffles into the kitchen with her empty chocolate cup, puffy-faced but better, a hint of a smile. She picks up a card of the over-sized spangles and notes the way they catch the light from the ceiling lamp. "They're beautiful," she says. "I think they're perfect."

Margo snorts. "You would."

Elaine blushes and leaves the card on the table and slips out of the room, but takes her revenge by practicing piano scales.

SADIE WANTS respite—that she knows—but wanting respite is different from, say, wanting hot chocolate or something grander. This week she's actually had respite: no sign of migraines and no sign of Jo, who is angry with her for once again suggesting Celia see a doctor. Jo says she does *not believe in* doctors, as one might not believe in leprechauns. It isn't clear what Jo does believe in, or what she thinks will help Celia, who for months has complained of dizziness and headaches.

Sadie's last attempt to get Celia medical care, in September, was in all ways a fiasco. She'd persuaded Dr. Weintraub to make a house call, and he had not been daunted by Celia's unwashed state, her matted hair, her distraction. But Celia would not answer his questions and would not let him touch her even to take her pulse. He took a stethoscope out of his bag and Jo, who was hovering, swore at him. She called him a *death mongrel* and insisted he leave the house immediately.

Sadie took Jo's arm and tried to tug her out into the hallway, away from the doctor, from Celia. "What's gotten into you?"

Jo shook her off. "I'll call the police," she said. "Don't think I won't."

Then Celia fled. And as Dr. Weintraub hurried out of the

house, it seemed as if he'd discovered Sadie herself unwashed and belligerent. She left Lancaster without speaking to her sisters and slowly drove to Dr. Weintraub's office, where she paid his house call fee and pretended not to be mortified. She asked for his discretion with regard to her family.

"Of course," he said. He gazed at her through black-framed glasses, his hair balding in a pattern like Bill's, and added dryly, "Apparently I am not the doctor for your sister."

Over the past several weeks, Sadie has left ice packs and aspirin and her own migraine pills at Lancaster, but Celia's complaints have persisted, and more than once Sadie's found her in midafternoon lying in the dark of her bedroom. This week Sadie suggested Celia have a phone consultation with a doctor, and for a moment it seemed Celia would consider it, but Celia replied quietly, "They just make things worse."

Jo started in, telling Sadie to keep her nose in her own business, and then Sadie lost her own patience—she should not have, she knows that—and smacked the coffee table with her hand and announced that Jo was being ridiculous. This helped no one. Sadie returned to her own house, and neither Jo nor Celia called.

It was time to relent, and Sadie found guilty relief in relenting. She had her own family to watch out for, other matters to contend with: the creeping strangeness of time, the effort to ignore it.

AFTER HER FATHER'S death, the world devolved into a rougher, less refined place, and Sadie became sharply aware of Bill as an anchor, a solid if not an easy anchor, without whom she might drift out of ordinary life into the ether. Too much drifting—beyond novels, beyond sleep—and you are lost, maybe the way Celia is. Bill does not drift, or condone drifting of most sorts, except when listening to music, slow jazz and show tunes on the radio. Another side of him unfurls then, a quiet attentive side, as when he is piecing together a mystery, or momentarily arranging the flowers he brings home for her each week. He loses his bluster when he listens to music, yet remains entirely, unflaggingly Bill. And when there's no bad news, when Bill's attentive and sweet, there is a delicate smoothness to the air, an ease in the way her body moves. She likes their public life as a couple, the dinners and temple work, the dances and the Saturday night restaurants. Isn't this what she wanted? A world away from Lancaster, a world of proper dressing and music and polite waiters smiling as they seat her at the corner table? And at night in bed, when she and Bill are finished with the business of touching and pleasure and lostness, she's comforted by the strong if temporary sense that there is only this world of the bed, with its clean linens and warmth, their sleep-closeness one of a safe if not wholly harmonious ship.

Whose marriage is, after all, wholly harmonious? Whose family? Bill is a man of strong opinions, his stubbornness irks her—you can see where Margo's comes from—but she tries not to react, instead training her mind on errands. It's true, Bill is stern with his daughters, they do not know him beyond the sternness at times, and yet he is devoted to them. The house does not sink into the ground, they are fed and bought dresses and offered dance lessons, treated to restaurants and chocolate and boxes of bubble gum. They want for nothing. They are loved if not understood and if not in a way they understand. Sadie wanted a good life. He has made one for all of them.

Tonight she finds him again after the girls have gone to bed, and the house itself seems an animal asleep. Bill is sitting on the edge of the bed in the blue-striped pajamas she gave him, rubbing a spot in the middle of his forehead and setting his glasses on the night table. Bluish half-circles swell below his eyes. He's pale from working too much again. It's late enough that he should not receive calls from patients: that sort of emergency is rare, though it occurs. When it does he drops whatever he is doing and disappears to his other world, the dental world, returning in the small hours. He can be a kind of dental hero, but heroism wears everyone out.

"What's this with Elaine?" he says.

"It's over," Sadie says. "She drank hot chocolate. She's fine."

"And Margo?"

"Nervous about her play. No more than that."

"I don't like her tone with you."

"She's fine."

And then he waits. It's the time when she might tell him about Lancaster, or of occasional news from his family, but today she will say nothing. Let him enjoy that silence, the lack of calls, the fact that the telephone ringing was only thirteen-year-old Daphne Farber. Bill waits and understanding dawns, marked by his relieved smile before the yawn and the goodnight kiss.

The yawn then, the goodnight kiss. In ten minutes he is asleep. In the morning he's gone before she's fully dressed. The girls quietly eat their scrambled eggs and toast and gather their schoolbooks. Margo studiously ignores Elaine, remaining unaware of three blue spangles stitched to Elaine's notebook, beside Elaine's curving signature.

SOMETIMES A FREE afternoon downtown—Main Street flooded with coats and hats, a rush of voices, and the brick buildings gilded and slightly pink, the clouds orange and violet before dusk—seems wholly enough. It is a good life, she's sure, though she doesn't know why it seems so tentative and airy, or why the past seems to spring up at her as if in defiance, or how to name what she feels, even to Anna, her closest friend. She is at the art museum with Anna, gazing at a marble statue she's seen many times before, and the quality of another time begins to superimpose itself on the day: a time before she had children, when she would visit the statue and pretend she was in Italy. She'd close her eyes and picture cities she'd only read about, letting Buffalo melt beneath a brilliant light. She told no one of these moments: she did not know if anyone other than Celia might have them. But here she is with Anna, and here is the statue, and she is not closing her eyes, and nonetheless the moment of Italy rushes upon her. Her face is hot, her breathing too fast. In her peripheral vision, an imaginary Florence rises, and Rome, a shimmering sense of the Sistine Chapel's nearness, a feeling of light. She's forgotten that the mind can do such things, and she is concentrating on the statue's blank white marble pedestal, trying to name this leap in memory, when Anna asks if she's all right. Apparently she is weeping. On hearing Anna's voice she stops.

She isn't sure how to answer, caught like this. She could say, *I was missing my father,* which Anna would understand, of course. Anna misses her own late father. But even as the words form themselves they seem partial and inadequate, true and untrue. The world without Sadie's father continues to shock her, as she was shocked initially. The air became drained of color, which she did not expect. Even the depth of her attachment shocked her: he had been a difficult and private man, and yet there it was, the world for a time drained of color. But here the color rushes back, the Italy moment she'd forgotten. How ungraspable everything seems— Anna, the museum, the fact of a country called Italy, the fact of years, the marvel of light, her daughters, the fleeing of moments only glimpsed, the fleeing of her father. Light fell on Italy. Had her father seen light fall on Italy? How little she'd known him. How little she knows the world.

But Anna is waiting, and they are in a gallery, and other people stroll the gallery. She's tearing up in public.

"Sadie, what is it?" Anna says.

"I don't know."

Anna nods. "Would you like to sit down?"

But Sadie does not know the answer to that either: for the moment all certainties seem elusive. Maybe she wants to sit, maybe she does not. The uncertainty seems to bubble beneath her ribs and expand into her throat. Another wave of heat begins in her face. Anna takes her hand.

"Let's sit for a minute," Anna says. "My shoes pinch today."

"They pinch?" Sadie refocuses on Anna's sable leather pumps. They are beautiful troublesome shoes. "I didn't know." The two women study Anna's small feet. It's all a matter of locating the problem, isn't it?

"It's only the second time I've worn them."

There is the immediate need for relief from the pinching, and the decision then to go to the ladies' lounge where they might try to stretch the offending shoe and find some tissue to pad Anna's foot. Does Anna have moleskin at home? They leave the gallery and the Italian statue and in the lounge Anna fusses with her shoe and Sadie reapplies lipstick. Sadie is no longer weepy; the weepiness, the entire wave of feeling, seems to have passed. Perhaps they should get something sweet, she tells Anna. She's had enough art for one day. There might be just enough time to stop for coffee before the school day ends, before Anna's sons and Sadie's daughters reappear, and Sadie and Anna again become mothers.

IF SHE HAD more time, perhaps she would feel surer of herself. There's always a feeling of hurry, of catching up, only glimpsing each moment before it shifts. She would like to be prepared, but only the small gestures seem manageable: school clothes for the girls, dry cleaning, groceries. She wants to be a good mother, gives motherhood her best effort. Sometimes her daughters listen to her and sometimes they do not. It's Rosalie who persuades Margo to use the spangles Sadie bought, telling her "they need to be *bold* for shows." Rosalie Margo listens to in a way she will not listen to Sadie, and for an afternoon, Sadie is caught between gratitude and hurt, unable to settle into the casual pleasure of the day. She is unnecessarily formal with Rosalie, who is unnecessarily formal in return.

She wants her daughters to be happy, and for the most part they seem so. The opening night of *Anything Goes*, Margo's elated, but also on stage transformed to a girl more glamorous and adult than the Margo Sadie knows, an heiress on a luxury liner, someone Sadie has in fact never met. This she is unprepared for; she is unnerved. The spangles are convincing, perhaps too much so, and it's a relief to see Margo backstage after the play, clutching her bouquet of sweetheart roses, returned to her headstrong, familiar self. *Stay Margo*, Sadie thinks. There will be three more performances, and Sadie has promised to attend the closing show, if not every single performance. She loves her daughter. "You were marvelous," Sadie tells Margo. "I can't wait to see it again."

SHE WOULD LIKE to forestall crisis—this too is not the same as desire—and the days can seem a shoring up against disaster. She has become skilled at averting small, imaginable crises, at pushing the larger threats to the shadows of thought, but it requires vigilance. And she's not ready, the Thursday morning the telephone rings, and it isn't Jo—there's a flicker of relief—but Buffalo General Hospital—the flicker doused. Celia's been admitted, having fallen unconscious on a city bus. The woman on the phone is kind, almost familiar, the call itself both shocking and plainly factual. There's a moment of paralysis, a searching for words, and finally the release of adrenaline. Then motion replaces feeling, and the early particularities of the day recede, everything but the call recedes.

When Sadie arrives at the hospital, she is fixed on the reception desk. Poise depends on taking one issue at a time, negotiating the larger problem but addressing the smaller ones, the question of Celia's location, her status, her doctor. It is the kind of situation in which crying or losing one's temper is out of the question: you do not compound a collapse with another type of collapse. Sadie is directed to a green-and-beige waiting room, where a few people— a couple of women, an old man—swim in their separate worries and Irving fidgets in his chair.

"Unresponsive so far," Irving says. "That's what the doctor said. Ten minutes ago, maybe." His voice seems altered by the sea fog of the room, the words also tinted green and beige in the thick static air. An old man glances up at Sadie and does not look away. On the far side of the room, a ballooning woman in a violet dress studies her feet. Irving remembers to greet Sadie then: he kisses her on the cheek and offers her his small silver flask, which she declines.

"Where's Jo?"

"Got me," Irving says. "They called her."

The waiting room crowds up for a while, empties, but remains a jittery sea fog. In his chair Irving appears smaller than usual, as if shrunken by unhappiness and worry, which surprises Sadie: she usually sees this expression when he's panicked about money. It's the expression that frightens her into writing checks, and check writing will not work today. She'll have to find another way to harness fear.

From the public telephone she calls Bill and then Rosalie, who will meet the girls after school. She tries to telephone Lancaster, tries to telephone the store, but the phones ring emptily, and she hangs up and replaces the coin and dials again. The numbers distract her, as does the circular movement of her fingers over the

heavy dial: after four or five attempts, she's lost in a light trance, almost forgetting her purpose.

In the waiting room, it seems Irving cannot get hold of himself.
The bobbing of his right knee sends tremors into the floor and her
own chair, and he seems to be chewing his lips—she's afraid he'll
start bleeding, the way he's working them. It's as if he has been
drinking coffee, pots of it, rather than whiskey from his flask. She
sets her hand on top of his, the way she might to calm one of her
daughters, but she only feels the tremor more profoundly. This
will not do. "I'll stay here," Sadie says. "Why don't you find yourself something to eat?"

"Yes?" He seems to rise into himself then, his face a shade
closer to the Irving she prefers.

SADIE'S ALONE when a doctor named Grafton calls her from the
waiting room to offer the absurd explanation that Celia has had a
stroke.

"She's too young for that," Sadie says.

"It's uncommon," he says. "But it happens. I'm sorry."

"Maybe she's anemic," Sadie says.

"She might be," he says. "But that would be a separate problem."

Where is Bill? Because he could speak to Dr. Grafton more
easily, more *scientifically*: Anemia is just as scientific as stroke, isn't
it? Why not anemia? Why not simple exhaustion? *She was tired, she
collapsed.*

There is the peculiar drift of not-knowing: she watches herself
speak to Dr. Grafton, hears herself say, "Can you test her for that?"

Dr. Grafton says, "Yes, but there's the primary problem. Right
now it's hard to tell what the damage is."

She nods. When might he know more? When might she see
Celia? The light in the room seems stark and cool. Her blue suit is
the one she put on this morning, her blue pumps the ones she
bought with Anna. She asks Dr. Grafton what might have caused
this. He does not know. When he leaves her, she returns to the
public telephone, dials and lets the phone ring at Lancaster. She
pictures Celia at home, the real Celia approaching the phone, as if
it's some other Celia here in the hospital.

After two hours Sadie is allowed, briefly, into Celia's room. Irving has not returned. There are tubes attached to Celia's arms, but
Celia is asleep, and she seems simply like Celia on a bed. Her
mouth is oddly curved, but her breathing is not so very different
from ordinary sleep breathing, and her forehead is an ordinary
temperature. Celia seems peaceful asleep, though it is not clear
what sort of peace this is.

"Celia?" Sadie says. "How are you feeling? You took a fall on
the bus."

Celia sleeps, breathes. What does she know? If she dreams,
does she dream the same way she did last week? There's a slight
movement—the flickering of an eyelid or the movement of Sadie's
own shadow, Sadie cannot tell.

IN THE LATE afternoon Sadie finds Jo at Lancaster, housecleaning:
she is dusting the dining room. She's come from the store, she says.
She is busy. She does not have time for conversation with Sadie.

"I'll give you a hand," Sadie says.

"Thanks, no," Jo says. She hums tunelessly to herself.

"Listen, Jo," Sadie says. "Celia had a stroke. I know you got the
call from the hospital."

Jo pushes her dustrag over the dining room table in hard circles, and the sharp smell of linseed oil rises. She does not look
Sadie in the eye.

"The doctor thinks it was severe," Sadie says, and the rag continues its circles, the table shines, the humming persists. "It's very
upsetting. I know."

"What do you know?" Jo steps away and turns to the china
cabinet.

AND WHAT, Dr. Grafton asks, does Sadie want? She sits in his office with Bill, and this is not a question Bill can answer, only Sadie
can answer, because Jo will not visit the hospital or speak to the
doctor. Five days have passed and Irving has still not returned to
see Celia, who is awake in her room. No one knows what awake
means, however: her eyes seem unfocused, and she's unable to
speak. She's lost movement on the left side of her body.

Now Sadie must determine what is best for Celia, after years of Celia resisting her judgment. She couldn't get Celia to a doctor, or convince her to wash: now Celia has a doctor, now she is clean, now there is a strange and horrifying ease in her presence. And now Celia will require round-the-clock care, Dr. Grafton says. He mentions live-in nurses. He mentions a nursing home. "She can't stay here much longer," Dr. Grafton says. "Mrs. Feldstein, what do you want?"

She hears him clearly, but the question seems patently wrong, not at all in keeping with matters of desire; nor, if rephrased, the sort of question Sadie ought to answer, that anyone but Celia should answer.

"Dear?" Bill's voice is a mix of tenderness and warning, a reminder of their life.

What choice can she make, without Jo, who will not visit the hospital, who will not even speak of Celia's stroke? Jo who will not tolerate nurses, and cannot possibly care for Celia alone. Nor can Sadie, with or without Jo.

"Mrs. Feldstein?"

Yes. She is Mrs. Feldstein. Mrs. William Feldstein. A woman in command of herself. She meets Dr. Grafton's gaze, and he holds out a sheet of paper, which she takes.

"There's nothing available in a Jewish home," Dr. Grafton says.

She's holding a list of nursing homes. She reads it carefully, as a woman in command of herself would.

"Shall we try the Sisters of Mercy? I can look at it tomorrow," she says. The sureness in her tone surprises her, but here is the decision, here is what they will live with. "Shall we move her there next week?"

SHE DOES NOT know what it will take to prevent Celia from feeling lost, to explain this to Jo, to make the Sisters of Mercy acceptable. It's all a matter of effort, isn't it? Bill kisses her in the hospital parking lot and drives back to his office, where his patients are waiting. Snow clouds have thickened over the lake, vast toy animals herded onto a bed. Then the wind shifts, and there's a piercing loneliness, and Sadie finds her car. She starts the ignition, the radio plays big-band and she eases into traffic, driving toward what she thinks of as her life: this seems to have a border on Upper Main. The snow begins to fall, the traffic slows, and the big band changes to a jingle for coffee. Then she is north of the border. Here is Hertel Avenue, and she continues on. Here is her own street, her calm red brick house. Rosalie has cleaned the living room and dining room. On the coffee table there's a vase of pink roses from Bill, today's mail: the electric bill, the *Jewish Review,* an invitation to a baby shower, an invitation to a temple dance. This afternoon she'll market and pick up the dry cleaning and drive Elaine to her piano lessons. Later she and Bill will take the girls to dinner at the Towne Casino, a separate world of white tablecloths, attentive waiters, elegant men and women sipping amber drinks. An oasis of good fortune, Sadie thinks, and for the evening that oasis will be her world. *Anything Goes* has been a success, and Margo is wholly Margo again. It's Margo's chance to celebrate, and this is what she wants.

CHAPTER 26

Goldie

1950

U ntil now she's continued to picture Celia as a woman permanently in her twenties, dark hair bobbed and windblown, lipstick red, uneven, eyes hazel: pinpoints of intensity. An image from the time of their mother's death? Probably earlier, because of the vibrancy and motion. Irving and Jo also seem static to her, Irving hardly more than a boy (nothing he has done truly contradicts this), Jo slim, sharp, but prone to quiet mooning. Goldie thinks of her father as a man who died in the prime of his life, hearty in his rectitude, though he had of course become old. They all seem to her fixed in the place that she left them. Only Sadie has altered with time: the monthly news of Sadie's daughters and husband, the photographs, the descriptions of evenings at concerts and theater—worlds not belonging to Lancaster—have revealed an older, sturdier, more elaborate Sadie.

This is not the first time she's detected bewilderment in Sadie's letters, but now the statement is more direct, a rawer admission. *We are all shocked about Celia. Every day I am shocked.* And maybe it's this, the directness, bringing the bewilderment alive in Venice: Celia is no longer Celia, and the family has altered irrevocably. An uneasy, swimming sensation rises at the thought of Lancaster, though the sensation doesn't last. That house is part of someone else's life, and her own life in Venice she does not question: there is a weight to her small history, the daily conversations with her friend Emily, her sometimes-lover Ted, talk with vendors at the fruit market and the bakery, the postman, the librarian, the other waitresses, the neighbors on her block. She isn't so much rooted as held by the web of conversation and the accumulating knowledge of the shore. And although the beach shifts, the town seems solid enough, unlikely to disappear. If she travels, Venice will remain itself: what ever made her believe otherwise?

From California it's hard to imagine the kind of winter she grew up with: she can picture snow, but papery snow contained by a frame, like a stage imitation. It's now winter in Buffalo, the most forbidding time, yet visiting seems possible. She has the means to go, a week's vacation. There will be wind off the lake, ice, and the snow, which she's never missed. She has missed the hush of it, how snow empties the city; then there is space for you to walk and think without noise and the interruption of passing voices. This is something Celia seemed to understand—what it meant to walk on uncrowded streets. It is not clear what Celia understands now, Sadie says, and so far she does not walk, but it's hard to say she is unhappy. One can only guess. Goldie can't begin to picture her: Celia-in-her-twenties has been replaced with haze.

SHE BOARDS a plane. She has never before boarded a plane, and air travel proves to be stranger and less strange than she imagined: the enclosed cabin makes her uneasy, as does the odd, perky formality of the stewardess, but the speed and noise and tilting ascent impress her, the sky is very blue, and Los Angeles becomes a tiny model town, miniaturized like places from the past. The stewardess brings trays of food and pours coffee, and then Goldie dozes off to the droning engines. It's a long trip, requiring a change of planes, and when she lands in Chicago she feels as if she has in fact reached another country. There's a chapped paleness to the landscape, and in the airport a preponderance of fur coats. Her own is a heavy cotton—not even wool—though it seemed warm enough when she packed. She chose her clothing with care, but what she's wearing now—cotton blouse, loose cardigan, slacks, closed-toed shoes—is too flimsy. She has in fact forgotten winter.

A smaller plane continues to Buffalo, the flight noisier still, taking on roller-coaster qualities around the lakes. Out the window she can see only gray fog, then deep red and purple reflections on a bed of clouds, then gray fog going darker. When the plane descends into Buffalo it's evening, though an evening brightened by airport lights and snow and a ceiling of cloud. The snow is not falling when she arrives but several inches cover the fields near the airport, still white and uncrusted. The terminal itself seems spare and muted, and in its spareness Sadie appears anomalous: a petite, porcelain-skinned woman in a fur-trimmed coat, a fur-trimmed hat, the dark fur setting off blue eyes and the pale skin and rose-colored lipstick. Her eyes are wet but there's a certainty in her quick stride and almost deft way of hugging Goldie, kissing her on the cheek—a softness, a flowery perfume—then separating from her again, drawing the precise lines of her affection.

"It's good to see you," she says, her voice the one Goldie remembers, but more dense.

Maybe *good* is the right word. Goldie does not know: the moment seems to her sliced open, geologic layers revealing themselves, delicate in the chilly air. Is *good* the same as *immediate*? "How are you?" Goldie says. "There's new snow, isn't there?"

Sadie offers her a coat, camel wool, insisting she put it on right away, and as Goldie slides her arms into it, a man steps up beside her and lifts the coat onto her shoulders. Bill, now balding and serious. He waits for her hands to pop through the sleeves, extends his own cool hand for her to shake.

"How are you, Goldie?" he says. "Good to see you." Then he picks up her small bag and steers her and Sadie in the direction of the luggage claim. His rounder, older appearance does not surprise her—she's seen photographs—but his manner is that of somebody's father. As if in the intervening years he has not only aged but leaped generations.

Bill pulls the car up to the airport entrance, and as Goldie opens the passenger door there is along with the dry stillness, a

rush of sound from the radio—jazzy piano, swishing drums. Then
they drive through light snow, past blank flat fields near the airport
and then more houses, clusters of them, and eventually neighborhoods that seem almost familiar but in fact are not. It's the trees
Goldie remembers, silhouetted maples and oaks; and the preponderance of chimneys, like periscopes above the rooftops, peering
through the snow at the swollen sky and the passing traffic. The
houses—their windows squares of yellow light—are still somehow
eclipsed by the snow, and the streets seem narrower. Sadie talks
over the band music, she is telling Goldie about a house, not her
own—Lancaster. Something about *matters to sort out.* Something
about *a need for time.* "Of course that's your house too," Sadie says.
"But for now, it might be simpler to stay at our place."

The cold seems to deepen as they drive on smaller streets, and
it occurs to Goldie to say thank you.

"Don't be silly." Sadie twists around and peers over the top
of her seat, her face ringed by fur. "Stay with us anytime."

"You're more than welcome," Bill says.

"We should talk tomorrow." Sadie squints at Goldie. "You must
be exhausted."

Goldie *is* tired, enough that she could sleep in the car: the fact
of falling snow and the lake air seem both strange and utterly ordinary, and already she has to close her eyes to imagine the warm
seawater smell and the strong light through her apartment windows, and there is for a moment a mix of place, as if bright snow is
falling through the windows onto her apartment floor.

Bill and Sadie's house is set back from the street, a red brick
three-story with a wide lawn and a driveway curving past a large
oak. Bill parks and holds open the car doors for Sadie and Goldie
and collects the luggage, and they enter the house through a side
door leading to a short hall, where they shake off snow, remove
their coats and shoes. Beyond, there's a white-and-blue kitchen
and girls drinking from mugs. Young women, really, the older one
more mature than Goldie expected. They are dark-haired and
dark-eyed, more Bill's complexion than Sadie's, but they are at a
glance Sadie's girls. Margo's nose and cheeks, the shape of Elaine's

face, yes, but something else, the way they hold themselves, the way they say hello and their own names. Margo's more poised, Elaine a little dreamier: they are like that in the photographs Sadie's sent, but despite the photographs, the girls seem to have dropped from the sky fully grown. The substance of them shocks Goldie, their smooth skin and knowing expressions, their soapy girl scent mixing with the kitchen's sweet bakery smell. Why was she thinking of children? They are likely too old for the shells she brought them from the beach; the Mexican bracelets might be all right.

The girls drink hot chocolate, and Sadie offers Goldie a cup: on snowy evenings, girls drink hot chocolate. She'd forgotten. And she would like to drink hot chocolate; she would like to be a girl drinking hot chocolate, a girl like one of Sadie's, rather than the girl she once was. There is something irresistible about falling into a chair, receiving the hot sweet drink. But in the warm kitchen her drowsiness is deepening again, and time seems to have stretched. There is talk of California, postcard California—Hollywood, palm trees, sun-washed beaches—but she's having trouble keeping up with conversation.

"How about this?" Sadie says. "We'll bring your chocolate to the guest room."

SHE IS NOT used to sleeping and waking in a family household, and in the morning she's startled to hear footsteps in the hall, the water tap, murmuring voices close by; and then the sounds seem a kind of protective shield. They comfort her but already she remembers the intensities of family routines, the way one's attention is pulled and refocused and pulled again. You must defer the moment of reentering that world if you can. Goldie keeps her door closed until she's heard the sounds of Bill going to work, and soon after the sounds of Margo and Elaine leaving for school. Then in the bathroom down the hall she washes; returning, she finds on her bed a wool skirt and a fine-knit sweater and a pair of stockings, which more or less fit. Downstairs, in the kitchen, there's a table setting laid out, coffee and muffins, and then Sadie herself appears, today in a slate blue suit, asking if Goldie would like scrambled eggs.

.   .   .

SADIE HAS befriended the nuns. She's two steps through the door of the Sisters of Mercy, and already greeting them: *Sister Mary Catherine, hello, how are you? Sister Agnes, hello. Hello, Sister Bernadette.* The nuns are not at all spectral or stern: they move quietly, without rushing. There is something appealing in their nun-ness, Goldie thinks. *Mrs. Feldstein, good morning,* they say. *Nice to meet you, Miss Cohen.* Celia is a little more alert today, they say, she finished her breakfast; and thank you for that box of chocolates.

At the Sisters of Mercy the light green linoleum shines; the walls have been recently painted, and there's a strong smell of bleach. It doesn't quite cover the odor of urine and illness, which hits Goldie in waves. Her eyes sting, and her head seems buzzy and light, her quickening pulse a sharpness below the skin. It isn't only the Sisters of Mercy she's frightened of: the odors are a trapdoor to other sickrooms, other years, the echo of being there with Sadie. And she is afraid of Celia—was she always? Yes. Of course, yes. Though mainly of what Celia would require, not Celia as herself.

Sadie does not seem unnerved, though she has always been a good actress. Her gait is purposeful and when she waves Goldie in the direction of Celia's room, her smile, though small and brief, appears real.

THE WOMAN in the room sits in a wheelchair. At first glance, she is not the same person Goldie remembers; she's not even definitively female. Her face seems oddly young, but static, with a droop on the left side. Her hair is very short, salt-and-pepper, starting to curl.

"Celia, good morning," Sadie says, and kisses her on the cheek. There is no change in Celia's expression. "Goldie's here."

Sadie seats Goldie in a wooden chair beside the wheelchair, and it's then that Goldie first gazes directly into Celia's eyes, which are the same hazel as always. Celia's watchful, or seems so. And Goldie is timid; gingerly, she touches Celia's left hand.

"The right hand is better," Sadie says. "Celia's got movement there, she can probably feel you."

"How are you, Celia? It's Goldie." As if introduction is warranted. She takes Celia's right hand then, which is warm and oddly soft, like powder under skin. The limpness is unnerving: Goldie resists the impulse to let go and leave the room. Celia's eyes stay on her, intent, as if Goldie's mind is transparent and Celia sees exactly what she's thinking, what she has ever thought. Goldie's face flushes warm; there's a rush of grief; and she breaks away from Celia's gaze.

"Are you ready?" Sadie says. She's removed her coat and arranged herself on a wooden chair, the slate blue suit and stockings and shapely heels incongruous against the beige walls and green linoleum.

Celia's gaze shifts to Sadie. There's a book on Sadie's lap, a novel, which Sadie opens. The one she's picked is a romance, lively and improbable. It has a character named Edward, who in a gentlemanly way flirts with beautiful, witty Anita. Celia stays fixed on Sadie. Is Celia calm? There is no simple way to tell; there is no simple way to tell anything about her. Sadie reads on, but Goldie can't focus on the plot. Instead she concentrates on the shapes of certain words—*Anita, cocktail, parkway*—the cadence of Sadie's voice, which seems more important than anything. There is a moment then of being held, of the room and the three of them and the order of all things drawn together by Sadie's voice and the diffuse light filling plain space.

When they leave the nursing home, Sadie's mood seems unchanged: a pragmatic brightness, reassuring but opaque. Was Sadie always so opaque, or was it simply that Goldie had thought her transparent? *Every day I am shocked.* But you have to look closely to see the doubt flicker. And Sadie *is* more solid than she used to be, more assured. Today Goldie feels less so: it's only noon, she's already rattled, and they have yet to visit the house and Jo, and Irving, who on the telephone sounded like a quiz show host. Falling snow cuts visibility but Sadie is not driving toward Lancaster— that much Goldie can tell.

"Is it like that most days with Celia?"

"About like that. Sometimes there's a little more spark." Sadie glances at Goldie. "We'll go to the house after lunch."

They stop at a coffee shop in Sadie's neighborhood, and it's comforting to sit quietly and eat soup and sandwiches and drink hot cups of coffee. Goldie doesn't remember this place: she barely remembers this neighborhood, which edges into suburb. The city's changed, Sadie says, they'll have to tour downtown. She and Bill will take Goldie out, maybe Irving will come along.

"By the way," Sadie says, "Jo's a little odd."

"Is that new?"

"Well, no, of course not. But yes. I mean more than a little odd. She's upset about Celia."

"I'd imagine," Goldie says.

"She's fine when she's calm. If not, she might seem cruel. I thought you should know."

EVEN WITH the fortification of soup, Goldie's sense of time—of hours, of years—is off-kilter, and it's difficult to get her bearings. Did she feel this way before the Sisters of Mercy? The air keeps filling with snow, and Sadie leads her, first to shops to buy Goldie gloves, a hat, a lamb's wool cardigan, then to the old neighborhood.

"We'll just stop by the house for tea," Sadie tells her. The car slides a couple of feet as they turn from Delaware onto Lancaster, then regains traction. Sadie does not seem to notice. "If you want to stay longer, just say so."

From the outside, the house appears well cared for, but the snow is melted in patches and the path is shoveled haphazardly, which gives it a shabbier air. Goldie's sense of proportion is off: the house seems smaller than she expected, though it's substantial, and the place she'd imagined from California was the size of a snapshot. Inside, Goldie is immediately aware of a smell she thinks of only as the past, or *there*—now *here*—the complicated smell of wood oil and hot steam pipes, rust and cooked sugar and old tobacco smoke. The hall and parlor are covered in the rose wallpaper their mother chose, as if their mother's desire for delicate things were still alive, separate from the body. More reassuring than unnerving, Goldie decides, but the snapshot image wasn't wrong: she seems to be walking through a photograph. There is no apparent dust and yet the house has the feeling of dust, and when she turns from the rose wallpaper she feels herself a dusty blankness.

It is a house, and here is Jo, plump and pale, dressed up in a ma-roon wool skirt suit and pearl earrings, her hair pinned back. She has gone to some effort. But there *is* something wrong with her, and not just with her teeth, which are a tea-stained ruin. She does not touch Goldie or hug her, but shrinks back as if a passing touch will burn her. Sadie ignores this, leans in and kisses Jo on the cheek. There is no sign of Irving, who has promised to meet them before dinner.

"Hang up your coat if you like." Jo waves at a full coatrack. "You probably want to look around. I've moved a few things."

Perhaps Jo has moved an ashtray or a vase, but it seems that like the wallpaper, nothing has changed in the rooms downstairs: in the parlor her father's chair and pipe stand are stationed in the places he preferred, the carpets and sofa the same though faded, and as she walks through the dining room and lower halls there is the thickening sensation of an underlit museum. The kitchen seems identical to the kitchen of memory—or could her mind be correcting? Upstairs, their father's room remains as it was, seem-ingly inhabited but for the extremity of order. Goldie checks a drawer and finds his shirts in wrappers from the cleaners. The suits in his closet are arranged by color. Behind her, Sadie sighs but says nothing. It's Goldie's own room and the rooms of her siblings that have changed: the bedroom she once shared with Sadie is white and almost empty; Jo's room immaculate and pale yellow. Irving's room is a sea of clothes, the furniture covered by shirts and under-clothes and trousers.

"Where is he, anyway?" Sadie says.

Jo shrugs, the same eye-rolling shrug she's made since she was six. She tells Goldie, "He's not here much," and for a moment there seems to be an opening: yes, Goldie remembers this, the mutual eye-rolling over Irving, their small head-shaking society. This time she isn't sure what the gesture implies, but it isn't hard to nod.

In Celia's room the bureau is covered with knickknacks and costume jewelry, pots of rouge and bottles of perfume; scarves in blues, greens, and yellows hang off the rocking chair. It seems a functional disorder, the single clue to Celia's absence the basket of clean laundry near the door: Celia never folded anything. Two cats stare up from the bed, one calico, one gray, and Goldie sits on the quilt's edge and holds out her hand for them to sniff.

"I've been looking after them," Jo says. There's a slight haughtiness to her tone.

"I'm sure Celia's glad for that," Goldie says.

"She would be," Jo says.

"How about some tea?" Sadie says.

But Jo's taking Goldie's measure. "It's been a few months, you know."

And there is Sadie's warning look. Upset, yes, Jo's edgy when she's upset.

"Let's get the tea," Sadie says.

"All right. Let's," Goldie says. The cats remain unblinking on the bed, and Sadie starts down the hall, Goldie following, Jo nearly at her side.

Jo touches Goldie's arm and stops, shaking her head. "She's dead, you know."

Sadie turns. "Don't start with this."

"What are you talking about?" Goldie says.

"Celia. You heard me," Jo says.

"Jo, she's not dead," Goldie says. "I just saw her."

"How would you know? You don't know Celia. Celia's dead."

"Stop it, Jo," Sadie says. "Would you please go downstairs?"

"I just saw her." Goldie pictures Celia's hazel eyes tracking her, tracking Sadie in the small plain room, and there's a warm flush to Goldie's face, her pulse beginning to speed.

"Sadie tell you to say that?"

"I saw her. She isn't dead."

"That's a lie," Jo says. "She's dead."

And a droning rises fully now, not unlike approaching bees. Goldie feels a splitting pressure, as if her ribs might separate and push into her lungs. The swarming and splitting and pressure collide, one vast lush rage: for an instant she is breathless and dizzy, and as the air rushes back, her right hand moves of its own volition, an open-handed slap, which catches Jo not on the face but the side of the head. Jo shoves her fast against the wall, the hard flat surface like a live thing striking her shoulder, and Sadie shouts, "Stop this," and wedges herself between them.

Goldie's skin feels strangely hot, Sadie's hand on her arm cool, and there's a wash of lilac scent.

"Go into the bedroom," Sadie says, herding Goldie to a door, pushing her inside, and closing the door fast. Through the dark wood Goldie can hear ragged breathing, and then Sadie's voice: "Go downstairs Jo. Now." As if she is disciplining a child.

THE AIR IS close and stale, and Goldie is quivering, her own breathing thick; the room is disintegrating into objects gathered without purpose. She's trapped between the wooden door and the iced windows; she shuts her eyes and covers her ears, the old mired feeling upon her—a sense of perpetual dying, perpetual turning away—and she concentrates on breathing. If she waits, the room will take its proper form: this she remembers. She counts to thirty and Jo is still in the hall: beyond the door there's whispering. Celia's not dead, though not all right and Jo isn't all right either. Goldie herself is anything but dead, though once she might have been.

The bedroom is Irving's, soiled shirts layered on chairs, and dust like silt over the bowl of glass marbles, an empty brown suit hanging on a rack. She sits on the unmade bed and tries to catch her breath. Her parents are dead but Celia is not. Something has happened to Jo, a kind of inversion. Something has happened to all of them—how is it that she struck Jo? She doesn't remember striking anyone before, not like this: as a girl she slapped Irving's and Celia's hands when they tried to steal sweets.

Outside snow is falling thickly. Eighteen degrees, the radio said, and the snowflakes are fine and small, half the windowpane etched in frost. It seems that she has always sat before a window etched in frost, she has always lived between the wooden door and the patterned glass. California? How hard it is to sense that life. She opens the window for air, a gesture from her old life—wasn't she always opening windows, even in winter? How is it, she wonders, that the living die and the dead surreptitiously live?

More sounds in the hallway. "Come on, Jo," Sadie says. "I said leave her be." And Jo is a silence, and then they are both retreating footsteps.

Bits of snow drift in the open window, and she can hear steps on the back stairs. Goldie envisions Sadie and Jo moving through the house, the past as proximate as the tree beyond the window— the undeniable echo of her sisters as girls. For an instant time wavers: she can almost sense the moment her mother wakes for tea, her father pacing downstairs. But the moment doesn't take hold, its release accompanied by a sharp pang. The movements downstairs seem askew: Irving's room is over the dining room here, farther back than hers was.

Venice Beach: she lives in Venice Beach. She is fifty-four years old. She's visiting her sisters, who are not dead. In this house she does not belong. As for the city, it's hard to tell. She can stay in Buffalo long enough to see Celia a few more times, to repeat Sadie's daily routine of greeting the nuns and smoothing lotion on Celia's hands and reading; long enough to see the Falls again, now rimmed with thick green ice, the river flowing underneath, snow blurring the boundary between countries, between river and shore. She can go to the pictures with Sadie, or with Sadie's daughters. For a few days she'll stay at their house, then fly back to California.

For now, she's too raw and quivery to face Jo: God knows what Jo will say next. When she's certain Jo and Sadie are in the kitchen, Goldie slips out of the bedroom and crosses the hallway to the front stairs. She'll wait in Sadie's car, or, better, catch a cab on Delaware to Sadie's house. She would like to breathe and swallow properly, would like to stop the quivering, and walking will help: it always helps. But at the bottom of the stairs she hesitates. The interior doors are open and she can peer down the hallway to the kitchen, where Jo and Sadie sit at the table. There's murmuring— Sadie's. Jo's head is slightly bowed and Sadie is stroking her hair. They do not look up. Despite the open space of the hall, the sensation is of gazing through window glass.

Goldie slips through the foyer and out of the house. She's starting down the porch steps when a blue Ford with a cap of snow pulls into the driveway. The driver's door opens and a man in a chestnut overcoat and fedora steps out. It is and is not her father, an altered image—shorter, his body moving more loosely—yet still the same face. He is surprisingly beautiful. She stands in the walkway, watching him, unsure of what to say, but he is crossing the snow of the lawn, he is holding out his arms. Her life astonishes her: he is calling her name.

ACKNOWLEDGMENTS

Many thanks to Gail Hochman and to Robin Desser for their guidance and faith
in the novel, as well to their assistants, Joanne Brownstein and Diana Tejerina.
I'm grateful to Helen Herzog Zell for her exceptional support; to Ann Patchett
and Elizabeth McCracken for their remarkable kindness and encouragement;
to Nicholas Delbanco, Peter Ho Davies, and my other colleagues at the University of Michigan, as well as to dear colleagues at the University of Wisconsin and the University of Florida. During the writing of *The First Desire*, the
Bogliasco Foundation, the Brecht's House Society, the Ragdale Foundation,
Blue Mountain Center, the Millay Colony, the Fine Arts Work Center in
Provincetown, and the National Endowment for the Arts all provided generous
support.

The research collections at the Buffalo Public Library and the Buffalo and
Erie County Historical Society and Mark Goldman's histories of Buffalo were
particularly helpful, as were my conversations with many family members and
friends, among them Ben and Lenore Polk and Tillie and the late Bert Gross.
I am deeply grateful to Carin Clevidence, Ann Harleman, Rick Hilles,
Ronna Johnson, Lynne Raughley, Linda Reisman, Helen Schulman, Heather
Sellers, and Therese Stanton for their invaluable manuscript readings and
comments; and to Jesse Lee Kercheval, Dale Kushner, the Wisconsin Insti-
tute for Creative Writing, and the Providence Area Writers for their early
and ongoing support of my work. This book would not have been possible without the generosity of these friends and of my family and other
loved ones, including Jeanne Reisman, Leonard Goldschmidt, and Deborah
Goldschmidt, Linda and Jack Reisman, David Reisman and Betsy Abram-
son, Robert and Rena Reisman, Janet Gross, Lo Wunder, and Sue Cooperman,

Leonard and Judith Katz, Jenny, Doug, Olivia, and Taylor Boone, Margaret Lewis, Jill and Isabella Polk, Kenneth Kidd, Brandy Kershner, Pamela Gilbert, Bill Waltz and Brett Astor, Pamela Perry, Dorothy Antczak, and Lyn Bell Rose.

My profound gratitude and love to Rick Hilles, who teaches me joy.